THE
FORGOTTEN
GIRL

THE
FORGOTTEN
GIRL

RIO YOUERS

ST. MARTIN'S PRESS ⚏ NEW YORK

THE FORGOTTEN GIRL. Copyright © 2017 by Rio Youers.
All rights reserved. Printed in the United States of America. For information,
address St. Martin's Press, 175 Fifth Avenue, New York, N.Y. 10010.

www.stmartins.com

The Library of Congress Cataloging-in-Publication Data is available upon request.

ISBN 978-1-250-07239-9 (hardcover)
ISBN 978-1-4668-8405-2 (e-book)

Our books may be purchased in bulk for promotional, educational, or business use.
Please contact your local bookseller or the Macmillan Corporate and Premium Sales
Department at 1-800-221-7945, extension 5442, or by e-mail at
MacmillanSpecialMarkets@macmillan.com.

First Edition: June 2017

10 9 8 7 6 5 4 3 2 1

For Emily, Lily, and Charlie
Family Hug

One

I'm not a coward. This will become evident as we move forward, but I want to put it out there nonetheless. A definitive, no-bullshit statement: I am *not* a coward. I'll admit that I'm sensitive, and that my stomach tightens at the mere suggestion of confrontation; I'll walk away from an argument before it gets too heated. I inherited this from my mom: a gentle-hearted pacifist and vegetarian who, like Linda Mc-Cartney, died of cancer anyway. *Violence is how stupid people negotiate,* she once said to me. I was maybe twelve or thirteen at the time. I smiled and told her that she was brilliant and beautiful. *I'm paraphrasing Asimov,* she replied, kissing my forehead. Mom never took credit for anything.

I got into a few scrapes in high school. It happens when you're just south of ordinary. I was never the instigator, though, and I always tried to make peace. It's not that I was afraid of getting hurt; I simply found the whole exchanging-blows thing unnecessary. So I proffered the white flag and bore the chickenshit denomination. I could forgo being popular for those few ugly years of adolescence, if it meant keeping my integrity. But allow me to state again: I am *not* a coward. I wasn't in high school, and I'm not now. I just have zero capacity for violence.

Or so I thought.

His fist jackhammered the left side of my face—three swift, blunt blows that sent fluorescent particles swirling across my field of vision. The pain felt as if it were wrapped in cloth: a thing both large and round-edged. My cheek swelled and blood spouted from a cut beneath my eye. I slumped to my knees. My emotions shifted from fear and confusion to outright terror. These men were going to kill me.

I crawled a short distance and watched the blood drip between my hands. I imagined them having to scrub it later with bleach, perhaps using a toothbrush to get into the fine cracks in the cement. They would dispose of my body efficiently. My crazy father would assume I'd been abducted by aliens.

"Please . . ." Blood dripped from my mouth, too. The inside of my cheek had been smashed against my teeth.

Another thug—boots like Frankenstein's monster—kicked me in the stomach and all the air rushed out of me. I rolled onto my side, knees drawn to my chest. More of those fluorescent particles whirled before my eyes. I blinked them away and staggered to my feet. There was another thug—how many of these guys *were* there?—guarding the door and I stumbled toward him. I thrust my shoulder into his chest and bounced off him. He shoved me back into the middle of the room. I turned a slow circle, wiping my face with trembling hands.

"What do you *want* from me?"

My vision swam. Five of them. No . . . six. Maybe seven. They surrounded me, as robust as trees, and all grim-faced. That was when I started to cry. And no, that *doesn't* make me a chickenshit. Jesus, I was terrified—*anybody* would cry. Even those ballsy, testosterone-jacked Neanderthals from high school.

My tears brought no pity, though. No reprieve. Some brick-headed dude with fists as hard as bowling balls dropped me with one punch. My head struck the cement floor and chimed. I felt it then: the first toxic pangs of rage. I thought of the many confrontations I'd turned my back on—the punches I could have thrown but hadn't. It was like I had banked all my aggression and now I was cashing it in. Adrenaline surged like a whale breaching. I got to my feet and made fists of my own. Be damned if I'd go down without a fight.

I stepped toward the thug with the monstrous boots and threw a sizzling right hook. I imagined it an asteroid that would impact the planet of his skull and split it to the core. Instead, I tripped over my own feet and my fist sailed harmlessly wide. I caught my balance in time for one of those boots to connect with my bony ass. Down I went again. The rage was flushed from me, as if it had never been there to begin with. I curled onto my side and whimpered. Thug one—Jackhammer—rolled me onto my back. He placed his foot on my chest like a victorious barbarian.

"Tie this skinny motherfucker up," he said.

So I have this theory: that we all have tunnel vision; we move through life seeing only what's directly in front of us, with little interest in the periphery. I mean, when was the last time you *really* looked around, a 360-degree appreciation of your environment, where you note—at once—the architecture of that building, the sun-washed red of that stop sign, the black car idling in a different spot every day? We see these things, but—because they exist beyond the conveyor belt of our lives—we rarely absorb them. It's a remarkable form of blindness.

My old man once claimed that we have microchips implanted into our brains at birth, that we're essentially automatons hardwired to certain corporate logos and propaganda. Conspiracy-theorist paranoia, of course, but I can't help but believe that *something* is scrambling the signal. *Something* is blinding us.

They'd been watching me the past few days. That black car idling first outside the Bank of America, then in the Cracker Barrel parking lot. That stranger standing two behind me in the line at the post office. That brick-headed dude walking past my apartment every few hours, often wearing a different jacket. They occupied the periphery, but I didn't really *see* them because I—like everybody else—have tunnel vision.

It had been an average Tuesday: get up at 9 a.m., a breakfast of quinoa flakes with almond milk, thirty minutes of Ashtanga yoga, shower and teeth. Tuesday mornings I busk beneath the Tall Man statue in Green River Park. It's a sedate vibe, where people go to read, relax, just *be*. I play Joan Baez, James Taylor, Jim Croce. Mellow tunes to complement the setting, and the money in my guitar case at the end of the session suggests that people appreciate it. Tuesday afternoons I hit the sidewalk outside the Liquor Monkey, where I break out the blue-collar rock. After a couple of hours there, I go to the bank to unload the small change. Then I buy bread, return to Green River Park, and feed the birds: a little spray of color at the end of the day. Sometimes I'll play to them, too. Sweet acoustic melodies. Birds dig it.

Average Tuesday, then I returned home and everything was turned upside down. The door to my apartment hung ajar and I stepped inside tentatively, wondering if Mr. Bauman, my landlord, had let himself in for some reason, and forgot to close the door afterward. Stepping into my living room, I saw this wasn't the case: my apartment had been ransacked. Bookshelves had been cleared. Drawers had been emptied. Chairs were overturned and my few pictures shattered in their frames. In the bedroom, my clothes were strewn across the floor and my mattress flipped. There was similar disarray in the kitchen and bathroom. I dropped my guitar and it struck a muted, tuneless chord from inside the case.

"What the hell?" I said. There was too much chaos to tell if anything was missing. I stepped into the kitchen, where I kept a roll of twenties— maybe four hundred dollars—in a Ziploc bag at the bottom of an empty cookie jar. The jar was broken. The money was still there.

"What the *hell*?"

My computer hadn't been stolen, either, but I suspected it had been tampered with. I always put it into sleep mode and closed the lid, but now it was open and wide awake, my Beatles-themed screensaver going through the motions. It occurred to me then that whoever had turned over my apartment wasn't interested in money. They wanted information.

A case of mistaken identity. Must be. Because I had no information. I was a twenty-six-year-old street performer from Green Ridge, New Jersey. I didn't mingle in other people's affairs. I kept blissfully to myself. Just south of ordinary, remember?

Something else occurred to me: that the door to my apartment hadn't been forced, which meant they'd either picked the lock, or Mr. Bauman had let them in. I thought I should pay him a visit—he'd need to know what had happened anyway—before calling the police.

The landlord's apartment was on the first floor (I was on the third) and the quickest way down was the stairwell. The elevator worked but it was slow as hell and swayed ominously as it descended. I'd just rounded the second flight of stairs when I came across two of the thugs blocking my way to the exit. Even then it didn't click—I didn't *see* them. I scooched to one side so we could pass without bumping shoulders, but instead one of them grabbed my T-shirt and threw me against the wall. My head cracked off the concrete and I saw the first of those fluorescent particles. I realized then that—for some unknown reason— I was in shit of the deepest variety.

I tried doing what I always do in the face of confrontation: I turned away. Or in this case, *ran* away. A deft spin-move took me out of the thug's clutches and I darted toward the stairs, heading for the second floor. Footsteps echoed around me. I looked up and saw another thug—Brickhead—descending from the third. Only one option available: I crashed through the doorway onto the second floor and staggered toward the windows at the far end of the hallway. The fire escape was only accessible through the apartments, but I hoped—courtesy of too many cheesy action movies—that I might be able to leap into a dumpster, or perhaps onto the back of a truck.

Voices behind me: thug one and thug two, with their unmoved expressions and granite shoulders. I passed the elevator and saw it standing open. It appeared I had another choice after all. The doors rattled closed as I reeled toward them, but I squeezed through the gap and into the stale-smelling cube. I saw the thugs in the inch-wide strip of hallway before the doors came together. Frantically, I punched *P* for the parking garage. There was a moment's hesitation—a pondering of counterweights and pulleys. I thought the doors would obligingly open again, allowing my pursuers access, then I heard a reluctant *ding* and the car began its descent.

Slowly.

There was a dulled mirror on one side and I noted my reflection wildly drawn: screwball cousin to the coolheaded dude who'd sat down to his quinoa flakes that morning. The car swayed and clanged like antique clockwork. I imagined the thugs patiently making their way to the parking garage. The doors would open and they'd be waiting. I tried the emergency button, hoping the car would stop—that the frickin' Bat-Signal would illuminate the sky over Green Ridge. The red light above it sputtered but that was all. "*Help me,*" I shrieked, jabbing the button like a kid with a video game. "*This is Harvey Anderson, apartment eighteen. I'm being—*"

Cables swinging, creaking. The car stopped with a bang. I wondered if the emergency button had worked, after all, then the floor indicator displayed a mockingly bright *P* and the doors rumbled open.

The thugs were there. Four of them. They weren't dressed like secret service agents, and were nothing like the muscle you see on TV. They didn't have eye patches or neck tattoos. These looked like regular guys. Jeans and jackets. Designed to blend into the periphery.

"You've got the wrong man," I said.

One of them stepped into the elevator. A baton telescoped from his sleeve. It swept toward me with a hummingbird purr—caught the ridge of bone behind my right ear. I went down and wavered for a moment on the rim of consciousness. Another thug placed a cloth bag over my head. It smelled of oil. I dampened the fabric as I sucked for air.

And then . . . nothing.

Nothing until I came to in a small room with a cracked cement floor and cinderblock walls. A dim lightbulb buzzed behind a wire mesh set into the ceiling. A tender bump had risen behind my right ear and I examined it gingerly. It felt as large as a knot in a bed sheet.

The thugs circled me. I pushed to my knees and implored the blurred face of the one closest.

"What the *fuck,* man?"

They came at me.

Jackhammer first.

I was pushed into a creaky wooden chair and my wrists bound to the slats behind me. I bled onto my T-shirt and screamed. The thugs waited for me to burn myself out. My blood darkened and dried.

Jackhammer stepped toward me. I flinched as he reached out, placed his fingers beneath my chin, and tilted my head so I could see him.

"And now it's down to you," he said.

I rasped something. Begged him with my eyes.

"We've shown you how serious we are."

My blood was smeared across his knuckles.

"What do you want?" I asked.

"Information," Jackhammer replied. "Cooperate and we'll let you go. Hold back and we'll kill you."

There was no character to his voice. It could have been his shadow speaking. His face, too, was remarkably blank. No moles or scars. His eyes were not a striking shade of blue and his nose not too flat. I imagined describing him to police as "nondescript" and having them roll their eyes. The facial composite would look as generic as a grapefruit.

He removed his fingers from beneath my chin. My head slumped.

"It's your choice," he said.

"You've got the wrong man," I said.

"Harvey Nathanial Anderson. Born: zero-four, zero-four, eighty-nine. Mother: Heather June Anderson. Deceased. Father: Gordon Anderson. Served with the Ninth Infantry Division in Vietnam. Lost the left half of his face to fragments from a Viet Cong grenade."

Lost his mind, too.

"How am I doing, Harvey?"

"Is this about my father?"

"Your father doesn't concern me," Jackhammer said. "To be honest, *you* don't concern me, either."

"Then what *is* it about?"

His nostrils flared as he inhaled. He brought his hands together in a bony ball and leaned forward, studying my expression, looking for any hint of recognition.

"Sally Starling," he said.

There had been three unsolved murders in Green Ridge in the last three years. All women. Beaten, raped, stabbed to death. The killer was extremely careful, leaving no incriminating evidence. For a while the town was at condition orange. We even checked our peripheries, like the entire nation in the months following 9/11. It must have worked, because there hadn't been a murder for sixteen months. The towns-people had since slipped into their usual zombie state.

That name—Sally Starling—was *vaguely* familiar, and I wondered if she'd been one of the three victims. Perhaps if I hadn't been so scared, I could have identified it, but all I found in my mind was an empty space.

"I don't . . ." Tears filled my throat. I inhaled sharply and the sound was drain-like. "It's not . . . *please*—"

Jackhammer's fist drummed off my jaw and the chair teetered side-ways. A flare exploded in my skull and set an alarming glow over every-thing.

"Did I mention how serious we are?"

I spat a red ribbon from my mouth.

"Sally Starling."

He pronounced the name slowly. Four precise syllables. I churned through my bruised mind but there were only blanks. A terrible thought occurred to me: that if Sally was one of the murder victims, these guys likely believed I was her killer. They could be vigilantes, or Sally's stricken family, taking the law into their own hands.

I lowered my eyes and groaned miserably, then recalled Jackhammer saying that they wanted information. *Cooperate and we'll let you go,* he'd said. It didn't jive with the vigilante theory.

"I don't . . . don't—"

He hit me again. More an open-handed slap. My head rocked to the side so viciously that capillaries erupted in my neck.

"*NO,*" I screamed. "*Jesus fucking Christ.*" I coughed up blood and snot and spat it down the front of my T-shirt. The pain encircled me. "I'll help you if I can. I swear. I fucking *SWEAR.*"

Jackhammer's lip flared. He flexed his fingers.

"Sally Starling," he said. "Where is she?"

"I don't know, man. I don't even know who she is."

"You're lying."

"I *swear.*"

"*WHERE IS SHE?*"

That diamond of a fist drew back yet again and I braced myself, thinking the next blow would shut out the lights, perhaps cause permanent brain damage. I thought, bizarrely, of Swan Connor, Green Ridge's celebrity resident. Swan had been a big-time record producer in the seventies and eighties—back when people actually bought records and there was money to be made. He was always so engaging and bright, happy to share an anecdote or a smile, but a recent stroke had turned him into a maundering imbecile. I'd seen him just the week before, stumbling down Main with the aid of two canes. He was drooling like a teething infant and had a thick green booger on his upper lip. That would be *me* after this punch landed. There'd be deep crevasses in my brain where cognitive functions and motor skills used to live. I would eat mashed potatoes with plenty of ketchup. I would wear eight-dollar track pants and maunder with Swan.

I waited, but the punch never landed. Another thug had stepped forward and placed his hand on Jackhammer's chest.

"She got to him," he said.

"I know," Jackhammer said.

"She's powerful."

"I know that, too."

I had no idea what they were talking about, but—for the time be-ing, at least—the beating had stopped and that was a positive. Albeit a meager one. I lowered my head and started to cry again. Jackhammer loomed over me. He rolled back my head and used his thumb and fore-finger to peel my swollen eye wide.

"We should make sure," he said.

We often think of our memory as a vast library containing volumes of information—a place where "books" are stored and sometimes lost. It's a romantic notion, but an inaccurate one. In truth, it's more like a fac-tory, with forklifts speeding along the neural pathways and production lines operating 24/7. In recalling a childhood Christmas, for instance, we don't send some dusty librarian to hunt through the holiday depart-ment, but rather assemble a team of neurons from pertinent regions of the brain to encode and reconstruct the desired memory. It's an effi-cient system, but complex and susceptible to malfunction.

Memories deteriorate. They get lost forever. I don't know—nobody does—whether they actually disappear, or if the conjunctions neces-sary to reconstruction become damaged. I favor the latter theory. You ever smell something—a perfume, home cooking—that whips you back in time, floods your brain with recollection? Sure you have. I like to believe that all lost memories are equally recoverable. They just need the correct stimulus.

It's a little different when certain memories have been stolen—plucked from your head like they were never there to begin with. Sci-entists argue that this isn't possible, but I know that it is.

"We need to find her."

"I can't help you."

"We'll see about that."

Jackhammer had procured a chair from somewhere and sat opposite me. His expression hadn't changed. He could have been waiting for a bus. Again, I considered my father's theory about microchips in the brain and automatons. Maybe he wasn't so crazy.

"We are proceeding under the assumption that you are telling the truth, and that Ms. Starling has performed her little party trick on you." He linked his fingers and leaned toward me. The chair creaked, offering the impression of a tree bowing in the wind. "Let's just see if there's anything left."

I nodded, as if that were all fine with me. As if they were suddenly being reasonable. Something warm trickled from my swollen left eye.

"Sally Starling isn't her real name," Jackhammer said. His blank eyes felt like the backs of cold spoons, placed on my cheeks. "She was born Miranda Farrow, June 1991. That makes her twenty-four years old. She used the name Charlotte Prowse after her parents abandoned her at age fifteen, then became Sally Starling when she moved to Green Ridge six years ago. Places of employment include Marzipan's Kitchen, Pennywise Used Books, and the Health Nut."

I knew those places well, but nothing stirred in my brain.

"Her last known address was apartment eighteen, Passaic Heights, Green Ridge, New Jersey."

My address.

"We spoke to the landlord: Mr. Ralph Bauman. He told us that you and Ms. Starling had been living there for five years. Good tenants. Quiet. Always paid your rent on time. He hadn't seen her for a week or so, but had no reason to believe she'd moved out. She certainly didn't notify him. No forwarding address or number where she could be reached."

"This is . . ." I couldn't find the right words. My body was slumped and something inside my skull hissed like a cracked pipe. "This is all news to me."

A folder appeared in Jackhammer's hand. I didn't see which of the thugs had handed it to him. Possibly the one who purchased his footwear at the same place as Frankenstein's monster. From it, Jackhammer pulled a sheet of paper. He studied it for a moment, then held it up for me to read.

"The rental agreement for your apartment," he said. "Signed August twentieth, 2010, by co-tenants Harvey N. Anderson and Sally Starling. Tell me, Harvey . . . is this your signature?"

I looked at my strike-through scrawl, identifiable even through the tears in my eyes, and nodded. Sally Starling's signature—a vivacious, bubble-like cursive—sat beside mine. I was positive I'd never seen it before.

"Mr. Bauman was kind enough to make a copy," Jackhammer said. I thought I detected a smile in his voice, but when he lowered the agreement I saw that his mouth was a humorless gray line. "We can be *very* persuasive."

"Yes," I said stupidly.

"Jogging any memories, Harvey?"

"No."

"Nothing?"

"Nothing."

He blinked, slid the agreement back into the folder, and took out a color photograph. It was a headshot. Sally Starling, I assumed. Tousled, mousy hair. No makeup. The kind of girl my heart gallops for. She had a zit on her chin that she hadn't tried to hide. There was a crusty something—perhaps dried tzatziki—on the bib of her Health Nut apron.

"Seems absurd," Jackhammer said, "to ask if you recognize a woman you lived with for five years."

"I don't recognize her," I mumbled. The woman in the photograph— agreeable as she was in her crunchy, *au naturel* way—was a stranger to me.

"Very private, your girlfriend," Jackhammer said. "Very *careful*. Like you, she doesn't own a cell phone or subscribe to social media—the things that tie you to society. It was difficult to find a current photograph of her. But once we determined her location and the alias she'd adopted, we found this: the Health Nut's employee of the month for February 2015."

I looked at her again, because it was far more appealing than looking at my blood on the floor, or any one of my dour tormentors. She had hazel eyes, the color of turned leaves, and her nose was slightly off-center. Her face shape, though, was perfectly oval, and I imagined how it would complement the cup of my palm—how I could cradle her brow or jaw, and it would be the counterpart to my hand. I wondered if the rest of our bodies would enjoy a similar harmony, and if we'd make love like strawberries and cream.

"Anything, Harvey?"

And yeah, there was . . . *something*. But was it a memory, or imagination? I closed my eyes and concentrated. A woman, swaying her hips to music I couldn't hear. Her dress was knee-length. It switched between blue and yellow.

"Harvey?"

"Dancing," I said distantly.

"Sally?"

Impossible to tell. She had no face.

"Tell us what you see."

That blue/yellow dress flickering around her knees. Her arms making flowing motions. I pushed deeper, but there was nothing more. It was a sketch done in pencils, partially erased.

My eyes crept open. Jackhammer was leaning forward in the chair, only inches from me. I could smell his breath, which had decidedly more personality than his face.

"Harvey?"

"I think I've been brainwashed," I said.

He stood quickly and the chair toppled backward. I thought he was going to beat the dancing woman from my mind. Instead, he ran a hand through his average hair, righted the chair, and looked at the others.

"Make the call," he said.

I can't tell you how long I was in that boxlike room, alone and bleeding, tied to a chair. There was no window, so I couldn't use the light to measure time, and my body clock had been damaged by Jackhammer's fists. It could have been a day, or three days, or a week. I faded in and out like a ghost in an old movie, never unconscious or asleep, but caught in a surreal daze where pain and fear were ever present. My throat was too dry to scream.

Escape was out of the question; I was too weak, and the thugs kept guard outside the door. I heard them shuffling their feet, clearing their throats. If they spoke to one another, I didn't hear them. I told myself that if they were going to kill me, they would have already. It was a small comfort.

So time passed in mysterious excerpts. I suffered deeply and prayed shallowly, and worried for my father, whom these thugs knew all about, and who was delicate and paranoid. I imagined them bringing him here, wide-eyed and confused, and Jackhammer pressing a gun to his forehead. *Dig deep, Harvey,* the thug would say expressionlessly. *Tell us about the dancing girl.* And my old man would puff out his chest and regard me through his single whirling eye. *Goddamn Russian sleeper agents,* he'd say. *The red hammer is falling.*

My wrists flexed weakly at the rope binding me to the chair. I counted my pains and wept. It felt like a circular saw was buzzing around the inside of my skull, scoring the bone, and with any sudden movement my head would fragment like a fortune cookie. My dreadlocks—clotted as cows' tails—had absorbed blood like sponges.

I faded in . . . and out.

Was it average Wednesday? Or slightly-better-than-average Friday? Out . . . and in.

Three words kept floating into my mind, and sometimes they'd lodge there like arrows in a bull's-eye: *Make the call.* What did that mean? Who were they calling? It couldn't be good, right? *Let him go.* Now *that* was good. But *make the call* . . . no, that sent unpleasant vibes racing through me.

I default to my mom in moments of duress. She was a beacon of strength—my *only* beacon of strength—when she was alive, and I could always rely on her celestial wisdom. On this occasion, however, I turned to the girl without a face—the dancing girl. She lured me with the timing of her hips, the flash of her dress, and I went to her meekly. *Who are you?* I asked, stepping into the partially erased scene. *Why can't I remember you?* I took her featureless face in my hand and cradled it perfectly, and I knew for certain, from somewhere deeper than my mind, that this *was* a memory.

Who are you?

I felt the tick of her hips against mine. The warming pressure of her breasts. I searched for greater detail—my brain fighting to pull together elements that simply weren't there. I cupped the other side of her face and that, too, was perfect.

Sally . . . is that your name?

Her hair smelled of nothing. Her skin smelled of nothing.

Why can't I . . . ?

Time passed. Sometimes I was wide awake, with a wildfire of emotion burning through me. Other times I slumbered in that exhausted daze. Eventually, the door opened and Brickhead strolled in. He placed smelling salts beneath my nose and I popped to full alertness. A series of cracked sounds eked from my mouth. He held a small glass of water to my lips and I drank with my throat pumping.

"Please let me go," I said, and followed him with my eyes as he left, slamming the door behind him.

Sally danced in my mind.

Make the call.

Moments later the door opened again, and in crawled the spider.

Two

He was an older man—just into his sixties, I thought—with a pale, lined face and dark eyes. His forehead was dominated by angular eyebrows and a silvered widow's peak that glimmered in the overhead light. He wore an unremarkable gray suit, given character by a red flower pinned to his lapel.

"Harvey," he said. His voice was sure and strong. I detected a hint of the South in his accent. He took the seat opposite me (a pillow had been placed on it, I noticed), his long arms and legs folding neatly as he made himself comfortable.

"Who are you?" I asked.

"I see my hunt dogs have been heavy-handed with you." He gestured with one finger at my battered face. "They find the aggressive approach to be expedient. I'm always called upon as a last resort—when their weakling minds are empty of ideas."

The thugs appeared unfazed by this insult. They formed a semicircle behind the older man.

"Who are you?" I asked again.

"You"—the finger pointed now, straight as a ruler—"don't need to know. Suffice to say that Miranda Farrow—or Sally Starling, as you know her—knows me very well. Almost as well as I know myself."

I shrugged and winced, then shifted in the chair. My left leg was numb. I imagined that if they ever cut my binds, it would take me ten minutes to stand. Another twenty to walk to the door. The man in the suit watched me, breathing coolly.

"I need to find her," he said. "She took something extremely valuable from me."

"And you think I know where she is?"

"That's what I'm here to find out."

"Are you going to torture me?"

A thin smile touched his lips. He regarded me with those Emperor Ming eyes, and I could only imagine the wickedness behind them. A new, great fear rose through my stomach and lodged in my throat. I lowered my head and trembled.

"We searched your computer as well as your apartment," he said. The smile had slipped from his face but that cool air remained. "We went through all your files and folders, your browsing history, your e-mail. Came up empty. But it's easy to erase data from a computer. You just right-click and hit delete. Empty your trash and it's gone forever. You can even wipe your entire hard drive. It's effortless."

This was a nightmare. It *had* to be. A long, brutal nightmare.

"The human brain is a wildly different creature," he continued. "We immodestly think of it as some kind of supercomputer, but it's far more complex. We have our instincts, our emotions, our memories. A surfeit of knowledge and experience. Erasing this data is more demanding than a simple right-click. There are methods, of course—lobotomies, electroconvulsive therapy—and medications that repress emotional triggers. But to go into the brain and hand-select certain memories for deletion . . . impossible. So how do we begin to explain what has happened to you?"

I shook my head. My eye was drawn to the red flower on the man's lapel. Two shades lighter than my blood.

"Your other memories are intact," he said. The lines at the edges of his eyes deepened. "You know your name, where you live, where you went to school. I'm sure you remember events from your childhood, computer passwords, the lyrics to your favorite songs. Everything appears in working order. And yet you cannot remember the woman you lived with for five years."

"I still think you've got the wrong man," I said. "You tell me I know this woman, but the only proof you've got is a rental agreement that could've been forged. So what are you going to do? Torture me—*kill* me—for information I don't have?"

"I know this is upsetting for you."

"Just let me *go*."

He sat back in the seat and regarded me silently. His eyes were like hands, touching where they shouldn't.

"I can't help you," I said.

"I need to be sure of that."

"But I don't—"

"It's incredibly difficult to track a person who leaves such dainty footprints." He smiled again. Full and false. "Miranda—sorry, *Sally*— puts down few roots, and adopts an unremarkable image so that she doesn't stand out."

I considered the periphery and sighed.

"No driver's license, social security number, or passport. She worked for mom-and-pop stores and was paid under the table, limiting her paper trail." His eyebrows came together, forming a bird shape across his forehead. Not a sparrow or chickadee, either, but a raptor. Something with claws. "Nonetheless, my hunt dogs sniffed around Green Ridge. They discovered where she lived and worked, and that her boyfriend busks for quarters outside the Liquor Monkey. Other than that—and although she lived in Green Ridge for six years—nobody knew anything about her. A dainty footprint, indeed."

The thugs stood silently, like monoliths, staring straight ahead. *Hunt dogs*, the man called them. I wondered how much power he wielded and felt sick inside.

"That doesn't explain why I can't remember her," I said.

"Then allow me to spell it out for you," the man said, and I detected the first suggestion of impatience in his voice. "Sally Starling possesses a unique and powerful ability. Just like we can erase data from a computer hard drive, she can—*selectively*—erase the memories from a person's mind."

"Bullshit," I said. Growing up with my old man—who believed in government-engineered hurricanes and little green men—I had become remarkably adept at sniffing out bullshit. Hell, I was a hunt dog for bullshit.

"She fled Green Ridge a few days ago, a frightened girl, no doubt, forced to begin a new life in a new city, with a new name and a fabricated background. Before leaving, she cleared your apartment of anything that could be associated with her. Photographs. Clothes. Possessions. Any triggers . . . gone. There's nothing on your computer, so it's fair to assume she scrubbed that data, too. Simply accessed the relevant files and hit delete. She did the same thing with your mind."

"Bullshit," I said again, but my heart made a forlorn, hurt sound in my chest, and that sickening feeling deepened. "You're saying this woman—my so-called girlfriend—deleted parts of my mind?"

"Your memories, yes. Specifically, your memories of her."

"Why would she do that?"

"Because her life is fraught with danger, and she doesn't want you involved." He spread his long-fingered hands. "This is the only way she could make a clean break without worrying that you might follow."

"I guess she didn't count on you guys getting to me."

"She knew we'd find you, I'm sure, but likely thought your absence of memory would protect you."

The bird shape took wing again. His dark eyes gleamed.

"She was wrong."

"As I've already noted, the human brain is expansive and intricate. Given the additional complexities of memory, it's entirely possible Sally left something in your mind."

I closed my eyes and there she was, swaying her hips, matching the rhythm of a song I couldn't remember.

"Even if she has," I began hesitantly, my good eye slowly opening, finding that red flower again. "Even if I suddenly remember everything about her, I still wouldn't know where she is. If what you're saying is true, she would never have told me."

"That's true, but in the time you spent together, she may have mentioned something—a longing, a wanderlust—that could offer some clue as to where she went." He extended his upper body toward me, his hands curled into bony fists. "That's all we want, Harvey. A slice of information. A partial of that dainty footprint."

"I've got nothing," I said. "I'm a waste of time, I promise you."

"He remembers something about a dancing girl," Jackhammer offered.

"That could be *anyone*," I said, knowing it wasn't. "A scene from a movie. A drunk aunt at a wedding."

"Explore it," the man in the suit said.

"I *have*." I shook my head. It rattled with pain. "It's too hazy. She doesn't even have a *face*, for God's sake."

"We'll soon see," the man said. He receded into the seat and breathed deeply. I sensed the tension illuminating his chest, like neon in a plasma globe, that would snap colorfully toward me if I dared touch him. Not that I could, of course. Or would. My fear, already ramped up, created a similar thrum. If we bumped chests, it'd be like lightsabers colliding.

"I want to go home," I said. A hopeless statement. It made me feel so small.

"Some scientists believe," the man said by way of a reply, "that when we store a memory, we do so multiple times throughout the cortex. It's kind of like backing up your hard drive. If information becomes lost or damaged, there are ways of restoring it."

"Hypnosis," I muttered.

"Perhaps," he replied. "Although the theory suggests we draw upon the backup without being aware we are doing so—our brains instantly retrieving information from the nearest undamaged source."

I looked at his eyebrows again, recalling the hypnotists I'd seen depicted in countless movies and comic books, usually with spiraling eyes and mysterious rays emanating from their skulls. *See THE GREAT*

MESMERO demonstrate his amazing MIND-BENDING abilities. They all had stupid names, and they all had the same eyebrows as this dude.

"Are you going to hypnotize me?"

"No," he replied. Another thin smile. "My method is far more . . . effective."

That didn't sound altogether reassuring.

"But I would like to avoid that," he said. "If possible."

"Yes," I said.

"I need you to explore your memories, Harvey. The smallest detail could unlock any duplicates Ms. Starling may have missed, and trigger at least a partial recall."

"I tried that already," I said, gesturing toward the muscle standing blandly behind him. "With your goons—your dogs. I've got nothing."

"I urge you to try again. Try harder." His upper lip flared. I saw his teeth. Neat and white. "The alternative will not be pleasant."

A knife held to my throat would not have been more threatening. I swallowed blood and nodded weakly.

"Good." He leaned toward me again, bowed over his bunched fists. "Concentrate on the dancing girl. *Explore* her. Every minute detail."

"There's nothing to explore," I said. "She's dancing. That's all."

"Where is she? A party? A nightclub?"

"I don't know; it's just an empty space."

"Is she dancing with you? Are you with friends?"

"I don't have many friends," I said. "I find people to be overrated. Go figure."

"What is she dancing to?"

"I can't hear anything."

"Music is a powerful memory trigger."

"There *is* no music."

"*Concentrate!*" It was the first time he lost his cool. An eruption of anger that had the dull impact of an underwater explosion. I leapt in the seat as much as my binds would allow. Even the hunt dogs flinched.

"I'm trying," I whispered.

"Not hard enough." He rose to his feet and took a long stride toward me. I pulled away and almost spilled backward. "Last chance, Harvey."

His closeness unnerved me. The dice-like clack of his teeth when he spoke. The hollows of his temples, which I could see now, veined with blue and deep enough to cup eggs. He looked like he'd crawled from the pages of a comic book. Not one of the good guys, either. This put me in mind of something my old man always said, that the world had gone tits-up because there were too many supervillains.

"Go *deep*," he implored.

I shook my head and sniveled. A string of snot glued itself to my upper lip.

The man retreated. I gazed at that odd red flower as he backed away. His chest crackled impatiently and his nostrils flared. He was hoping for some kind of neural connection—a memory cascade—but there was nothing. If Sally Starling really had removed all my memories of her, she had been incredibly efficient. Only the dancing girl remained, and I began to wonder if that was deliberate.

"Okay," the man said. "It's time to do this the hard way." His long body affected a precise right angle as he leaned forward. I noticed his flower wasn't a flower at all, but a cluster of red feathers.

"The hard way?" I said. Voice like ash.

He wasn't smiling anymore.

He looked at the thugs—the hunt dogs—and nodded once. Frankenstein's Boots broke from the semicircle, left the room. The door slapped closed behind him. I smelled dust and rusty water. I'd thought I was in the basement of some old house, but imagined now an abandoned warehouse with a polluted stream running beside it. The kind of place where bodies were dumped.

"What's going on?" I searched the man's dark eyes, my shoulders rolling as I struggled against the ropes. "I told you everything I know."

He nodded, as if he believed me, when clearly he did not. The heels of his fine shoes tapped off the cement floor as he stepped closer. Would he wipe the blood off them himself, I wondered, or have one of the hunt dogs do it for him?

"Please," I begged. "Whatever you're thinking of doing—"

"I need to look for myself."

"What? I . . . *what?*"

"This will be excruciating," he said. "Not so much pain, but an un-fathomable sense of violation. You will cry and scream and plead. It will feel like your brain is being unspooled from the inside out."

"No—"

"Like your mind has been raped a thousand times."

"Please, no—"

"And when I'm finished, you'll feel haunted, degraded, and shared." The bird on his brow again. A savage thing, and so close. "The night-mares will never stop."

The door opened. Boots entered pushing a wheelchair ahead of him. An oxygen mask was looped over one of the handles. The sight of it silenced me. I blinked in shock. The fear now was beyond scale, shaped like a thing reaching.

"What are you going to *do* to me?"

The man didn't reply. He took off his gray jacket and placed it care-fully over the back of the chair.

"Let's begin," he said.

Three

He crawled into my mind. Spider. I felt each of his eight legs tapping and the soft thump of his abdomen along my consciousness. It was, instantly, the most harrowing and invasive thing I'd ever experienced. Ice replaced the marrow in my skeleton. I screamed and curled stiffly at the waist, as if some drawstring connected to my spine had been pulled tight.

He was cold and slick and plump.

Now, let's see . . .

I heard him clearly, as though he'd spoken out loud. That soft, southern tinge. He was *inside me*, scurrying along my memories and dreams. I tried to shake him loose—jibbing and rattling in my chair—but he held tight. I envisioned the sole of some gigantic sneaker slamming down and crushing his fat body into the grooves of my brain.

A sneaker? That's cute, Harvey.

"Get out of my—" Blood frothed at the corners of my mouth and I spluttered, drawing deep, gurgling breaths. I finished the sentence in my mind: *—FUCKING HEAD.*

He skittered, explored. His many legs stretched, touching neurons throughout my brain, acting as conductors that drew the separate elements of memory together. I tried to thwart him, to imagine a blank brick wall, but he was beyond that. He crawled into the folds of my temporal lobe, stimulating electric impulses, uncovering memories with formidable ease.

Is this Mom? Why, she's pretty.

Fuck you, man.

She stood in a stroke of sunlight at our living room window, her hair so gold it was almost white. I recall this with unnerving clarity; the day she told me she had breast cancer. The memory shifted to her lying in an eco-coffin made from hand-woven rattan and organic cotton. Her face was a pastel mask.

The spider burrowed. I jerked and cried out, the cords in my neck announcing themselves like tension wires.

Get OUT.

Not until I'm satisfied.

They're my memories . . . MINE.

Mr. Kinshaw, my science teacher in eighth grade, crying at his desk after calling Jermaine Robinson a "stupid little nigger," knowing his career was over. Sitting alone in the school cafeteria after someone had pinned a sign—STINK-HIPPIE—to the back of my sweater, and it was Mr. Kinshaw who had removed it. Watching my old man sharpen lengths of bamboo for a Vietnamese punji trap he was building in the backyard.

Where is she?

My teeth clattered and blood vessels cracked in my good eye. It felt like I was being electrocuted, but there was no pain, only a stream of cold energy. The chair creaked and scraped across the floor.

Snapshots of my first guitar; my first kiss; combing Mom's hair while she sang "God Bless the Child"; picking peaches at Uncle Johnny's farm; jamming with Steve Van Zandt at a bar on the shore; masturbating in the shower; masturbating in the kitchen; masturbating on a train.

The spider crawled. He saw it all.

My memories. *My* life.

Blood trickled from the corners of my mouth. The ice in my bones melted and I voided myself, bladder and bowel.

The spider said, *This hasn't even started to be uncomfortable yet.*

He went deeper.

And he found her. The dancing girl. He groaned with a sad kind of satisfaction and gathered the memory close, as if it were precious, as if it were his.

There you are. My little bird.

He crawled into the middle of her empty face and paused there. His fat abdomen throbbed as he worked to recall her features, using his legs to bridge damaged connection points, but to no avail; her face—as she had appeared in this moment—was gone. He assembled a likeness based on the employee of the month photograph Jackhammer had shown me, but it wasn't the same.

I know it's you. I can feel *you.*

I felt her, too, and wondered if she was connected to his soul like she was connected to mine. Did our respective—and perhaps opposite— emotions resonate equally?

The spider scurried along the angle of her jaw, onto her throat, then onto her dress. Another pause as he repaired a damaged connection, and her dress stopped switching color. Blue. It was blue. Recalling this singular detail caused a miniature cascade, and the scene gained greater depth.

Her dress was blue. Exactly the same color as the sky. We were outside. A clear, hot day. Sound and smell of the ocean. People milling around. Sunglasses and tanning oils. The wooden planks beneath our feet were laid in a herringbone pattern. In the distance, the faded green shell of a building with punched-out glass and a sign that read CASINO.

Where is this? the spider asked.

It's the boardwalk at Asbury Park.

When?

I don't know.

He delved deeper. His long legs ticked and grabbed, the fine hairs on them sensitive to all brain activity. My eyes looped back inside my skull and I yammered senselessly. I felt the warmth of my body waste but everything else was cold.

More detail emerged, like an old film being brought into focus. The boardwalk flushed with life: lovers holding hands, people pushing bicycles, joggers wending like fish, their muscles wet in the heat. The dancing girl laughed and threw her arms wide. Her mousy hair caught the merest breeze and flowed around that invisible face.

You can't hide forever.

Aromas of grilled fish, lemongrass, coconut. There was a restaurant to the right with boardwalk seating. A three-piece band, tucked in the corner, played their instruments silently. A slow-tempo number, judging from the way they played, and the rhythmic tick of Sally's hips.

What song are they playing?

I can't remember.

You're a musician. Do you recognize the guitar chords?

I was looking mainly at Sally when this memory was recorded, but I caught glimpses: C . . . E-seven . . . G-seven. Could be one of ten—*fifty*—thousand songs.

That doesn't help, I said.

His legs curled with agitation. He first explored my brain to see if I was telling the truth, then attempted to repair the damage, hoping the music—such an effective trigger, as he'd already noted—would activate a more detailed cascade.

But the song, like her face, was gone.

He scurried from my mind in an instant and I screamed, slumped forward. Pressure in my face, like hot dough filling the front of my skull, oozing into the cavities and fissures, cooling slowly. Blood leaked from my mouth and nose. I vomited bile in strands thin as spiderweb.

I wasn't the only one hurt and bleeding; the man had slumped into the wheelchair. He wheezed and trembled—made weak grabbing motions with his right hand. Boots stepped forward, looped the oxygen mask over his face, turned it on. The man—the *spider*—sucked long, clean breaths into his chest. The inside of the mask fogged. Blinking my tears away, I saw tiny drops of blood in the corners of his eyes. His face appeared more deeply lined, and his hair more white than silver.

I don't know how long he sucked on that oxygen, his breathing growing deeper, steadier. Maybe as long as an hour. Time was beyond me. Eventually, he lowered the mask and gestured for Jackhammer to come close.

"It's a long shot," he said, and coughed. His lips were dry, tinged blue. He took another shot of oxygen, then continued: "Asbury Park, New Jersey. I don't think she's there, but sniff around. And go gently."

Jackhammer nodded. "You want me to go alone?"

"Is Corvino still MIA?"

"Yes."

"Then no . . . definitely don't go alone."

Jackhammer left with thug four. I prayed it was the last time I'd ever set eyes on him.

"Can you still feel me inside you?" the spider asked.

"I can feel where you've been," I murmured. "Your legs."

They gave me more water. I drank some of it, but most spilled down my chin. I shivered and ached.

"I still feel the girl." The spider's voice was cracked and whispery. His hands trembled when he moved them. "Nine years later, I can feel the impact—the emptiness of what she took from me. A great famishment of the mind."

I shifted my upper body and groaned. My shoulders throbbed and my wrists felt slick, bleeding where the rope had chafed them.

"She took memories from you," the spider continued. "But you feel no emptiness. And why? Because she was like a surgeon, operating so precisely and efficiently that you're unaware of anything missing."

I considered this enigmatic girl, blithe enough to swirl in the ocean

THE FORGOTTEN GIRL • 29

breeze, dangerous enough to excise entire moments from my life. She terrified, fascinated, mystified me. I wanted to track her down and reclaim my memories. I wanted to run away and never look back.

"With me, she was a bird—a beautiful, savage bird." The spider blinked, and a single bloody tear trickled from his left eye. "She clawed away so many memories, leaving me with morsels of everything. Just enough to feel loss."

"You're suffering?"

"Yes." He pulled on the oxygen once again. "I am."

Good, I thought.

"She took my power, too. *Much* of my power." He wiped his face. Smeared one of the tears. A pink smudge colored his cheek like rouge. "As you can see"—he indicated his weakened state—"I'm not the force I used to be. I'm like a car running on a single cylinder, or a battery at five percent power. As soon as I find her, I'm taking back what's mine. And more besides."

He was a monster to me. The thought of him with greater power was terrifying.

"I wouldn't help you if I could," I said.

"You have no say in the matter."

I felt him scratching at my mind again. Mockingly. His eyes grew hazy and he cleared them with another blast of oxygen.

"I would kill you now," he said. "Split your brain like a tomato."

"Why don't you?"

"You're a link to the girl, however broken." Another red tear curled from his eye. "You may be of use to me yet."

I shook my ruined head and listened to the cold hiss of oxygen through the mask.

He attacked me again. A final scurry through my mind to ensure he'd left no stone unturned. I found energy enough to scream, and to vomit most of the water they'd given me. Then I drifted to the edge of consciousness, barely attached to who—*where*—I was, but feeling the spider's plump body squeezing into my most secret places.

. . .

I felt devitalized, picked apart . . . as empty and faded as the casino at Asbury Park, with my glass shattered and the wind blowing through me. Eventually, I found the strength to gather the pieces of my brain—separated along their fissures, clogged with cobwebs—and slot them together with a watchmaker's care.

I opened my eyes. The walls swam into focus first. Too close, too solid. Then I saw the spider, huddled in the wheelchair, his gray suit drooping off his withered frame, his face raglike beneath the oxygen mask.

One of the hunt dogs—his face a smudge—stepped toward me. The knife in his hand was small but sharp. I clenched my entire body, except for my jaw, which trembled.

"You might be tempted to go to the police," he said blandly. "But consider, carefully, what you'll tell them, and if they'll believe you. And then look over your shoulder. We just might be there."

He stepped behind me, cut my binds.

I spilled to the floor and stayed there for some time.

I lay in my hot stink as the pain in my head waned to a dull but constant thud. When I looked up, I saw that I was alone in the room. I cried and rolled onto my side. My ribs screamed and my spine fired off a series of explosive cracks.

Deep, burning breaths. Time ticked unevenly.

At length, I pushed myself to my knees, and then to my feet. I managed two agonizing steps before the door swung open.

The spider walked in.

I collapsed again.

He was stronger. Walked with a silver-tipped cane, but there was no wheelchair, no oxygen mask. His face, though, was the same gray color as the walls.

The thin smile had returned.

"Some people," he said, "find the best way to remember something is to write it down. Others prefer repetition, visualization techniques, or mnemonics."

I struggled to one knee and looked up at him, trying not to feel like a serf before his king.

"I find," he said, "that creating associations is incredibly effective."

He pulled the cluster of red feathers from his lapel, plucked one of them free, twirled it before my eyes.

"You won't forget me . . . will you?"

I shook my head.

"No." That feather was so red. "You won't."

I hated being on one knee, so I fought the pain and struggled to my feet. Our eyes came level. His were penetrating. Mine tear-struck and sore.

The feather followed me. He blew on it, and it bristled.

"I don't think Sally Starling will contact you," he said. "But if she does, you should alert me immediately. Likewise, if you happen upon information that may be of use, or uncover some deeply buried memory strand . . ."

Fuck you, I thought. I didn't care if he read my mind.

"The pain. The threat," he said, and his dark eyebrows took wing. "The humiliation. The violation. I'm sure you'll do anything to avoid a repeat of what has happened here. Or something worse."

The feather rolled between his thumb and forefinger, so bright it could burn.

"You're on my radar now. If you try to run away, or even *consider* keeping information from me . . . I want you to look at this feather."

He took my hand, placed it in my palm.

"This is how you'll remember me."

I kept the red feather. It's a little worse for wear (we've had some adventures, that feather and I), but still bright and remarkable, each filament replete with the memory of what I endured.

Not that I needed *association* to help me remember. That particular ordeal runs deep—so deep that I don't think even Sally could remove it from my brain. Some memories, for better or worse, touch the soul. That's just the way it is.

It was the same with Sally. She was a *part* of me, occupying a place the spider could never reach, and it didn't take me long to realize that I needed to find her. For the sake of my sanity, of course, but also because—as powerful as she was—I wanted to protect her. That may sound crazy, given what I went through, but hey . . . she was my girl. I knew this even though I couldn't remember a damn thing about her.

So yeah, I kept the feather. Partly to remind me that bad things exist in the periphery, and that sometimes they can spill right in front of your eyes. But mostly to emphasize what Sally would go through if the spider and his hunt dogs ever caught up with her.

The pain. The threat. The humiliation. The violation.

I turned the feather from an ugly association to a symbol of justness and determination.

You're on my radar now. If you try to run away, or even consider *keeping information from me . . .*

My old man was a Jedi Master when it came to bullshit, but he was right on the money when he said that there were too many supervillains in the world. I'd spent my whole life turning my back on confrontation. But not this time. I couldn't—*wouldn't*—let them win.

Not a coward, remember?

That red feather . . .

My tiny superhero cape.

Moment: Baby-Blue Schwinn

*C*adillac Jack's *is on the corner of Columbus and Main, a shimmering diner that would show up on Google Earth like a uranium spill. It has an over-the-top fifties vibe that you adore: waitresses wearing poodle skirts and bobby socks, swirling between tables. The Wurlitzer is just for show, but the music being pumped through the speakers is pure rock and roll—Danny and the Juniors, Dion and the Belmonts, Bill Haley and His Comets. It's impossible to sit down to your Blueberry Hill pancakes and not feel like you've walked onto the set of* Happy Days.

You used to go there with Mom every Sunday morning. She'd order the Jimmy Durante fruit cup and a lemon tea. You'd mostly go with the pancakes, but sometimes the Brando omelet—all that gooey American cheese—was too tempting to resist. Mom knew the words to all those rock-and-roll classics, and she'd sing along while you ate. Then she'd make a huge fruity grin out of her orange peel and come in for a kiss. Writing this down won't help you remember everything—time steals as well as it heals—but never forget how much you loved your mom, and how much she loved you.

You dined there every now and then after Mom died, but it wasn't the same. It felt lonely, even with the bouncy, bubblegum vibe. So you found a new breakfast joint at the other end of town: Marzipan's Kitchen—a different dining experience, to say the least. Where Cadillac Jack's has neon and polished chrome, Marzipan's has faux wood paneling and checkered tablecloths. There are pictures on one wall of spooky dudes from the Civil War era, and another wall is decorated, floor to ceiling, with Beanie Babies, each nailed into place through their little heart tags. It has quirk, like Marzipan herself—a sixty-something widow with Smurf-blue hair and coprolalia. "White or whole wheat, fuck-Jesus-fucking-whore-fuck?" she will ask, and you'll coolly reply that whole wheat is preferable. Her profane outbursts—a somewhat rare symptom of Tourette's—ensure the characterful little restaurant is always busy. People love to be entertained.

You'd never have set foot in Marzipan's Kitchen if Mom hadn't died and you'd continued breakfasting at Cadillac Jack's. Mom's death came with many silver linings, which shouldn't surprise you at all, given her glimmering and selfless nature. The quirk of Marzipan's Kitchen is one. Sally is another.

She's the new waitress. Yin-yang earrings. Beads in her hair. An adorable belly accentuating the front of her T-shirt: the female form at Her loveliest. The first thing she says to you, utterly un-waitresslike, is: "You'd look good with long hair. You have the perfect face shape—beautiful cheekbones. Also, we're out of whole-grain bagels."

"Re: the bagels," you reply with the slightest of smiles, "don't sweat it; I was considering an English muffin. Re: the hair, my eyelashes are too long; I'd look like a Las Vegas lion tamer."

"Maybe dreadlocks?" she ventures.

"It's a consideration," you say.

One other thing about Marzipan's Kitchen, real sweet: For those dining alone, Marzipan will often bring out a mannequin and sit it across the table from them. Conversation is encouraged, and sometimes, if Marzipan is in a good mood, the mannequin will foot the bill. It's quite common to see diners getting into the zany spirit of things, discussing a cornucopia of topics with their fiberglass friends. Nobody blinks an eye, either. Marzipan's is liberating like that. Good for the soul, as well as the belly.

"Is this your girlfriend?" Sally asks.

Your mannequin has cracked blue eyes and sultry lips. She wears a paisley headscarf and has two left hands.

"My sister," you say. "We were just discussing Britain's appointment of the first female poet laureate. I don't have a girlfriend."

Sally slides into the booth, bumping your mannequin across the seat. She tilts stiffly, head resting against the wall.

"I listened to you play yesterday at Green River Park." Color has bloomed in Sally's cheeks, red as the checks in the tablecloth. "You were playing to the birds. I wanted to hug you."

"Sometimes they sing along," you say, and there's a quaver to your voice; your heart is tripping. "It's better than money."

"I'm new in town," Sally says. She licks her lips. "I don't know many people. Do you know what you're having?"

"I've lived here all my life," you reply. "I don't know many people, either. I'll take the American cheese omelet."

"Did I mention the bagel situation?"

You want to kiss her right there, right then.

You eat at Marzipan's Kitchen more frequently—three, four times a week—until you finally pluck up the courage to ask Sally on a date. Even then, you can't really do it. You say, "I don't have a car," in the most arbitrary manner, but she knows what you're trying to say, and she says, "That's okay; I have a bicycle," and your voice quavers, "Where shall we go?" and she says, "As far as I can pedal."

That evening, she screeches to a halt outside your apartment on a baby-blue Schwinn, bubbly wine and a punnet of strawberries in the basket. You climb on behind her with your guitar strapped to your back, and she pedals to Buttermilk Falls. You drink the wine and get giggly. You eat the strawberries and get sticky.

"Pretend I'm a bird," she says.

You play. She sings.

The waterfall turns from white to pink in the setting sun.

"I have something for you," she says. "Shhhh . . . don't tell Marzipan." And she takes from the pocket of her skirt a long chestnut-colored wig. "It belonged to your sister. Try it on."

You smile and tug the wig onto your head. Sally helps straighten it, her face alive and as full of color as the waterfall. She brushes errant strands from your face, tucks them behind your ears.

"I was right," she says.

"Lion tamer?" you say.

"You're beautiful," she says.

Her lips glisten, moist with strawberry juice and wine, and you want to kiss it all away. Instead you run a hand through your chestnut hair, pick up your guitar, and play Van Morrison's "Someone Like You."

The birds settle around you.

Four

I've always been resilient. I'm not sure if that's much of a superpower—*Is it a bird? Is it a plane? No, it's RESILIENT MAN!*—but it got me through some scrapes in high school, and it got me out of that cold cinderblock room, where I'd spilled mind and blood in ample measures. I first crawled, then staggered, then limped, but I got out . . . found myself in an industrial wasteland; the rusted skeletons of factories, derelict warehouses, piles of reinforced concrete. Beyond overgrown railroad tracks and a sagging chain link fence, I discovered a narrow stream clogged with faded trash. I stripped, washed my clothes, washed my body, then lay in the brown grass until everything dried. Bullfrogs droned around me. I slept, and awoke to the singed light of an August evening. Distantly—across the stream and a near-apocalyptic expanse of low-income housing—I watched Newark's bulky skyline wink with light.

I was forty miles from home.

My wallet was intact. Not exactly bursting at the seams, but the seventy-three dollars I'd earned from average Tuesday's busking was still there. I caught a bus to Parsippany, then the last bus to Green Ridge.

I'd cleaned myself up the best I could, but I was still bedraggled and bloodstained. That said, neither driver had any problem letting me ride. Hey, this is Jersey.

The second bus was nearly empty. I sat with my head resting against the window, feeling every bump in the road. There was a copy of the *Star-Ledger* on the seat across from me and I was tempted to snag it, see what the date was, but realized I didn't actually care. I was in pieces. I'd worry about the date after I'd been picked up and put back together.

Westbound on I-80, toward Green Ridge. I wished for the next stop to be a place without pain. It was dull and constant. I took the red feather from my pocket and studied it.

This is how you'll remember me.

I wiped moisture from my swollen eye, then blew on the feather. It swayed left and right. I thought not of the spider, but of the dancing girl. Sky-blue dress, hips ticking. I bastardized the partial memory— pulled her into my arms as the Atlantic boomed and the three-piece silently played. I turned her invisible face to mine and kissed where I thought her lips would be.

The bus rumbled. I smelled exhaust through a half open window. The headlights of oncoming vehicles passed across my face like thoughts. East of Green Ridge a nondescript black car pulled into the lane beside the bus. Brickhead was in the passenger seat. He looked at me and nodded, as if we had an agreement.

I flipped him the bird.

Fuck him.

It was almost midnight by the time I made it back to my apartment. It was anarchy, of course, everything flipped inside out, turned over. I didn't correct a single thing, or even tend my wounds. I fell deathlike across my sofa cushions and slept for eighteen hours.

Dull thumping on the door, like someone beating it with a Christmas ham. I rose groggily, tripping over shit on my way to the hallway, slurring, "I'm coming, already," as the door bounced in its frame. I braved the peephole, thinking it might be the hunt dogs, but it was only Mr. Bauman, my landlord. I breathed a sigh of relief, threw the lock, popped the door.

"Jesus Christ," he said. "What happened to you?"

"Bar fight," I said.

"Jesus *Christ.*"

Bauman was small and ropy, third-generation English, but fancied himself Italian—a forty-year-old guido wannabe with blown-out hair and a spray-on tan. He wore too much gold and had his teeth bleached every three months. The tattoo on the inside of his forearm read GIUDO 4EVR.

"How can I help you, Mr. Bauman?"

He shifted from one foot to the other, trying to get a look over my shoulder. I rolled my eyes, held the door wide, showed him the mayhem.

"Those guys you let into my apartment," I said. "They had a party."

"They were looking for your girlfriend," he explained. "Concerned family members, they said."

"Yeah, they were all heart."

"Jesus, what a goddamn mess." He ran the tip of one forefinger across his eyebrows. "Hey, any damage is your responsibility. Understood?"

I nodded.

"So about the girl," he continued, puffing out his chest. "I figure she was the breadwinner, with you being, you know, like a bum."

They see the dreadlocks and baggy clothes, the guitar case open for loose change and dollar bills. They don't see the craft, the commitment, the clean teeth and fingernails.

"A street performer," I said.

"Yeah, yeah. Whatever. Anyways, she used to pay in cash, first of every month. I know she ain't around anymore, so I'm just checking you're good for it."

The rent—$860 a month—was the last thing on my mind. I could probably cover it with my busking, but I had savings (actually, a generous inheritance, courtesy of Mom) in the bank, unless Sally had wiped me of that, too.

"I'm good for it," I said.

"Music to my ears," he said, pointing at his temples. "You're late once, I put you out on your ass. *Capisce?*"

"I'm good for it," I repeated.

"Well okay." Bauman puffed out his chest again, then waved a hand at the mess behind me. "And clean that shit up. Jesus."

He swaggered away. I called his name.

"Mr. Bauman . . ."

He stopped, looked over one shoulder, eyebrow cocked.

In an ideal world, I would *never* discuss personal matters with my idiotic landlord. But I was confused, upset. All I had was a partial memory and something inside—an emotion—that I couldn't pin down. I wasn't leaving my apartment anytime soon, and I knew my old man wouldn't answer the phone, so right then, Ralph "*GIUDO 4EVR*" Bauman was my only option.

"You saw us together, right?" I asked. "Me and Sally?"

He regarded me suspiciously, as if I was trying to trick him. He made a gesture with his upper body—almost a shrug, not quite a nod—that I couldn't read.

"It's just . . ." I stepped toward him, lowering my voice. "We broke up, you know? It was kind of sudden, and I'm still trying to get my head around it. But maybe I wasn't as happy as I *thought* I was. Now, I respect you, Mr. Bauman. You're a man of the world—a man who knows a thing or two about the fairer sex. *Capisce?*"

I wanted to shoot myself in the face for saying that, but Bauman nodded, groomed his eyebrows again.

"So I'm wondering—from your point of view—how we looked together . . ."

"Looked?"

"You know . . . did we look happy?" I took a deep breath. It hurt my bruised ribs. "You think we were in love?"

He stepped back quickly, as if I'd set fire to his sneakers.

"What? I look like Dr. frickin' Phil to you now?"

"C'mon, man. I've been to hell and back." My swollen face was evidence of that. "I just want to know if she was worth it."

He set his jaw and nodded, responding to the bitterness in my tone, as I knew he would.

"I don't know what goes on behind closed doors," he said. "I ain't no snooper, but I guess, to me . . ." He made a "more or less" gesture with his hand, his rings winking in the overhead light. ". . . To me, you looked pretty good. Cut from the same cloth, my ma would say."

"Right," I said.

"I don't know . . . when I saw you together, you were always smiling, I guess." He rubbed his chin and shrugged. "She must've been doing something right."

I hooked a thumb into my pocket, brushed the red feather.

"You think I should go after her?" I asked.

"I think you should fix your face," he said. "Then I think you should clean your apartment. After that, it's your call. All's I care about is eight-sixty a month."

She swirled in my mind again and I reached for her. Bauman said that we were cut from same cloth, and that I was always smiling when he saw me with her. There *had* to be something there—something worth chasing, *protecting*. That strange emotion deepened. The thought of her alone and scared didn't sit comfortably with me.

I pulled my shoulders square—felt a little of my strength return.

"Mr. Bauman," I said. "One more thing."

He was almost at the stairway. His sneakers squeaked as he stopped, swiveled at the waist, and looked at me.

"What day is it?" I asked.

"Friday," he said.

Five

So it was slightly-better-than-average Friday. Or, on this occasion, woeful-shitty-painful Friday. Fortunately, there were only five hours and forty-three minutes of it remaining. I showered with the water cranked hotter than was comfortable, concentrating the jet on the achiest places. It was altogether excruciating. The blood that flowed from my dreads was like terracotta paint from a brush. The water ran tepid before I was clean.

Three Advil, and each felt like a finger bone in my buckled mouth. I crossed my junked living room to the window, peered through the blinds. A casual glance showed all was well on Franklin Street. The setting sun inked slender shadows along the sidewalks. Traffic rumbled and honked. The patio outside Juke Johnny's was thronged with clientele; happy hour ran until 8 p.m. Fridays.

The scene was a wholesome slice of American pie, until I checked the periphery. There was an unmarked silver cargo van outside Cramp Hardware, no doubt loaded with tracking equipment and nondescript muscle. A dude in a Yankees cap stood in the doorway of a beauty salon, playing with his cell phone but occasionally stealing glances at my window. Something winked—a camera lens, perhaps—from the top floor of the office building across the street, where the workers would have left hours ago, and even the cleaners would have packed up by now.

They were everywhere.

Or maybe—*maybe*—it was just a cargo van parked for the evening, a dude waiting for his ride, the evening sun glinting off the office windows.

Jesus Christ, I was turning into my father.

The Advil numbed me, body and mind. I shuffled through my apartment, making a half-assed effort to clean up. This amounted to sweeping up some broken glass, brushing crumbs from my kitchen counter, and flipping my mattress back onto the box spring.

It was a start.

I boiled an egg. It sat unbroken in its cup, my appetite—such as it was—gone in the time it took to cool. I found a clear space on the floor and strummed my guitar, more interested in the abrasions on my wrists than any chord I was playing. Eventually, I popped two more Advil and went to bed, but not before cracking the blinds one last time.

It was too dark to see anything.

I woke in the small hours, positive the hunt dogs were in my apartment. I couldn't hear them, but I *felt* them. I fumbled for my lamp but it was broken on the floor. Pain crimped the left side of my body as I rolled out of bed. I stumbled into the hallway and hit the light.

Nothing. Just the shit show as I had left it. Didn't mean they weren't there. In a closet, perhaps. Behind the shower curtain.

"Motherfuckers," I breathed, sliding into the kitchen, grabbing a breadknife from the counter. I gave it a couple of experimental swipes and it made a sharp, satisfying sound, although the thought of having to use it was only marginally better than the thought of being back in that cinderblock room.

"Motherfuckers."

Into the living room. The light from the hallway made deep shadows of the corners. Easy to imagine the hunt dogs skulking there. That they wouldn't bother hiding, or even skulking—would simply grab me like they had before—didn't factor into my logic. I was scared and paranoid. The mind runs at least three paces left of center at such times.

"I can see you," I said, even though I couldn't. My hand crawled along the wall, found the light switch, flicked it. The shadows disappeared. I saw my jumbled living room and nothing else. I checked behind the sofa, the coffee table, even behind the plastic banana tree. It was then that I began to suspect my emotions were getting the better of me.

I lowered the knife.

So tired, I thought.

But yes I checked the closets, yes I checked behind the shower curtain, yes I checked the kitchen cupboards.

"I'm losing my mind."

I couldn't live like this. No fucking way. I looked out the window again at Franklin Street bathed in 3 a.m. atmosphere, sidewalks bare, the stoplight red. How long before I stopped living like a frightened mouse?

I returned the breadknife to the kitchen drawer, then grabbed my bloodstained jeans and took the red feather from the front pocket. I sat on the windowsill with one leg hanging, the blinds partway open, looking from the silent street to the feather. I relived it all—pain, threat, humiliation, violation—many times, hoping it would wane with repetition. The fear was boundless. The dread weighed me down.

Everything . . . red as the feather in my hand.

There was anger, too. It gathered inside me. Along with that other deep emotion—that Sally thing—that perhaps I was afraid of admitting to. And yes, these emotions were also red.

I twirled the feather.

5:40 a.m. The sky paled. A delivery truck grumbled to the intersection of Franklin and Main.

The light changed.

The next few days were spent healing and cleaning. By Wednesday my apartment was more or less back to normal and I could do some light exercise. I hadn't spoken to a single soul since Bauman had thumped on my door. I left my apartment only to check my mail. On one occasion I found my mailbox open, and surmised the hunt dogs had been there before me, obviously hoping to intercept any possible correspondence from Sally. I wondered if Bauman had given them a key along with a copy of the rental agreement, then realized he wouldn't have to. It was a basic lock, any doofus with a pick could open it.

They were probably checking my e-mail, too. You didn't need to be an elite black hatter to gain access to a Gmail account. I considered changing my password, for all the good it would do, but didn't bother. I had nothing to hide, and if Sally was careful enough to wipe my computer's hard drive *and* my memory, she certainly wasn't about to send me an e-mail.

Loneliness kicked in on Thursday. Okay, I'm not Captain Sociable, I admit to that, but I'm not a recluse, either. I missed being outside, amid the buzz of day-to-day life. I missed the sunshine on my face, the metallic glow of the river, the sound of the halyard tapping the flagpole in Veterans Square. I missed playing my guitar at Green River Park and smiling at the townsfolk who dropped money into my case. And the birds, man, pecking breadcrumbs and chirping along to Cat Stevens. Yeah, I really missed the birds.

The walls of my apartment had never seemed so close. I opened the windows and gulped the sunshiny air, but it didn't help with the loneliness. I ended up taking a load of washing to the laundry facilities on the ground floor and waiting around for someone to talk to. Eventually, some old cat shuffled in with an empty basket and I chatted to him while he folded. We had nothing in common. We discussed the exorbitant per-unit price of the detergent in the vending machine. It was the dullest, shittiest conversation I've ever had. I retreated to my apartment, more depressed than when I'd left.

Saturday (still-hurting-and-hating-my-shitty-life Saturday) I thought, *Fuck it,* and grabbed my guitar, headed outside. I got as far as the front step before a wave of fear broke through me and I shrank back to my claustrophobic coop. It took an hour for my heartbeat to return to normal.

Determined not to be outdone, I broke up a handful of graham crackers, then opened both windows in my living room and scattered the crumbs on the ledge. First little dude on the scene was a bright-eyed oriole with a pretty voice. I started to play my guitar and two house wrens joined the party. Pretty soon the ledge was hopping, and I smiled for the first time in over a week.

It wasn't Green River Park, with the smell of the water and the summery breeze in my hair, but it was better than nothing.

Feeling somewhat buoyed, I tried calling my dad. A waste of time and hope. I knew he wouldn't answer; he was convinced that the NSA was spying on the nation's telephone and Internet communications, using backdoor loopholes to violate the privacy of 320 million blissfully ignorant Americans. He had a working landline, but used it only to call *Truth Matters USA* (the nation's number-one show for conspiracy theorists and idiots) and to order pizza.

Mom insisted that he wasn't always so unstable. They'd first met in 1966. Mom was a ten-year-old schoolgirl, and Dad, nineteen, along with two other young men from Green Ridge, had been paraded into her classroom by the principal. "These fine young Americans," the principal fiercely intoned, "from here, your very own hometown, will soon be sent overseas to fight the slope-eyed devils of Asia. Know that they are fighting for a people who are not our friends, neighbors, or cousins, but who live half a world away: the Vietnamese, besieged by tyrannous and vile communists." He whispered the last word for maximum sinister effect. "*Communists!*" Again, emphasized this time with a stomp of the foot. "Who but America will stand against the unjust, and will go gun-in-hand to fight for the freedom of others?" And apparently the principal became quite emotional and had to excuse himself, at which point the children asked the three brave men any number of informed questions, like, "What kind of dog is your favorite?" and "Do you know Gomer Pyle?" But it was Mom—in pigtails and horn-rimmed glasses—who stood up and, instead of asking a question, offered the peace sign, which she had seen some pretty groovy teenagers exhibiting at a protest in Green River Park, and it was only the jug-eared man in the middle—my dad—who returned the gesture.

After training at Fort Riley, Kansas, he was deployed with Charlie Company, 4th/47th, 9th Infantry Division, in January of '67. He saw nine months of service before a Viet Cong ambush cut down his platoon on the outskirts of a village in Long An province. Thirteen of the "Old Reliables" were killed. Dad—who lost the left side of his face when a VC frag grenade exploded less than twenty feet from him—was one of the lucky ones.

He spent ten weeks at hospitals in Saigon, Japan, and the US, before being discharged from the army on Christmas Eve of '67. Adorned with his Bronze Star and Purple Heart (actually, they were rolled up in a sock in his luggage), he returned to Green Ridge, and following a handshake from the mayor and some frigid flag waving, he was all but ignored. Perhaps it was his grotesque injury, or the growing tension over the war, but people became very uncomfortable around him. Except for little Heather June Fountain, now eleven years old, who remembered the young man who had come to her classroom and returned the peace sign. She started to go to his house after school and read to him on his front porch, only for fifteen minutes or so, but it was a part of the day they both looked forward to. Time passed. The books went from *The Wolves of Willoughby Chase* and *A Wrinkle in Time* to *The Catcher in the Rye* and *Slaughterhouse-Five*. Also, the townspeople adjudged that if a girl just out of pigtails could engage so agreeably with the unfortunate young veteran, then they should make a greater effort. Dad was thus employed at the textile mill, where he spent three years operating a spinning frame, and then at the post office—but way in back, where he couldn't be seen, sorting parcels.

Mom said this was when the cracks started to appear. He had frequent nightmares and flashbacks. One time he locked himself in the safe at the post office and refused to come out until they'd swept the area for mines. In the mid-seventies, after the last US troops had returned from 'Nam, his fears shifted from the Viet Cong and their assorted weaponry to . . . well, just about everything else: asteroids, Russians, politicians, aliens, nuclear war, demonic possession, oil companies. Mom assured me that, for all these occasions of frailty, Dad was often discerning and considerate. He once—using Swan Connor's music industry contacts—arranged for Little Anthony and the Imperials to doo-wop in Mr. and Mrs. Fountain's backyard: a little thank-you for being so selfless in regard to their daughter.

It wasn't until the late seventies that Mom and Dad's relationship ventured into a more romantic territory. Mom—now in her early twenties—was promoted to assistant editor at the Green Ridge *Sentinel,* and my dad was so thrilled for her that he scooped her into his arms and danced her around the garden. Mom responded by kissing him on the mouth, thereby initiating their romantic involvement. There was a delicate period at the beginning where Dad struggled with confidence issues, and it must have been difficult for him to separate—but not disassociate—the woman with whom he now shared a bed from the little girl in pigtails who'd read to him after school. It took time, but he got there. *They* got there.

They were married in the summer of 1982. A nonreligious ceremony in Green River Park. They honeymooned in the Poconos before renting a three-bedroom split-level on Wilson Avenue.

I came along seven years later.

One of my earliest memories is of Dad blowing raspberries on my belly, his face struck with joy and not at all unusual. A rare memory, in that he is clearly delighted. I have searched my brain—a spider to myself—for similar moments of happiness, but they are obscured by occasions of distance and insecurity. Like the time he hollowed out a tree trunk and lived inside it for a week, and Mom had to feed him through a hole made by a woodpecker. Or when he drew an eye and half a mouth on the scarred side of his face and walked around as if we wouldn't notice (and we—God love us—pretended not to). Mom had hoped the responsibility of a child would complete his healing, and draw out his beautiful inner character. In fact, the opposite happened: Dad feared the world more. He feared it for *me*.

I used to blame him for my social shortcomings, which wasn't fair. He was an older dad—forty-two when I was born—so wasn't inclined to run around with me on his shoulders or shoot hoops in the yard. Even so, I wondered if I could relate more to other kids if my old man—like theirs—had taken me to baseball games or taught me how to fly a kite. He *did* introduce me to his vinyl collection, a universe of sound that kindled my love of music. He also taught me some evasive driving techniques in case I ever got into a high-speed car chase with terrorists or shapeshifters, and what to do in the event of an alien invasion.

Mom was my balance—my go-to parent on the many occasions I needed one. Her death had the paradoxical effect of further rifting my relationship with Dad, in that we'd lost our common denominator, and bringing us closer together, in that all we had was each other. I thought college would provide the distance we needed. I applied to Mom's alma mater—Vassar—and got in, but dropped out after a year because I couldn't bear the thought of Dad being totally alone. He'd moved from Wilson Avenue to a converted barn in the country outside Green Ridge. I rented an apartment and visited dutifully.

We each found our coping mechanism—our *groove*. I started busking (made pretty good money, too) while Dad distanced himself from reality. He ascribed to wilder conspiracy theories, wrote articles about the microchips implanted in our brains and how Kentucky Fried Chicken causes impotence in African-American males. He scrutinized the night sky for extraterrestrial activity, and used what he'd learned in the Mekong Delta to turn his sprawling, jungly land into a death zone of booby traps. He also adopted stray cats, believing them to be reincarnations of deceased celebrities. I once discovered one of Johnny Carson's hairballs in my granola.

But I loved him, in spite of his eccentricities. And as I sat holed up in my apartment, alone and afraid, I longed for him to relinquish his distrust and answer the goddamn telephone. I couldn't ask him about Sally or if the hunt dogs had been snooping around (assuming the likelihood—not to the mention the irony—of my phone having been tapped), but to hear his voice would be enough . . . to feel his strange comfort.

Jesus, I wanted my dad.

So I called him, and of course he didn't answer. I tried several times, because persistence usually pays off. But not on this occasion.

I tried not to fear the worst as the phone rang and rang at the other end: that the hunt dogs *had* paid him a visit—that he'd responded aggressively to their inquiries, and as a result was slumped in the living room with a bullet to the head. I quashed this terrible thought by telling myself that the hunt dogs—for all their threats—had no interest in killing. Not with the spider crawling around, who could do all the damage he wanted with the power of his mind.

No, the old man was alive and kicking, probably deconstructing the Zapruder film or listening to *Truth Matters USA*. He just didn't like answering the phone. I promised myself I'd go see him just as soon as I could leave the apartment.

I wasn't ready for that yet, but I was getting there.

I burned the next forty-eight hours eating and sleeping, and by Tuesday felt more like my old self. Not 100 percent, but a little stronger, for sure. My bruises were yellow and black and the cut beneath my eye was healing nicely. I tried to leave the apartment again—I needed sustenance; my refrigerator was empty of everything but a few shriveled mushrooms—and this time made it all the way to Main Street before fear and paranoia sent me scampering back into my shell. I studied the red feather while repeating the mantra, "Fuck you, I'm not a coward. I won't be bullied, so fuck you . . ." That evening I tried again—didn't make it as far as the Health Nut, but got to the Happy Filler Gas and Convenience, two blocks west. I bought trail mix, eggs, and protein bars. On Friday morning I managed a full Ashtanga routine. It left me hurting, breathless, but exhilarated.

I played four songs at Green River Park that afternoon. A nervous, distracted effort. I strummed a few bum chords and forgot the words twice. Didn't make a dime. Even so, this was as close to normal—to average—as I'd been for some time, and I was foolish enough to believe that things might be looking up.

Sally, meanwhile, was never far away. That single, incomplete memory pushed and enticed, and I wondered, not for the first time, if she'd left it for a reason. She dominated my dreams, too. Sometimes as a lover: raw, feverish fantasies. More often as a scared, lonely girl running from something that slathered and swooped. In each case, I woke with her name on my lips, clutching the empty half of the bed, knowing beyond all doubt that she should have been there. She should have been next to me.

Six

The last day of August was the kind of hot that drained everything of its vitality. Ninety-three by midday, the streets were languid and blurred in the heat haze. I stood on the front steps of my apartment building, guitar in hand, and scanned the periphery for threats. Seeing nothing suspicious—although it was difficult to be certain in the glare—I crossed Franklin and walked a block to Posy's Florist. Here I selected a modest arrangement of reds and yellows, then walked another four blocks to the bus stop.

I checked every storefront window along the way, every doorway and parked car. By the time I made it to the Columbus Avenue stop my upper body was coated in sweat and my heart was clamoring. I set my guitar down, assessed my surroundings again, then sat on the bench and waited. Seven minutes until the 270 arrived, which would take me to within a five-minute walk of Rose Hill Cemetery. This would mark the farthest I'd ventured since crawling from that cinderblock room. I was on edge, but it would take more than paranoia to keep me from visiting Mom's grave.

August 31. The tenth anniversary of her death.

Behind me, the Barista King was doing small business on this sweltering day. I considered grabbing something full of ice and caffeine, then Swan Connor maundered over—two canes clacking—and dropped onto the bench beside me. He smacked his gummy lips together and said, "Jub." If I moved now, it'd look like I was moving because of him. I had no idea how much thought he was capable of, but I didn't want him to think that.

"Hello, Mr. Connor."

"Jub."

His hair stood in creamy tufts. There was a clump of orange goo in his right ear and a blob of dried oatmeal on his chin. My heart ached for him, this man who had once been so sharp, generous, and successful, who'd worked with some of the biggest names in the music industry, and was now—one stroke later—little more than vegetable matter. I'd lost my memories of Sally. Swan had lost *everything*. I couldn't begin to imagine what that was like.

He'd watched me play a few times, and it always felt like I was auditioning. "You're good, kid," he once said to me. "But you need to write your own material. And cut your hair. White guys with dreadlocks don't sell records. They look like bums." I smiled, thanked him, and told him that I didn't want to sell records, that I was happy playing to the birds. He laughed and said I was crazier than my dad.

The bright flowers caught his eye. He half pointed at them.

"Jub."

"They're for my mom," I said. "You remember her, right? Heather Anderson. Married to Gord."

He made a mumbling sound and maybe nodded. He'd gone to school with Dad, and they'd remained friendly until Dad's psychological concerns became too significant a factor. Mom had known him, too, of course, but never really took to him. "He's a peculiar duck," I remember her saying. "I guess that's what you get for hanging out with Frank Zappa." And I had corrected her: "No, Mom, he's a peculiar *swan*." And we'd laughed until there were tears in our eyes.

I wondered what Mom would do if she were sitting with me now, but I didn't have to wonder long; I knew. I plucked a flower—a brilliant red gerbera—from the bouquet and threaded it through one of Swan's buttonholes. It stood out against his dour clothing like a stoplight. It transformed him. He looked, suddenly, *lighter.*

"There," I said, managing a smile. "That color suits you."

The 270 rumbled onto Columbus and toward the stop. I got to my feet, grabbed my guitar. Swan sniffed his flower and his eyes flooded with grateful tears.

"Jub," he said.

"You're welcome, Mr. Connor."

Rose Hill is a beautiful cemetery on the outskirts of Green Ridge, thirty-eight peace-filled acres landscaped with towering evergreens, modern sculpture, and a man-made lake. I walked a winding path toward Mom's grave, breathing the clean air and trying to focus on my reason for being there: Mom. Only Mom. Recent events had reinforced how much I missed her, and the ten years since her death seemed now a blur, perhaps because so many of the intervening memories had been erased.

There was a music of birdsong, of the summer breeze and branches waving. It accompanied me as I stepped off the path and strode between the graves until I came to the stone that bore my mother's name. No unnecessary dates or epitaphs. Just her name and a single encompassing word: BELOVED.

I dropped to my knees. Pushed my fingers through the grass there.

It was an ideal spot, neighbored by a tubular sculpture through which the breeze piped dreamily, and close enough to the lake to hear it lapping. Mom purchased this plot when she learned that her breast cancer had bypassed "curable," and gone directly to stage IV. She had drawn the money from her retirement savings and remarked, with the driest, most heartbreaking smile, that this was entirely appropriate. I remember visiting the location with her in the weeks before the cancer took hold, and assessing its natural beauty as if we were going to build a house there. I had escaped to the lake to cry. Mom had remained dry-eyed throughout. So brave. So strong.

I brought my hand to my face, smelled the grass between my fingers.

"Hi," I said.

A yellow rose had been laid at the base of the stone. Dad had been here before me. Not *long* before, judging by the rose's freshness. I had actually tried calling him again to see if he wanted to meet, but—true to form—he hadn't answered. The rose, at least, assured me he was still alive.

There was a note, too. Occasionally, Dad would scribble a little something—a random Mom memory—and leave it on her grave. In reading these notes (and they were always written in the second person, addressing *himself*, to emphasize memory over emotion), I had discovered things about their life together that I would otherwise never have known. Like how they used to enjoy bicycle rides at sunrise, and how each chose the other's ice cream flavor. It was sad and sweet. And yes, I found it baffling that my father was too insecure to answer the phone, but had no problem leaving a note—however cryptic and anonymous—in a public place. People deal with their grief in different ways, I guess.

This one read:

> You sit, mostly, with one hand covering your face, without her to lower it, and kiss you, and tell you not to hide. "A full moon shines brighter," she would say. You couldn't hold all her love, if your arms were twice the size.

I sat with my own memories for an hour or so, not speaking, lost in occasions of happiness and wonderment. Grief, too. But I found what I'd been looking for: Mom. Only Mom. And the recent pain faded. The fear, too. All thoughts of Sally, the spider, and the hunt dogs were temporarily suspended.

Mom's favorite song was John Lennon's "Woman." It was written for Yoko Ono, but it works for moms, too.

I took out my guitar, started to play.

The sculpture piped in tune.

To be absent from the real world—with all its strangeness and paranoia—felt entirely wonderful. If only it could have continued.

I wasn't alone at Rose Hill.

Snapping my guitar back into its case, I became aware of someone watching me. Not a new sensation, by any means, but this felt distinctly different. I stood up and retreated from Mom's grave, swiveling my head, scrutinizing the shadowy spaces between the stones and trees. I'd taken no more than a dozen steps when a muscular arm appeared from behind a marble obelisk. Before I could even flinch, I was dragged backward and thrown against the monument with a jarring thud.

"Hello, Harvey," Jackhammer said.

The sight of his grapefruit face sent cold water rushing through my stomach. I squirmed out of his grasp and wheeled toward the path, unsure of my direction, but it didn't matter anyway; I lost balance and tumbled to the ground. Jackhammer was on me in a moment. He pressed the heel of his boot against my throat just hard enough to keep me from struggling.

"I suggest you keep your cool," he said, his voice low and bland. "This is a social visit, but it can turn nasty in a hurry."

I wheezed in reply, twisting my neck enough for him to see me nod. He lifted his boot and with his boundless strength—sickeningly fa-miliar to me—hoisted me to my feet. I staggered, dropped my guitar case, and flopped against another grave marker. Sweat dripped from my brow and my heart galloped.

"What do you want?" I managed.

"Thought I'd check in," he said, spreading his hands in a casual manner. "See if any memories had resurfaced, or if there's anything you should tell us."

"Nothing," I said. "I'm just trying to get on with my life."

He looked at me carefully, his eyes narrowed. I'd been thinking about Sally constantly—*dreaming* about her—and I wondered if that showed in my expression.

"Do I need to call my boss?" he asked.

The spider. I blanched—couldn't help myself—and shook my head.

An elderly lady shuffled close, carrying flowers that had wilted in the heat. She gave us a curious glare before moving along. Elsewhere, I heard the breeze excite the trees and the arrhythmic tapping of a woodpecker.

Jackhammer waited for the lady to amble out of view before looming close, prodding me hard in the chest with his forefinger.

"We can get to you anytime, anywhere," he warned. "You need to think about that if you're trying to hide something."

"Your boss makes it hard to hide anything," I said.

His lips twitched. Almost a smile. He retreated a step and his impressive chest expanded as he inhaled.

"So?" he asked.

"So what?"

"Anything you need to divulge?"

"No."

"Have you contacted anybody who knew Sally?"

"I've barely left my apartment," I replied. "My landlord wanted to know if I could make rent. That's about it."

He searched my eyes but all he saw was fear. He then clamped my face between his concrete fingers, tilting it this way and that, examining my wounds.

"We really roughed you up, huh?"

I twisted away from him.

"Yeah, you did."

"Two reasons for that. Firstly: We find it an effective method of procuring information." He pushed his face close to mine. His rancid breath was as familiar as his strength. "Secondly: It serves as a precursor to what will happen should you withhold information or cross us in any way."

I nodded, recalling the wet-meat sound of his fist against my face.

"We *will* fuck you up, Harvey," he whispered. "We'll crush everything you know and love. And when you're bleeding from every hole in your body, begging to die, my boss will pick through your tiny little mind and find what you've been keeping from us. Sound like a good time to you?"

I wiped sweat from my throat and sighed. Distantly, a mockingbird called colorfully and I heard music on the breeze. Some other son, perhaps, playing his mother's favorite song.

"How long?" I asked Jackhammer.

His face was grapefruit-bland again, except for one raised eyebrow.

"How long before I get my life back?" I drew myself to my full height. I was taller than Jackhammer by at least three inches, but he still over-shadowed me. "How long before you realize that I'm no use to you?"

He shook his head, as if that were any kind of reply. I wondered if his soul was as dry as the bones beneath me.

"Just leave me alone," I said.

He slipped away without another word, with barely an expression. Gone in a moment. Blended with the shadows.

Jackhammer's motive was to reintroduce fear, and it worked, but there was another, unexpected effect; walking to the bus stop and then rid-ing into town, I contemplated how Jackhammer had violated Rose Hill—the most peaceful, unblemished place I knew—when he could have more easily come to my apartment. It was an unnecessary move that underscored the hunt dogs' callousness, and in turn reminded me what would happen to Sally if they ever tracked her down. Anger overshadowed my fear. There was something else—so subtle that it took a moment to place: a sense of triumph. Jackhammer had revealed a certain vulnerability. His threats were formidable, but they were *desperate.* Sally's trail had gone cold and they were hanging on to the pos-sibility that timid, terrified Harvey might recall some crucial detail, and point them to where the little fox was hiding.

Motherfuckers had nothing.

The anger stirred me. *Riled* me. It also exposed that indefinite emo-tion inside—the one I'd been afraid of admitting to. And it was love. Of *course* it was. I loved a girl I couldn't remember, and that made *total* sense to me. Because love is quite apart from memory. It runs deeper, like a hole in space that exists even after the star has exploded.

I returned to my apartment, where my only company was a half-eaten protein bar and a plastic banana plant. I played furious music until my neighbors hammered. I twirled the red feather and considered my empty life.

Not *quite* empty; Sally was out there.

Somewhere.

Cancer destroyed my mother. She went from hale to ashes in a matter of months and all I could do was watch. The darkness that followed Sally was different but no less destructive. Despite the threats—the nightmarish associations the red feather was supposed to incite—I knew I had to do something.

I looked out my window at Franklin Street, then over the gray rooftops at a scoop of Jersey and the haystack world beyond.

"Where are you?"

I dreamed about her again that night, dancing in a rain of red feathers. She drew me into her arms and set her ticking hips close to mine. *I'm going to find you,* I whispered in her ear, and might have said more but she stopped me, her mouth against mine.

I closed my eyes and we swayed to soundless music.

Seven

Marzipan's Kitchen had lost none of its character. The checkered tablecloths, Beanie Babies, and pictures of spooky nineteenth-century dudes were still in place, and Marzipan was as endearing and foul-mouthed as ever. The only visible change was her hair, which had run through every color in the rainbow before settling—at least for now—on angel white.

Two things hit me as I stepped through the door. The first was the aroma of home-cooked food, eliciting empty sounds from my stomach. The second thing was Sally. Her energy was so palpable that I almost expected to feel her hand slip into mine, or see her sway from the kitchen carrying plates of steaming food. Even if the hunt dogs hadn't so violently repositioned her in my mind, the warmth and character of Marzipan's Kitchen would have. I think the result would've been the same, too—the certainty of having lost someone precious, along with a bullheaded determination to find her again.

I hovered in the doorway, barely tethered, until Marzipan shuffled over in her slippers, her white hair gelled into an impressive rhino horn.

"Harv," she said, flapping a hand at the dining area. "Sit anywhere, but it's quiet today so I'll be closing soon. Fuck you."

"Yeah . . . okay." I gave my head a little shake, blinked distantly, and grabbed a table against the spooky-dude wall. Marzipan was right; it was quiet, with only three other tables occupied—two couples and a redheaded woman sitting opposite her mannequin, engaged in lively conversation. I zoned them out and focused on the Sally vibe, absorbing every minim of sensory stimuli in the hope that some lost memory would float to the surface.

My mind drifted. My eyes glazed over. A woman appeared in the seat opposite, as if placed there by the power of will. Her head was tilted at a carefree angle and a wave of brown hair covered one side of her face.

Okay, for one second—maybe two—I thought it was Sally, but only because I was so deep in the vibe. My heart dropped a beat before I realized my mistake.

"I don't often bring you company," Marzipan said, adjusting the mannequin's position so that she didn't fall off the chair. "You're usually here with Sally."

"Yeah, well," I muttered. "She left me."

"I know that. I had some men here asking about her."

"Oh yeah?"

"IRS, they said, but I didn't believe them."

"You tell them anything?"

"What's to tell?" she said. "They wanted to know where Sally was. I told them I didn't know."

"Right," I said. "I told them the same thing."

Marzipan placed one finger beneath my chin, tilting my damaged face toward the light.

"I guess they didn't believe you?" she said.

"You guess right," I said, touching my scar. "But it's true. I don't know where she is. She just took off."

"Not for the first time, I bet." Marzipan screwed her eyes shut and made a zipping motion across her lips. This was one of her physical tics, which helped suppress the profanities. She took a deep breath, held up one hand, and said, "Sally was a quiet one. In my experience, quiet people tend to have the most secrets. But secrets cast shadows, Harv, and sometimes the only option is to run where there's more light."

"Yeah," I said. "I think you're right."

Marzipan nodded, satisfied, then took my order: her famous tomato soup with homemade bread (my stomach was crying out for real food; I was so fucking sick of protein bars), but when it arrived I barely touched it. A slurp of the soup. A nibble of the bread. My appetite had fizzled, unlike Sally's energy, which swirled around me in a way it didn't anywhere else, not even in the apartment we'd apparently shared.

I rode the vibe again, like a surfer on a wave, taking it as far as I could. I even employed the breathing technique I use during yoga, hoping to attain a heightened awareness. It helped; I blotted out the ambient noise and felt Sally more deeply, but no memories were uncovered.

Rousing myself from this near-meditative state, I noted that my soup had turned cold and that the other diners had vacated. It was just me and my mannequin, who regarded me from behind that veil of tawny hair.

"I don't know what to do," I said to her. "How do you help someone you can't even find?"

No reply.

"How do you find someone you can't remember?"

Still nothing. I shrugged, took a ten from my wallet, and tossed it on the table. I was about to leave when the door opened and our very own chief of police stepped in. Brian Newirth. Perceptive, unruffled, classically handsome.

"Harvey," he said, approaching my table. "I haven't seen you around much. Mind if I sit?"

"Sure," I said, "but I was just leaving."

"Stay awhile," he said. "We need to talk."

"My performer's license is up to date," I said with a nervous smile.

"Good to know," he said, sliding the mannequin over so that he could sit opposite. "That's not what I want to talk about."

Marzipan poked her head up from the kitchen. Chief Newirth caught her eye and ordered coffee. She made the zipping motion and disappeared. I looked from the chief to the mannequin and back again.

"Looks like you've got my undivided attention," I said.

"Good," he said.

Our conversation was neither brief nor pleasant, even though Chief Newirth did his utmost to maintain a neighborly tone. It caught me off guard, mainly because—with my own catalog of concerns—I hadn't thought about the Green Ridge murders for some time. They may have popped into my head now and then, but I hadn't really *considered* them: the victims, the families, the impact on the town.

Twenty minutes with Newirth, though, brought everything to the fore with new and chilling implication.

If I'd believed things couldn't get any worse, I was wrong.

The first victim was Melissa Wynne. Twenty-five years old. Green Ridge born and raised. She was a single mother, well-liked, worked two jobs. I knew her as well as I knew anybody in town, which is to say, not well. Her kid used to enjoy watching me play. He'd sit in his stroller clapping his chubby little hands. Kept pretty good time, too.

Melissa's body was found on the morning of August 15, 2012. I say "found" but there was no attempt to hide her. She'd been wrapped in garbage bags and dumped in the middle of the Shoe-Nuff parking lot. There was no clear motive, and the few persons of interest—Melissa's ex-husband, two recent lovers—had solid alibis. The killer had been either very careful, or very lucky.

The town bubbled for a couple of weeks. We carpeted the Shoe-Nuff parking lot with flowers, as if Melissa had any affinity with the place other than that her corpse was discovered there. We held a candlelight vigil at Green River Park, beautifully attended, and set our candles floating downstream afterward. Homicide detectives appealed for information and knocked on doors, and the good folk of Green Ridge assisted them wherever possible.

By Labor Day things were largely back to normal. Melissa's murder was no longer the topic of every conversation, and state police had switched their focus to other major crimes. We were asked to remain vigilant, though, and to report any suspicious activity. I can't speak for everybody, but I'd say this heightened awareness of the periphery lasted a few more weeks. Maybe.

Victim two: Latisha Paffrey, twenty-nine years old, originally from Atlanta, Georgia. Her body was discovered in the doorway of Granger Insurance on the morning of July 20, 2013. The similarities to Melissa's murder were irrefutable. Both were African-American females in their twenties. Both were bound in garbage bags and dumped in public locations. Both were raped vaginally and anally, and beaten about the skull with a flat-faced instrument. One slight variation in the MO: Melissa had been stabbed twenty-three times in the torso, Latisha six times. Still, there was little doubt they were dealing with the same killer.

The investigation escalated. Police scrutinized every tenuous connection between the two victims. They cross-examined mutual associates, and looked for links to other sexual homicides within a one-hundred-mile radius. Suspects were rounded up and interrogated. Three local men were arrested and later released. Even I—one of the town's oddballs—was brought in to aid with inquiries. The questions were on the plus side of intimidating, but I didn't mind; the police were doing their job, and I had nothing to hide.

The investigation sent ripples through the community, ruffled feathers, but bore no fruit. Much like the hunt dogs, police used strong-arm techniques in the absence of solid evidence, hoping to scare out a lead or, better yet, a confession.

They got nothing.

Nine months passed. The town lowered its guard.

Victim three: Grace Potts, discovered at the foot of the monument in Veterans Square. She complicated the pattern in that she was Caucasian, thirty-two years old, but everything else was consistent: bruising and tearing around the genitalia; eleven puncture wounds to the torso; blunt force trauma to the skull. Police efforts again intensified. More forensic analysis, cross-referencing, interrogations—a forcible joint endeavor by Green Ridge police and the state's major crimes unit that, unfortunately, netted the same results.

No worthwhile leads. No witnesses. No apparent motive. Forensic pathologists found no conclusive trace evidence or DNA. The killer was brutal, but meticulous. He clearly didn't want to make the investigators' jobs too easy.

I imagined him among us, not skulking and wolflike, but blending in—just an everyday dude who buys his groceries at ShopRite and his suds at the Liquor Monkey, but twisted inside, and laughing as the police chased their tails.

With no dependable evidence and a shortage of resources and manpower, the investigation was turned over to the county's cold case unit in June 2015.

But cold didn't mean dead, and while the people of Green Ridge had lapsed again in their vigilance, the police had not.

I never had a problem with Chief Newirth. He was one of the good guys, a proud American intent on serving his community as honestly and efficiently as possible. He'd been chief for twelve years, deputy chief for eight years before that. I couldn't remember a time when he didn't embody Green Ridge's law enforcement. But there was more to him than the badge; he organized events for local charities, ran a boxing gym in Bryant Grove (Green Ridge's low-income neighborhood), and talked at schools throughout the Skylands Region about such issues as firearm safety and substance abuse. He also donned the red suit in Green Ridge's celebrated Santa Claus Parade.

Yeah, one of the good guys.

I studied his calm brown eyes as he stirred sweetener into his coffee, thinking he looked incongruous beside the mannequin, as if *he* were the one out of place. He lifted the mug to his lips, took a sip, shook his head. "Not great," he said. "Been on the plate too long." He added another sweetener, stirred again, then asked, "Where's Sally?"

A conversation with law enforcement will always set a person on edge, even when they've done nothing wrong. I didn't think this could be anything serious, though, given that we were in a public location (sharing a table with a mannequin, by God). Nonetheless, I found the chief's casual approach concerning.

I told myself to be cool—I'd done nothing wrong.

"She left me," I said. "Skipped town."

"You don't know where?"

I shook my head.

Chief Newirth nodded, took another sip of coffee, curled his upper lip. I recalled one of the hunt dogs warning me about talking to the police. *Consider, carefully, what you'll tell them, and if they'll believe you,* he'd said. *And then look over your shoulder. We just might be there.* I glanced from the chief to the restaurant's front window, expecting to see a shadowy figure leaning against a streetlight, or a nondescript black car parked across the road. I saw nothing suspicious, but felt suddenly as if I were trapped between two immovable objects.

"No forwarding address?" Chief Newirth pressed. "No cell phone, or number where she can be reached?"

"Nothing," I said.

"She just . . . disappeared?"

"I guess."

"You guess?"

I nodded vaguely, because the only information I had would make me sound crazy. *She stole my memories, Chief, then I was accosted by a group of thugs led by a dangerous mind reader I call the spider.* I linked my hands to keep them from trembling. How could I be so blameless, yet look so guilty?

"It's not unheard of, but it *is* unusual," Chief Newirth remarked. "In my experience, there's often some contact after a breakup, if only to tie up loose ends."

Another vague nod. Chief Newirth watched me while he sipped his coffee. I couldn't hold his gaze.

"Of course, unusual doesn't mean suspicious." The chief set his mug down and spread his hands. "But the fact remains that a young woman has disappeared without trace, which raises certain concerns in light of our town's recent history."

It took a moment, but the weight of his words dropped onto my shoulders, and the air rushed from my lungs so fast that I needed to grab the table to remain balanced.

"Wait a second," I gasped, and now I had no problem looking him in the eye. "Sally's not dead. She just . . . left town. It happens."

Chief Newirth took another sip of coffee and his hand was remarkably steady. "I have a responsibility, Harvey. I need to report anything untoward to the county prosecutor's office, no matter how insignificant it may seem. So I'm gathering the pieces and trying to make them fit. You understand that, right?"

"Sure," I said. "And I'll help you any way I can. But honestly, sir, Sally just left. I don't know where she is, and that's the truth."

"I get the feeling," he said, pointing to my left cheek, "this is connected somehow."

I touched the crescent scar, feeling a knot of ruptured tissue beneath the surface, but it was otherwise healed. I told my landlord that I'd been in a bar fight, but that bullshit wouldn't fly with Chief Newirth. The whole truth wasn't an option, either, so I plugged for something close.

"Some guys came looking for Sally." My voice cracked. There was a pitcher of tap water on the table. I poured a glass and downed it in three pelicanlike gulps. "Let's just say they were more forceful in their interrogation techniques."

"This isn't an interrogation," the chief said calmly.

"I know that, sir." Hearing those words helped, but they didn't stop my heart from hammering.

"I heard about those guys," the chief said. "I've made some inquiries, but haven't been able to locate them for questioning."

"You won't," I said. "They're invisible. I can't tell you anything about them. I can't even tell you what they look like."

"Nobody's invisible, Harvey. Some people are just better at hiding than others."

Tell me about it, I thought.

"I also ran a background on Sally," Newirth continued. "Actually, I didn't, because she *has* no background. Not as Sally Starling, at least. So she's either an illegal immigrant, a fugitive, or is on the run for some other reason."

"Okay," I said.

"Did she ever mention her past to you? Talk about her parents, or her childhood?"

I frowned. If I told the truth—*I don't remember*—it would look like I was avoiding the question. If I made something up, he'd see through it. Either way, I looked guilty.

"She's a quiet girl," I said, echoing what Marzipan had said. "Very private."

"You didn't know *anything* about her? That didn't bother you?"

"I knew what I needed to know," I said. "And I'm a private person, too. It was all very cool."

"No driver's license, social security number . . . Jesus, Harvey, that didn't seem *odd* to you?"

"I don't remember it being an issue," I said. One hundred percent true.

Chief Newirth held up one hand, as if I were a lost cause, like his coffee—of which he took another sip, sneered again. He was persistent. Got to give him that.

"Anyway," he said, turning his cool brown eyes back to me. "Sally. No background. On the run. These heavies show up in town—bounty hunters or loan sharks—around the time she disappears. They snoop around. They rough you up. Are you with me, Harvey?"

I nodded. Cat was on the money.

"The pieces fit," he said. "I don't like them, and there are things I don't quite understand, but they *fit*. When the prosecutor's office enquires into unusual activity, I can lay this out. No problem. Keep calm and carry on, as the T-shirts say."

"Okay," I said, and my discomfort lessened, albeit marginally. "Totally do that, then."

"*Except*," the chief added, leaning across the table, the expression in his eyes more probing than cool. "A detail came to light recently that . . . hey, it's probably nothing, but I need to address it before doing anything else."

I nodded. I had no idea what emotions my body language conveyed—guilt, confusion, fear—but at that moment I aimed for absolute honesty.

"I'll help you if I can," I said.

"That's what I like to hear," he said with a smile. He considered his coffee again, then pushed the mug to one side. I tried a smile of my own, hoping it didn't look as false as it felt.

"You still live at Passaic Heights?" the chief asked.

"Yeah."

"One-bedroom apartment?"

"Yeah."

"Does it have a garden area? Anywhere for residents to grow flowers or vegetables?"

"Nothing like that," I said, wondering where this was going. "There's a small, paved area in back where the stoners hang out, but that's about as horticultural as it gets."

"That's what I thought," the chief said. "And have you been doing any gardening on the side, perhaps to make a few extra bucks now that you're on your own?"

"Gardening?" I shook my head, frowning. "No, sir. That's not really my thing."

"Right." Chief Newirth settled back in his seat. His badge caught a pellet of light. "So tell me, Harvey . . . what use would you have for a shovel?"

He appeared to have deviated from his original line of inquiry, and I wondered if the bad coffee had rattled his usually perceptive brain. I shook my head again.

"A shovel?"

"Yeah, you know . . . for gardening. Or digging holes."

"I know what a shovel is, I just . . ." I looked at the mannequin, as if she could provide an explanation, then back at the chief. "Honestly, sir, I don't know what you're talking about."

He nodded, took a notepad from his breast pocket, flipped a few pages. "Friday, August seventh. Five forty-eight p.m. You bought a shovel from Cramp Hardware. A Razor-Back digging shovel with a forty-nine-inch fiberglass handle. That's a quality tool, Harvey. Tough to break. You obviously planned on digging a deep hole."

I looked at him, jaw hanging.

"I have a copy of the sales receipt in my office," he said, tucking the notepad back into his pocket.

"You've made a mistake," I said, and I was sure of it. "It wasn't me."

"The store clerk and another customer say otherwise," the chief said. "Well, they said it was the tall guy with dreadlocks who plays guitar outside the Liquor Monkey."

"Wrong," I said, shaking my head.

"You're also on the store's security cam," the chief added. "Large as life, holding a shovel."

"What?"

"I can arrange for you to see it, if you need your memory jogged."

And that was it: my memory. Whatever use I had with a shovel, it was connected to Sally, and she had deleted it from my mind. I lowered my head and sighed. *What have you done, Sally?* I thought. *What have I done?*

"August seventh," the chief said. "That's around the time Sally disappeared, right?"

I threw my mind back, but it was all a blur. I shrugged and said, "I guess."

"It was the last day she worked at the Health Nut. Joy Brady showed me the schedule. Sally worked nine 'til two. She was supposed to work the morning shift on the eighth, but didn't show up."

My eyes—so heavy—rolled up to Chief Newirth's. I figured if I wasn't under arrest, I could just go home. You see it in the movies all the time—the suspect being grilled by police. *Am I under arrest? No? Well, fuck you.* And they get up and leave, those cool motherfuckers. My legs were trembling, though, and I felt sick inside. I wasn't going anywhere.

"So," Chief Newirth said. "You want to explain why you bought a shovel on the day your girlfriend disappeared without a trace?"

Yeah, I thought. *I do want to explain it.* But I could only stutter and blink, feeling as empty-headed as the mannequin. Eventually, three words—the truth—stumbled from my lips:

"I don't remember."

"That's not very helpful, Harvey."

"But I *don't,*" I warbled, and elaborated with something that didn't feel *too* much like a lie. "Ever since those thugs beat me up, I've struggled to remember certain things. Maybe it's post-concussion syndrome.

Or brain damage. Shit, I don't know, but there *has* to be some rational explanation for this."

"I hope you're right," Chief Newirth said.

"What . . . you think because I bought a shovel that I killed my girlfriend? Buried her someplace?"

"I didn't say that."

"And that I likely killed the other women, too?"

"I'm not accusing you, Harvey." His eyes remained calm. He linked his fingers and studied me over the top of them. "I'm looking for answers. That's all."

"It's bullshit," I snapped.

A shrill voice from the kitchen: "*Cocksucker!*" We both turned and saw Marzipan frantically making the zipping motion. She saw us looking and ducked—"*Fuckity-fuck*"—out of sight. A little break in the tension, for which I was grateful. I breathed through my nose. Found a shred of calm and pulled it close.

"It's bullshit," I said again, but in a quiet, controlled voice, and I looked at Chief Newirth with all the honesty I could muster. "Besides, it doesn't fit the killer's MO. Those women weren't buried, they were dumped out in the open."

"An MO isn't a signature, Harvey. It can change according to the conditions of the crime." He leaned across the table again. "I have to look into this. You know that, right?"

"I haven't done anything wrong," I insisted.

"No one is saying you have," the chief said. "No missing-persons report has been filed. No dead body has been discovered. As of right now, there isn't a crime. And buying a shovel isn't against the law."

"Right," I said.

"But something doesn't fit. I *know* it." He tapped the side of his head and winked. "Cop intuition."

My head drooped. The sick feeling inside bubbled through my pores and from my eyes. I wanted to run away.

"I like you, Harvey," Chief Newirth said. "I've known you all your life. You sat on my knee every Christmas and you never asked for much. I know what kind of person you are."

I wasn't sure if he was trying to reassure or coax me, but his tone was kind and I gravitated to it—came close to reaching across the table and clasping his hands.

"I want to help you," he said. "But you have to help me, too. If you hear from Sally, let me know. If you remember why you bought the shovel, you need to tell me. Because right now there's a question mark over your head, and I want to be able to erase it."

Walking home took longer than it should have. I ambled distractedly, took a few wrong turns. My mind was a scrambled, aching bird's nest of thought.

Again, I told myself that I'd done nothing wrong, but how could I be sure of that? I knew Sally wasn't dead; she had to be alive to steal my memories. But I'd done *something* with a shovel on the night she disappeared—something she saw fit to delete—and that troubled me.

I walked with my shoulders drawn tight and my hands jammed into my pockets. I scoped the streets for hunt dogs, but really, it felt as if the whole world were watching me.

I didn't sleep that night; I tossed and turned my way into the small hours with one question—*What did you do, Harvey?*—banging through my mind. Eventually, the sun nudged over the horizon and colored a new day. I longed for it to be average. Quinoa flakes for breakfast. Busking in Green River Park. Feeding the birds.

Life wasn't average anymore.

I *tried*, though. I managed three mouthfuls of cereal before my appetite shriveled. I pushed the bowl aside, then spun from my apartment and crossed the road to Cramp Hardware. According to Chief Newirth, I'd purchased a Razor-Back digging shovel with a forty-nine-inch fiberglass handle. They had three in stock. I took one off the rack, expecting the memory of some heinous crime to recur the moment I touched it.

I got nothing.

What did you do, Harvey?

I tested the shovel's weight and feel, then made a few manly dig-ging motions.

Still nothing.

The store clerk eyed me curiously. I wondered if it was the same dude who'd reported my purchase to Chief Newirth.

"Help you?" he called across the store.

I shook my head, returned the shovel to the rack, and left.

Two hunt-dog sightings that afternoon. I *think*. The black car in Juke Johnny's parking lot looked suspicious, with its tinted windows and Alabama plates (the hunt dogs had no discernible accent, but the spider definitely carried a hint of the South), and I thought I saw Brickhead hovering in the doorway of the Sushi Stop, although it was difficult to be sure because of the amount of people scooting in and out. By the time I got a clear view, he was gone.

I wandered the streets for hours, everything bubbling in my mind: Sally, the spider, the hunt dogs, the shovel. I tried to find some order, some *sense*. My head ached. My eyes thumped.

One thing was certain: It was time to make a move. I was done with being scared and alone. No more swimming in circles like a goldfish in a bowl.

Back at my apartment, I threw some shit in a backpack, slung it on my shoulder. A cursory—pointless—look out the window. The black car with Alabama plates had gone. If the hunt dogs were out there, they had blended in perfectly.

They couldn't stop me anyway.

I knew what I had to do.

Eight

Fear convolutes truths and cripples reason. It turns a maybe into an absolutely. Most emotions are like waves, they crash and recede. Fear is like a hand grenade; once the pin is pulled, who can say how much damage it will cause?

I sat at the back of the bus and noticed the tailing car: a silver Chevy Impala with New York plates. It stopped when we did, pulling to the side of the road, then rejoining the traffic as we rumbled away. A coincidence, perhaps—could have been someone stopping to program a GPS or send a text message—but my paranoia painted the man behind the wheel: bland face, square shoulders, heavy hands. The passenger and rear seats were similarly occupied.

They had seen me leave my apartment building with a backpack on one shoulder. They were staying close.

I took the red feather from my wallet, bringing the spider's words to mind: *The pain. The threat. The humiliation. The violation. I'm sure you'll do anything to avoid a repeat of what has happened here. Or something worse.*

The Impala was five car lengths behind. The setting sun rippled off its windshield like a burning flag. I couldn't see the driver—couldn't even see if there was a passenger.

You're on my radar now. If you try to run away, or even consider *keeping information from me . . . I want you to look at this feather.*

I looked at it: a deep, bloody red within the gloom of the bus.

"This is how you'll remember me," I whispered.

We made a left turn onto Ramapo Avenue and the Impala, after a moment, followed. My eye tracked to the backpack on the seat beside me. Nothing much in there. A pair of jeans. Two clean T-shirts. A travel bag loaded with toiletries. Not exactly my worldly possessions. But was I *trying to run away?* Was that what this was, or how the hunt dogs might see it? Would they intercept me before I reached my destination?

The pit of my stomach turned cold.

"Don't let them stop you," I murmured, trying not to lose my resolve. "It might not even *be* them."

But then Jackhammer spoke up in my mind, and his voice was very convincing: *We* will *fuck you up, Harvey.* I shrank into my seat—could almost smell his breath. *We'll crush everything you know and love.*

That was when the fear kicked in, crippling reason, turning a maybe into an absolutely. The hunt dogs *were* in the Impala. Four—no, *five* of them, armed with stun guns, brass knuckles, slip-joint pliers for extracting my teeth. They were going to fuck me up. Make me bleed from every hole in my body.

The coldness in my stomach turned to nausea. I screwed my eyes shut, shook my head. The red feather fluttered between my trembling fingers. I clung desperately to that other thing it represented: the *fight* in me; the determination not to let the bad guys win.

You're not *a coward. Don't let them stop you.*

A right turn. The Impala followed.

You've got this, Harvey.

We clipped an amber light that turned red before the Impala reached it, forcing it to stop. Within moments, there was some distance and a good deal of traffic between us. No time to breathe easy, though; they'd catch up as soon as we made our next stop.

My chest boomed. I popped the narrow top window and gulped air that tasted like exhaust and steel. Not pleasant, but it cleared my head enough to know that I had to get off the bus. I sat down again, looking down the narrow aisle and through the bus's expansive front windshield. We were approaching Spruce Plaza—a crummy strip mall at the edge of town. I could get off here, then catch another bus home. No harm done. My life of doubt and suppression would resume. At least until I was ready to try again.

Or . . .

I looked at the red feather.

Or I could get off, then run. If I did it before the hunt dogs caught up, they'd think I was still on the bus—would follow it to the end of the line.

A huge risk, but it just might work.

Ahead, the strip mall glimmered in the evening gloom. I pulled the cord. The bell sounded and the bus immediately slowed. I grabbed my backpack and stumbled down the aisle. The doors opened with a pneumatic hiss. I disembarked and looked toward town. No sign of the Impala.

Indecision halted me. Grab a bus home, or run?

Two choices, Harvey: coward or hero.

"I'm not a coward," I insisted.

In the distance, a silver Impala with New York plates edged into view.

I made my decision.

I ran.

My long legs scissored across the parking lot and I slipped behind a jacked-up Silverado, taller than me. I peered through the cab windows but couldn't see the road, then dashed for the Applebee's at the end of the strip. The hostess noted my discomposure and took a step back rather than greet me. "Just grabbing a beer," I mumbled, sliding around her as I looked over my shoulder, trying to see through the windows, but the light was fading and I saw nothing but reflections.

I skirted the bar and walked across the restaurant. The dinner rush was on and I figured I could slip through the kitchen and hit the back-door before anybody noticed me. It almost played out this way, but some dude with dreadlocks like mine—bundled beneath his hairnet like a couple of caught octopuses—saw me and offered a fraternal,

"Right on," before realizing that I shouldn't be there. His jaw dropped and he held up one hand, which I couldn't help but high-five, then he said, "Bro," in an inquisitive voice, and I replied, "Bro," in a more assured one, before sidestepping a caddy of dirty dishes and pushing through the backdoor. It opened on a service alley littered with crushed cigarette butts, empty crates, and—against the far wall—dumpsters lined end to end like train carriages.

I heard a car's tires squealing and my imagination conjured a shot of a silver Impala careening toward the alley. Had they seen me striding across the parking lot, or entering the glaring, neon-lit restaurant? They would send two men in the front, then the car would race—tires screeching—around back to cut me off. I stood paralyzed for a moment, waiting for them to advance on me. Then I jerked into action. I ran at the nearest dumpster—sprung off it catlike and over the wall. It was a deeper drop on the other side and I landed awkwardly. Twisted my ankle. Wobbled and fell on my ass. I picked myself up and limped across gray scrubland, then ducked into the gap between two buildings. A raccoon woke and blinked bright eyes at me, then hissed and found a gap of its own. I pushed on, pinballing off the walls, emerging into another lot where several cars were parked. I slunk from one to the next, edged onto the sidewalk. The road wasn't busy. I stumbled across, cut through someone's yard, scaled their back fence. Here was more scrub, sloping to a play area and basketball court. There were a few kids shooting hoops and teenage girls on bleachers smoking, lost in their cell phones. I exited the play area and headed north, keeping to the shadows where possible.

My legs were loose, coated in sweat. My heart was a gun. I scanned like a periscope the entire time. I flinched at every passing car.

I limped half a mile before resting behind a derelict diner off Route 94.

Almost full dark.

Even hidden from the road, with the sky dark but for a burn mark in the west, I couldn't shake the feeling I was being watched. I massaged my swollen ankle and rested for as long as I dared, then moved on.

The road was both the safest and most dangerous place to be. Easy to follow, but also easy to *be* followed. I had left Green Ridge behind and ventured into its scenic backdrop: a rugged tract of Kittatinny Valley, marked with freshwater wetlands, ravines, and forests, dominated by a broad limestone ridge that gave the town below its name. I took Buckhorn Road off Route 94. Traffic was infrequent but fast-moving and I ducked out of sight whenever possible. It made for slow going. After two miles and close to an hour, I arrived at a small gas station about to close for the night. I bought aspirin for my ankle and a flashlight the size of my thumb. The attendant was old and slow-ass. I shifted nervously as he rang up my change. The fluorescents made me feel as exposed as a specimen on a microscope slide.

Outside again, I merged with the darkness and shoveled three aspirin into my mouth. I continued another mile or so down Buckhorn Road before scaling a moderate outcrop and—flashlight in hand—cutting through a thicket of ragged trees and shrubs. I paused for a moment. The silence was eerie and sweet. I believed—perhaps prematurely—that I'd broken away from the hunt dogs. For the first time since this ordeal began, I didn't feel like I was being watched or followed.

I took a rigorous breath, cupped the drum of my chest, managed a weak smile. Pushing through the thicket, I joined the Silver Rock Trail, zigzagging northwest toward Spirit Lake. In the bright of day, I would be afforded a stunning view of the valley and the Kittatinnies beyond. Now I saw stars and whatever fell within the cone of my flashlight.

Ten minutes on the trail. The uneven ground was tough on my ankle. I rested atop a boulder, sprawled like a lynx, then mopped the sweat from my face and dry-crunched another aspirin. Somewhat enlivened, I rejoined the trail for another half mile—jumped a foot in the air when several deer broke from the forest line to my right and bounced beyond the flashlight's glow. I swore at them under my breath and pushed on.

I had walked this trail dozens of times during daylight hours, but never at night. I was jarred by how unfamiliar it felt, only seeing a tiny portion at a time, as if it were being stitched together ahead of me—and unstitched behind—as I limped along. The sounds were foreign, too. Hoots and creaks. Something tapping. A distant, cold yowling. Even the silences were different. They were purer . . . longer. During the day, this shard of Appalachian wilderness was as natural to me as the walk to Green River Park. At night, it felt like I didn't belong.

I recognized, thankfully, where the trail veered from my destination. I clambered up a steep incline, grabbing roots and tough grasses to hoist myself up. A brief respite at the top, plucking burs from my clothes and hair, catching my breath. I used another moment to get my bearings, then moved on. The stars dissolved as the forest folded around me. I inhaled scents of hemlock and beech. The ground crunched beneath my feet, then became stonier. I came to Fellow Creek, twenty feet wide at this point. It trickled musically, feeding Spirit Lake a mile northwest, which in turn drained into the Delaware. I crossed without pausing, but carefully. The water flowed around my knees but no higher. The ground was wetter on the other side and my flashlight picked out the glimmering shells of what had to be a hundred bog turtles. I tiptoed among them, holding my breath, like a man in a minefield.

The ground elevated steeply, then leveled out. I ducked beneath branches, pushed through spiny shrubs and ferns, and eventually heard the traffic on Ribbon Road. This is where the bus would have stopped had I stayed on it. I was getting close—ten minutes away, at most. I fetched a relieved sigh and continued through the dense forest.

That was when I heard something behind me.

I whirled with a gasp, flashlight sweeping, and saw—thirty feet away— an indistinct shape flicker between the trees. It was gone in a blink. Too nimble to be a bear, and too big—too *upright*—to be a deer. A trick of light and shadow, perhaps. Or a hallucination brought on by fatigue. The fear, though—still with its claws in me, and always apt to cripple reason—screamed that it was the hunt dogs. They had followed me after all.

I broke into a painful, hobbling run, directing my flashlight in vaguely the right direction and following it as if tugged by a rope. Branches whipped my face and snagged my hair. I stumbled over a rock, fell into a shallow ditch, scrambled to my feet. I managed half a dozen awkward steps before bouncing off a tree and falling again.

A confusion of noise: critters breaking, startled, through the understory; the canopy rattling; the blood pounding in my skull. Still on my ass, I turned three-sixty with the flashlight. Branches swayed. Shadows pounced. I popped to my feet and staggered through the foliage.

The ground dipped suddenly and I would have fallen again, but grabbed a low-hanging branch and stayed on my feet. The forest settled around me and I dared a glance over my shoulder—saw nothing out of the ordinary.

Didn't stop.

I emerged from the trees moments later, into high grass that ticked in the breeze. Walking backward, I studied the forest line, expecting the hunt dogs—or a black bear, frothing at the mouth—to appear. Nothing did. I counted fifty ragged breaths. Still nothing.

Just your mind playing tricks with you, I thought. *Jesus, Harvey . . . paranoid much?*

I turned dizzily, trying to get my bearings, to figure out if I was in the right place. My flashlight picked out tall weeds, a knotted fencepost, the bole of a familiar oak. I passed beneath its sprawling branches with the light angled upward. An untroubled owl regarded me with huge eyes.

I edged from beneath the oak, then heard the ominous *snick* of my right foot triggering the trap.

Fuck.

I tried to move—wasn't quick enough.

There was a whipping sound, followed by something closing around my swollen ankle. Suddenly I was hoisted upward, turned upside down, hanging by one leg from a rope tied to a branch.

I twirled helplessly, pathetically, like a broken yo-yo. I didn't know whether to laugh or cry.

A flashlight—more ostentatious than mine—bloomed in the distance. It cut a broad triangle of daylight into the darkness, narrowing as it approached. I twirled slowly, shielding my eyes, until the light was lowered and I saw a hunched man shape behind it. He stepped closer, breathing heavily. I twirled again and watched the scarred balloon of his face float into the light.

"Harvey," he growled.

Yeah, I was in the right place.

"Hi, Dad," I said.

Moment: Human Nature

W*hat does* eccentric *mean, anyway?" she asks, plucking a maple leaf from an overhanging branch. "Different? Odd? Should a person be labeled because they dare to live outside the box? And if so, wouldn't* individual *be a nicer label?"*

She brings the leaf to her face, inhales deeply, like someone breathing the ocean from a shell. Her smile is small, delightful, as if she and the leaf share some secret.

"You're so kindhearted," you say. "Do you always see the best in people?"

"For as long as I'm able," she replies. "It's a better way to live."

You walk from the stop on Ribbon Road to Dad's house. The air is tinted green and deliciously scented. This is the first time you have made the walk with Sally. With anybody. *And your heart, brother: wham and bam. You are so nervous.*

"Consider this fair warning," you say. "You can give me your full assessment after you've met him."

"I'm sure he's wonderful."

You've had girlfriends before. Brief misadventures with the fairer sex that left you hurting/confused/resentful. Remember Delores Covington, skater girl and pyromaniac? Dating her was like being a contestant on a

Japanese game show. Then there was Eloise Dance. Pixie eyes. Voice like Betty Boop. Slept with a loaded .357 beneath her pillow. These relationships did not last long, nor were they particularly serious, but they left you wondering what was required for two people to find true happiness. Did their shapes have to align to begin with, or was there some magic relationship cement that was used to patch the gaps? You'd asked Dad, because he'd found happiness with Mom, and because . . . well, a boy should *be able to turn to his father for anything, including matters of the heart.* "Even the best relationships are balancing acts," *he'd said.* "They take time, patience, and exactness." *Remarkably coherent.* Normal, *even. And then he'd said,* "Unless you're co-existing with a reptilian, in which case there's nothing you can do."

Thankfully, Sally has provided a clearer response. Not in what she says, but in who she is: sweet, intelligent, considerate, mysterious. Simply put: easy to love. No surprise that you want her to meet your old man. A true test of compatibility. If she loves you after this, she'll love you through anything.

"Do you think I'm eccentric?" *she asks, pushing the leaf into her hair.* "Different?"

"Sure," *you say.* "That's why I dig you."

"Dig? That's sweet."

"Aw, you know . . ."

A truck rolls westbound and you step to the edge of the shoulder until it has passed. The wind gust it creates ripples your clothes and lifts Sally's hair, but the leaf stays in place.

"Maybe I'm more different than you think," *she says.*

Dad's barn house comes into view, with its rutted driveway and perilous yard. A cat is poised statuelike atop a fencepost—doesn't deign to look as you pass. "Hey, kitty," *Sally says, and does the kissy-kissy thing, but the cat only flicks her tail and stares straight ahead. Cats manage arrogance and cool better than any creature alive.*

"I told you about the cats, right?" *you ask.*

"I'm ready," *Sally says.*

You have cleared the visit with Dad, of course. You know better than to show up out of the blue with your new girlfriend. He'd pissed and grumbled for a few weeks, but finally succumbed. "Expect no airs," *he had announced.* "No graces." *As if he were capable of either. But—having navigated the* yard without mishap—you enter his house to find it cleaner than it has been in years, with scented candles flickering and Brahms on the stereo. There's an open bottle of merlot on the kitchen table. Several cats skate comically across the newly polished floor.

Dad—while not as presentable as the house—has no doubt made an effort. He wears a faded paisley shirt tucked into clean dress pants, with a cravat fashioned from one of Mom's old headscarves. A long black wig covers the left side of his face, hiding the scars.

"Miss Starling . . ." He greets Sally with an elegant handshake and a pompous, affected tone of voice. "An absolute delight to make your acquaintance."

"Likewise," Sally says, then tilts her head to one side. "Do you like my leaf? It's a maple."

"Like it? I love it." He lets go of Sally's hand and snaps his fingers. "Harvey, be a darling and pour the wine."

His posturing is sweetly intended, but makes for a more peculiar atmosphere. You think it a shame that you can't fully relax, and don't know whether to blame yourself or Dad for that. All you want is for the old man to not embarrass you or upset Sally. You don't think it too much to ask.

The real Dad briefly appears when an overweight cat flops onto the sofa beside Sally, and she ill-advisedly asks his name.

"That," he says, adjusting his cravat, "is lovable Hollywood actor Dom DeLuise. Can you see the resemblance?"

"Actually," Sally says, "I can."

"He's been with me for about five weeks. A part of the family now."

Dom mewls and licks his balls.

"Harvey will confirm this," Dad continues, flicking a finger in your direction. "Within days—sometimes hours—of a celebrity's death, a stray or feral cat appears on my doorstep. Make of that what you will."

"Reincarnation?" Sally asks.

"Or some form of possession."

"Or," you venture, "complete coincidence."

"Poor Harvey," Dad says, and gives you a dismissive look.

"Well, cats are connected to the spirit world," Sally notes. She glances at you. Her mouth twitches and her eyes brim with fondness.

"Yes. They're also remarkable companions." Dad scoops one from the floor and places her on his lap. "They have all the qualities you hope to see in people: loyalty, independence, intelligence, cleanliness . . ."

A ruthless killer instinct, *you almost add.*

"I have seventeen of them," Dad says. "This beautiful lady"—he holds up the cat on his lap—"is Katharine Hepburn."

When Sally leaves the room a moment later, you take the opportunity to address Dad's behavior.

"What happened to no airs or graces?" you ask.

"I thought I'd make an effort," Dad replies.

"But it's a mask, Dad. It's false."

"Isn't that what you want?"

"What I want," you insist, "is for you to be yourself."

"No. You don't."

Sally returns full of bounce and color. She suggests you all take advantage of the June sunshine and go for a walk.

"There must be some amazing trails around here," she says.

"There are," Dad says. "You go, the two of you. I need to feed the cats."

"Come with us," you say halfheartedly.

"You go," he says again.

Sunlight floods the trees. They shine with color and movement, parting on the banks of Spirit Lake like beautiful gates. The water flickers, dark and gold. A blue heron skims the northern edge and disappears across the wetlands.

"The lake looks still enough to walk across," Sally says.

You smile and kiss her. To the west, the Kittatinny Ridge looms through the summer haze. There are no traffic sounds, but you hear the trees and the life within them, everything calling.

Sally takes off her shoes, lifts her skirt, and wades to her thighs. You have no inclination to join her, only watch. She quavers and tells you that the fish are tickling her calves. Amid the sun glare, she is sublime.

"Don't go too far," you warn. "It gets deep in a hurry."

"I'll stay where it's safe," she says. "It's what I do best."

You sit on the shale. It cracks and slides, then settles. Sally emerges after a moment and lies beside you with her skirt still pulled up. You draw patterns in the water on her thighs. Her eyes are closed. She quavers again.

"You're like him," she says later, when her legs have dried and her skirt is back around her knees.

"Him?"

"Your dad."

You'd been slouching on one elbow but now you sit upright and look at her with a questioning expression. She smiles and takes your hand. You pull it free.

"How can you say that?" you ask. "You haven't even met him. What you've seen . . . it's not real."

"I'm a good judge of character," Sally says.

"Not on this occasion."

"Your distrust of people. Your insecurity and individualism." She takes your hand again. "You're more like him than you want to admit."

"Insecurity?"

Sally holds her thumb and forefinger an inch apart.

You shake your head and look across the water. Not angry, but a little hurt, although you can't work out if it's because Sally is so wrong, or so right.

"Hey, this doesn't have to get frosty," she says. "Your dad has a big heart, and you don't take in that many cats without being kind and caring. You have those qualities, too."

"Well, gee. Thanks."

"And sure, he's a little out there—"

"A lot out there."

"But I'm willing to bet he's strong inside, and that he can step up when needed."

You recall how he once devised plans for a gigantic Faraday cage to be built around the house, and how he spent three weeks analyzing Microsoft Word's Wingdings font for anti-Semitic messages. But you also recall the man who sat at Mom's bedside for hours on end, reading Shakespeare to her (admittedly, in the style of Richard Burton), holding her hand while she slept, feeding her tiny drops of food, like a sick lamb.

"Yeah, well . . ." You shrug, trail off.

"There's nothing to be ashamed of," Sally says.

"I take after my mom," you insist.

You walk back in near silence and find Dad sitting in the gloom of his living room. The long black wig is gone. He wears a plain T-shirt, blue jeans, and athletic socks with holes in them. Several cats are arranged like gargoyles around him.

No music plays. The candles have been snuffed out.

"Dad?" you say, trying to study his face in the light coming through the windows. "Everything okay?"

"You were right, Harvey," he says. "It's no good pretending to be someone I'm not."

You inch closer. Dad shifts in his chair and looks at Sally.

"Clearly, that wasn't my real hair," he says to her. "It was a Morticia Addams Halloween wig. I bought it at the dollar store."

Sally presses her lips together.

"The way I dressed and spoke . . . that was a lie, too." He shakes his head. "I wanted to make a good first impression. Not for me. For Harvey."

"Dad—"

He shushes you by raising a hand. The ruined side of his face catches the light. Sally doesn't flinch.

"Harvey loved his mom so much," he continues. The gleam in his eye lasts a second, then fades. "I always felt he was ashamed of me. On this occasion, I wanted him to be proud."

You want to tell him you are *proud, but can't. That—like the wig—would be a lie. You lower your head and shuffle your feet.*

Sally, who always sees the best in people, at least for as long as she's able, says: "I know who you are."

He regards her with an expectant expression, and is about to say something when his attention is diverted by movement at the living room window. His single eye widens. His upper lip twitches. You turn and see a cat sitting on the outside ledge, pawing at the glass.

"Hello, friend," Dad says. He crosses the room, opens the window, and the cat leaps into his arms. "Where did you come from?"

You play along because you have hurt Dad's feelings enough for one day. You fetch the new cat a bowl of water and stroke behind his ears. He's an American shorthair, black with a dirty white ruff. His eyes are bright drops of hazel, exactly the same color as Sally's.

"*Ed McMahon died the other day,*" *you offer, and look around for Johnny Carson, who you'd last seen clawing the drapes in the entranceway.*

"*Hmm,*" *Dad says, then shakes his head.* "*No. I don't think so. Sally?*"

"*I don't think so, either,*" *Sally says.*

Dad has a flat-screen TV in the corner of his living room, which he calls his Window of Lies. He finds the remote and turns it on—flicks from a Cialis commercial to Fox News, where a reporter stands outside the UCLA Medical Center, babbling into her microphone while the lower third announces in sensational uppercase that Michael Jackson—the king of pop—is dead.

You turn as one and look at the cat.

He meows and blinks brightly.

The remainder of the evening passes in a surreal haze. You eat supper on the rear deck while Dad recounts war stories, all of which you've heard before, then retire to the living room for more wine. The radio plays nonstop Michael Jackson songs. Sally pirouettes with tears in her eyes. She sings along to some of them. Her voice is beautiful. Carefree, but with measured tenderness.

When "Human Nature" comes on she says, "I love this song," and pirouettes again, then grabs Dad from where he sits on the sofa and dances him around the room. He is hesitant at first—definitely self-conscious about being so close to her—then relaxes and follows her lead. After a moment, he presses his scarred face to the top of her head.

Sally looks at you and winks. She still has the leaf in her hair.

Michael Jackson curls up on your lap and sleeps.

Nine

I stayed with Dad for three days. I thought the change of scene would help me get my shit together, but I also longed for echoes of yesteryear—for *normalcy*. Sure, the old man had alarming levels of bullcrap flying through his head on a constant basis, but this was the person I knew and loved, and who had a hand—a small one—in raising me.

"Why are you here?" he asked on the night I arrived, after cutting me down from the tree and all but carrying me to the house. I lay on the sofa while he bandaged my throbbing ankle, and thought about how best to answer.

"I wanted to see you," I replied, keeping it simple.

"See me? At ten o'clock on a Wednesday night?" He raised his only eyebrow. "You're not drunk, you're not high, and you're not displaying signs of an alien abduction."

I gave him a Vulcan salute just to fuck with him.

He finished wrapping my ankle, securing the bandage with a strip of first-aid tape. He'd done a pretty good job, all told.

"Are you going to tell me what's going on?"

"Nothing to tell," I said.

"You're lying." Dad raised an admonitory finger. "Does this have anything to do with the men who came looking for Sally?"

Information. This was another reason for going to Dad's. I wasn't sure how much he could provide, but it was safe to assume he'd seen me and Sally together on numerous occasions. He knew things about *us*, and might be able to repair connection points where the spider could not.

"When were they here?" I asked.

"August tenth," he replied at once. "Seven fourteen. A hot evening. Swampy, almost."

"Good memory," I said. August tenth was the day before they'd grabbed me.

"I wrote everything down," Dad said. "Including what I remember of the conversation. I plan to tell the guys on *Truth Matters* all about it."

I looked at him blankly.

"The men claimed to be from a privately funded organization investigating extraterrestrial activity," Dad explained. "They had reason to believe Sally was from the Alpha Draconis star system, and that you—all of us—could be in danger."

The hunt dogs, using fear to obtain information. They'd terrorized me, and had told Marzipan they were from the IRS (which made me wonder how thorough she was with her bookkeeping). With all of Dad's paranoia and fear, they would have been spoiled for choice.

"What did you tell them?" I asked.

"Not a whole lot," Dad said. "I can't say why, but I didn't trust them. Instinct, I guess. Anyway, I told them I didn't know where Sally was, but that I'd keep my eye on the sky."

"Did they hurt you?"

"No. Why would they hurt me?"

I bit my lip. He was the only person in the world who would believe the crazy shit I was going through, and the last person I wanted to tell.

"Is that what this is all about?" Dad touched my face, running his thumb over my new scar. "Is that what *this* is all about?"

I pulled away from him. "Yeah. Maybe. I don't know." I looked at him with a mostly honest expression. "I'm still trying to work it all out."

He narrowed his eye and furrowed half a brow.

"But I can tell you this," I said. "Sally *isn't* from Alpha Draconis."

"Shit, I know that." He squared his shoulders defensively. "You think I don't know how to identify a reptilian? I wrote a book about it, after all."

He had. It was called *Reptilians Among Us*. Its opening sentence read: *We all know that Barack Obama is a negro, but what you probably don't realize is that he's actually a lizard, too.* It was rejected by every publishing house in New York City.

"Men like that don't come looking for you unless you've ruffled a few feathers," Dad said. "I liked Sally. She had a big heart, but I always thought there was something peculiar about her."

"Peculiar how?"

"The way she'd tighten up when she talked about herself," Dad replied. "You must remember that."

"No," I said.

"Yeah, well, love can blind a man," Dad said. "Me . . . I got the feeling she was hiding something, and I guess I was right. She hit the road and left you with nothing but questions."

"True dat."

"Doesn't make her a lizard, though."

"No," I said. "Just alone somewhere. And scared."

"You don't know where she is?"

"No, but I'm going to find her."

Lou Reed sauntered into the room. He meowed and brushed against Dad's leg. Dad lifted him into one arm, nuzzled his wiry ruff, and kissed him between the ears.

"I don't like your lies, Harvey." Dad regarded me with a no-nonsense expression and raised that finger again. "If you're in trouble, I want to know about it. I want to help."

"It's nothing I can't handle." I sat up, put a little pressure on my left ankle, and winced. It was better, but still sore. "And you're already helping . . . letting me stay here. I appreciate it."

His nostrils flared. I think he was caught between wanting to read me the riot act and showing me the same affection he was showing Lou. Either way, I found his concern quite touching.

"Just a few days," I said.

"Stay as long as you want," he said.

Something surprising happened in those three days: I saw Dad in a more paternal light—due largely to his concern, but also to my unusual predicament—and for the first time in forever, I actually enjoyed his company.

We spent one night watching the skies over Spirit Lake. A few burly clouds masked the stars to the north but it was otherwise clear. Dad claimed to have seen a UFO crash into the lake in the summer of '57, and that the area had been closed to the public for almost two months afterward. "Saw a lot of unusual traffic on Ribbon Road during that time," he told me. "Big old Lincolns with government plates, military vehicles, trucks with covered beds. They wouldn't say what they were doing, but I knew; they were dragging the lake, finding the truth in however many pieces, and driving it all away." Almost certainly the fruit of imagination (he was ten years old at the time), this nonetheless sparked his fascination with all things extraterrestrial and conspiratorial. 'Nam did the rest.

The lake was a sacred place for Dad. He could often be found sitting in a lawn chair on the shore, pointing his homemade radio telescope at the sky and taking readings, or reclining pensively on the rocks with nothing but his memories. He said he was waiting for another UFO sighting, but that wasn't all of it. The area was a favorite location in the months before Mom became too sick to leave the house. I have memories of them stumbling across the shale hand in hand, giggling wildly whenever one of them lost balance; of him getting close enough to a blue heron to hand-feed it a fish, and Mom squealing euphorically; of them wading to their waists—fully dressed—for no good reason, then driving home afterward soaked and happy.

It was his church—a place of both intimacy and huge distance, where Dad felt closer to the things he believed, but which could never be proved. When I asked why he so often went there, he replied, "We always come back for the things we've lost." To this day, I don't know if he was talking about the aliens looking for their downed ship, or Mom.

We were there that night to watch the skies, so Dad said, although I suspect it was really an opportunity for father and son to bond. Either way, I embraced it. Dad informed me that he'd been getting "spikes" on his radio telescope for the past two hours. "I had it tuned to 1420 megahertz, which is a protected spectrum. This means the spikes were unquestionably extraterrestrial." He dropped ass into the lawn chair beside mine, rifled through a nearby cooler, and handed me a frosty-cold beer. "This is a *great* night for a sighting." I had my doubts, seeing as his "radio telescope" was in fact a DirecTV satellite dish connected to an arrangement of gizmos from RadioShack. Who knows what he was tuning in to. The "spikes" could have been some horny teenager Snapchatting cock shots to his girlfriend. But hey, Dad seemed happy, and what else were we going to do? Go fishing?

We listened to the water against the shoreline, as rhythmic as a heartbeat, to the coyotes yipping and howling, to the sounds of our bodies working—breathing and sniffing and yawning. Dad pointed out constellations while I feigned interest. He told me the story of the '57 UFO crash for the ten thousandth time. We talked about Ebola and *Back to the Future* and whether or not Mama Cass choked to death on a ham sandwich. We drank steadily, but not too much. We avoided politics and barely talked about Mom and didn't see any UFOs.

With a single beer left in the cooler and a contented vibe between us, I decided to ask about Sally, hoping to do so in a way that didn't sound like I'd lost my mind.

"I thought she was the one," I said, and sighed dramatically. "She was cool, right? I'm not just imagining that because I miss her?"

"Yeah, she had that cool hippie thing going on," Dad said. "Definitely your type."

A deliberate pause, as if I were reminiscing about Sally's cool hippie thing. Dad stretched out a yawn. His scars glimmered in the dim battery-powered lamp posted between our seats.

I asked, "What did you like most about her?"

"She danced spontaneously," Dad replied with barely a second to think about it. "I admired her energy. She had a pretty singing voice, too."

"Yeah," I said, as if I remembered it. "She did."

"I like that she never judged me," Dad continued. "Most people do, but she took everything I said in her stride, whether she believed it or not. I'm sure she was just being polite, but I liked that about her."

"Right," I said.

"Like I already said, she was a peculiar girl. No denying that. But in some ways—her sweetness, her tenderness and patience—she was a lot like your mother."

I had opened my mind. I imagined the neural pathways flowing with activity. No blockages or breaks. It was like turning on a tap. The connection points fizzled with life and glowed. My brain crackled vibrantly.

One decent memory, I thought. *That's all it'll take to trigger a cascade.* I envisioned pushing the first domino; rolling a snowball downhill; flicking a smoldering cigarette butt into brittle grass.

I was ready.

"Any particular memories?" I invited.

"Sure," Dad said, but when it came to recounting them, he mostly faltered and frowned. It can be hard to recall memories on demand, and Dad was no spring chicken. He partially uncovered a few things, like when Sally sang a selection of Nina Simone—or was it Etta James?—songs by candlelight during a power outage, and how for his birthday she'd recited Rudyard Kipling's "If—" from atop the kitchen table. He recalled that he first met Sally on the day Michael Jackson died/arrived. "Or was that the second time? No, it was definitely the first. She wore a leaf in her hair. A maple, I think." These were not the clear, dependable memories I'd hoped for, and they did nothing to begin the cascade. At the very least, it was nice hearing Dad talk about Sally. He did so with a fondness that made me want to find her even more.

"All these years searching," I said, pointing at the stars. Dad thought I'd changed the subject but I hadn't. "Against the odds, with nothing to go on but phantoms and gut instinct . . . how'd you keep from losing faith?"

Dad finished the last beer and dropped the empty into the cooler.

He sighed and said nothing for a long time, and I wondered if he'd thought my question rhetorical, or if he'd even heard it. Then he turned to me with a contemplative smile.

"Really, son, it's a matter of belief, and how it defines us." His eye tracked skyward again, as if drawn by a magnet. "I'm more afraid of *not* believing than I am of not finding what I'm looking for."

Pale light spilled through the trees as we made our way home, with the dawn chorus in full voice. Dad carried the lawn chairs and lamp, and I—favoring my sore ankle—the heavier cooler. We didn't speak until we reached his land, veering around the many holes and traps. Something occurred to me as I looked at all the places he'd been digging. It was a long shot, but I saw no harm in asking.

"This is going to sound crazy, but did I buy you a shovel recently? As a belated Father's Day present or something?"

"Last time you bought me a Father's Day present," he said, "Mom was alive to watch me unwrap it."

"Right, okay." I sighed. "Well, a birthday present, then."

"Do you even know when my birthday is?"

"March twelfth."

"March fifteenth, and no, you didn't buy me a shovel." He stopped, turned, and held the lamp up to my face. "What's with all the questions, Harvey? Is there something wrong with your memory?"

"Occasional blackouts," I said, forcing a smile. "It's a vegetarian thing."

"Sure it is." He lowered the lamp and started walking again, but not before tipping an amused wink. "Or maybe your girlfriend really *did* wipe your mind before returning to Alpha Draconis."

"Could be that, too," I said.

I followed him back to the house and asked no more questions.

I called Chief Newirth to let him know where I was; I didn't want him thinking I'd skipped town after our conversation. That would look about as innocent as buying a shovel on the day my girlfriend disappeared. He told me to keep him in the loop. I didn't like how—over

a phone line, and with only a few words—I was able to detect the suspicion in his voice. Or maybe that was the old paranoia creeping in.

The next forty-eight hours were spent looking after myself. I slept
well, ate good food, and made time to read. Not for pleasure—for
information. I learned more about Sally, in small part from the half
memories that Dad shared, but mainly from an old notebook I uncovered. Additionally, Dad had an abundance of reference materials.
Magazines. Books. Newspapers. Audio and video recordings. I even
took his old truck to the library in Newton (I didn't want to go to
Green Ridge—just the thought of being back there made me anxious)
and supplemented my research online. I turned pages until the words
blurred and my head throbbed, but it was worth it; I procured critical
information. Not only about Sally.

I also found out about the spider.

Ten

Dad's library was an airless jungle of crammed shelves and teetering stacks, predominately non-fiction books with titles like *Corporation: Evil* and *The Assassination Nation*, and yellowed newspapers, some of which dated as far back as the Vietnam War. I'd ventured in knowing there was little chance of finding anything to my taste, but quite charmed by the idea of losing myself in a good novel. Dad had assured me he owned several modern classics, so I figured I'd at least try looking for them before venturing to the bookstore.

I made sturdy footstools out of encyclopedias and used them to reach the top shelves. I removed titles placed like Jenga blocks, searched through wavering stacks, and upended boxes that clearly hadn't been opened for years. Eventually—on the verge of defeat—I disinterred a copy of Orwell's *1984* and ran it around the room like I'd scored a touchdown. With everything so precariously placed, disaster was inevitable; I brushed a tower of books as tall as me and it toppled spectacularly. The shock wave caused a second and third tower to fall. I groaned, slipped the paperback into the back pocket of my jeans, and set about fixing the mess. It was then that I came across the book Dad had written, *Reptilians Among Us,* an eight-hundred-page doorstop he'd self-published after failing to win interest with the major presses. Its black cover was adorned with insipid green lettering and a collage of well-known faces, all Photoshopped with lizard eyes and forked tongues. It was actually kind of wonderful.

Intrigued, I turned to page one and started reading, but didn't get beyond those opening two lines. I imagine the publishers' slush readers had stopped at exactly the same place. I rippled a few pages and saw pictures of the Alpha Draconis star system and President Obama and some old movie star whose name I couldn't recall. I jumped to another set of pictures somewhere near the middle and saw David Bowie as Ziggy Stardust and, top right on the right-hand page, a darkly handsome face that made me scream, snap the book closed, and throw it across the room.

"Jesus Christ," I said, backing up, looking at the book where it landed, fearfully, as if it were a poisonous snake or a fat black . . .

Spider, I thought.

It was him, I knew it. He was younger in the picture, obviously, his face not as deeply lined, his widow's peak more black than silver, but those Emperor Ming eyes and angular brows were unmistakable. I exhaled steadily and rubbed the gooseflesh from my forearms, still feeling him—his many legs—crawling through my brain. I reeled from the room and went downstairs, crossed the kitchen to the backdoor. "You okay?" Dad asked, because clearly I didn't *look* okay, but I grunted something vaguely positive and stepped outside. The air was sunshiny and clean and I took deep gulps of it, until my trembling had eased and the sweat on my throat had dried. Several cats curled around my legs. I scooped one of them into my arms and clutched her.

The picture pulled at me, though, and within an hour I found myself back in Dad's library. This time I was armed; I had my red feather. What nightmares could an old black-and-white picture possibly evoke with such a vivid reminder already clenched in my fist? I retrieved *Reptilians Among Us* from where I'd thrown it and flipped the pages until I saw him again. A smiling head shot. I recalled that he'd smiled often in the moments before violating my mind.

I touched his face—ran my finger from his striking brow to his nose, over his smiling lips and then to his throat, where I made a swift cutting motion. "Fuck you," I said, then slammed the flat of my fist—the one holding the feather—down between his eyes. "Fuck you." I struck the picture again. "*FUCK YOU.*" And again. The page creased. My voice echoed through the house. I didn't care.

Did it help, this mimicry of violence? A little, perhaps; I was still nauseous, but could look at the picture without rage—could focus on the caption beneath it: *Former Tennessee Senator DOMINIC LANG used reptilian mind control to coerce terror suspects at Guantánamo Bay.* Fucker had a name. He'd always be the spider, but with a name I could find out more about him. Jesus, I knew he didn't hatch from an egg or ride the E train from Alpha Draconis, but as a former senator, his story—or at least some of it—would be available to me.

I'd started reading Sun Tzu's *The Art of War* when I was fifteen, not because I had any intention of going to war, but because it seemed like a hip thing to do. Much of it was beyond me; not difficult to understand, just not relatable. I had memorized several quotes, though, because they sounded smart and cool. One of them came to mind as I looked at the spider's picture again. *If you know the enemy and know yourself, you need not fear the result of a hundred battles.*

I parked the feather in my dreads, freeing up both hands, and flipped to the back of Dad's book. There wasn't an index, so I started skimming for that name, Dominic Lang. I'd take anything written by Dad with a truckload of salt, of course, but it was somewhere to start.

After thirty minutes—and with a tight, achy knot in my skull—I'd found only a couple of references that didn't reveal much, so rather than go through the entire book, I took it downstairs. Dad was in the living room sorting through his vinyl records, placing some of them in a box with the word BUNKER written on the side in permanent marker. I found this curious, but didn't have time to think about it. I opened *Reptilians Among Us,* pointed at the spider's picture, and said to Dad, "What can you tell me about this man?"

Dad's murky blue iris floated behind his monocle, which he wore for reading. He couldn't wear glasses because he only had one ear.

"Dominic Lang," he said, and sneered. "Reptilian. Possibly an over-lord. The media called him the 'Terrorist Whisperer.' He made a fortune interrogating prisoners of war with what he called 'advanced intellec-tive analysis,' and what *I* call 'reptilian mind control.'"

"What else?" I asked.

He told me what he knew. I extrapolated several feasible details, then asked if any of the books in his library could provide further read-ing. I don't know if he thought I'd taken a sudden interest in his bizarre humanoid theories, but he scuttled away and returned with an armful of books. Some would offer scant and unreliable information. *Aliens on the Hill,* for instance, and *The Babylonian Brotherhood.* Others—*The In-terrogation Files* and *Beyond the Chamber*—would prove more valuable.

"What's this all about?" Dad asked, watching as I sorted through the titles.

"I'm not sure," I said. "Maybe nothing."

"You're not going to tell me?"

I smiled apologetically, found a quiet corner, and started to read.

Most of the books had indices, so I found what I was looking for quickly. With certain information revealed, I was able to dig deeper . . . and deeper. Over the next several hours, I delved into yet more books, both at Dad's house and at the library in Newton. I scoured the Inter-net, cross-referenced everything, and made copious notes in a legal pad with the words KNOW YOUR ENEMY scrawled across the front.

The red feather was my bookmark.

This is what I learned:

Dominic Lang's twin died in utero and for six weeks he shared the womb with that little corpse. He would one day tell his constituents—holy-rolling Republicans, by and large—that the hand of God had cradled him before unmaking his brother, and that he'd been born with a divine blueprint in his pocket. What he *didn't* tell them was that he'd hogged all the blood and nutrients in the womb, effectively starv-ing his twin. In a leaked e-mail exchange with his former legislative director, Lang purportedly wrote, "I'd have bitten off that little fucker's head if it meant only one of us was getting out of there alive." Lang fervently denied this, of course—claimed his e-mail account had been hijacked by terrorists or heathens. His God-fearing majority believed every word.

May 9, 1953. Lang was born at thirty-four weeks. The only son of Rudolph and Patricia Lang—a diplomat and English teacher, respectively—he was not, by any measure, a healthy infant. In addition to the complications of being born premature, his heart was enlarged and his blood pressure too high. Doctors said he might not live through the night, which almost proved the case when, not even twelve hours old, his heart stopped beating. By some miracle the medical staff revived him, and although he went on to grow big and strong, it was clear he was not like other children. He was withdrawn, inaccessible—didn't voice a single word until he was eight years old. In 1958, he was diagnosed with autism, a term that was new to most Americans, and largely misunderstood. Some specialists suggested the condition was due to his heart having stopped beating and his brain being denied oxygen. Others maintained that a cerebral imbalance was common in survivors of twin-to-twin transfusion syndrome.

Beyond the traumatic first hours of Lang's life and the subsequent neurological concerns, I didn't discover much about his childhood. I thought I might read about how he'd manipulated his teachers with mind control, or killed everybody at the high school prom. There was nothing like that. I learned that he was homeschooled, partly because his mother refused to admit him to a remedial facility, mostly because his father's job took them all over the world. They lived in Hong Kong, Malaysia, India, and Switzerland. It was here that a neurologist declared Lang's autism a grave misdiagnosis, adding that he was a boy of "intimidating mental capacity." This was as close as I got to finding any suggestion of telepathic ability.

The family returned to their home state of Tennessee in 1967. Lang, now fourteen years old, attended a conventional school for the first time: Conasauga High, where he excelled. I don't know if he had friends, girlfriends, boyfriends, if he was on the track team or in the drama club. The only mention of his high school years was that he scored a perfect 1600 on his SATs. He went on to Laurel State University in Georgia, a small but prestigious school, where he majored in psychology and graduated summa cum laude in 1975.

Lang showed his political aspirations at Laurel State by running for student-government president. There were two other candidates. One of these, along with her running mate, stepped down only days into the campaign. The remaining candidate was a wildly popular senior named Mitt Grover, whose father was a Laurel State alumnus who'd pumped tens of thousands of dollars into the school coffers over the years. Simply put, Lang could run the tightest campaign and address the most important issues, but there was no way he was getting elected.

A local news station televised the election debate. I found stills but no video. The story came courtesy of the *Macon Telegraph* archives.

Everything was going well for Grover and his running mate. They had just made their opening statements to rapturous applause, and Grover in particular glowed with confidence. The *Telegraph* noted how the handsome young senior appeared "entirely in his element," and that his opponent, Lang, "shifted uncomfortably during the applause." There's a still of Grover standing with one fist aloft, as if he'd already won, with Lang off to the side looking like he'd rather be anywhere else in the world. They each fielded two questions put forward by students (Grover, again, to roof-shaking acclamation) and it was while answering a third question that Grover started to slur his words. There were ripples of unease from the audience, which turned to concern when blood dripped from Grover's nose onto his pristine white shirt. He didn't appear to notice. In fact, he must have thought the shouts of alarm were yet more plaudits, because he raised his fist again, slurred, "Go Wildcats," and dropped dead on the stage.

The autopsy concluded that Grover had suffered a subarachnoid hemorrhage caused by a ruptured aneurysm. As the candles were lit and the flowers laid, the obligatory questions were raised as to how such a vibrant young man could have had his light extinguished so suddenly.

I think *I* know.

There's a chilling still of Grover lying facedown on the stage, his running mate kneeling beside him, already in tears, with Lang hovering in the background. The focus of the still is obviously Grover and his stricken comrade, so it's easy to overlook the intense expression on Lang's face. He is staring at Grover with his shoulders hunched and his Emperor Ming eyebrows forming a familiar bird shape—a *raptor* shape— across his brow. I remembered that bird shape clearly. I also remembered how he'd felt inside my brain, with his long spider legs ticking and gathering. I knew that with just one push—one *squeeze*—he could have ballooned every artery and turned my brain into pasta sauce.

Coincidence? Cold-blooded murder? It's impossible to know for sure. What I do know is that Grover's running mate was too emotional to continue the campaign, and the presidency was awarded to Lang.

There was another quiet period while Lang went to medical school, then completed his psychiatry residency at Yale. I bled the search engines for more brain-squeezing stories but found only dull biographical notes. He worked for a year at a psychiatric hospital in Connecticut, and returned to Tennessee in '86 to be close to his ailing father. After the old man died, Lang used a portion of his inheritance to establish his own clinic in Nashville. I found a picture of him standing outside the front doors, his arms wide and welcoming, that thin smile—anything *but* welcoming—touching his lips.

He met Gene Lyon in June of 1990.

I found no reference in books or online, due to the secrecy of their affair, but have subsequently learned how important—how *stabilizing*— Lyon was to Lang. They met at a fundraiser for then-gubernatorial candidate Jimmy Packer. It was attended by Tennessee's Republican elite and a handful of carefully selected businesspeople. Gene Lyon was the campaign's official photographer. At twenty-six, he was eleven years Lang's junior, but this didn't stop the men forming an immediate bond.

Lang said in a 2006 interview with *Harper's*: "Gene was both brazen and ambitious—a magnetic, if alarming, combination. He worked Packer's fundraiser with absolute professionalism, although I could tell his heart wasn't in it. Later, he said to me that he'd spent the day photographing falseness and pomp. When I asked what he'd rather be doing, he smiled and said, 'Getting my hands dirty.' I knew then we'd be friends forever."

Lyon would get more than his hands dirty. He went from photo-graphing Packer's failed gubernatorial run to the war-torn streets of Kuwait, where his lens captured the charred corpses of Iraqi soldiers and bombed, blackened buildings and dead civilians—children among them—piled like laundry. His most notable photograph is of a US Marine holding a ravaged four-year-old girl's hand and it's the marine, not the girl, who's in tears. The Gulf War was as far from falseness and pomp as it was possible to get. "It was a gallery of haunted images," Lyon said of his work there. "Of agonies and truths. I was emotionally torn, professionally replete."

He photographed burning villages in Bosnia and the victims of geno-cide wrapped in a thousand sheets. Another famous shot is of a bereft dog standing outside its shattered Srebrenica home. In Grozny, he immortalized a Chechen rebel who faced a squadron of Russian tanks armed only with a pistol. His exhibition at MoMA, titled *War, Children*, documented the Congo's child soldiers in emphatic colors. Efrain Rivas at the *New York Times* called it a "visceral education."

On May 15, 2004, a US warplane fired two missiles into a resi-dential neighborhood in Fallujah, Iraq, killing twenty-six people. Lyon—stationed in Baghdad—arrived with his camera later that same day. Given the recent, brutal killings of American contractors in the area, he was urged by US officials to remain glued to his military escort. He heeded the warning for the first two days and on day three slipped away to photograph the broken streets of the Jolan district. The last shot he ever took is of a half-naked child standing outside the bombed market-place where his father used to work.

In the first video, Lyon is on his knees with his hands cuffed behind his back. Four Islamist militants veiled by black kaffiyehs stand behind him. One holds a sword above Lyon's head. Lyon disjointedly intro-duces himself as Eugene Mark Lyon, an American photographer. He gives his date and city of birth. The militant with the sword demands the cessation of US airstrikes on civilian targets, and vows to paint the streets with American blood should a single missile fly.

The US government's dictum, *We don't negotiate with terrorists,* was underscored when, on May 21, American F16s targeted suspected militant positions in Ramadi and Fallujah. Thirteen women and nine children were among the dead.

I didn't watch the second video, and it needs no description here. After Lyon was decapitated, his head was placed in the *V* of his crossed ankles and photographed using his own camera. His body was discovered tied to a burned-out truck on the outskirts of Fallujah.

Dominic Lang made no official statement. That was left to Lyon's grieving family. The *New York Times* ran a four-page memorial and *Time* produced a Gene Lyon special issue. Any number of photojournalists and correspondents paid tribute, but it was two years before Lang mentioned his good friend's death and the effect it had on him.

This from the now defunct political magazine *365 Steps* (June 2006):

Everybody feels deep grief at some point in their lives. Mine was exacerbated by a sense of disappointment and betrayal. I felt *betrayed* by America. By the system. I kept imagining the luminaries on Capitol Hill—some of whom were friends, all of whom are now peers—making decisions from their positions of luxury while, seven thousand miles away, Gene was tormented, abused, and beheaded. I remember feeling they could have done more to save him, and I was furious. I wanted to turn myself into a flame and run through everybody responsible. But time eases grief and dampens those irrational responses, and with a cooler head I realized that I could use my gift more productively. That was when I closed the clinic and established Nova Oculus.

The CIA sanctioned Project MK-Ultra in the 1950s, a covert program that used—among other things—torture, hypnosis, and hallucinogens to analyze behavioral modification and mind control in human subjects. When Lang gained renown for his work with Nova Oculus, human-rights activists drew comparisons to MK-Ultra. Lang assured his critics he used no drugs, hypnosis, or coercive persuasion, only known intelligence coupled with the minutia of behavioral science. His was a peaceable and effective form of interrogation. Given the outcry in the wake of human-rights violations at Abu Ghraib prison in Iraq, Lang's work was not only embraced but celebrated. The CIA paid him vast sums of money to interrogate terrorism suspects both at home and at Guantánamo Bay, and the information he procured led to the capture or killing of several senior al-Qaeda operatives, the location of multiple strongholds, and the foiling of terrorist attacks in London, Toronto, and Boston.

Lang wasn't lying; he didn't use drugs to manipulate the prisoners' minds. He didn't use hypnosis or mind control. I know this from my own harrowing experience with him. He used telepathy, which he never denied, because it was never brought up. He may have given the impression of using "advanced intellective analysis," but really he was spidering through the folds of his subjects' brains, gathering intelligence, and being paid a king's ransom for doing so.

Suddenly, Lang had wealth, power, and influence.

This could only lead to one thing.

In a 2005 interview on *Larry King Live,* the eponymous host asked Lang: "You were the student-government president at your alma mater. Do you still have political ambitions, or did you get that out of your system at a young age?"

"I'm invested in the well-being of our country," Lang replied. "I want to make sure the right decisions are being made and that we're moving forward as a nation. As of this moment, I believe Tennessee is well represented in Congress. Should that change, I would certainly consider my options."

He didn't have to wait long. Two months later, Eldon Pie, Tennessee's long-serving Republican senator, resigned due to health complications. He'd suffered a debilitating stroke while playing golf (I don't know who he was playing with, but had to wonder if Lang was swinging the irons that day). With fourteen months until the midterms, Governor John Pryce appointed Lang to the vacant seat.

So there he was, a member of the 109th Congress. In his first PR move, Lang promised—in the interest of homeland security—to keep Nova Oculus operational, but that he would remove himself from the payroll, thereby nullifying any concern that a sitting senator might profit from a government contract. He said he had every intention of running for reelection in 2006, although rumors in regard to 2008 were already circulating. I found a photograph of Lang and Bush embracing at a Rangers game. It had been captioned, with the president confiding: *Don't worry, I'll keep the seat warm for you.*

Within four years, Lang could have gone from being a noted psychiatrist to the leader of the free world. Everything was on track. And then, less than two months before the midterms, something went very wrong.

To begin with, he withdrew from the Senate race without explanation, having already spent millions on his campaign. While Tennessee Republicans scrambled to find a replacement candidate, Lang dropped another bomb by resigning his seat in Congress, effective immediately. A member of his staff cited health reasons. There were rumors of brain cancer, heart failure, retrograde amnesia. I found a picture of him stepping from the back of a limousine appearing withered and pale, reminding me how he looked—frail, sucking on oxygen—after spidering through my mind. In December '06, he pulled the plug on Nova Oculus. At the subsequent press conference (appearing hardier but still far from healthy), he shed no light on the nature of his illness, but thanked everybody for their support, expressed how proud he was to have served his state and his country, and promised the rebirth of Nova Oculus—as well as a return to the political arena—as soon as he'd made a full recovery.

Then he faded from the public eye and from everybody's minds. The last article I found was from September '08 when he'd attended a Gene Lyon exhibition in Los Angeles.

The spider had done a commendable job of protecting his public image. I uncovered no dirt, no evil, other than the leaked e-mail about biting off his twin's head, which he denied, and my own suspicion that he'd brain-fucked Mitt Grover. There was more to him, though. He'd been *inside* me, remember, and I'd felt that evil pulsing off his plump little body. Just because Google hadn't been able to find it didn't mean it wasn't there.

I found no mention of Sally, either. Not that I was expecting to. Lang knew her by a different name, which I couldn't remember— Miranda something or other. I tried a few shot-in-the-dark searches and came up empty. Armed with my legal pad and pen, I used the information I had to make connections. They were tenuous, and there was still so much missing, but it was a start.

Nine years later, the spider had said. *I can feel the impact—the emptiness of what she took from me. A great famishment of the mind.*

Nine years ago: 2006, when he'd suddenly dropped out of the Tennessee senate race, resigned from office, and closed down his multimillion-dollar operation. There had been suggestions of cancer and amnesia, but it was Sally. She hadn't simply taken his memories, she'd clawed them away (his words), leaving him with just enough to feel loss. She'd taken his power, too. *I'm like a car running on a single cylinder,* he'd said. *Or a battery at five percent power.* Thirty minutes in my brain and he'd been left withered. How could he manage the demands of the Oval Office when he couldn't even breathe without aid?

But what was his connection to Sally? Had he recruited her for Nova Oculus—to keep the money rolling in while he made a run at the White House? Was she a threat to his power, his wealth? Whatever the circumstances, their paths had crossed and Lang had come out licking his wounds. He thought he was powerful, but he'd met his match.

No wonder he wanted to find her—to take back what was his. And as soon as he did, he would reestablish Nova Oculus. In light of the US Senate's recent report on CIA torture, it isn't a stretch to think there'd be considerable money involved in a nonviolent but efficient interrogation program. Dominic Lang would be back on his feet. The toast of the town. He would revive his political career, and then . . .

Don't worry, I'll keep the seat warm for you.

What happens when the most dangerous man on the planet becomes the most powerful? Or the most powerful becomes the most dangerous?

That copy of Orwell's *1984*—the one I'd rescued from Dad's library—sat around for a while. I didn't have time to read it, but I picked it up now and then and flipped through a few pages. It's one of those novels where you can open it anywhere and read something provocative or chilling or both, but one sentence stood out above all others:

Power is in tearing human minds to pieces and putting them together again in new shapes of your own choosing.

It unsettled me. It got under my skin and kept me awake at night. It evoked images of bug-eyed, fetus Lang sharing a womb with a tiny corpse, and Mitt Grover lying facedown with his handsome senior's brain all watermelon-smashed. *I felt* betrayed *by America,* he'd said in the *365 Steps* interview. *I wanted to turn myself into a flame and run through everybody responsible.* And I imagined him—President Lang—giving his State of the Union Address, and there we are, his fellow Americans, looking not at the eagle on his seal but at the raptor on his brow. How long before he tore our minds to pieces and put them together again in shapes of his own choosing? How long before he turned himself into a flame?

It was terrifying, entirely possible. All it takes is one tyrant with the power to surrender wills and manipulate. It's happening right now to 1.6 billion people, in countries like Somalia and North Korea and Sudan and Myanmar.

Power is in tearing human minds to pieces . . .

I'd felt that power (actually, I'd felt only 5 percent of that power), so it was easy to envision the aftermath: a cracked, smoldering nation, where the people had risen and their brains had been smashed, and where the brightest thing for miles in any direction was a single red feather laid upon the land.

This is how you'll remember me.

Eleven

I decided Sun Tzu was full of shit.

I knew the enemy and knew myself, and feared the result of a hundred battles more than ever. Not that there would *be* one hundred battles—just one swift, effortless execution. I was out of my league.

On my penultimate night at Dad's house, I sat with him at the kitchen table drinking heady, homemade wine and making ninja smoke bombs. Every twenty minutes or so one of us would stagger into the living room to flip the vinyl. We listened to Woodstock-era rock, the perfect soundtrack to my angst.

"Is all my hair going to fall out?" I asked, handling a crystallized concoction of sugar and potassium nitrate. "This shit can't be good for you."

"Just don't eat it," Dad said.

"Is this even legal?"

"Self-defense is one of our constitutional rights."

"We're making bombs," I said. "I'm pretty sure that's not legal."

"Think of them as explosives," Dad said. "There's a subtle difference."

I'd spent most of the day with the spider, bringing him to life through archived articles and bios. As out of my element as I was, it was a relief to be doing something else—*with* somebody else.

"How do you defend yourself with these anyway?" I asked. "It's just a puff of smoke, right?"

"It's a *lot* of smoke," Dad said. "We're not making party snappers here, son. These are the real deal."

"Right," I said.

"They create a diversion, giving you time to arm yourself or run. They also make one hell of a bang, which sets your adversary on the back foot."

"Cool," I said.

"I threw one at a bear once."

I smiled, put on the B side of Creedence Clearwater Revival's greatest hits, and glugged a little more wine into my glass. During this time—maybe three minutes—I didn't think of the spider at all. Then "Fortunate Son" crackled from the speakers with its line "Some folks are born made to wave the flag," and there he was, President Lang, mind-melting Congress and the nation.

"So," Dad said. "You've had a couple of days to get your head together. Are you any closer to finding what you're looking for?"

"I'm more informed," I said. "I'm not sure if that's a good thing."

"Information is power."

I shrugged; he'd paraphrased Sun Tzu. My theory—*my* art of war: Power is useless if you can't do anything with it.

My mind had been cranking, though, thinking up ways I could expose Lang as the dangerous son of a bitch I knew him to be. I wondered if I could present my notes to some visionary muckraker, who would sling enough shit at Lang to hobble any political revival. Trouble was, Lang wasn't news, and hadn't been since 2006. Also, the moment I mentioned telepathy or mind control, any journalist—muckraker or not—worth their salt would boot my bony ass out the door. I even entertained (it was more a guilty fantasy) the idea of hiring a hit man. Not that I knew where to find a hit man, even in Jersey. I could have asked my landlord, I suppose, who might know a man who knows a man. I didn't think this was a job for some *paisano* from South Trenton, though, but rather an elite assassin with a high-tech sniper rifle, who could take out his target from a distance while factoring in wind resistance and the Coriolis effect. Moreover, my peace-loving Mom would spin in her grave if I used my inheritance to put a hit on a sixty-two-year-old man.

I had to get real: Bringing down a future tyrant was not a job for a vegetarian street performer. What I needed was to find my girlfriend. To support and protect her. *That* was my part in this. For as long as Sally was safe, the spider would be defanged.

I sighed, measuring exact amounts of silver fulminate into little piles, which wasn't easy with trembling hands.

"So," Dad began, looking at me across the table. "Are you ready to tell me what's going on?"

I met his gaze for a second, then glanced away. Over the last couple of days—and certainly while reading about the spider—I had toyed with the idea of telling Dad everything. He would *believe* me. He might even take some of the weight from my shoulders. Ultimately, I decided not to; Dominic Lang was a dangerous motherfucker, and his supernatural ability made it impossible to keep anything from him. The less Dad knew, the safer he'd be.

"It's better you don't know," I said.

"Bullshit." Dad's eye whirled angrily. "I don't like being kept in the dark, Harvey. The goddamn government does enough of that. I sure as hell don't need it in my own house."

"I can leave if you want," I retorted, and now there was an edge to my voice. "I'll go right now."

"I don't want that." Dad glugged his wine and some spilled onto his chin. "You're my son, dammit. If you're in trouble, I want to protect you. Can't you understand that?"

I could; it was exactly my reason for wanting to find Sally.

"This isn't your fight," I said.

"Yeah, it is." Dad wiped his chin and sat back in his seat. "Anything happens to you, I bleed, too."

"That goes both ways."

He sighed, knowing he wouldn't get me to change my mind, but not knowing how conflicted I was. My lips trembled and I pushed down a rising tide of emotion. I was grateful when the record needed changing. It gave me an opportunity to leave the table. I selected something with enough flower power to diffuse the tension. It didn't really work.

"You're a hardheaded little bastard, you know that?" Dad shook his head and handled volatile materials recklessly. I kept a safe distance, fearing disaster, but curious to see how a dozen sleeping cats would react to the kitchen table suddenly exploding.

"I'm doing what I have to do," I said.

"At what cost?"

"Doing nothing will cost more."

"Time will tell." He sighed again, shrugged, then refilled his glass. "Until then, I can take comfort in knowing that you're tougher than you give yourself credit for and that whatever the hell you're up to, you'll do well not to underestimate yourself."

I wanted to hug him, and would have—explosions, be damned— had Michael Jackson not leapt onto the kitchen table and stepped dangerously close to the silver fulminate. I grabbed him quickly and hugged him instead.

Dad nodded, acknowledging the save. Our gazes locked and I saw in his eye, beyond the frustration and fear, maybe not the smartest man or the strongest, but a *good* man, and one to whom I was the most important thing in life.

"I appreciate you looking out for me," I said.

"I'm trying," he said.

We cleared the bomb-making detritus away without incident and took our wine into the living room. Dad ditched the psychedelic rock and brought us all the way into the eighties with Michael Jackson's *Thriller.* Stupidly, I looked at the cat to see what he would do.

He slept.

I was tired, too. It was late, almost midnight, but there was still tension between me and Dad and I wanted to fix that before hitting the hay.

"I read some of your book," I said hopefully. *"Reptilians Among Us.* It's . . . interesting. In places."

"Yeah, well, I couldn't get it published." Dad flapped a hand. "I had to go the vanity route."

"There's no shame in that."

"It took me five years to write that goddamn book," Dad growled. "I wanted to get *paid.*"

"So write another book," I said. "Write about home defense. Or your experiences in 'Nam. Put the Stars and Stripes on the cover and call it *Patriot.* We're Americans. We eat that shit up."

"I think I'm done with writing," Dad said, shaking his head. "I need someone to keep me from straying. I'm nothing without my editor."

"You mean Mom?" I said. "Jesus, Dad, she wasn't your editor, she was your *wife.*"

"She was everything."

My effort at easing the tension had resulted in Dad staring glumly into his wine. It reminded me of an unfortunate truth—that Dad and I would always take one step forward, and two steps back. This visit had gone a long way toward bringing us closer, but there were still cracks.

"I miss her," Dad said.

"I know."

Of *course* he missed her; Mom understood Dad in a way that no one else did or ever would. Including me. I once asked her—whiny little dick that I was—what she saw in him, why she put up with his violent war stories, his insecurities and anger. Mom patiently explained that so much of Dad's behavior was a show, a coping mechanism, which was a *good* thing, because too many soldiers came back from Vietnam, from the Gulf, from Afghanistan, without one. *It allows him to be a husband and a father,* she'd said. *Believe me, Harvey, there are worse men out there.*

"I miss her so much."

The teenager in me wanted to slip out of the room. The man I had become went to his side, took his hand.

"It's okay, Dad," I said. "It's all good."

He nodded and a tear dripped onto his cheek, and we sat there for a moment, hand in hand, while Michael Jackson sang "Beat It," which was kind of odd, but also kind of cool.

"You were at her grave," I said a moment later. "On the anniversary. I must have just missed you."

"I go as often as I can," Dad said. "It may be my favorite place in the world. Does that sound weird?"

"No," I said, and smiled. "Those notes you leave for her . . . so sweet."

"They help me remember the little things."

"Memories are important," I said, and nearly added, *I know that better than anyone,* but instead a long, musical yawn escaped me.

"You're tired," Dad said. "Go to bed."

"Yeah," I agreed. "Bed sounds good."

It really did, and I should have gone. I even stood up and took a couple of drowsy steps toward the stairs. And then a question popped into my head—a lame-ass, unnecessary question—that I asked really without thinking about it, and in so doing instigated another sleepless night, yet more reading, and a chain of chaotic events.

"So . . ." I looked at Dad over my shoulder. "What's the deal with the second person?"

"What second person?" he asked.

"You know, the narrative you use when you write those little notes for Mom." I struggled for a succinct way to explain it. "Using the pronoun 'you' instead of 'I' . . . like in a *Choose Your Own Adventure.*"

"Oh, right," Dad said. "I like that style."

"It's unusual," I said.

"It helps me focus on the memory. Not the emotion."

"Right," I said, and nodded. "That makes total sense."

"It should," Dad said. "I got the idea from you."

"From me?"

"From your journal."

"My journal?" The sleepy voice telling me to go to bed was enveloped by another voice insisting I stick around awhile. "I have a journal?"

"The one you started after Mom died," Dad said. He downed his wine and his single eye whirled. "You called it your Book of Moments, remember? You left it here . . . shit, I don't know, three, four years ago. I didn't think you'd mind if I read it."

"Four years ago . . . ?" I stepped toward him.

"You'd had a fight with Sally," Dad replied. "Nothing serious, you said, but you stayed with me until the dust settled."

I felt my head clearing, as if a small hole had been drilled into the back of my skull and the sleepiness was flowing out like sand.

"Do you still have it?" I asked.

"The journal?"

"Yeah."

"Sure," Dad said. "It's in the bunker."

I frowned, then recalled Dad packing some of his albums into a box marked BUNKER, thinking it peculiar, but being too distracted to ask him about it.

"Okay, let's pretend we've had a conversation about the bunker," I said. "I know all about it. I'm impressed by your forward thinking and preparedness. Now I just want to take a look for myself."

"It's not quite ready," Dad said. "I'm in the process of stockpiling it. Blankets. Batteries. Canned food . . ."

"Let's go, Dad."

"Medical supplies. RAD monitor. Chemicals for the toilet. I packed a box of your old stuff, too, in case you wanted to join me in the apocalypse."

"I can think of nothing better," I said. "Let's go check it out."

"What . . . now?"

I grabbed his hands and pulled him out of the chair.

"Yeah," I said. "Right now."

He'd buried a storage container in the garden like a giant coffin, painted it inside and out with a waterproof sealant, lined it with timber and drywall. Three vents led to the surface, these concealed on the outside by rocks and bushes. The door was reinforced steel, with several narrow steps leading to it, concealed by a trapdoor that blended with the environment. It was strewn with shelving, boxes, radio equipment, bottles of water, two cots—one of them, I supposed, for me: his apocalypse amigo.

"Still work to do," Dad said, turning on a lamp he'd wired to three car batteries. "More supplies, for a start. And I'm going to rig the power to the house with a genny for backup. When that runs dry, we're on to batteries and candles. Even so, I figure two of us can survive down here for at least twelve weeks. Long enough for any threat to pass."

"Sounds good," I said, looking around. The walls were brilliant white in the lamp's glare. He'd painted the floor white, too. It was like being inside a large refrigerator.

"These things aren't designed to be underground," Dad said, flicking his finger at all four walls. "I've reinforced it to withstand the pressure. The vents are filtered, too, so we won't die from radioactive fallout. Also, I want to finesse the trapdoor, get it to blend better so it won't be spotted by Russian drones."

"Good thinking," I said, not adding that the reinforced walls and air filtration system would do nothing to prevent us from killing each other—doubtless a more realistic threat. My attention had been diverted to a box beside one of the cots. It had my name on it.

I'm not sure my feet touched the ground. I flew around the cot and opened the box. The first thing I saw was a photograph of Sally (I recognized her face from the employee-of-the-month photo that Jackhammer had shown me). She wore a green bandanna in her hair and looked, I thought, quite lovely. I must have thought so at the time, because I was in the picture too, smiling broadly, my arm thrown around her. Judging by the length of my dreads, I guessed the picture was about two years old.

"Holy shit," I whispered, studying the photo, everything from the baby-blue Schwinn leaning against the wall behind us to Sally's faded Led Zeppelin T-shirt.

No memories stirred.

I continued through the box and found a photo of toothless baby me snuggled in Mom's arms, another of Mom on her own, another of me and Dad at the shore (I'm doing bunny ears behind his head and grinning as if I'm the first person in the world to have thought of it). There were a couple of mix tapes I'd made in my teens, my high school diploma, an unfinished screenplay I'd written when I was twelve. There were also new editions of three of my favorite novels: *Lord of the Flies*, *The Grapes of Wrath*, and *A Prayer for Owen Meany*. It was a little frustrating that Dad hadn't mentioned this stash while I'd been hunting for something to read, but I was more touched by the fact that he'd added them to the box—that he *knew* my favorites. Dude had been paying attention after all. I held up the Steinbeck and gave the old man a smile. He waved it off, curled up on the cot, and fell asleep moments later.

It was a box of words, keepsakes, and memories—things to cherish if the missiles flew, the Martians invaded, or if President Lang ever turned himself into a flame. At the bottom was a three-hundred-page notepad with a frayed cover. It was dog-eared, distended with the ink from a thousand pens. Nearly every page was busy with writing—*my* writing. I had no memory of it at all.

It was not a journal. Dad was wrong about that. There were no dates. No chronology or pattern. It was—just as I'd calligraphed on the front cover—a book of moments, written as they'd occurred to me. Some were very short. Others continued for pages.

All were written in the second person.

This was me putting memory before emotion, because I understood, even at sixteen, that emotions bend and flex, but memories are brittle. I turned to page one. *LIVIN' ON A PRAYER* was written on the top line in tight uppercase. Beneath this, several overwrought paragraphs about how Dad got into a high-speed car chase with Jon Bon Jovi after Jovi flipped him off at an all-way. I skipped a dozen or so pages and relived the moment I found a dead rattlesnake beneath the kitchen sink of my old apartment. Halfway in: the moment Eloise Dance, my ex-girlfriend, woke me up by tapping the barrel of a loaded .357 against my forehead. *Your balls shrivel to the size of pinheads*, I had written. *This isn't what you meant by starting the day with a bang.*

These and more. The memories either bubbled to the surface or they had never gone away, but in every case the connection was made. I was there again. This was *my* life. The second person added a layer of distance that I found more evocative. It was like being apprised by a wiser, more sensitive version of myself.

Until I got to the second half. The Sally years. I read these entries from inside a void. There were no connections. No cascades. I was a stranger inside my own head.

For the first time, I got a sense of Sally's power.

Terrifying.

I cracked a bottle of water and read through the night. I learned more about Sally—about *us*—than I could have hoped. Small things: how we met; how often we made love; which movies made her cry.

But also, crucially, I had a pretty good idea where she was hiding.

Twelve

I hit the road in Dad's old truck, which groaned and coughed and wouldn't go a tick over sixty. The cassette player worked, at least, so I could listen to the mix tapes I'd rescued from the bunker. I also rescued my Book of Moments and the photograph of me and Sally. My backpack was on the seat beside me, stuffed with freshly laundered clothes, and I tried not to think about what was in the glove compartment: a dozen smoke bombs nestled in an egg carton, and a loaded .38 Special.

Sally slides from you and lays gasping within the tangled sheets and pillows. Her hair is loose, spilling everywhere, and her rapid breathing pulls her stomach inward, deep as a cupped palm.

"Damn you," she says.

You roll onto your side and look at her. Run one finger from her cheekbone to her right breast, where a small black hair, fine as an eyelash, grows just above the areola. Sometimes she plucks this hair and sometimes she leaves it. You don't mind either way.

"Damn me?"

"For making me fall in love with you."

"Yeah," you say, and kiss the tip of her nose. "I'm a son of a bitch like that."

She smiles, then makes some order from the sheets and draws them mid-waist. You fold your arms around her and stay there for the next five minutes or so, caught in the afterglow, watching the many thoughts pass across her face. Eventually, she sits up, takes a deep breath, and shares one with you.

"Would you run away with me . . . if I needed you to?"

It's the sort of frivolous question people ask when they are recently in love. Perhaps to test the waters, or to indulge in fantasy. But two things stand out: first, the use of the word needed. *For you, it gives the question a solemn edge. Second, that her expression is entirely serious.*

"Run away?"

"Sure." She tries to smile but her lips only tremble. "Something you should know about me: I've moved around a lot in my life. I'm always looking for that one place to settle down, but when it feels like the walls are closing in, I hit the road."

"Walls? What do—?"

"It's complicated," she says.

You look at her blankly, sit up, draw your knees to your chest. Sally rests her head on your shoulder.

"Are you going to leave me?" you ask.

"No," she replies. "I'd want you to come, too."

"Where?"

Sally pulls the sheets higher. Her upper lip twitches. Body language you can't quite read. And yes, you love her, too—no doubt about that—but there is mystery here. There are secrets.

"Somewhere no one will find us," she says.

No hunt dogs in my rearview, which didn't surprise me; I'd spent much of the previous day scoping the perimeter of Dad's land, but saw no sign of them. To be absolutely sure, Dad and I went on a recon mission through the woods. We dressed in camouflage and smeared our faces with burnt cork. Dad was in his element. He commando-crawled with a KA-BAR knife between his teeth and communicated through tactical hand signals. I didn't know what the fuck he was motioning about, I just nodded and gave him the occasional thumbs-up.

We climbed trees and looked down on Ribbon Road like birds. We even approached Clover Hill from the north, which offered an elevated view of Dad's property, but there was no sign that anybody had been there.

"When do you leave?" Dad asked later that day. I was on the rear deck, glassing the forest line with one of his military telescopes.

"Tomorrow morning," I said. "I'll catch the early bus to Newark. Hop on a Greyhound from there."

I'd considered flying, but the idea of being locked in an airplane made me uncomfortable. I could hop off a bus whenever I wanted to. That wasn't possible at thirty thousand feet. Being on the ground gave me more options. More control.

"Where are you going?" Dad asked.

"That's classified information."

He sneered and his eye flashed impatiently, but he caught up with me an hour or so later—tossed me his truck keys.

"Take her," Dad said. "She's old but reliable. That three-fifty engine is one of GM's finer moments. Wherever you're going, she'll get you there."

Dad's truck: an '88 Silverado with as much rust as original paint. I wasn't going to decline the offer, though; I'd make better time on my own schedule, and detour if I needed to.

"Are you sure?" I said. "This is your truck, Dad. It's your link to the outside world."

"To hell with the outside world," Dad said. "Besides, the DMV pulled my license last year. Something about no longer meeting the minimum requirements."

He gestured at his eye and shrugged; I knew his monocle prescription had been changed in recent years, but didn't know how bad his vision was.

"I'm an accident waiting to happen," he said. "Take the truck, son."

Later that day, after I'd planned my route and packed my bag, I became convinced the hunt dogs were one step ahead of me—that they'd planted some kind of tracking device on the truck and would follow from a distance. So Dad and I checked the truck over. Dad took this very seriously. He popped the door panels and bed liner, shone a flashlight under the wheel arches, and looked under the hood.

"This is all because of Sally, huh?" he asked.

I ran an invisible zipper across my lips.

"You know, I learned some effective interrogation techniques in Vietnam." A half smile touched his lips, but there was no mirth in his voice. "I could just *make* you talk."

"Waterboarding. Tiger cages. Electrocution." I puffed out my chest and thought of the spider. "I've had worse."

He shook his head and disappeared beneath the hood. Moments later, his voice floated out to me:

"Don't get yourself killed for this girl."

"That's not in the game plan," I said.

Dad finished checking the engine compartment, then flicked off the flashlight and closed the hood decisively.

"Truck's clean," he said. "Rumble on, my son. And Godspeed."

I was reluctant to use my credit card on the road in case my activity was being tracked. Paranoia, maybe, but I had to play it smart. I wrote Dad a check for fifteen hundred dollars, which he exchanged for cash he kept in a shoebox under the bed. I also had my own cash, which brought the grand total to $1,986. If I stayed at cheap motels and avoided costly food bills, the money would last until I had a better idea what the future had in store.

Because I didn't know how long I'd be gone, or if I'd ever return, I mailed my landlord a check to cover two months' rent. I also made another call to Chief Newirth.

"I think I know where Sally is," I told him. "It may be a dead end, but I'm going to check it out."

"Where?" he asked.

"Rhode Island," I lied. "She has a cousin there."

"What about the shovel?"

"Still can't remember," I said. "Listen, I find Sally and the shovel becomes a nonissue. That may be the best I can do."

Silence at the end of the line. I don't know if Chief Newirth was contemplating stopping or assisting me, or if he was gauging where this ranked in terms of suspicious activity.

"One more thing, Chief . . ."

"I'm listening."

There was every possibility the hunt dogs would pay Dad another visit, and although he wouldn't be able to give them any information, that wouldn't stop them from doing to him what they'd done to me.

"Will you check on my dad while I'm gone?" I plucked a reason out of the air, something—I thought—entirely plausible. "He seems a little crazier than usual."

A pause. I heard him scribble something in a notepad.

"I'll stop by on my rounds," he said.

"Thank you."

"Good luck, Harvey," he said, and ended the call.

With the cash situation sorted and the truck checked for tracking devices, only one thing—one heartbreaking thing—remained to keep from drawing undue attention on the road.

"Do it," I said to Dad, handing him the scissors and clippers.

Dad cut his own hair all the time, and did a clean enough job despite only having one eye. I guess he was familiar with the shape of his head, and the way his hair grew. Even so, you'd think he'd never seen a pair of scissors before, the way he looked from them to my dreads and then back again.

"You sure?" he asked.

"Yeah."

He shook his head, turned his mouth down, circled me like a sculptor assessing a chunk of granite.

"Jesus, Harvey," he said. "Where do I even begin?"

Using both hands, I lifted my dreads into a tangled heap.

"Just take it all off," I said.

. . .

Six years to grow—to develop, nurture, and maintain. Forty-five minutes to remove, first severing the dreads close to my scalp with scissors, then running a number one across my skull, leaving me with a tight, velvetlike fuzz. Despite his initial reluctance, Dad soon relaxed—shit, he outright *enjoyed* himself. He put an old Dean Martin record on the turntable and spoke in a bad Italian accent (I have no idea why). He *flourished* the scissors, and used his monocle for detailed work. When he'd finished with my head, he trimmed my sideburns and neck hair, then shaved me with a warm, fragrant foam and a disposable razor. The end result was not barbershop perfect—there were a few nicks and patches—but it was good enough for me.

I looked in the mirror afterward and saw a different man. Smoother. Handsomer. And, with the curved scar beneath my left eye, *tougher*. Most importantly, I wouldn't be so goddamn conspicuous. Like Jackhammer and the rest of his happy pals, I could blend into the periphery.

"Severe," Dad said, examining his handiwork via the mirror.

"Had to be done," I said.

"You look good, though." He smiled and squeezed my shoulder. "You look like I did when they shipped me off to 'Nam."

I raised one eyebrow. "Like a soldier?"

"Yeah," he said. "Like you could win a fight."

The haircut was good, but the breakfast Dad cooked before I set out was even better. It was the greasiest, unhealthiest meal I'd had in a long time, and I loved every delicious mouthful. He kept shoveling food onto my plate, and I kept eating it. When I'd had enough, he replaced my empty plate with an egg carton.

"Take them with you," he said.

"Eggs for the road," I said. "What a great idea. If it's all the same to you, I think—"

"They're not eggs," Dad said.

I opened the carton and saw the ninja smoke bombs we'd made. A dozen tear-shaped pellets wrapped in duct tape, sitting on beds of cotton wool.

"Just in case," Dad said.

I nodded. My breakfast stirred uncomfortably. Despite looking like a soldier I hadn't planned for confrontation, simply because—should Lang and his hunt dogs appear—I had zero chance of victory.

"I don't think I'll need them," I said.

"Keep them in the glove compartment," Dad said, ignoring me. "The cotton wool will stop them from activating, even on the bumpiest road. Keep one in your pocket, though. A *loose* pocket. Away from keys and coins."

It was pointless arguing with him. I picked up the carton.

"Now, how about a firearm?" Dad said.

"No," I said. "Absolutely not."

"Just a little extra insurance."

"*No.*"

Now Dad backed off, or so I thought. When it came time to leave, he followed me out to the truck. I threw my backpack onto the bench seat, popped the glove compartment to slide the smoke bombs in, and that was when I noticed the revolver.

"I'm not taking it back," Dad said. "It goes with the truck. That's the deal."

"Jesus Christ, Dad," I said, stepping around the hood toward him. "I've never fired a gun in my life. You're making this trip *more* dangerous."

"Smith & Wesson thirty-eight special," Dad said. "The two-inch barrel makes it small enough to conceal just about anywhere. There are five rounds in the cylinder. Note the internal hammer; it's double action. You want to fire it, you aim and pull the trigger. That simple."

"I open windows for houseflies," I said. "What makes you think I could shoot a human being?"

"What if your life—Sally's life—depends on it?" Dad asked. "Anyway, you'll find a warning shot is *very* effective, either in the air or, better, at the assailant's feet. And you may not have to fire it at all; just having a heater in your hand will make most people think twice."

"Christ, Dad."

"You won't tell me what's going on? Fine. Okay. But this may be my only way to protect you." His nostrils flared and he said again, "I'm not taking it back."

I shook my head, thinking I would drop the gun out the window as I pulled away, then realizing I could use it as a bargaining chip.

"Okay," I said. "I'll take the gun, but you have to promise me that—should those heavy dudes return—you won't confront them, you won't even *speak* to them. Just lock yourself away. In your bunker, if possible. And don't come out until they've gone."

"You think they'll come back?"

"They might come looking for me," I said. "And they won't be in the mood for polite conversation."

"I can look after myself."

"*Promise* me, Dad. I'll feel a lot better about trekking halfway across the country if I know you're safe."

He pursed his lips and glanced away from me.

"Don't take these guys lightly," I warned him. "Tell me you'll lay low, or I'll dump the gun before I'm out of your driveway."

"Fine," he said, putting his hands up. "I'll keep an eye out. If I see them, I'll hit the bunker."

"Good. Thank you." I nodded, then exhaled. I hadn't been aware how quickly my heart was beating until I heard the flutter on my breath. I looked from the truck to the pale blue sky in the west—the direction I was heading—and then back at Dad.

"I should get going," I said.

Dad nodded, and I heard a flutter in his breath, too. Then he grabbed me and pulled me into a rigorous embrace. I felt the old muscle in his arms and chest tighten, then he whispered in my ear, "Be careful, son," and kissed me high on the cheek.

We separated. His eye was moist and he wiped it with the back of one hand.

"I love you, Harvey," he said.

"Love you, too, Dad."

Michael Jackson curled between his legs and meowed. Taking this as my cue, I climbed into the truck and cranked the ignition. The engine wheezed, coughed, and rumbled to life. Dad wiped his eye again, raised one hand. I gave him a peace sign and drove away.

I didn't want to look in the rearview but couldn't help myself. Dad stood at the top of his driveway with the cat nuzzled to his chest, one fist raised in a gesture of triumph and defiance—an image as beautiful as it was odd.

It summed him up perfectly.

"Goodbye, Dad," I said.

I hit Interstate 80 going westbound and didn't stop until the gas gauge read just below a quarter of a tank. I would have kept trucking until I hit the red, but didn't trust a twenty-seven-year-old gauge with a V8 that liked to drink. So I played it safe and gassed up just west of Milton, Pennsylvania. I'd been on the road three hours at that point, so I took the opportunity to stretch my legs.

Despite obsessively checking the rearview, and my every effort to ensure the hunt dogs were not following, I couldn't shake the paranoia. I eyed every vehicle that rolled into the gas station behind me. Some meathead threatened to knock me out because he thought I was staring at his girl, but I was just trying to see beyond the sun glare on his windshield. I raised a hand in apology, looked away, and imagined throwing a smoke bomb at his car. Pyrotechnics and gas stations don't play nicely together, but in my mind, with *this* douchebag . . . trust me, it was hilarious.

I hit traffic an hour or so later. There was an accident in the eastbound lane, so of course everybody heading west had to slow down for a look-see. My paranoia escalated as we inched bumper-to-bumper toward DuBois. I felt locked in, vulnerable. I may as well have been on a plane. I scoped around the truck like an owl, easing between lanes whenever a larger vehicle obscured my view. I told myself there was nothing to fear—that my paranoia was raw because I'd just set out. It would diminish with every mile I covered and I'd be back to my supercool self by the end of the day. Yeah, sure, maybe. But it didn't stop me from studying every vehicle that crawled beside or behind me.

And I saw them.

I *think*.

Three cars back in the outside lane. A silver midsize, seen via the rearview and then over my shoulder. A glimpse of the driver. Brickhead. Then a U-Haul truck eased into that lane and blocked my view. The air rushed from my lungs. An icy sweat broke across my skin. I turned off the stereo, needing to concentrate, but my mind was a whirlwind of dismay. I looked over my shoulder again, then my gaze flicked to the glove compartment. Suddenly, handling a gun didn't seem such a stretch for me.

"Make sure," I said, and stopped moving. The U-Haul truck passed on the outside, followed by a red Mustang and a silver Chevy—a smaller car with a middle-aged lady behind the wheel. I let a few more cars pass until the vehicle behind me let rip with the horn, then I edged into the outside lane, put my foot on the brake, and let the cars I'd been holding up zip past. A silver midsize was among them: a beat-to-shit Buick driven by a tattooed dude in a Steelers cap. This was not the car I'd seen, I was sure of it.

"Where did you go?"

It was possible I was seeing things, but I wasn't about to take any chances. I steered onto the shoulder and put my boot to the floor. The truck belched, groaned, and gradually picked up speed. Fellow road users expressed their disapproval by blasting their horns and maybe some called the cops. I don't know, didn't care, and didn't let it stop me. I checked the rearview to see if I was being followed—I wasn't—and kept going. A vehicle was parked on the shoulder ahead, hood raised, but even that couldn't slow me down; I veered around it, rumbled over the verge, tires cutting up grit and turf. A dirty cloud ballooned behind me as I bounced back onto the shoulder, nothing between the pedal and the floor.

A mile on, still nobody following, more vehicles giving me hell with their horns, and maybe I would have cut in but there was an exit coming up and I took it. The tires lost a little rubber as the road looped south, and I finally had to brake for the intersection. I turned right so I wouldn't have to wait for the green light, then made random turns, weaving through rural Pennsylvania. After fifteen long minutes of this—hands aching on the wheel, sweat in my eyes—I fishtailed into the parking lot of a country diner and rumbled around back so I couldn't be seen from the road.

I opened the glove compartment and saw the revolver inside. I thought about grabbing it but left it there. My legs were limp. My chest was full of sound. I settled back in the seat, closed my eyes, and breathed deeply.

Brickhead. Was it really him, or was paranoia playing tricks on me?

In lieu of the gun, I reached for the red feather. Studying its filaments, its color, a simple fact occurred to me: that I had only seen the hunt dogs twice—for certain—since crawling from that cinderblock room. The first time was on the bus out of Parsippany, when I'd flipped Brickhead the bird. Second time was when Jackhammer paid me a visit at the cemetery. I *thought* I'd seen them on many occasions, of course. Jesus, I was convinced they were hiding in my apartment, listening to my telephone calls. But the truth was, there had only been two definite sightings.

Was I fighting myself here? Was I my own worst enemy?

"You need to get a grip, Harv," I said.

It came down to this: If I truly believed I was being followed, I needed to head back to Jersey; no *way* could I risk leading the hunt dogs to Sally. If, however, I thought it more likely—and I *did*—that the only things following me were fear and paranoia, then I needed to seriously cowboy up before continuing west.

I twirled the feather. It was beginning to look a little beaten up, but was still vibrant. Still intact.

So . . . what's it going to be?

I'd already made my decision, of course. The hunt dogs had rattled my cage. Dominic Lang had rattled my *mind*. They had me—understandably—jumping at shadows, but that didn't make me a coward.

I put the feather away, gunned the truck, and headed back to the Interstate.

One last scan of the periphery.

"Okay," I said, and rumbled west.

Kansas bound.

Thirteen

Sea salt glitters on your shoulders. Sally walks beside you with air beneath her heels. Her hair is unkempt in the ocean breeze, half covering her face, and she makes no attempt to fix it. She looks tousled, a little drunk, and altogether alluring. You pull her into your arms and kiss her.

Fourth of July and the boardwalk is thronged. Everybody is sun-dark and smiling. Along with the singles, straight couples, and families, you see gay and mixed-race couples. They hold hands freely. Kiss openly. This is what you love about Asbury Park: You cannot judge or be *judged. It is a microcosm of a diverse and accepting society. The smiling faces prove that it can and does work.*

"Remember when you mentioned running away?" you ask.

"Vaguely," Sally says.

"I could live here," you say. "The beach life. The music scene. Not too far from Dad."

"I'm not sure it counts as running away if you stay in the same state." Sally's eyes glimmer behind her hair. "I'd at least want a different time zone."

You walk on, hand in hand. Beyond the sounds of the boardwalk, the roar of the ocean, you hear the parade marching along Cookman Avenue. This is soon drowned out by a three-piece band playing outside a crowded seafood restaurant. They are halfway through an old-time country number with a slow, swinging melody.

Sally is already dancing.

The song is one of Dad's favorites: "Abilene" by George Hamilton IV. As a kid, you thought it was just another country song about a girl, but Abilene is actually a town—in Texas, you assume.

You watch Sally. She rolls her hips in perfect time. Her blue dress sways. The love you feel for her in that moment is daunting. It pushes at you from inside. It fills empty spaces and burns recklessly. You have qualms—of course, what relationship is faultless?—but they are brought to their knees in surrender. And Sally can do that, with a kiss, a smile, a twirl. She has a way of making everything brighter.

She dances without inhibition, just another free-spirited soul on the boardwalk. Her arms and hair flow. Her dress bounces around her knees. Fragile as memory is, you think this is a moment that will stay with you forever.

The song ends and she falls into your arms. You hold and kiss her. She twirls again, takes you with her.

"Oh, Harvey," she says. "I think that was a sign."

"A sign?"

"Forget Asbury Park . . . let's move to Abilene."

"Right," you say. "Sure."

"A complete change of scene. A new beginning."

"Sounds great," you say. "I could learn some Merle Haggard songs. Wear a gun on my hip."

"I'm serious."

"You're drunk."

She holds her thumb and index finger an inch apart. "But Abilene . . . I'm feeling it, baby. It's safe and low-key. Slap-bang in the middle. The perfect place to disappear."

"Why would you need to disappear?"

Her mouth closes at once, as if she's said too much. She steps out of your arms and looks at the ocean.

"Sally?"

"It's just a figure of speech," she says, turning back to you. Her cheeks are

crimson. Her eyes are huge. You want to give her everything, but you're not sure if you can. There are moments when you don't even know who she is.

She presses herself close, stands on tiptoe, whispers in your ear.

"You have to admit . . . I'd look cute in a cowboy hat."

Her cheek brushes yours, then she is kissing you, both hands in your hair. She comes away smiling and you can't help it; you smile, too.

Everything brighter.

The night before leaving, I'd rifled through Dad's vinyl collection and found "Abilene" on an album called *Country Gold*. I dropped the needle and listened to it, focusing on Sally—that one memory of her dancing on the boardwalk. I matched the tick of her hips, the bounce of her dress to the song's easy tempo. I recalled the band—the drummer's rhythm, the guitarist's strumming pattern—and everything fit. This was the song from the memory . . . the song she'd erased.

I think that was a sign, Sally had said, as if she'd been looking—*waiting*—for a sign. *Let's move to Abilene.*

"The perfect place to disappear," I mumbled.

Dad had entered the room as the track faded. "One of my favorites," he said. "I didn't think you were into old-time country. What gives?"

Given that I was about to take off on a covert cross-country adventure, I didn't want Dad knowing that Abilene was on my radar.

"Thinking about making a mix tape for the journey," I said. "Random songs. Just to keep my mind fresh on the road."

"Good idea."

"Found this old track and it brought back a few memories, so . . ."

I trailed off. Dad nodded, lost in memories of his own, no doubt. It occurred to me then that I had no idea where Abilene was. I'd assumed Texas, but only because it was a country song. It could be in Oklahoma, Arkansas, Kentucky. And what if there was more than one? Abilene wasn't as common a town name as Clinton or Springfield, but I'd save a lot of miles by getting it right the first time.

"I always thought Abilene was a girl," I said carefully. "Until I actually listened to the lyrics."

"Prettiest town I've ever seen," Dad sang.

"Women there don't treat you mean," I sang with him, then smiled and casually asked. "It's in Texas, right?"

"There *is* an Abilene in Texas," Dad said. "But this was written about the one in Kansas."

A map of the United States unfurled in my mind. I threw a mental dart and hit the bull's eye.

"Kansas," I said, and recalled what Sally had said: "Slap-bang in the middle."

"Pretty much," Dad said. "It's where Eisenhower lived, and where he's buried. I know it because it's about twenty miles west of Fort Riley, where I did my basic training."

"That explains why you like the song so much."

"We'd go off-base from time to time. Me, Curly Tom, Billy Gomez. Head down to Abilene. There was always a bar playing that song, and always a woman waiting to treat you mean."

"The song lies," I said, smiling.

"Yeah, but you can still dance to it," Dad said. "And really, son, what more do you need?"

I had hoped to make the Illinois state line before calling it a day, but because of my detour through rural Pennsylvania there was no way. Resigned to this, not to mention tired and hungry, I stopped for the night in a little town west of Indianapolis. I found a motel that accepted cash payments, no questions asked. The Mexican restaurant on the next block played mariachi music through external speakers. I fairly danced through the door and loaded my face with tacos.

Afterward, I tried calling Dad from the motel but—as expected— he didn't answer. So I took a long shower, then collapsed into bed. I woke refreshed and found breakfast in a vending machine: Aquafina and a granola bar. I took a moment to enjoy the sunrise (I didn't even *consider* the periphery), sitting on the truck's rusty tailgate, swigging my water. Then I brushed my teeth, checked out, and hit the road.

Six hundred miles from Abilene. I estimated ten hours in the old

man's shitbanger. My intention was to stop for food and gas and nothing else. Unfortunately, it didn't work out that way; I blew a tire just
east of Columbia, Missouri. The spare was beneath the truck. It was
cracked, worn down to the plies, but inflated. It would get me to the
nearest auto shop but not much farther. I found a jack and tools behind
the bench seat and fought for an hour to release the spare. It finally
dropped and I switched it with the blown tire, which I tossed into the
bed, then drove slowly to a garage on the outskirts of Columbia. The
owner was a thickly bearded man with grease embedded in the cracks
on his hands and face who conducted business by way of his dog—an old
Great Dane with a dry, probing nose. "Rutherford says you're lucky we
had a no-show, otherwise you might've been waiting 'til tomorrow
a.m. . . . . Rutherford says the credit card machine's out of commission,
so we can only accept cash or check . . . I'm replacing the blown tire
and the spare, but Rutherford says the rest of your rubber is looking a
little thin, too."

I sat on an oily seat and waited, thumbing mindlessly through three-
year-old issues of *Easyriders* magazine while listening to Boxcar Willie's
greatest hits. The owner—GUNNER, according to the nametag on his
coveralls—worked at an undemanding pace and spoke to Rutherford
as if he was human. When it came time to pay, I took the cash from my
wallet and slid it across the counter toward Rutherford. He responded
with a deep, booming bark—*RAAAOOOF*—and I smiled for the first
time since leaving Jersey.

I was back on the road by 4:15, pushing the old Silverado to its full
thrilling sixty miles per hour, trying to make up for lost time.

I'd left my paranoia in Pennsylvania and spent the remainder of the
journey *freer*, clear-headed, but when I crossed into Kansas at just after
6 p.m., a different kind of anxiety set in. I was now only two hours
from Abilene, where—if I was right about it—I could bump into Sally
at any given time. The closer I got, the more nervous I became. Part of
it was not knowing how she'd react. Would she fall into my arms and
sob grateful tears? Would she reset my mind and take to her heels

again? Jesus, I didn't even know how *I'd* react. I had so many emotions inside that I wasn't sure which would bubble to the surface first. I *wanted* to kiss her—to scoop her into my arms and carry her away like Richard Gere in *An Officer and a Gentleman*. I was afraid, though—for all that I loved her—that my initial reaction would be less forgiving.

I passed a sign: ABILENE 50.

I realized the first words out of my mouth were all important. They would support everything that followed. After considerable thought, I decided on: *You don't have to be alone.* Simple. Powerful. Beautiful. Cue the kiss, the Richard Gere moment. I rehearsed it as the evening sun rippled across the horizon ahead of me, experimenting with levels of gravitas. I settled on an inflection that was sensitive but strong. It did nothing to help my nerves.

It was full dark by the time I reached Abilene.

I drove around to get a sense of the town's geography. It was a little larger than Green Ridge, with roughly the same population, but not as urbane or contemporary. The main thoroughfare, Buckeye Avenue, ran north to south with the downtown core made up primarily of family-run businesses—a lot of antique and gift stores, from what I could see. There were the usual places to eat: McDonald's, Burger King, Pizza Hut, and a sprinkling of home-style restaurants, the kind of places that would employ Sally without asking too many questions. The Eisenhower Center was to the south, along with a strip of "old town" buildings marked by a sign inviting you to CHECK ALL GUNS by order of Marshal J. B. "Wild Bill" Hickok. In keeping with the Old West flavor, the Smoky Valley Railroad offered tourists locomotive rides to the nearby town of Enterprise.

Abilene was not—as the song professed—the prettiest town I'd ever seen, but it *was* unmistakably charming, with one foot firmly planted in the nineteenth century. I drove around knowing I could never live in a place like this, and I didn't think Sally—assuming she was anything like me—could live here, either. But maybe that's the whole point of disappearing: going somewhere people would never expect.

. . .

I checked into a downtown motel, paid for two nights but was prepared to stay for as long as it took to check every mom-and-pop store,
restaurant, family farm, and lemonade stand in the area. I didn't waste
any time, either. Once in my room, I snagged the photograph of me
and Sally from the front pouch of my backpack, pulled on a clean shirt,
and hit the streets. Most of the places I needed to check had closed for
the night, but I'd seen a few bars while cruising around town. I figured
they were good places to start.

My head swiveled as I walked, checking every doorway and shadow.
I was so used to seeking out hunt dogs that this was second nature to
me. I had no proof that Sally was in Abilene, only a feeling—a *vibe*—
plucked from a two-page entry in my Book of Moments. Even so, I
expected to see her wherever my eye fell. At any point, she could be
inches away from me, or many thousands of miles. Both possibilities
set my heart racing.

I breathed air that was notably fresher than Jersey's, composed
myself, rehearsed my line. "You don't have to be alone." Over and over,
always with that delicate but essential inflection. I walked for ten minutes until the purr of live music drew me to a bar called the Steel Horse.
American beer signs flickered in the windows, which were either
smoked glass or dirty with exhaust fumes. Stepping inside, I smelled
barbecue, sweat, and graft.

It was open mic night, not exactly standing-room only but there
was a decent turnout. The clientele was primarily blue-collar male,
some still dressed in their work clothes, all drinking from bottles or
eating with their fingers. I grabbed a seat at the bar and ordered a beer.
Some dude on stage was giving his all to a Johnny Cash cover. I pretended to watch, but really I was scoping the room for Sally. Judging by
what I'd read in my Book of Moments, I didn't think the Steel Horse
was exactly her scene, but I couldn't afford to make assumptions.

No sign of her.

"That's Shane," the bartender said, gesturing at the kid on stage.
"He knows one damn song and plays it every week."

"At least it's a good song," I said.

"Not anymore." She dropped a wink and smiled—a middle-aged woman with lavish eye makeup and the bare midriff of a teen "You play?"

"On occasion."

"We have a house guitar," she said. "Let me know if you want it."

I finished my beer, then took her up on the offer. The guitar was a decent Epiphone and I played a thumping rendition of Tom Petty's "American Girl." It earned the enthusiastic reaction I was hoping for. Making my way back to the bar, I felt less nervy, less like a stranger, which I needed before asking about Sally.

I started with the bartender. I took the photograph from my pocket and slid it across the bar toward her.

"Have you seen this girl?" I asked. I had this rehearsed, too: just enough information, delivered with the slightest crack in my voice. "My girlfriend. She suffers from depression. We haven't seen her since the first week of August and we're real concerned."

We: as if I were asking on behalf of the family, a whole network of people who cared, when—going by what I'd written—she had no one who cared. Only me.

The bartender looked at the photograph carefully. I was glad I was in it, that we were both smiling and evidently in love. It made me look like her boyfriend, and not some deranged stalker. I had shoulder-length dreads in the photo, of course, and no scar beneath my eye. These differences aside, it was clearly me.

"No. Haven't seen her," the bartender said.

"Focus on her face," I said. "She'll likely have had a makeover: different clothes, a new hairstyle."

She looked again, narrowing her eyes, but then shook her head and handed the photo back to me. "Sorry, sweetie. Hope you find her."

I ordered another beer and walked it around the bar, hopping between tables, showing the photograph, getting the same negative responses. With every no, every shake of the head, my confidence waned. A few people said she looked familiar, but were too vague—or drunk—to be helpful. I left the Steel Horse feeling drained, unsettled, and overshadowed by the task ahead. I reminded myself that this was the first place I'd checked, and that Sally had a talent for making herself invisible.

Still, if she was in Abilene, I'd find her.

I checked two other places that night: a coffee shop called The Grind where a tableful of twentysomethings played *Cards Against Humanity,* and another bar—I don't even think it had a name—where some jacked freak with the Chiefs logo tattooed on his neck threatened to snap my "little goddamn bitch spine" if I didn't get the fuck out of his face.

Nobody recognized Sally.

I returned to my motel. It was midnight and I was dog tired. I took a shower and collapsed on the bed. Sleep came with a warm, dark blanket and enfolded me. My final thought of the day was, *Are you here, Sally? Are you close?*

Then I was gone.

Dominic Lang had told me that Sally blended with her environment, put down very few roots, and that because she had no credible ID, no social security number, was forced to work for businesses that didn't object to paying under the table. This reduced the number of places I had to check, but I still had some schlepping to do.

Over the next three days I got to know Abilene very well. I enquired at every non-franchise business I could find, from the mom-and-pop stores downtown to the farms scattered on the outskirts. I checked rental accommodations, the public library, the Eisenhower museum, even the Smoky Valley Railroad. The photograph passed from person to person. A string of hands and faces. It started to crease and fray. All for nothing.

I don't know how many variations of the word *no* there are, but I heard them all.

As the sun rose on my fourth morning in Abilene, I sat on the edge of the bed in my motel room feeling dispirited, not to mention foolish;

Sally had evaded Lang and the hunt dogs for nine years, and while I'd uncovered a significant piece of information, it was still crazy to think she'd be in the *first* place I looked. Just because Sally had mentioned Abilene, that didn't mean she'd be here, or that she hadn't changed her mind in the years since.

I took the photograph from my pocket, smoothing the creases with my fingers.

"Where the hell are you, Sally?"

There were two cities nearby: Salina and Junction City, each considerably larger than Abilene. I'd driven all the way out here, so thought I'd pay them a visit, make some inquiries. It was thin, but it was all I had.

Before this, I cruised the streets of Abilene one final time, romantically attached to the idea of finding Sally right at the end, waiting for a bus, maybe, or stepping out of a grocery store, bags bundled in her arms. Because life is like that sometimes. It throws these little moments at us. We attach words like *destiny* and *serendipity*, but really it's just life being wonderful.

It happens. It really does.

But not this time.

As if to epitomize my gloom, clouds rolled in from the west and a cold rain began to fall.

I checked out of my motel and put Abilene in the rearview.

It happened like this:

I'd planned to grab lunch in Salina, but eight miles west of Abilene I passed a cozy family restaurant called the Stovetop. It put me in mind of Marzipan's Kitchen so I pulled into the parking lot and went inside. As with every establishment I'd entered in the last few days, I wondered if I'd find Sally there. My expectation had been whittled down to nothing, but—almost a habit now—I rehearsed my line anyway. No sign of Sally. No surprise. My waitress was golden-haired and full of shimmering teeth. "Be right with you, sweetie," she said. I grabbed a seat by the window and ordered a grilled cheese without looking at the menu.

I sat there eating, looking at the folksy décor, contemplating my hopes, doubts, and disappointments. The best I could say about all this was that I *tried*, and if the hunt dogs found Sally before I did—if Dominic Lang took back his power and set fire to the world . . . well, it wouldn't be my fault.

I was still hungry after my grilled cheese so ordered a slice of peach pie off the specials board. While I waited for it to arrive, I fetched my backpack from the truck, took out my Book of Moments, and started to read. I looked for anything I'd missed, any tiny clue or something hidden between the lines.

"This your girlfriend?" the waitress asked. She had arrived with my pie and picked up the photograph of me and Sally from where I'd placed it on the table. It had been pressed between the pages of my book, trying to work out the creases.

"Uh, yeah," I said, dragging myself from my reading. "My girl-friend."

"Pretty smile."

"Yeah." I figured I may as well go through my routine. "She's missing. She suffers from depression, so we're all real concerned. I heard she was in the area."

"That's why you're out here?"

I nodded.

"How long's she been missing?"

"Since August."

"What's her name?"

It was useless giving a name because she would've changed it, but I had to say something.

"Sally."

The waitress shook her head, lips turned down. "Can't help you, sweetie." She placed the photograph back on the table. "Chet Nettle's new girl arrived at around that time, but her name's Clarice or Clara or some such."

A piece of peach pie fell off my fork and landed on the table with a splat.

"Chet Nettle?" Something fluttered in the pit of my stomach. My heart started to jump. "Where can I find him?"

"He runs a little farm store on Nineteen Hundred Avenue." She gave directions, using her entire arm to point, like a traffic cop. "Take Old Forty east, then south over the railroad tracks onto Eden Road. Carry on for a couple of miles and you'll come to Nineteen Hundred. Hang left and you'll find Nettle's just a little toot down on your right."

I pulled a twenty from my wallet and dropped it on the table.

"But, sweetie," the waitress said. "From what you told me, Chet won't be able to help."

"It's somewhere to start," I said. "Thank you."

I grabbed my book and backpack and whirled from the restaurant. Climbing into the truck, I told myself to calm down—this was likely a dead end. My heart disagreed, though. It sprang furiously. I felt it in my fingertips, in my throat, in the pockets beneath my eyes. Driving east on Old 40 and then south on Eden, I took gulps of fresh air, window open despite the rain. Fallen leaves swirled behind the truck as I motored through the farmlands southwest of Abilene. My hands made claws on the wheel.

I slowed down when I saw the sign for Nettle's. A long driveway led to a parking lot and farm store. There were a few stalls outside, produce glistening in the rain, and a wagon loaded with pumpkins.

She had dyed her hair dark brown and wore it in a ponytail. No cowboy hat, but she had the boots, the blue jeans. I stopped the truck and watched for a moment, tears stinging my eyes, as she loaded pumpkins from the wagon to the stall. Every now and then she'd wipe her hands down her jacket. I stumbled from the truck and tried walking toward her but my legs wobbled and I had to shoot out a hand, grab the hood.

She turned and saw me. I'd envisioned this moment a thousand times but it didn't go the way I planned. Her mouth fell open. A pumpkin dropped from her hands and didn't split but went *pok!-pok!* as it bounced along the ground. She shook her head and I shook mine.

I had a line. A *great* line. Powerful and beautiful. For the life of me, I couldn't remember what it was, so I said, "Hello, Sally," with a cracked voice and reached out with one hand. She came toward me, still shaking her head.

"Harvey," she said. "You shouldn't have come."

I recognized her only from the pictures, not from any memory. She had well and truly wiped herself from my mind. *We'll make new memories,* I thought, looking into her eyes, but she wasn't looking into mine. As she took my hand, I noticed she was looking over my shoulder at the driveway leading down to the road. I turned, and now it was *my* turn to be surprised.

Silver midsize. Brickhead behind the wheel. Jackhammer riding shotgun. They screeched to a halt twenty feet from my truck and the passenger window scrolled down. Jackhammer extended his arm, his meaty hand curled around a pistol.

"You shouldn't have come," Sally said again.

The sight of the gun and Jackhammer's expressionless face brought everything back in a hurry. I tried shielding Sally but was too slow. I heard a sound—*fzzzt*—and felt something zip past my shoulder. Sally gasped and staggered backward. I turned and saw the tranquilizer dart lodged in her throat, its fluorescent pink tailpiece too bright in the gray air.

She looked at me. Her eyes whirled.

"Silly Harvey," she said, and collapsed into my arms.

Fourteen

Jackhammer took aim at me and I ducked behind the truck before he could get off a clean shot. I watched through the driver and passenger side windows as he and Brickhead stepped from their car and strode toward us. Sally moaned. Her head flopped against my chest. I opened the driver's door and lay her across the bench seat. The .38 Special was in my backpack—I'd moved it there so it wouldn't be in the truck overnight—which had fallen into the passenger side foot well. I didn't have time to open the flap, dig around for the gun, and come up firing. A quick glance at Jackhammer and Brickhead confirmed I had only seconds before they were upon me. I reached across Sally with my long arms, popped open the glove compartment, and grabbed the egg carton. I recalled Dad telling me to put a smoke bomb in my pocket but of course I didn't listen. I could've saved valuable seconds—the difference, perhaps, between capture and escape.

Brickhead and Jackhammer closed in, separating to approach the truck from both sides. I scooped three smoke bombs into my palm, not knowing if they would work, just using whatever I had.

"Don't try anything stupid, Harvey," Jackhammer warned. It was like he'd read my mind. A quick glance showed him approaching the front of the truck cautiously, from behind his pistol. I took a deep breath and went for it.

I slipped from the cab, crouched behind the bed, and tossed the first smoke bomb high into the air. I prayed it would activate and not thud uselessly to the ground. I had nothing to worry about. There was a deeply satisfying bang and a pillar of white smoke that instantly enveloped their car. The hunt dogs swiveled on their heels, giving me a window. I leapt up and tossed the second smoke bomb at Jackhammer's feet. Again, the noise was startling. Jackhammer flailed and was lost in a swirl of smoke. A third explosion, a third impressive mushroom cloud—Dad was right, these were the real deal—as I threw the last pellet at Brickhead. The alarm on his face was deep enough to scar. He raised his hands and retreated behind the veil of smoke, which now formed a screen across the parking lot.

I couldn't see them. They couldn't see me.

I stood stupidly for a moment, looking at my handiwork, somewhat hypnotized by this warzone in miniature. Two more bangs: gunshots, fired blindly through the smoke from Brickhead's direction. The first punched through the truck's rusted tailgate and ricocheted off the bed. The second fizzed across my right arm. It scored my shirt and the skin beneath.

My turn to reel backward, to feel that boot-stamp of alarm. I dropped to one knee with a cry, then threw myself into the truck, pushing Sally along the bench seat until she butted against the passenger door. One glance over my shoulder showed the veil of smoke already dispersing. The hunt dogs stood shrouded, poised to attack.

I cranked the ignition. Dad's old truck gave a chesty cough and jumped to life.

I floored it.

A few consumers, and maybe Chet Nettle himself, had exited the store and were watching from the doorway with drop-jaw expressions. I tore past them, clipping one of the stalls with the truck's front end, scattering produce across the lot. I saw them duck for cover as I ripped around the side of the farm store, and knew they'd call 911 as soon as the smoke—literally—had cleared. Vandalism, gunshots, possible kidnapping, *bombs*. It wouldn't be long before every cop in Dickinson County was looking for a beat-to-shit Silverado with Jersey plates. I'd worry about that later, though. If there *was* a later. I had more immediate concerns.

I glanced over my shoulder and saw the hunt dogs heading back to their car, ready to give chase. A long sob bubbled from my chest. They were *here*. Fuckers had followed me from Jersey, tucked into the shadows, into the periphery, and the bullet that had scored my right arm assured me they were not playing games. Another wrong move from me—and God knows I'd made enough—and it was all over.

I considered circling back to the road, but the flat, straight blacktop favored the hunt dogs in their slick midsize. They'd catch up to me in no time. A couple of well-aimed shots and my tires would be blown to the rims. I had to stay off-road, at least until there was some distance between us.

I steered between two parked trucks and made a hard right into the yard behind the store. There was a barn ahead of me, both the front and rear doors open. I blew through it at the full sixty, dragging up a swirling tail of hay and feathers. On the other side I checked the rearview. The hunt dogs were there and catching fast. I tightened my grip on the wheel and broke left, crashing through a wooden fence—pieces flying—and into a freshly tilled field. The truck bounced and clattered but even at twenty-seven years old could take the knocks. I wasn't so sure about the remaining smoke bombs; the carton rattled across the seat and threatened to spill. Nine smoke bombs detonating in the cab was not a good scene, so I rolled down the window and ditched them. There was a volley of firecracker pops. Smoke funneled like a tornado. I watched through the rearview as the hunt dogs fishtailed around it. They balanced for a moment on two wheels—I thought they were going to flip—and then crashed back down to four. Dirt sprayed around them. Brickhead slowed to get the car under control, then roared after me again.

Another wooden fence loomed ahead, this sturdier than the last. I aimed the truck between two posts and kept my foot to the floor—crashed through with a jolt that pushed me against the wheel and bloodied my nose. Busted rails clattered over the hood, cracked the windshield, spun away behind me. I tore across two lanes of blacktop and missed a loaded cattle truck by inches. It offered a godlike horn blast that rattled my skeleton. Through fence number three—twin of the last—and the hood crumpled, the headlights blew. I lost the back end and slid across wet grass sloping upward. Pumping the accelerator, I steadied the wheel and regained control, but not before the hunt dogs had caught up to me. Jackhammer was hanging out the passenger window, gun in fist. I jerked left, then right. Two shots punched the tailgate. Out of nowhere, I drew on the evasive driving techniques Dad had taught me when I was fifteen years old (*You never know when you'll need to escape shapeshifters,* he'd said seriously). I touched the brake and the hunt dogs pulled abreast on my right side. The driver's window was down and I saw Jackhammer aiming across Brickhead. I steered into them before he could pull the trigger. Metal bounced off metal. In the heavier vehicle, the advantage was mine; I nudged their rear fender and sent them into a spin. The truck wobbled, too, but found its line and rumbled on.

The field rose and fell, leveled out, but the grass was slick and the tires slipped. Sally bounced on the seat. She thumped her head on the door panel but didn't wake. The dart was still lodged in her throat. I crashed through whip-thin trees and bushes, popped over railroad tracks with all four tires off the ground, landed with a thud that spilled Sally into the foot well.

The engine wheezed. Something else knocked beneath the hood. Dad's truck had taken a pounding and wasn't going to hold out much longer.

The silver midsize appeared in the rearview again.

"Sons of bitches," I moaned. My fingers locked around the steering wheel, knuckles aching. Here the ground was flat as a football field but punctuated by sagging trees. I weaved between them to keep Jackhammer from getting off a clean shot. He tried, though. I heard his handgun ringing above the struggling engine—kept my head low.

The field sloped suddenly and I was airborne again. The steering wheel was snatched from my hands on landing and I lost control—went sideways through brittle bush where birds were startled skyward. I jammed my foot on the gas, grabbed the wheel, and recovered. Another gunshot, loud and close. I screamed and waited for my blood to pepper the windshield but the bullet must have strayed. I went sideways again but this time I meant to, steering around a fat old oak before descending toward a stream. It was wide but shallow. I crossed it at a crawl but the spraying water gave me cover. Once clear, I picked up speed again but not too much. The needle hit forty and wouldn't go higher.

The hunt dogs were right behind me. Their car was beaten, too, steaming from beneath the hood.

"Come *on*," I screamed.

Through another fence, this made of high tensile wire that bowed like elastic before snapping. The grass on the other side was full and green, perfect for grazing.

"Shit," I said.

A field full of cows. Maybe a hundred of them. Hitherto unharmed by my vegetarian lifestyle, but now I had no choice but to go through the fuckers. I rapped the horn. The cows lowed and scattered, but slowly, and I was forced to brake, to weave. I cleared a path for the hunt dogs who roared up behind me. They crunched my rear bumper and I was thrown forward again, bouncing my cheekbone off the steering wheel this time and causing it to swell. A glance in the rearview showed Jackhammer taking aim. I stomped on the brake and went into a slide. The hunt dogs clipped my back end and lost control. I stopped, threw the transmission into reverse, and backed into them. A satisfying crunch as I punched a deep *V* into their rear passenger side door. It was met with a gunshot. The truck's narrow rear windshield exploded, showering the cab with glass. I screamed, jerked into drive, and hit the gas.

The hunt dogs followed.

Most of the cows had bolted in the opposite direction. I steered toward them and again they scattered, thundering on either side of the truck. I clipped one and sent it spinning behind me and the hunt dogs had to zigzag to avoid it. Brickhead fought for control on the slick grass and I saw my opportunity; I slowed down until we were level and steered a hard left, slamming into them from the side. They veered away at speed and I watched what unfolded with fascinated horror.

They drove through a cluster of cows that toppled over the hood, sagged the windshield, crushed the roof. Mooing, broken-legged things, but they gave as good as they got. The battered midsize wobbled out of control, then flipped. Three times, four . . . five. It landed hard on its roof, a tangle of steel and shattered pieces, wheels splayed on their axles. Smoke gushed from the engine compartment.

I slowed down but didn't stop, afraid I wouldn't get going again. I saw Jackhammer's bloodstained arm flop from the broken window. If he and Brickhead weren't dead, they were definitely close.

I wasn't going to stick around to find out.

Several cows butted defensively against the truck. I nudged around them, then picked up speed. I drove through the hole in the fence I'd already made, then trundled west until I found a road.

Dad's truck rattled and knocked. I crawled one mile to the next, away from the scene.

I thought I heard sirens but might have imagined that.

I drove for almost two hours, keeping to the back roads, my speed sinking from thirty-five to twenty until finally I had to ditch the truck. No bad thing. I had a feeling the police were looking for me, not to mention a few irate farmers. More concerning still: The hunt dogs knew the truck. Jackhammer and Brickhead were perhaps out of the picture, but the spider had more goons at his disposal. Given how they'd tracked me, I had to assume the truck was bugged, not while it was parked at Dad's house—we'd checked it thoroughly—but when I was already on the road. They'd likely planted a tracking device when I'd stopped for a bite to eat.

I thought I'd have to drive it into a forest and leave it, but went one better, disposing of it completely so that the license plate or VIN couldn't be traced to Dad. I followed a rutted trail to the edge of a small lake. A rocky embankment dropped sharply to the water. I pulled Sally from the foot well and lay her on the soft grass—plucked the dart from her throat and threw it into the weeds. She stirred. Her eyelids fluttered but she didn't wake. I grabbed my backpack, ejected mix tape Vol. II, dropped the truck into neutral. It started rolling immediately and I lunged backward with a gasp. I watched the tailgate—pocked with rust and bullet holes—disappear over the embankment. There was a crunching sound as it struck and bounced over the rocks, then a booming splash as it met the water. I crawled toward the edge and looked down. The old truck was ass-up in the lake. It had worked hard and died like a hero.

"Sorry, Dad."

I took a T-shirt from my backpack, scuttled down to the water, soaked it through. I used it to wash the blood from my nose and arm, then as a compress against my swollen cheek. It was soothing. I closed my eyes and sighed. I dipped it in the water again, returned to Sally, wiped the trickle of blood from her throat, and then mopped her brow.

Only then did I let it in. Everything that had happened—that was *happening*—crowded my mind: Sally, the hunt dogs, the chase, this war I found myself fighting—a war I didn't want and couldn't win. Like Sally, all I could do was run. We were in this together.

By the time I'd regained an iota of composure, Dad's truck had sunk completely from view. A few bubbles disturbed the surface, but that was all.

I wondered if the tracking device, if not still working, would lead the hunt dogs to its last known location. If so, they could be here at any moment. I held my breath and listened but all I heard was the rain in the trees.

I took the .38 Special from my backpack and tucked it into the waistband of my jeans.

We had to get moving and Sally was still out.

I don't know how much strength and energy you can distil from adrenaline, but I hoisted Sally—easily one-thirty in her cowboy boots—onto my shoulders and carried her until the sun went down. I maintained a westerly direction, using the sky as my compass, and stayed away from roads and buildings—from *people*; a man carrying an unconscious woman on his shoulders can only raise suspicion.

So I crashed through thickets and crossed streams and navigated woodland where the trees were dense and birds sang angrily. I rested seldom and for never longer than five minutes. It stopped raining. I was grateful for that. The clouds thinned and I watched a fingernail moon rise. Too dark to keep walking, I found a derelict barn filled with old engine parts and a bed of damp straw. I made it more comfortable with clothes from my backpack and lay Sally down, kissed her forehead. I pulled the gun from my jeans, sat on an engine block, and kept my eye on the open barn door.

I didn't sleep. Not a wink.

Fifteen

"Why did you come?"

"Because I love you."

"Not a good enough reason."

"I think it is, but here's another reason: Because you took something from me."

"If you've come this far, you'll know it's because I had to."

"Yeah, maybe. Which leads me to the third reason for tracking you down: answers . . . I think I deserve some answers."

Sally sighed and looked away from me.

"We were together for six years," I said. "I'm pretty sure you know everything there is to know about me. Not because you stole it from my mind, but because I *shared* it. Call me crazy, but I figure that's what you do in a relationship."

"A normal relationship, yes."

"Isn't that what you want?"

"It's all I've ever wanted."

"It begins with honesty," I said. "For six years I was in the dark. It seems everything I knew about you was a lie. Including your name."

She looked at me.

"Miranda," I said.

She seemed surprised that I knew this. Her eyes widened then flickered, a mite regretful, perhaps. A lock of hair spilled across her cheek and I reached without thinking, curled it behind one ear. It felt *wrong*, somehow, to touch her like this. I loved her, yes, but I didn't know her.

"It's self-preservation," she said. "I live very carefully, Harvey. And that's the thing: I can restore your memories, give you all the answers, but we can never be together. My life is too dangerous."

"I'm a part of your life," I said. "A part of your danger. We're in this together."

"No," she said.

It was early morning, the sky charcoal in the west, rimmed with milky light in the east. The trees were tangled silhouettes and the birdsong was mayhem. We sat outside the barn, which creaked and whistled in the breeze, our breaths frosting the air. I took a moment to gather my thoughts, and the line I'd rehearsed a thousand times—which had deserted me when I first saw Sally—finally dropped into my mind. It didn't seem nearly as powerful now, but it was the best I had.

I wanted to touch her again.

"You don't have to be alone."

We walked maybe a mile with the sun rising at our backs, following a stream through the woods, then taking a beaten pathway that skirted a pond where cricket frogs chirped. It ended in a clearing, at the other side of which we found a bush drooping with plump red raspberries. They were chilled with dew and we gathered them greedily, ate in silence. Our hands and faces sticky, we walked on, listening to our feet on the ground and the constant whistle of nature, and then, eventually, traffic sounds. We followed these to a road and walked the shoulder and some twenty minutes later arrived at a village called Moon.

A weathered sign placed us fifty-five miles west of Salina, which put us eighty or so miles from where I'd shaken the hunt dogs. A good distance. Unfortunately, we were only seven or eight miles from where I'd dumped the truck. I shared my theory of how the tracking device would draw the hunt dogs to the lake, which meant they could be closing in.

"We need distance," I said. "And fast."

I had wanted to buy a bottle of water in Moon, maybe see if there was somewhere we could catch a bus or taxi. Sally shook her head.

"This is a tiny village. Maybe two hundred people. We buy anything or talk to anyone, we leave a footprint. You need to be smarter, Harvey."

"So what do we do?"

"How much money do you have in your wallet?"

We walked another two hours, maybe five miles, cutting across farmland typical of the central plains. We stayed within earshot of traffic, emerging intermittently until we found what we were looking for: a gas station with a sandwich joint attached. My dry mouth clicked and my stomach growled. We *did* eat, but we weren't there for the food.

"We're going to buy a ride," Sally said, and took a long swig of water. We'd already downed a bottle each. "The seekers could have bus and train terminals in all the big towns around here covered. So we need to go farther. Out of state."

Seekers. What I—and Lang, to be fair—called the hunt dogs. Sally's terminology reminded me that she had been doing this since 2006. A fifteen-year-old girl on the run. I ached for her.

"Whatever you say," I said.

"So what are we looking for?"

"Vehicles with out of state plates," I said, and tore into my foot-long. Mayo dripped down my chin and I didn't care.

"Right," she said. "Gas stations—even small ones like this—see people from all over the country, so they're great for buying rides. Ideally, we're looking for a young couple like us. Open-minded types who could use the extra cash. Failing that, a dude in a suit; businessmen don't like sharing their cars, but they *do* like money."

We were sitting at a table in the sandwich joint watching the vehicles rumble up to the pumps. All sky-blue Kansas plates so far.

"We can't just hitch a ride?" I asked.

"Time is against us," Sally said. "We can buy a ride a lot quicker than we can hitch one."

"Okay." I nodded, took another mouthful of sandwich. "Whatever it takes."

"Our story: I'm a writer, you're a musician. We're going to a rock festival in . . . wherever: somewhere between here and where they're headed. We're traveling bohemian-style, seeing the land, just a few clothes in a backpack. It's like Woodstock, baby. It's romantic."

"Sounds good," I said. "Believable."

"Not my first rodeo," Sally said.

This was an ideal time to ask about previous rodeos—the food had revived me; I burned with questions—but just then a Cadillac with New Mexico plates pulled in and the moment was lost. Sally had turned away from me, looking to see who got out of the car.

"I'll let you do the talking," I said.

"Good idea."

But it was a no-go: a middle-aged female driver with angry lines across her brow, snapping into a cell phone as she gassed up.

"She looks like a barrel of laughs," I said. "Let's go to Albuquerque with her."

"Even if she was all smiles and sunbeams, she wouldn't help us out. Women traveling alone are understandably cautious about giving rides to strangers. Show her a hundred bucks and all she'll see is a fistful of red flags. She might even call the cops."

"We don't want that," I said. "Let's stick to greedy, gullible guys."

"You're learning." Sally looked at me, the slightest of smiles on her face. "Is this the life you want, Harvey?"

"It's the life I've got," I replied and then, attempting levity, "I think the extreme haircut shows how committed I am."

"That's the only smart thing you've done," Sally remarked. "But it takes more than that."

"I know," I said. "And I'm ready; I'm in this for the long haul."

"You don't have to be. We go our separate ways and the target switches to me. It's always been me."

I thought of the way the hunt dogs' car had plowed into the cows and flipped, its roof partially crushed and its wheels splayed. More particularly I thought of Jackhammer's bloodstained arm flopping through the broken window.

"I'm not so sure about that," I said.

Sally lowered her eyes, finished her sandwich and water, wiped her mouth with a napkin.

"You should freshen up," she said. "You don't smell great. Change your T-shirt. Wash your face. It'll help."

"Right," I said, and grabbed my backpack; I *did* smell a little funky. "I'll be right back."

The restroom was at the back of the dining area and I pushed the door open on a dimly lit cube smelling of disinfectant with a bucket and mop in one corner, a toilet without a seat, and a sink bolted to the wall. The water was lukewarm but felt good on my face. I took off my shirt, soaped my armpits and splashed them clean. No towels, so I let them air-dry while I brushed my teeth. It was only when I was smearing deodorant into my pits and across my chest that I realized my mistake, my *stupidity*. I looked at my ridiculous face in the mirror—eyes wide, jaw loose—while Sally's words struck a mocking note in my mind.

You need to be smarter, Harvey.

I pulled on the same smelly T-shirt I'd taken off, snatched up my backpack, darted from the restroom with such zeal that the door cracked against the wall and the mop toppled to the floor. I reeled into the dining area and saw, with zero surprise, that Sally had gone. Our table by the window was empty but for our sandwich wrappers and empty water bottles.

"Shit," I muttered, still hiking down my T-shirt. "Shit fucking shit."

Of *course* she was gone. She didn't want me in her dangerous life. She'd taken this opportunity to remove herself—*again*—and was likely sitting in the passenger seat of a car heading . . . Jesus Christ, could be *anywhere*; we were in the middle of the country. Throw a goddamn dart at the map.

"*Fuck*," I snapped, everything inside me sinking. Weaving across the dining area, cursing out loud, I realized I was leaving a pretty deep footprint. If the hunt dogs came here asking questions, the staff would have no problem remembering me. *Tall dude with a scar on his face? Mouth like a sewer? Yeah, he was here.* Sally reminded me again that I needed to be smarter, and I told the voice to shut up, to just shut the fuck—

The thought snapped like it had been frozen and tapped once with a hammer. I had exited the sandwich joint into the toxin-scented air and there was Sally, hands casually on hips, talking to some immaculate business type in a shirt-and-tie combo. He had a neatly groomed goatee and boot-polish hair. His cufflinks blinked in the light as he pumped premium fuel into a Lexus with Oklahoma plates.

I stepped slowly toward them, my jets cooling as if they too had been frozen. The smile on my face covered everything I felt inside.

Sally turned toward me and beamed.

"Baby," she said. "Three hundred dollars gets us to Tulsa."

"Only if *he* sits in the back," Mr. Immaculate added, wrinkling his nose at me.

"Deal," I said.

We were five hours from Tulsa and with every mile my anxiety lifted. We put the gas station behind us, along with the lake where I'd dumped Dad's faithful old truck. The clock on Mr. Immaculate's dash read 11:15 and by 2:30 we had Kansas in the rearview. It was like removing a burdensome weight from my shoulders.

I wanted to believe Sally felt a similar relief but it was difficult to gauge her mood. She wore her mask throughout the trip and told some fabulous lies. She was incredibly convincing, too. It made me wonder if I'd fallen in love with the real Sally, or one of her many characters: crunchy, alternative Sally Starling, who threaded beads into her hair and didn't wear perfumes, and who probably knew a dozen kick-ass quinoa recipes. If she were to stand before me, stripped of her masks and fabrications, would I love her still?

I was glad to be in the back. I didn't have to talk. Didn't have to lie.

I caught a few z's but not many. Mostly I listened to the conversation up front and the thrum of the road, but I also paid attention to the thin place that's inside us all: the point at which heart and mind come together.

Mr. Immaculate dropped us in Sand Springs, a suburb of Tulsa, about seven miles west of the city proper. It was a little after 4 p.m. and we were hungry, in need of a shower, and I, at least, wanted to plummet stonelike into a bed and sleep for a day.

"We should find a motel," I said. "Get cleaned up. Plan our next move."

"We?" Sally asked, looking at me with one eyebrow raised. "There is no *we*, Harvey. I got us out of the danger zone. Now you go your way, I go mine."

"You can't be serious," I said.

She walked away from me, head down. I shouldered my pack and hurried after her. We were on Second Street, four lanes of clean road, not especially busy even at this time. There were people around, though, and I didn't want to make a scene—didn't want to shriek that I'd spent so much of my time pining for her, wanting to care for and protect her, that I'd traveled halfway across the country looking for her and be damned if I was going to let her shrug her shoulders and walk away. Actually, I *did* want to shriek those things, and more, but instead I strolled beside her with my lip buttoned, at least until we made a right on Main and parked ourselves on a bench outside the library. The late afternoon breeze made the tree behind us shake its leaves.

"You know what I think?" I said.

Sally looked at me with dark, tired eyes.

"I think you wanted me to find you." I gave that a moment to sink in, then continued. "Not as soon as I did, of course, but down the line . . . a year—five years—from now. You left the door a little way open."

"That's very sweet, Harvey," Sally said. "And very wrong."

"Really?" I tapped my brow. "You leave one memory in my head—

the memory of you dancing to 'Abilene,' which just happens to be the town you ran away to."

"I erased the soundtrack."

"Yeah, you did. But I wrote it down in my Book of Moments, which you *knew,* because you stole the memory of me having written it."

Sally slumped, shaking her head. "I knew that goddamn book would bite me in the ass."

"You probably figured it was buried beneath a pile of shit in my dad's house, and that I'd come across it after he died." I smiled and spread my hands. "Well, I came across it a lot sooner than that. And here I am."

"Bravo, Harvey. Now get out of here."

"No can do," I said, unable to keep the frustration from my voice. "Unlike you, I can't just shut off my emotions, move on to the next . . . whatever."

"I do what it takes to stay safe."

"Help me understand," I said. "Let me in."

"I considered letting you in," Sally said. "I told you I can't stay in one place for too long, and asked if you'd run away with me. Okay, so I didn't expect you to bounce off the walls with enthusiasm, but if you'd shown even a shred of interest, I would have opened up to you. Not completely, just a little, then a little more. But this life, Harvey, this constant danger . . . it's not for you. Never has been. Never will be."

"I don't remember that conversation," I said. "For obvious reasons. But it must have had some effect on me because I wrote it down. And from what I read, you were a little sketchy. So you'll excuse me for not dropping everything and running off into the *sunset* with you."

We'd done a good job of keeping our voices down, but mine rose during this last sentence, an impatient blip that earned stares from the folks passing on Main. I took a deep breath and listened to the leaves chatter. Two flags—American and Oklahoma state—rippled from a nearby pole, and I found their colors, set against the deepening sky, quite tranquil.

"Since you left," I began in a perfectly level voice, "I have been beaten up, my mind has been violated, and my apartment has been flipped upside down. I've been tormented, threatened, terrorized, spied on, and pursued. I got into a high-speed vehicle chase that may have resulted in the deaths of two men. Oh yeah, and I did *something* with a shovel on the night you disappeared. I don't know what, but I have a feeling I wasn't planting azaleas. As a result of this unexplained activity, I find myself on Chief Newirth's very short list of suspects in the unsolved Green Ridge murders."

"Jesus," Sally said, and dropped her face into her hands.

"So this life of danger you're talking about . . . guess what, sugarbean: I'm already living it."

"What a goddamn mess," Sally said. She looked at me. There were tears in her eyes. "I'm sorry, Harvey."

"Everything that has happened," I said. "Everything I've done . . . I can't go back, Sally. This is my life now. You understand that, right?"

"Yeah, and we're safer apart," Sally said. "Trust me, it's hard enough to make one person disappear, let alone two."

"Two sets of eyes are better than one," I insisted. "We can look out for each other."

"They'd find us twice as fast."

"We're good together."

"Romantic and true, but it doesn't matter."

"It does," I said firmly. "Don't you get it, Sally? You stole my memories, but you couldn't steal what I feel for you. I fucking *love* you, and I want to help protect you."

"*Protect* me?" Sally said, and now it was her turn to win a few curious stares. "You led the seekers right *to* me. I was happy in Abilene. I had a job, a place to live. I was making myself invisible, and you led them right to my fucking feet."

"Yeah, well," I mumbled. "The truck had some kind of tracking device on it. That won't happen again."

Sally rolled her eyes, and in that second looked nothing like the girl in the Health Nut employee-of-the-month photograph, and even less like the pretty girl in the Led Zeppelin T-shirt and green bandanna. I wondered if this was closer to the *real* Sally.

"The girl I fell in love with," I said gently. "The girl in here." I placed a hand on my chest. "Was she real, or just one of your characters?"

Sally's tears were real. I knew that.

"What do you believe?" she said.

I recalled UFO-watching on Spirit Lake, where the lapping of the water was as clear and sweet as my old man's voice. *Really, son,* he'd said, *it's a matter of belief, and how it defines us.* I looked at the sky, just as he had, not full of stars but darkening toward evening. *I'm more afraid of* not *believing than I am of not finding what I'm looking for.*

I wiped Sally's tears away.

"She was real," I said.

Sally smiled and nodded.

"And did she love me?" I asked.

"Very much."

"Does she still?"

"Very much."

I was still adjusting to the fact that I had found her, and to every vibrant emotion running through me, not least the incongruity of both loving her and knowing nothing about her. I trusted my heart, though. Even if it was punched with holes.

"I should know better than to fall in love," Sally said, and wiped a grimy sleeve across her cheeks. "I just couldn't help myself, you're the best person I've ever known."

And with that she got to her feet and started to walk away.

"Sally."

She kept walking.

"*Sally!*"

She stopped but didn't turn around.

"I'm worth fighting for." My voice was strong, but when I stood up my legs were trembling. I took two shaky steps toward her. "*We're* worth fighting for."

"But I'm scared for myself," she said, still with her back to me. "Every second of every day. I can't live being scared for you, too."

"We can do this," I said.

She whirled, suddenly brimming with energy, and strode—*ran*—toward me, threw herself into my arms with such passion that I was knocked backward into the bench. I buckled at the knees, sat down hard. Sally straddled me.

"You say you can't go back," she said. Her forehead was pressed to mine, her lips brushed my lips and she had her hands clasped at the back of my neck. "Do you know what that means, Harvey? Do you really? You'll never see your father again. You'll never place another flower on your mother's grave. You'll have to change your name. Change your appearance—your *personality*. The life you knew is over. Are you ready for that?"

She didn't wait for a response; I felt her then, in my mind, just like I had felt the spider. But she didn't crawl or squirm. She lay herself on my brain, as soft and red as the feather in my pocket. My eyes trickled back into my skull and I groaned. I felt a momentary heat, uncomfortable but not entirely unpleasant, then she was gone, as if that feather had been blown away by the wind.

I gasped, looking at her through watery eyes. My heart gibbered and every inch of my skin had tightened with gooseflesh.

"What—?"

She cut me off—kissed me. No small peck on the lips, but a full-mouth smash, tongues touching. I didn't want it to end but she pulled away, breathless, her hands still clasped behind my neck. I cupped one side of her face and yes, it fit my hand perfectly.

"Do I still have my memories?" I asked.

"I didn't touch them." She sighed. "Not this time. I just needed to see what you were thinking."

"And?"

She grabbed my hands, dragged me to my feet.

"Come on," she said.

Sixteen

We walked until we found a motel that didn't require a credit card on file, which took almost an hour. Time enough for Sally to answer a few questions, but neither of us had the stamina for further conversation. All we wanted was a steaming shower and a soft bed. I *did* mention that I'd be glad when she didn't feel like a stranger—thinking out loud, more than anything—and Sally wrapped her hand around mine and assured me she'd give everything back, but that this wasn't the time or place.

"It'll take time and energy," she said. "And we'd need to move quickly afterward."

I wanted to ask why, of course, but I only nodded, squeezed her hand, and we walked with our arms swinging, occasionally bumping shoulders in our weariness.

The sun departed in layers of showy color and the streetlights sizzled around us. Eventually, we saw the sign for the motel in the distance. It was gaudy white neon, its letter *M* blinking fitfully. Still, it could have been Shangri-La. Sally kissed me again, unexpectedly, and I smiled.

It was my favorite part of the day.

. . .

I asked Sally if she wanted her own room and she told me not to be silly. We shared, and even though there were two beds, we slept in the same one. Pink and clean from our showers, bellies loaded with pizza, we lay in the darkness with a foot of mattress between us. This shrank to six inches, and then three. I felt her body heat and smelled the hotel shampoo in her hair. She reached for me beneath the covers, found my hand. I curled my arm around her and we spooned, nothing more. The way her face molded to my hand was the way her body molded to mine in miniature. We stayed that way until morning.

"I'd hoped Abilene would be the place I could finally settle down," Sally said. "I had this fantasy: maybe ten years from now, or whenever the danger had passed, working in a bookstore or coffee shop . . . just another day. Then the door opens and there you are, maybe with a goatee, a few silver threads in your hair, and some deeply sexy lines around your eyes. You step toward me and . . . well, you know how the rest of the fantasy goes."

"I can imagine," I said.

"I made a list of back-up towns in case Abilene didn't work out," Sally continued. "Safe communities. Low crime rate. Unassuming, yet energetic. Towns where I'd feel safe."

"Right," I said. "Where the hunt dogs wouldn't think to look."

"Hunt dogs?"

"That's what I call our mutual friends."

"It's nasty," Sally said. "Perfect, too. I like it."

"Well, 'seekers' makes them sound like a sixties folk group," I said with a dry smile. "And trust me, they ain't that."

"Trust me, I *know*."

We'd slept until late morning and only woke then because housekeeping knocked (in our tiredness, we'd neglected to hang the DO NOT DISTURB sign on the door). I barked a no thank you, blinked blearily, then propped myself on one elbow to watch Sally as she stirred. Playfully, I tickled the tip of her nose. She smiled from that fuzzy place between awake and asleep and batted my hand away. Then she tugged me close and kissed my bruised cheek. It's a weird feeling to find yourself falling in love with someone you're already in love with.

We showered long and hard again, then dressed in clothes that smelled of sweat or straw or both. I suggested finding a store and revitalizing our wardrobe. Sally—the brains of the operation, but who still had Kansas cowshit on her boots—said it could wait until after breakfast.

So there we were, in a diner not so different from Cadillac Jack's, me with my Brando—which is how I'll think of an American cheese omelet until the end of my days—and Sally with her fruit cup. Just like Mom.

"There's a town in Northern California," Sally said, popping a chunk of cantaloupe into her mouth. She chewed and swallowed and a thread of juice trickled down her chin. "Called Ryder. Ten thousand people, give or take. It's on the ocean. A cool, cosmopolitan vibe. I've heard it described as San Fran's little sister."

I nodded approvingly; I'd never been to the west coast, but my inner Jerry Garcia assured me I'd dig it.

"Another town on the shortlist," Sally continued. "Paisley, Colorado. Insanely picturesque, between the mountains and the lake. Low crime rate. Strong economy. They also have an annual writer's festival that draws some pretty big names."

"Sounds great," I said. And it did. It also made me wonder—with so many perfect little towns sprinkled across the country—why she ever chose Green Ridge. I swilled my eggs back with a mouthful of tepid coffee and asked her.

"An element of subterfuge," she said. "Whoever would think to look for me in Jersey?" She accented the last word—*Joisey*—and smiled. "But really, it's a sweet little town in the Skylands. I thought I'd check it out, and I'm glad I did."

Her hand crept across the table, looped around mine. A gentle squeeze before returning to her fruit cup. I just about purred.

We finished our breakfast, paid up, and left. The plan now was to buy Sally whatever she needed in the way of feminine products, and to buy us both some new clothes. Despite unforeseen expenses—a blown tire and a three-hundred-dollar ride to Tulsa—I still had a wad of bills in my wallet, although I wondered how long it would be before I'd need to buy a cheap guitar and go to work.

We took a cab into downtown Tulsa where the shopping was better and the streets somewhat livelier. They still felt subdued, though, but I put that down to being used to the bustle of Manhattan, the tight anger of Newark. Even so, walking through the Pearl and Brady Arts District, I felt myself becoming more transparent. The footprint I'd left in Sand Springs was definitely—to use a spiderism—daintier here.

"Why not a city?" I asked Sally, who'd paused to look in the window of a store called Stomp! where headless mannequins posed in colorful garb, all of them clutching fake smartphones.

Sally looked at me and smiled. "Huh?"

"A city?" I said. "It *has* to be easier to disappear in a city. Dense. Crowded. Diverse. We'd be needles in a haystack."

"You're right," Sally said, and continued walking.

"So let's go to LA," I said, skipping along beside her. "Or Philly or Seattle. Let's be invisible."

She stopped again and I bumped into her, gently, but I steadied her with both hands. She tilted her face toward mine. I thought she was going to kiss me, but, ever careful, she whispered in my ear.

"This ability I have," she said. "This power. It's like living with a warhead in my pocket. The more people there are around me, the more chance it has of detonating. And believe me, Harvey, the last thing I want to do is go bang."

I considered the brief puff of smoke I'd raised with my ninja smoke bombs, and the difference in our respective superhero abilities seemed suddenly Pacificlike.

"I've done the math," she assured me. "Small towns. But not *too* small. America is full of them. We find the right one, and if we don't draw attention to ourselves, we can remain invisible for a very long time."

"Sounds good," I said.

Now she kissed me.

"I know."

. . .

We loaded ourselves with shopping bags, Sally buying more than me; I was a light traveler and could comfortably run a pair of jeans for five days, but women—thank God—are more heavenly creatures. So Sally bought shoes and skirts and jeans and underwear and tops and I don't know what from Walgreens. She capped her purchases with a suitcase in which to keep it all. My wallet was notably lighter, but I couldn't really complain given that I'd plucked her from Kansas with only the clothes on her back.

We used the lavish restrooms of a four-star hotel to freshen up and get changed. I trashed the contents of my backpack—mostly old clothes that needed replacing anyway. The only items I didn't throw away were my mix tapes, my Book of Moments, an old Flaming Lips T-shirt that I couldn't bring myself to part with, and the .38 Special. I hadn't told Sally about the gun and didn't know if I would. I was holding on to the hope that, like us, it would remain hidden.

I pulled the tags off a new T-shirt and pair of jeans, slipped into them, then splashed my face with cold water. I was in and out in five minutes. It took Sally considerably longer. I waited in the lobby, sitting in a chair that was more stylish than comfortable. Guests whizzed by, dragging luggage, talking on cell phones, lost in their own busy worlds. I heard clinking glasses and the buzz of conversation from the bar, while the hotel's discreet sound system piped orchestral renditions of country hits. A string of clocks behind the front desk displayed times from around the world. Each one checked off ten minutes. Then fifteen. I looked at the door to the ladies' restroom and frowned, as if this would speed Sally along. Every time it opened I expected it to be her. My concern incrementally deepened when it wasn't.

I willed myself to calm down, but a mean voice at the back of my mind insisted that Sally was gone. Outta here. Riding the Greyhound to Somewhere, USA. I wiped my eyes and wondered if it would always be like this. Twenty years from now, returning to an empty house, or whenever Sally was running late, would I worry that she'd left me— not even a Dear John—or that the hunt dogs had grabbed her?

Yeah, probably. This was the life I'd chosen, after all. I might adjust to it, but it would never be easy.

"Not for as long as the spider is alive," I muttered to myself, and that was when it lodged in my mind—I mean *really* lodged: *Kill him. Kill the fucker.* I'd thought it before, of course, but flippantly: hiring an elite assassin who could run a bullet through his skull from a mile away. This time it was different. It felt like a spark, like the beginning of a plan. I saw Lang in my mind, gray-faced and sucking on oxygen, then recalled Sally whispering that her power was like living with a warhead in her pocket. *And believe me, Harvey,* she'd said. *The last thing I want to do is go bang.*

I pulled my wallet from the pocket of my new jeans, took out the red feather, and twirled it. The shaft was kinked and the barbs splayed—it had seen better days, for sure—but when I spun it between forefinger and thumb, it looked like fire.

Kill the fucker.

Yeah, a defiant thought, but hotheaded, ultimately foolish. If it was that easy—or even *possible*—Sally would have done it already.

The thought lingered, though, at least for the next ten minutes, until the ladies' restroom door opened and Sally walked out tugging her suitcase. She looked at me and grinned. The relief was so huge that I rose unwittingly to my feet, as if lighter.

"Sorry," she said. "Becoming a new person takes time."

She spread her arms and offered a single, glamorous twirl. The shitkicker boots and practical Levi's were gone. She now wore skinny jeans, baby-blue Vans, and a loose sweater. Her hair was wrapped in a polkadot scarf.

"What do you think?" she said.

"Yeah," I said, and smiled.

This was more like the Sally I didn't remember.

We decided then, on the spot, to make Ryder, California, our new home. If we didn't immediately jive with the town (although we both had a feeling we would), we'd hightail it to the Rockies.

"When do we leave?" I asked Sally.

"As soon as possible," she said.

There was a Greyhound leaving Tulsa at 3:15 a.m., scheduled to arrive in San Jose, California, forty-two hours later. We could sleep, talk, and play the license plate game, but forty-two hours, man, on a *bus*. I thought I might go crazy.

We decided to break it into two—Jesus, maybe even three—parts. For now, I bought two tickets to Cypress, New Mexico, arriving at 3:20 p.m. Twelve hours was still ugly, but it was doable.

"We've got time to kill," Sally said. "Maybe we should find a bar. Grab a drink and something to eat."

"Yeah," I said.

"We can talk, too," she said.

I nodded. I knew what that meant.

We were drawn to a bar two blocks south of the bus terminal, music jumping through the open doors, dirty country with a rock edge. We sat, we ate, we listened to the band. Sally bounced to her feet at one point and danced, swaying her hips, just like the girl in my memory. Her energy was infectious. I laughed and clapped my hands, and then— what the hell—I danced, too. Correction: I moved my body moronically. I can keep time on guitar, I have a fine sense of rhythm, but I turn to shit on a dance floor. Sally appreciated the effort, then took pity and swayed into my arms. I didn't let go. She made me look better.

We returned to our table and finished eating as the band wrapped its opening set. The background music kicked in to keep everybody hopping. It was loud, but not as loud as the band, so I heard Sally perfectly when she leaned across the table and said:

"I didn't want to hurt anybody."

The way she said it—resentful and sad—more than the words themselves made my stomach tighten. I took a shaky breath and looked at her with what I hoped was a cool and accepting expression.

"I was manipulated," she continued. "And scared. I might have handled it differently, but I was just a kid."

The music faded to a distant thump. Our server came and cleared our plates. We ordered more drinks. I wanted something stronger but stuck to beer. When our server had left, Sally reached across the table and clasped my hand.

"Are you ready for this?"

"Yeah," I replied.

"If you're going to commit to this lifestyle, you need to know who I am."

"Yeah."

"And if you're going to run away with me, you need to know what you're running from."

"Dominic Lang," I said.

She gave me the same surprised expression as when I'd called her Miranda.

"I've done my homework," I said.

"What do you know?"

I offered a synopsis of what I'd learned. Enough for her to know I hadn't simply read his Wikipedia page.

"He was in here," I finished, pressing a finger to my forehead. Pressing *hard,* to indicate how deep he'd gone. "He was in here, looking for you."

"I'm sorry."

"I call him the spider."

Our drinks arrived. I drained half my beer in a single, dry-throated hit.

"There's a room in my mind," Sally said a moment later. "*Deep* in my mind. It's full of other people's memories. Terrorists. Rapists. Murderers. I don't go there very often."

I lost the music then. Couldn't tell you what was playing. I lost all the other tables and everybody sitting at them. I lost the flashing TVs and fizzing neon signs. My attention was on Sally. Absolutely.

"There's a high-security vault at the back of the room," she continued. "It has a steel-reinforced concrete door with bolts as thick as your leg. Inside the vault is a box wrapped in chains. This is where I keep Dominic Lang's memories. This is where I keep his power."

A tear flashed from Sally's left eye, leaving a thin trail. This was my first glimpse beneath the mask. I saw nothing beyond nature. Only a fragile, frightened girl. The girl I thought I'd find.

"He's dangerous, Harvey."

"I know."

"Power-obsessed. And obsessed with *me*—with what I have inside."

I reached across the table, used my thumb to wipe the tear track from her cheek. But there was another. And another.

"My parents took me to him when I was eight years old," she said. "He recognized my ability, then manipulated and blackmailed me—used me to subdue his more powerful targets. For seven years I was his secret weapon."

She clasped my hand again, hard enough to make the bones pang.

"For seven years I was his red bird."

Seventeen

It was during his year at Oakwood Psychiatric Hospital in Connecticut that Dr. Dominic Lang wrote a paper propounding the similarities between psychic ability and mental illness. He suggested a widespread misdiagnosis of brain diseases such as schizophrenia, and through data collected over the next four years, estimated that ninety percent of "true" psychics reside in mental institutions.

"*True* psychics?" I asked Sally. "What does that mean?"

"Not the charlatans," Sally said. "Not the boardwalk fortune-tellers or two-bit intuitives. True psychics are a rarer breed, many of them highly troubled, most seemingly insane."

I recalled what I'd read about Lang: diagnosed with autism at five years old, didn't speak until he was eight. Not a normal kid, by any means.

"You need a conduit," Sally said. "You need to link your rational mind to your irrational psychic energy. Once you have a conduit, you have access. Once you have access . . . well, that's when the magic can happen."

It began with a patient named Edwin Elder, a diagnosed paranoid schizophrenic who spent his days doped up on phenothiazines, and when coming down would stand in a corner and rattle his head against the walls. Elder had found a home at Oakwood after killing his parents with a shingling hatchet, then sitting their corpses on the front deck—Mom with a whiskey sour, Dad with a book—for all to see. Lang, thirty-two and fresh off his psychiatry residency at Yale, had taken an interest in Elder during his initial assessment. Elder had been restrained, his medication wearing off. It was the perfect opportunity for Lang to crawl into his mind, where he felt a familiar and suffocating presence.

"The psychic coil," Sally said. We had left the bar by this point and were sitting in the bus terminal, huddled beneath Sally's new jacket. "It's what generates our power."

I imagined an electromagnetic coil buried deep inside the brain, inducing toothaches, migraines, debilitating nausea. It put me in mind of Dad, who'd gone through a phase of protecting himself against what he called "dirty electricity." This was when the tinfoil hat sat permanently atop his noggin, and when he'd designed plans to build a gigantic Faraday cage around the house.

"This may sound crazy," I said. "But when you say psychic coil, I think of electromagnetic pollution."

"Not crazy," Sally said. "You're actually close to the mark. The brain generates electricity, after all."

"Enough to power a lightbulb," I said. "Hey, I learned *something* in fifth grade."

"Right. Now think on a bigger—*much* bigger—metaphysical level: an aggressive energy producing symptoms in line with mental disorders like schizophrenia and bipolar. And the only way to control this energy is to get on the same circuit. Connect and flow."

"That's why you need a conduit."

"Which, according to Lang's research, fewer than ten percent of true psychics have."

Edwin Elder was not one of the 10 percent. Lang quickly determined that antipsychotic medications appeared to calm him only because they dampened his psychic energy. In no way a cure, they also hindered functionality in other areas of his brain. With or without medication, Elder was a hopeless cause.

Lang wrote: *The patient has exceptional psychic ability, perhaps equal to my own. However, he is unable to connect and interact with it. He may as well be a worm, blind, wriggling in the dirt. I could step on him at any time.*

Inspired by this development, Lang searched the minds of Oakwood's demented populace and discovered an untapped psychic coil in four out of fifty-two diagnosed schizophrenics. He visited other institutions across the Northeast and collected similar data. It was the same in the South; after leaving Oakwood, Lang toured hospitals from Tallahassee to Dallas, where the results were consistent: Between 5 and 10 percent of all patients with schizophrenia-like disorders had crippling levels of psychic energy.

"What was the point of this research?" I asked. "Was he gauging his power?"

"He was trying to understand it," Sally replied. "At least to begin with. You have to bear in mind that Lang was a complex and confused individual. It was the same with his sexual orientation, up until the point he met Gene Lyon, who made that aspect of his life much clearer. Gene was an emotional and sexual center for him. An anchor. And that's what Lang was looking for in his research: a way to become centered. Then, maybe, he'd see what he was capable of."

I thought of Mitt Grover dropping dead during the election debate at Laurel State, his brain a handful of wet pieces, and surmised Lang already had a pretty good idea what he was capable of.

"He was bad in the womb," I said. "I can't believe he didn't have wickedness on his mind."

"Perhaps," Sally said. "But, baby, there's only one thing more dangerous than someone with power, and that's someone in a position to use it."

Dominic Lang inherited a comfortable sum of money after his father died in February of '87. He invested most of it, but allocated a generous chunk to two things: to opening his own psychiatric clinic in downtown Nashville and to supporting his research. Regarding the latter, he used his contacts at Yale to put out a call for anyone with "paranormal, extrasensory, or nonrational sensitivities" to step forward for paid, noninvasive experiments.

It was frustrating work. Most of the people he saw were frauds: carnival chiselers and third-rate mediums, all unable to demonstrate a single psychic act on demand. They'd complain that the conditions were not right or that their pathway to the spirit world was in some way hindered. Lang didn't need to crawl into their minds to know their psychic coil had no rumble, no flash.

Occasionally, though, a true would show up with a vibrant coil and a passable conduit. The first through his door was an eighteen-year-old girl with greasy hair, Taco Bell breath, and self-harm scars on her forearms. Lang touched her mind, felt the coil. A low, buzzing energy.

"Tell me about the marks on your arms," he said.

"You know what they are," the girl—her name was Rose Gibb—said. "Sometimes I cut myself."

"Why?"

"It distracts me."

"From?"

"There's a muscle in my brain," Rose said. "It keeps flexing."

Lang took Rose to a room in the basement larger than his office, white concrete walls and floor, whispering fluorescent lights. It was set up with various stations, each with their own props: mirrors and sheets of glass, dollar-store vases, a pyramid of empty soda cans, a pile of knotted rags. It was ugly, unscientific, utilitarian.

"The flexing in your brain," he said to Rose. "It's not a muscle. It's energy. A kind of electricity. We call it the psychic coil."

Rose started to pick her cuticles, already agitated.

"Every living person has a psychic coil," Lang continued, trying to soothe her with a smile. "For most people it's buried deep. They don't even know it's there. Other people—the truly unlucky ones—know it's there but have no access to it."

Rose looked at her tattered sneakers and shuddered.

"And then there are people like you," Lang said. "The rarest of the rare, an infinitesimal percentage of the population, who are aware of the coil"—Lang made a flexing gesture with his hand—"and can inter-act with it."

"No," Rose said. "It's not . . . I don't—"

"The fact that you haven't been institutionalized tells me you can access it."

Rose shook her head.

"Can you read or influence my mind?" Lang asked.

"No."

"Can you predict the future?"

"No."

"I didn't think so." Lang nodded, then gestured at the stations around him. "So why don't you show me what you *can* do."

Rose mumbled something and shrugged.

"You say you harm yourself as a distraction, but truthfully, it's so that you don't harm others." Lang raised his eyebrows, hands spread. "I admire that. It shows you have a good heart, despite everything. But it's okay to blow off some steam here. There's nothing in this room that can't be replaced."

"It hurts when I do it," Rose said, head low.

"I know."

"I get headaches . . . nosebleeds."

"I know."

Rose looked toward the mirrors and something flashed behind her eyes, then it was gone. She looked at her sneakers again.

"Your father abuses you," Lang said, sharing what he'd seen when looking for her coil. "When you were nine years old he got you drunk, and you woke up to find him snacking between your legs. He once mas-turbated into your hair and made you wear it to school, stiff and un-washed. Then there was the time—"

"*STOP!*" Rose screamed. Tears sprang from her eyes. She reeled toward the mirrors and Lang followed. He watched as she focused, zany-eyed and drooling—as a crack appeared in the center of the larg-est mirror and splintered to the edge. She twisted her hands, as if wringing water from an invisible cloth, and with a final effort the cor-ner of the mirror broke away and shattered on the floor.

"Yes," Lang said. He wiped his mouth. "Good girl."

"No more," she whimpered. Blood spurted from her left nostril. The crotch of her jeans darkened with urine and she collapsed to the floor. Lang left her there while he wrote in her file: *Minimal psychokinetic ability. Moderate physical reaction inc. bleeding (nose) and voiding (bladder). It appears that a conduit doesn't necessarily translate to power. V. interesting.*

Rose woke a few hours later. Lang gave her Advil for her headache, a Kleenex for her nose, then handed her a hundred dollars in cash and sent her on her way.

He never saw her again, but he *did* see her father.

Sally did, too.

"More trues appeared over the next few years," Sally said. "Slowly to begin with, then in a steady trickle. Lang ran his tests and discovered varying levels of power depending on a number of factors, from age and personality to their relationship with the coil. Some could shatter the mirrors without blinking. Others could set fire to the pile of knotted rags or pluck surface thoughts from Lang's mind. Then there were trues—those with less effective conduits—who could barely topple the soda cans. It seemed no two were quite the same, although they all had one thing in common."

"And that was?"

"They were troubled," Sally said. "Depressed, addicted, suicidal."

"Because they were outcasts?"

"Maybe, but more likely because the coil is oppressive, and they turned to drugs or self-harm to help cope with it. There's also a theory that psychic ability is triggered through stress. Like Rose, a lot of these people were born into ugly lives. They didn't stand a chance from day one, so it's possible their coils were activated in infancy and strengthened during the course of their lives."

"That might explain Lang's power," I suggested. "A different kind of stress, though; he spent six weeks in the womb with a corpse, and the first hours of his life were touch and go. His heart actually stopped beating at one point."

Sally nodded. "Near-death experiences are also linked to increased psychic sensitivity. Lang was half a day old when he had his. His baby brain—like all babies'—was a sponge. If there's any hoodoo between here and the other side, he took a massive shot and absorbed it all."

I imagined Lang at thirty-four weeks, kitten-sized, his head swollen to accommodate not a brain but an electromagnetic coil. Blue light pulsed through the gaps of his unformed skull. He had electricity for eyes.

"Lang continued his research," Sally said, snuggling closer to me beneath the jacket. "He recorded data and got answers to some of his questions, but it didn't help that—of the trues he'd met—not one of them had his level of power."

"Because he had nothing to compare against."

"Right, and that was when things got sinister. He'd always planned on using his ability to attain wealth and power, but was wary of other trues. So his research switched gears. He stopped looking for under-standing, and started looking for threats."

A metallic voice overhead announced our bus was boarding. Sally lifted her head from my chest. It was after 3 a.m. and her eyes were tiny weights. Mine, too. I had a feeling we'd sleep until we were half-way across Texas.

"Did he find them?" I asked.

"He found what he considered to be *potential* threats. And he sub-dued them."

Once again, I thought of Mitt Grover lying dead on the stage, and knew exactly what Sally meant by *subdued*.

"After a lifetime of confusion and anger," she continued. "Of feeling sexually and energetically suppressed, Lang was determined to become one of the most powerful men on the planet, and God help anybody who got in his way."

"Jesus Christ," I said.

"Right," Sally said. "And then he met me."

The first four hours of our bus ride to Cypress were spent sleeping. Not deeply, but enough to take the edge off the tiredness. I woke with Sally's head on my shoulder and a crick in my neck. I judged from the road signs and license plates that we were still in Oklahoma. Behind us, the horizon was a simmering red line.

We rolled into Elk City's Greyhound terminal, which was also a Hutch's convenience store, a short time later. There was a thirty-minute layover, which gave us a chance to stretch our legs, freshen up in the restrooms, and grab a quick breakfast. We were still seven hours from Cypress, but we got back on the bus feeling somewhat refreshed.

"I bought this," I said, holding up a jumbo book of literature-themed crosswords. "Page eighteen is dedicated to *Pride and Prejudice*. Word of warning: Austen is spelled with an E."

"You're an idiot," Sally said, but she was smiling.

"Or," I said, "you can carry on with your story. Tell me about you and Lang."

"Are those my choices?"

"Not all of them. We could always make out like teenagers." I curled my tongue, flicked the tip. "Gross everybody out. Get tossed off the bus for lewd behavior."

"Lewd sounds good," she said. "But maybe later."

We watched the flat grassland of southwestern Oklahoma scroll past the window, dotted with billboards promising salvation and legal expertise and the waistline you always wanted. After a few moments, Sally's hand crept into mine.

"All right," she said. "Me and Lang."

"Take your time," I said. "There's a long road ahead of us."

She nodded, looking at me but not really seeing me. She was in the room deep in her mind, then in the high-security vault, pulling the chains off the box so that she could access Lang's memories and continue sharing them with me. I couldn't imagine how difficult this was for her, hotwiring conjunctions and reconstructing events from Lang's life as if they were her own. She didn't flinch, though. Not once.

"He used to fantasize about eating me," she said. "He had my vital organs slow-roasted and arranged on silver platters. A way of ingesting my powers."

"Whoa," I said.

"One of his dark reveries," she said. "He'd never have done it."

"Still fucked up."

"Yeah." She settled back in her seat, adjusting her hand so that our fingers interlocked. "He obsessed over my power, but couldn't have it. And he couldn't eat me, obviously, so he *used* me. But I'm getting ahead of myself. Let's go back to the beginning—the beginning of *me*, I mean. Let me tell you about a couple of trailer-trash, alcoholic, good-for-nothing scumbags called Steven Farrow and Tatum Moore."

The tone of her voice had changed. I detected anger, disappointment.

"Let me tell you about Mom and Dad."

Coil In Harmony was the perfect setup. To the outside world it looked like just another support group for wasters, junkies, and bottom-feeders. On the inside, it was a way for trues to share their feelings, their stories, to get to know and understand one another. For Lang—who established the group—it was an opportunity to see what happened when you brought a group of moderately powerful trues together. Would sparks fly? Would a leader, or aggressor, emerge? Could they join forces—link their energies like batteries—to create an all-powerful super coil?

September 15, 1990. A bio-PK named Steven Farrow walked into a Coil In Harmony meeting expecting only to walk out with the honorarium he'd been promised for attending. He got more than that.

"Back up a second," I said. "Bio-PK?"

"Biopsychokinetic," Sally said. "Someone who can mentally affect biological systems, either their own or somebody else's. If they're good people, they can use their ability to heal—to drive out viruses, stop bleeding, that kind of thing. If they're *not* so good, and they're powerful enough . . . well, they can cause heart attacks and strokes, kill a person just by looking at them."

"Like Lang," I said.

"His primary power." Sally nodded. "He was also a formidable tele-path with substantial mind-control abilities. Not so much anymore; I seriously damaged his coil when I tore through his mind."

"Five percent," I said. "That's what he told me—he's like a battery running at five-percent power."

"I should have shut him down completely," Sally said, and gave her head a little shake. "That was a mistake. A *big* mistake. But anyway: Steven Farrow. Steve-O to his dumbass redneck pals. Daddy to me. Not a good person, but a decently powerful bio-PK. He could raise your heart rate or give you a stinker of a headache. His preference, though, was to constrict bone tissue until it fractured. He called himself the bonesnapper."

The story of how Sally's parents met was something she plucked from both their minds over the years. Not deliberately, but she caught occasional flashes, like a radio picking up bursts of interference.

"No child should have to see what their parents are thinking," she said. "This whole psychic power thing . . . it's a double-edged sword, believe me."

Steve-O attended the inaugural Coil In Harmony meeting with no intention of "sharing." He just wanted to pick his nose for a couple of hours and get paid. There were eight trues present. One of them was twenty-three-year-old Tatum Moore, a bottle-blond jizz magnet (plucked from Steve-O's mind, *not* mine) dressed in a faded denim jacket and spray-on jeans. It wasn't long before they started shooting eyes at each other. Steve-O sent a little bio-PK mojo her way—making her heart fairly gallop, causing certain areas of her body to flush—and Tatum reciprocated with a dose of mind control, willing Steve-O to massage his crotch through his jeans until a quietly impressive porker had formed.

Fast forward a couple of hours and they're slinging swill at some dive bar on the next block, and not long after that are bumping uglies—*very* uglies—on the backseat of Steve-O's Grand Am.

"Everyone," Sally said bitterly, "should be so magically conceived."

There was more to the fairytale: how Steve-O refused to take responsibility after finding out that Tatum—as he so charmingly put it—had a trout in the well; how he'd one-eightied that decision and moved her into his trailer in West Tennessee, promising to be the best fuckin' daddy in McNairy County; how they'd argued over just about everything, resorting to psychic brawls that left them with fat lips and broken bones; how Steve-O had kicked the booze and amphetamines for almost two weeks and come close—*so* fuckin' close—to landing a job at the Chewalla Hoggery. There was so much anger and resentment, and for a while it didn't look like Steve-O would go the distance, but in June of '91 Tatum gave birth to a healthy baby girl and Steve-O was there. Drunk as shit but *there*. "Oh, Potato, we made the cutest little crumb-snatcher," he wept, holding his daughter for the first time, and those tears were *real*. "She's so fuckin' special." And he didn't know the half of it.

"You know what's crazy?" Sally said, raising her shoulders to emphasize the irony. "If Lang hadn't set up those Coil In Harmony meetings, my parents would never have met, and I would never have been born."

"That *is* crazy," I said, looking out the window as we crossed the Texas state line. There was a mild throb behind my eyes. Tiredness probably, but I had spent the last thirty minutes trying to align the sweet, pretty girl sitting next to me with the trailer-trash assholes tumbling around in my mind. It seemed the only thing she'd inherited was their supersensory powers, exponentially amped.

"Are they still alive?" I asked.

"I think so," Sally said. "I haven't had any contact with them since they put me on a bus and told me to never come home. Last I heard, Mom had shacked up with an Elvis impersonator in Tinsel, Tennessee. I don't know where Dad is."

Our hands were sweaty but still locked and I gave her fingers a light squeeze. Her head found my shoulder again. I liked it there.

"I used to tell you they were dead, and that I couldn't remember them, so that you didn't ask too many questions." Sally shrugged. "It wasn't entirely a lie; they're dead to *me*."

We were silent for a long time, lost in our own thoughts. I closed my eyes and willed the dull ache behind them to fade, which it did; I drifted into an unexpected, pleasant doze, and snapped awake with surprised little head movements when we stopped an hour or so later in Amarillo.

Another lengthy layover. Everybody off the bus.

It was 12:30 by the time we got rolling again. We were now less than three hours from Cypress, and had both agreed that with sleeping, layovers, and conversation, it hadn't been too shitty a journey.

"Let's spend one night in Cypress," Sally suggested. "Catch another bus early tomorrow. See if we can make it deep into Cali before stopping again."

"Sounds good," I said.

A young dude had joined the bus in Amarillo and sat close to us, manspreading across two seats, head resting on his backpack while he fucked around with his phone. Up to this point, we'd managed to keep some distance from the other passengers and our voices below the hum of the engine, so there was no chance of being overheard. Now, with the manspreader so close, Sally was reluctant to continue her story.

"Everyone's a potential threat," she whispered. "Even if they don't mean to be." And she made a tapping motion with her thumbs. I looked at the dude's cell phone and imagined the Tweet: #Greyhound to Albuquerque. Overheard chick in next seat claiming she has psychic powers. This is going to be a long journey. #freakshow #helpme.

"It's cool," I said. "We can talk later."

As it turned out, we didn't need to. The manspreader pulled a set of Bose cans from his backpack, wrapped them around his head, and zoned out to his music.

"Problem solved," I said.

Sally nodded. She continued.

The early nineties: Sally—then Miranda Farrow—grew up in a trailer on the outskirts of Ramer, Tennessee, and it was clear from the outset that she was far beyond ordinary.

"Most parents are afraid their kid will drink bleach or swallow a button," she said. "Mine were more concerned I'd turn one of them into a drooling zombie. When I was three years old, I told Mom that Dad had been 'naked kissing' Rhonda-Shawn Colton—I'd seen it in his mind, clear as I used to see Barney the Dinosaur on our crummy little TV—and he ran his belt across the backs of my legs for peeking where I had no business. Well, I didn't like *that* very much, so I jumped into his mind again, gave it a tiny pinch, and for the next two weeks he was wearing diapers and eating through a straw."

Meanwhile, back in Nashville, Dominic Lang had met Gene Lyon and fallen head over heels, and while Lyon was out of the country photographing dead Iraqi soldiers and the horrors of ethnic cleansing, Lang was continuing his search for threats. He held regular Coil In Harmony meetings, singling out anybody with greater than average power. He also contacted parapsychologists across the world and scoured the news for phenomena suggestive of psychic ability. Persons of interest were tracked down and tested.

"There were a lot of dead ends," Sally said. "But every now and then he'd encounter someone with considerable power. It didn't matter that they were on the skids, or that they were too strung out to know their own names. He shut them down, just the same."

"Brain-popped them?" I asked.

"Yeah, but he was careful about it," Sally said. "And too cowardly to challenge them directly. He'd follow them, learn their habits, and strike when they least expected it."

"And nobody suspected anything?"

"There weren't enough of them to arouse suspicion," Sally said. "Maybe six over a four-year period. And there was nothing tying them to Lang. No prescriptions or medical records. They were guinea pigs, not patients. Also, we're talking about down-and-outs, drug addicts, alcoholics. That they suffered heart attacks or strokes was hardly suspicious."

We passed a sign that read TUCUMCARI 33, our last stop before Cypress. Beyond the pale strip of the interstate, the High Plains of eastern New Mexico stretched as far as the eye could see, all brittle scrub and cracked earth.

"Everything was falling into place for Lang," Sally said. "He was in love, his clinic was prospering, and he was eliminating powerful trues. He was also moving in more influential circles: hobnobbing with Tennessee's upper class, increasing his stock. Unfortunately, the same couldn't be said for our dysfunctional tribe."

The young Farrow-Moore family had been evicted from their trailer on the outskirts of Ramer and were living out of Steve-O's '79 Grand Am. Steve-O earned a little scratch selling marijuana, but it wasn't enough to keep him in booze, let alone feed the kid. Tatum, for her part, tried using mind control to rob a couple of liquor stores, but was so whacked on drugs that she only managed to give herself a migraine and piss her pants. She found money in other ways, but again it wasn't enough. Eventually, Steve-O decided to drive them to the shrink in Nashville—who was well-to-do and well connected—to see if eight-year-old Miranda had any earning potential with her ability.

"They were thinking of a TV show or stage act," Sally said, smiling sadly. "But Lang had other ideas."

Rose Gibb (she of the Taco Bell breath) told Lang that she had a muscle in her brain that kept flexing. Eleven years later, little Sally Starling/ Miranda Farrow—wearing a Tweety Bird T-shirt, her hair in pigtails— sat in the same office, stared across the same desk into the same striking eyes, and offered a more imaginative description.

"It's a bird," she said. "I keep it in a cage."

"We told her to do that," Steve-O piped up proudly. "Shit goes tits-up when the bird gets out."

Lang sneered in Steve-O's direction, then turned his attention back to Sally.

"Is it like . . . ?" He pointed at Sally's T-shirt.

"No," Sally said. "Tweety is a *happy* bird."

"Oh, so the bird in your head isn't happy?"

Sally shook her head.

"Does it have yellow feathers?"

"No," Sally replied. "They're red."

Lang nodded calmly but that one word, *red,* sent flags of the same color rippling through his soul. He made a show of writing in his notepad while pulling a screen across his mind, just in case the girl decided to take a peek inside.

After a moment he asked her, "Do you know what kind of doctor I am?"

Sally nodded. "Daddy says you're a headshrinker."

"Well shit, I didn't *say* that," Steve-O said. "She must've plucked it from the ol' noodle."

"Yes," Lang said, ignoring him. "Another name for it is psychiatrist. My job is to analyze people's minds and help them. Do you know what *analyze* means?"

Sally shook her head. Her pigtails swayed.

"It means to look at something very carefully." Lang flipped to a clean page in his notepad and drew two basic pictures. The first was of a frowning face with a question mark over its head. The second was of a smiley face. He linked the two sketches with a looping arrow. "I help people go from this"—he tapped the frowning face—"to this." Then the smiley face.

"Got it," Sally said brightly.

"You're an intelligent young lady." Lang displayed a smiley face of his own, entirely false. "I wonder . . . could I take a look at your mind? Just a peek."

"You mean . . ."

"Go inside," Lang said, and again, "A *peek,* I swear."

Sally stiffened in her chair. Her eyes flashed unsurely. Tatum stepped forward and placed her hand on her daughter's shoulder.

"You sure about this, Doc?"

"It'll be fine," Lang assured her. "Won't it, Miranda?"

"I . . . I guess."

"Just be careful," Tatum said. "And don't poke the cage."

The smile dropped from Lang's face. His eyebrows took wing and he crept into Sally's mind. Normally, when reading trues, he followed the thrum, the *pressure,* and was able to estimate the power in their coils. With Sally, he was immediately blinded: a shimmering red mist, as if a flare had been dropped at the back of her mind. There was some-thing else—something *beyond* the mist: a bristling, vibrant energy. He imagined an exotic bird with cocked, special feathers, poised inside its cage with its red eyes narrowed. Helpless, *enthralled*, Lang crawled toward it, reaching out—

He was kicked back so forcefully that his chair rolled across the room, struck the far wall, and spilled him to the floor. His scalp siz-zled. Blood leaked from his ears.

Jesus Christ, what the fuck was THAT?

Steve-O hooted and clapped his hands. "She's a little shotgun, ain't she?"

Christ FUCK.

"I bet someone in TV land would pay a lot of cabbage for her talents."

"You put this girl anywhere near a TV camera," Lang hissed, look-ing at Sally with wide, bewildered eyes, "and she'll be burned at the stake within a week."

He tried getting up but his legs weren't there. He thumped against the wall, slid sideways, and dropped to his knees.

"Shit," he said.

Tatum cracked a smile—couldn't help herself—then wiped it from her face, stepped toward Lang, and held out her hand.

"Told you not to poke the damn cage," she said.

Lang had written: *She is remarkable. Terrifying. Short of dosing her up with antipsychotics—suppressing her coil over a matter of weeks (months?)— I see no way of weakening her.*

"He wanted you dead?" I asked. "An eight-year-old girl?"

"He could've wiped me out at any time," Sally said. "Not with psy-chic power, but a bullet would do it. A contract kill."

"What stopped him?"

"The fact that he could *use* me," Sally said. "Why bury a weapon when you can strap it to your shoulder?"

"Why need a weapon at all?" I countered. "Dude was powerful enough to do his own dirty work."

"He was also a damn coward," Sally said. "Sure, he could take out the deadbeats—and only when their backs were turned—but there were bigger fish out there."

Lang, in his increasing obsession and paranoia, had begun to suspect the greatest threats were already in positions of power, either in government or pulling the strings through secret societies. These individuals could not be enticed with a paltry honorarium. They were wealthy, powerful, and hidden. An unknown quantity. It terrified him.

"How do you begin to track them down?" Sally said. "They were phantoms. The secrets *within* a secret society. It played on Lang's every fear, kept him awake at night. Eventually, he realized they would come to him if he made enough noise. And when they did, he'd be ready."

I thought of the feather in my pocket. For Lang, it was an expression of power, control, and fear.

"Red bird," I said.

"He had me right where he wanted me," Sally said.

Tucumcari in the rearview. Cypress dead ahead. One more hour and we could breathe the desert air and eat food that didn't come from a packet, at least until tomorrow when we'd board bus number two and do it all again. But it didn't matter, because every little click of the odometer took us closer to our final destination: Ryder, California, where I'd live a different life with a different name, where I'd shoulder Sally's past—her darkness—and carry it as if it were my own.

Some fat dude had taken the seat behind us, which kept Sally from talking until he fell asleep, his snores louder than the tires rumbling off the blacktop. Every now and then his fat knees would press annoyingly into the back of my seat and I wanted to bark at him to cut it out, but didn't want to wake him so had to endure it. Sally's story, thankfully, offered something else to focus on.

"Lang wanted to keep me close, so he housed us in a modern two-bedroom apartment in downtown Nashville. Beat the hell out of the trailer and it for damn sure beat the hell out of the Grand Am. He helped Dad get a maintenance job at a retirement home, which basically amounted to mowing the lawn and changing a few lightbulbs, and he fixed Mom up with some part-time work answering the phone at a car dealership. All Lang asked in return was for me to assist in his research, which would occasionally involve accompanying him to para-psychology departments at universities across the country. Mom and Dad gave permission willingly, with big stupid grins on their faces. 'Absolutely, strange but generous man, *do* take our little girl away for a week at a time, just don't kick us out of our wonderful new home.' So yeah, they were bought, and easily, but he knew he'd have to work a little harder to win me over."

A chain of Harleys muscled by in the passing lane, chrome flashing in the sunlight. A perfect day for a ride, I thought, with the perfect road—historic Route 66—like a ribbon beneath their wheels. To our right was the Union Pacific railroad with a line of hills in the distance, tan-colored, the desert between stitched with mesquite and tumble-weed. For a second it felt like I'd been dropped into someone's vision of quintessential America—where Old Glory flew proud and the buffalo roamed—but then fat boy screwed his knees into the back of my seat again and Sally continued with her surreal life story.

"Lang needed emotional leverage," she said. "He had big plans for me, and he wanted to make sure I did whatever he said, no questions asked. That's when he brought in Kirby Gibb—Rose's piece-of-shit father, who turned out to have a string of pedophile convictions as long as your arm, and who'd just served time for possession of child pornog-raphy: over three hundred videotapes found in a box in his attic. Trust me, Gibb was a nasty, dirty, fucking *shitty* human being, and Lang locked me in a room with him. No windows or furniture. Just plain con-crete walls and a bare floor. Before leaving us alone, Lang whispered that Gibb wanted to do bad things to me. *Very* bad things. He wasn't lying."

"You can spare me the details," I said. "But you made this mother-fucker pay, right?"

"In seconds," Sally said. "Just the way he looked at me made my skin prickle. I lifted a few memories from his mind, saw some of the terrible things he'd done, and that was enough; I opened the cage door and let the red bird fly."

"Good," I said.

"One second he was rubbing the front of his pants, the next he was twitching on the floor with his tongue hanging out. I emptied his mind. Took everything. How to walk, talk, think. *Everything*."

"Jesus," I said.

"I didn't kill him," Sally said. "I could have. Easily. Not that it made any difference; Lang had his emotional leverage. I was so scared he'd tell someone what I'd done that, from that moment on, I did whatever he wanted."

It was seven years of being on guard, of eliminating threats, possible threats, and anybody who placed a roadblock between Lang and his idea of power, whether that entailed a leather seat in the Oval Office, or a throne of bones at the top of the world. But he wouldn't get there with all guns blazing. It required exactness, time, a series of strategic, chesslike maneuvers. So he greased as many wheels as he could and expanded his social and political circles. Sally, meanwhile, grew up in a relatively comfortable environment. She went to school, made friends, listened to boy bands, and watched *Gilmore Girls*. Her parents still went at each other like cat and mouse—like *psychic* cat and mouse—but were off the hard drugs and had managed to hold on to their jobs. Life was almost normal. *Almost*.

"Once or twice a year I'd be called upon to 'assist' Lang," Sally said. "We'd attend corporate events, fundraisers, dinner parties. I'd pretend to be his niece—all pretty in my dress—and he'd point out the threat: maybe a high-profile journalist, or a congressperson, or corporate bigwig—all true psychics, *very* powerful people, who'd used their ability to fast-track their way up the ladder. I don't know if they were threats but they were certainly dangerous, and Lang wanted them out of the picture."

"As in . . . dead?" I asked.

Sally nodded. Her eyes, already tired, were now rimmed with sadness, with distance. "I weakened them, shut down their coils, got them to the point where they couldn't fight back. Lang swept in and finished them off. It was like shooting a tranquilized lion."

I shook my head, took her hand.

"I didn't want to hurt anyone," she said. "You believe me, don't you?"

"You know I do."

"I was in too deep, though." She squeezed my hand tightly. "There were times when I thought about shutting Lang down, just like he fantasized about slow-roasting my organs, but Mom and Dad were happy and I didn't want to mess things up."

"But you *did* shut him down."

"Eventually," Sally said. "Gene died in 2004 and Lang took it very hard. He'd lost his best friend, his emotional center. It changed him, and accelerated his plans. Lang had always moved with precision, but now he moved recklessly, and with anger. He wanted the White House, and he wanted blood."

"Whose blood?"

"Everybody's," Sally replied. "He blamed *America*—our star-spangled ideology—for Gene's death. There was no attempt to rescue or even locate Gene. On the contrary, he was used to prove a point. We are America, and we will not be bullied. We are America, and we will not negotiate with terrorists. It garnered sympathy and support—gold dust for any administration at war. Lang, however, was fucking *irate*."

"He wanted to turn himself into a flame," I said.

"What he *really* wanted was to stand on top of the Hill and let the red bird fly."

Five miles from Cypress. The manspreader mumbled along to whatever music pumped through his cans, leafing through a comic book about zombies and robots. Behind us, the fat dude had woken up but was wearing a jumbo bag of Chex Mix like a mask. The smell of processed cheddar and sweat made my nostrils tingle. I was so fucking ready to get off that bus.

"Lang established Nova Oculus: mindreading disguised as cross-examination and behavioral science. It quickly won him power and influence, not to mention greater wealth. As his political career escalated, he used me to keep the company going and the money rolling in. I was flown to the Middle East and Guantánamo Bay and to secret locations across the States. I never spoke with the terror suspects, I just downloaded the relevant memories, then passed the information to Lang when I got home. I was a human memory stick, and I hated it. It wasn't just the locations—the squalid cells with blood and shit smeared all over the walls. It wasn't just that I was constantly being taken away from my school, my friends. It was the memories I lifted, the terrible things these people had done. So much death. So many screams."

Sally ran both hands down her face and sighed. I looked through the bus's front windshield and saw the sun-bleached outskirts of Cypress, buildings scattered amid the dust and scrub off old Route 66, the flashing lights of a casino.

"I had three choices," Sally continued. "I could endure it and whatever long-term psychological damage it caused; I could tell my parents—maybe persuade them to run away with me in the night; or I could shut down Lang's coil, cripple his mind."

"So you shut him down," I said.

"Actually, I told my parents first. I told them that, while they thought I was at some university or other in California, I was actually at a US installation on the outskirts of Kabul, stealing plans and mutilations from terrorists' minds."

"And they did nothing?"

"They were furious," Sally said, nodding as she remembered. "Maybe because they wanted a cut of the money I was making for Lang. Maybe because they didn't like being lied to and used. And yeah, I guess they were concerned about me, too. At the same time, they didn't want to give up a good thing, so Dad went to Lang to see what could be done."

The bus slowed with a hiss and pulled up at the stop—a silver pole with the skinny dog logo painted on it, jutting at an angle from the sidewalk. Sally and I disembarked gleefully. We were the only ones. The driver pulled Sally's luggage from the storage compartment (mine was small enough to carry on) and I tipped him five bucks. He muttered something from beneath his mustache, then got back behind the wheel, whooshed the doors closed, and grumbled on to Albuquerque. The bus's big, dusty ass was the best thing I'd seen in hours.

Then it was just me and Sally and some Mexican dude on the corner selling Route 66 T-shirts out of a suitcase. His eyes sparkled from deep within complicated whorls of facial hair.

"*Camisetas,*" he said, displaying one of the T-shirts. "*Diez dólares.*"

"Maybe later, brother," I said, and pointed across an abandoned, weedy lot to the rear of what looked like a motel with several bikes parked on slants outside the rooms. Sally nodded tiredly. There may have been nicer places to stay in Cypress, but we were too tired to go hunting.

"They fought," Sally said after a few steps, the casters on her luggage rattling over the uneven surface of the lot. "I went with Dad but he told me to stay outside. Man Business, he said, although he wanted his fifteen-year-old daughter there just in case he needed protection. As it turned out, he did. But to begin with I stayed outside, and I heard them talking, then Dad's voice got louder and before long they were shouting at each other. Pretty soon, there were crashing, breaking sounds, and I went in to find them wrestling on Lang's study floor. Dad knew he was no match for Lang in a psychic battle so went at him the old-fashioned way. It was actually kind of heroic, although I think he was doing it more for the money than for me. Anyway, Lang fired a psychic bullet into Dad's brain and Dad flopped off to one side, convulsing, blood trickling from his ears. He would have been dead within seconds if I hadn't intervened."

It *was* a motel. The Gran Palma, two stories of dirty white stucco with red doors faded pink in the sun. The mechanical backs of air-conditioning units whirred and dripped from every window. There was a rottweiler on a chain outside the front office.

We held up for a moment, blinking in the bright afternoon sunlight.

"I'll never forget the look on Lang's face when he saw me," Sally said. "His mouth was a big, dumbstruck *O* of terror. He'd gone from being a dominant, consuming presence to a little boy about to load his jockeys. I didn't care, and I didn't let up. I opened the cage door and the bird came out screeching. There was nothing delicate or precise about the attack; I went at him like a bird would, flapping and squawking, tearing pieces away. He tried to fight back—I felt him scratching in my mind like a little cockroach—then all his lights blew out. I took ninety percent of his memories, maybe more, and left his coil black and smoking. He collapsed on the floor. A twitching, drooling sack of shit. I knew he wasn't dead but thought he was close. Dad had just enough strength to leave Lang's house. I threw him across the backseat of his car, yanked the keys from his pocket, and drove us both home."

"Christ," I said. I ran a hand along my jaw, stubble rasping. "That's like . . ." I trailed off and shrugged. There were no words.

"Fucked up," Sally offered.

Okay, so there *were* words.

"We packed our bags and laid low at a hotel just outside Memphis, but Lang found us within a few days and sent his muscle. Mom took care of them—made them turn their guns on each other—but it was a close call. A couple of hours later, she and Dad put me on a bus out of town with five hundred bucks and a backpack stuffed with clothes. They told me to change my name, to run if I ever sensed danger, to never use my powers, and to never, under *any* circumstances, come home. 'You fucked everything up, you little bitch,' Dad said, and that was the last thing either of them said to me. The bus pulled away. I got off in Indiana, caught another bus to Chicago, then another to Osceola, Nebraska. By that time my name was Charlotte Prowse. I cut my hair real short, found a job folding laundry, and worked on losing my southern twang. And now you know who I am, Harvey, and who I'm running from."

I wiped sweat from the back of my neck and nodded.

Sally pointed back across the abandoned lot to where the silver pole poked crookedly from the sidewalk. "Another bus will be along soon, just in case you want to—"

I pulled her into my arms and kissed her fiercely. It wasn't great, if I'm being honest. It was a somewhat awkward, smelly moment that would never win the MTV Best Kiss award. But it *was* passionate, and it conveyed exactly what I intended: for Sally to know that I wasn't going anywhere. Not now. Not ever.

"Read my mind," I said.

I fucking love you, dammit.

A splash of red, and she smiled.

"I fucking love you, too," she said.

Our room was on the upper level. It was cool and dark and smelled of dog. The bed was soft, though, and the shower worked. It would do.

Sally kicked off her sneakers and collapsed on the bed. I joined her, thinking I would fall quickly to sleep, but something worked the edges of my mind—three words that had lodged into place at the hotel in Tulsa, and hadn't strayed far since.

Kill the fucker.

"Where does he live?" I asked Sally.

"No," Sally said. "Get it out of your head, baby. That won't work."

Kill the fucker.

"It might."

I'd always thought I was nonviolent—my mother's son—but recent events had given me reason to climb the tree I'd hitherto been hugging, and take a good look at the real world.

"He's weak, Sally," I said. "You should have seen him after he crawled through my head—sagging like an empty bag, sucking on oxygen. You'd annihilate him. We could stop running."

"He'll have protection," Sally said. "Armed guards. Dogs. Surveillance cameras. All kinds of security equipment. You'd be dead within seconds, and I'd be dosed up with antipsychotics. As soon as Lang gets into my head, he gets his memories back. His power, too."

"But—"

"No, Harvey," she said, and there was a snap to her voice. I imagined the bird in her head bristling its feathers. "All it takes is one goon to sneak up behind me with a tranquilizer gun and it's all over. So get this dumbass idea out of your head right now. We run. That's what we do."

I sighed, then rolled over, propped on one elbow. I touched Sally's cheek and her eyes flicked toward me in the gloom.

"I don't want you to have to run," I said. "I want this to be over."

"I know," she said. "And it will be. Lang is sixty-two years old. Not old, but not young, either. One day—hopefully not too many years from now—I'm going to go online and see that his Wikipedia entry has been updated with a date of death. *Then* it will be over."

She rolled onto her side, too. Our hands met in the middle.

"Then," she said again. "Only then."

Eighteen

Cypress wasn't so much a town as a bad idea, where two lanes of Route 66 defied I-40, lined with jaded businesses that depended primarily on the trade of bikers and Route 66 enthusiasts. There were two motels that rivaled each other for shittiness, a casino called Banditos, a raucous biker bar called Your Kicks, and any number of desperate, half-shuttered stores all selling the same crappy souvenirs.

"One night," I said to Sally. "Then we're taillights."

We had slept for three hours and showered vigorously, and emerged into a purple desert evening where cicadas called from dusty yuccas and quick, dark lizards disappeared the moment you noticed them. There was a peppery scent to the air and the breeze was gritty, carrying the thud of rock music from the biker bar. Bleached trash rattled in storefront doorways and along the edges of the road.

Sally and I turned left out of the motel and headed toward Route 66. The plan was to find somewhere half-decent to eat (we weren't hopeful), but first, to buy tickets on the earliest bus west. There was no depot—only that silver pole jutting from the sidewalk—but we found a ticket machine in the 7-Eleven on the corner of Guadalupe and 66. I tapped the screen and brought up a fifteen-hour run to Blythe, California, leaving at 5:30 a.m.

"There are a couple of long layovers," I said. "We can stretch our legs, get something to eat. It might not be too bad, and we'll be out of here before sunrise."

"Do it," Sally said.

The machine only took credit cards, though, and I definitely did *not* want to leave a digital footprint here—one that pointed in the direction we were going—so I persuaded a hairy-ass biker to use his card, and paid him the cash with an extra twenty bucks on top.

"Either your card is maxed or you're on the run," he said, tucking the notes into his wallet.

"The first one," I said. "Hey, you know anywhere good around here to eat?"

"Your Kicks does the best chimichangas this side of the border," he said, and I don't know why, but I found this tattooed, leather-clad near-wolf saying the word *chimichangas* quite endearing.

"We're there," I said.

We left the 7-Eleven and followed the distorted thump of rock music, although the bar wasn't hard to find: a brazen, flashing structure on 66, mesh on the windows, the parking lot choked with hogs and choppers. It was more of the same inside, the walls bedecked with Route 66 and Harley-Davidson memorabilia, TVs in cages, an open space on the floor for dancing and/or fighting. Grizzly bikers circled tables and lined the bar, their backs as rounded as barrels. Female bikers—some silver-haired and beautiful—punctuated the ruggedness like rhinestones.

"They'd better be damn good chimichangas," I whispered to Sally, and she laughed—a simply gorgeous sound—then strode to an empty table. I followed, feeling infinitely safe with her: the cutest little warhead in town.

It wasn't set in stone, but we figured staying for one drink after we'd eaten, then heading back to the motel. We had to get up stupid-ass early to be on the 5:30 bus to Blythe, and getting as much sleep as possible beforehand was the smart thing to do. However, smartness is apt to go bye-bye when you plug a beer into my fist and load the jukebox with classic rock. Not only that, but the bikers proved to be friendly old bears, buying us drinks, showing us their scars and tattoos. When "Touch Me" by The Doors came on the juke, Sally bounded from her seat and hit the dance floor at a whirl. A sleuth of biker guys and gals followed, and pretty soon the joint was jumping. I knew then that an early night wasn't in the cards.

I loved every moment, though. Sally did, too. I saw how she laughed—how she *lived*—without burden. Her delicate arms, the softness of her face, the lightness of her step, belied the terrifying energy she had inside.

"Dance with me, Harvey." She beckoned, shimmering from everywhere.

I caught her hand and danced, my own burdens hovering just north of my shoulders, and I remember thinking that we could do this. We could live and be happy. We could run and dance at the same time.

"I'm glad you found me," she whispered.

I pulled her close. Our bodies connected—they locked. "There," I said, but kindly, and kissed her, and for the next few hours, there she stayed.

It was just shy of midnight by the time we made it back to the motel. We weren't drunk but we had a buzz going, as much from the good times as the booze. I punched a 5 a.m. wakeup into the clock on the nightstand, giving us thirty minutes to get showered, dressed, and out the door. Time enough for a couple of cats who weren't too crazy about making themselves pretty.

"We got five hours," I said. "Better get sleeping."

We didn't get much.

"Wake up, baby . . . it's time."

I felt Sally's body close and warm and turned my head, blinking in the darkness. The glowing digits on the clock read 3:53. "Whuufuck?" I groaned. "What's going . . . it's only . . ." My head thumped back on the pillow and I would have gone down but Sally shook me gently, whispered close to my ear:

"It's time."

I groaned again and half sat up, turning toward her. She reached for the light on the nightstand, flicked the switch. I squinted, looked at the clock again—maybe I'd read it wrong. But no: 3:54.

"It's early, baby, we—"

"I'm restoring your memories," she said. "All of them. Right now. But we have to move quickly afterward."

It took a second for this to sink in, and when it did I sat up fully, not quite bushy-tailed but not sleepy, either. A loop of nervousness and excitement hummed to life deep inside me. It made everything run faster.

"Something happened when I attacked Lang," she said. Her voice was low and serious, but steady, and I don't know if that made me feel better or worse. "I wounded him so deeply that I left a piece of myself behind. Imagine a car hitting someone hard enough to leave paint chips embedded in the skin."

A graphic image, but it worked.

"We're connected," she continued. "It's a thin thread, but it's there— it's *real*. I can feel him sometimes, and I know he can feel me."

This triggered a memory: Lang slumped in his chair, drawing feebly on his oxygen. *I can still feel the girl,* he'd said, his voice little more than a whisper. *Nine years later, I can feel the impact—the emptiness of what she took from me.*

"He's been using this thread to hunt for me," Sally said. "But it's too thin, too weak. *Most* of the time. When I use my ability—and I'm not talking about little mind grabs; I mean when I *really* use it, when I let the red bird fly—the thread expands and sends out a pulse. It's like a blip on a radar, and it tells Lang where I am."

"Holy shit," I said.

"Lang sends the hunt dogs to come looking for me, to sniff out any and all information. They could be here in a day or in a couple of hours, depending on how close they are. This is why I had to leave Green Ridge—and you—in an awful hurry. And it's why we have to haul ass after I give you your memories back."

"Which explains why we're doing this now," I said, flapping a hand in a vaguely westerly direction. "Right before we hop on a bus and blow this chimichanga stand."

"You got it," Sally said.

"Then let's do this thing. I'm ready."

She nodded. Her eyes glimmered in the dim light. I took a deep breath and flexed my fingers, feeling like I was about to do something dangerous but exhilarating. A walk across hot coals, perhaps, or a bungee jump. I thought Sally would clasp the sides of my head and go all spooky-eyed, or at least raise one hand to better direct her energy. Instead she surprised the hell out of me by peeling off her T-shirt and tossing it onto the floor. Her breasts swayed gently with her body movement, and I thought the sublime shape of them would complement my palm in the same way her face did. I'd seen them before, of course, but couldn't *remember* seeing them, so this was like the first time. I have to say—for me, at least—they were perfect.

"Right on," I said.

The panties came next. She peeled them over her thighs, over her knees, then kicked them from the tips of her toes, revealing an unkempt triangle of pubic hair the same dark color as her eyebrows.

"Is this how it's normally done?" I asked.

"No," Sally said, dragging me on top of her. "But it's how we're doing it."

Her hair had the same peppery smell of the Cypress air and I dipped my face into it and filled my lungs. When I kissed the shelf of her jaw she turned her head and the side of her throat rose, too inviting, and the taste of her there was watery sweet—how rain tastes, unscented but fresh—and she sighed, batted a loose fist against my shoulder. I lifted her at the small of her back and she bowed. My mouth found her breast, first around, then upon her nipple, not biting or sucking, just holding it gently, feeling it knot against my tongue. "Here," she said. "Baby, here." And she ushered me to her mouth, but also—my hand— between her legs. I pressed with my tongue, with three fingers, and a storm of red feathers swirled through my mind.

We were inside each other. Surreal. A contradiction. It was like being dry underwater. Hollow and full.

I followed her through darkness, not a red bird, but a naked girl who ran as she would through a field of flowers. Red light spooled from her hair and body, an endless ribbon that pulsed softly and shimmered. I ran beside, passed through, caught hold of it. By its glow I saw pieces of nothing and bulky chunks of everything. There was no symmetry or continuity—only Sally and the light she left behind.

I was silent and screaming.

What did you expect? The Sally and Harvey photo album? A home movie reeling off all of our wonderful moments together? It doesn't work that way, baby. Memories are made up of scattered, breakable components. They're new things built from old pieces. It's like making art out of junk.

The ground softened, disappeared. I fell and the red light wrapped around me like a sash and lifted me, then set me down on a narrow bridge that spanned a canyon with no bottom. Sally waited on the other side and I crossed quickly. Around her, I heard ten thousand sounds and saw things crumble, then reform, subtly different. The sky was full of red lightning and stars and so many things rained from it but didn't land.

Locating the memories was the easy part; I was the leading lady, after all. The hard part was reconstructing them in your mind, then recording the sequences—those billions of neurons working at starlight speed. Then I closed out the memories and sabotaged the processes needed for recall.

So what's happening now? I asked, except I didn't have to ask anything.

I'm using the sequences I recorded like a blueprint, Sally replied. *I'm repairing the connection points, soldering the neurons, getting everything back the way it was.*

I watched a baby-blue Schwinn topple from the darkness above and my mouth filled with the taste of strawberries. Sally danced within her own red glow. I heard "Abilene." The lightning jagged brightly. I looked up and saw Michael Jackson—the cat, not the superstar—and a mannequin with two left hands.

I think it's working, I said.

Come with me.

I followed the girl, the light, so like a flame, but in my mind it was a giant red feather rippling. I traversed rivers flowing with mental bric-a-brac and scaled awkward peaks that rippled beneath my hands and feet.

Nearly there.

I was breathless but didn't stop. I crossed chasms, sometimes latching on to the feather, other times needing a bridge. Before long, though—no matter how quickly my heart ran, or how shallow my breaths—I could make the leap on my own.

Do you remember?

Sally slowed down . . . stopped. I caught up to her with my chest tight and my legs trembling. Tiny insects vibrated in the evening air and a pink waterfall roared. Above this, I heard music: my version of Van Morrison's "Someone Like You." I felt a comfortable weight against my body and looked down to see my guitar—my old Washburn with its split bridge and buzzing top E. I strummed and it was perfectly in tune.

The ground steadied beneath me. No lightning, only the sky, pink and blue, smeared with dusty cloud, like a chalkboard.

Do you remember me now?

. . .

"Yes," I breathed and pressed my forehead to hers, said it again, but louder: "Yes." My face was curtained with sweat and the pit of my stomach danced. I groaned as if I was hurt but only the opposite was true. I pulled out of Sally very slowly and her body responded by curling gently.

"Baby," she moaned.

I kissed her eyes.

"Baby."

We lay beside each other for . . . I don't know how long, catching our breaths, full of color. We never stopped touching. Our lips, our hands, our feet; there was always at least one part of bodies making contact. Not our minds, though. The bird was back in its cage.

"I could stay here forever," I said. "This moment, right now."

"If only," she said.

"Right," I said. "He knows where you are."

"To within a five-, maybe ten-mile radius, but there are no other towns around here, so yeah, he knows."

"We'd better hustle."

"As long as we make that five-thirty bus, everything's cool."

"What if they get here quickly," I asked. "Follow the bus?"

"They won't know we're on it," Sally replied. "I checked the schedule. Three buses pass through here in the next two hours. Eight before midday. We might have caught any one of them, heading in any direction. Also, we might be driving or walking."

"Right," I said.

"Only thing they'll know is that I *was* here." Sally kissed my chin. "So take a moment, baby. It's all good."

My chest rose as I inhaled, then I half rolled toward Sally, touched her lips, slowly trailed my fingers to her right breast, played with the fine black hair sprouting from the soft skin there. I'd mentioned this hair in my Book of Moments, but now I *remembered* it—the many times I'd brushed my tongue across it, plucked it tenderly between my teeth. I did so again now, then lay my head down. Her heart drummed beautifully.

"Your favorite song is 'Ruby Tuesday'—the Melanie Safka version," I said. "You once found twenty dollars on the number nine bus and gave it to the homeless dude who hangs out on the corner of Trenton and Main. Pickles make you gag. You've read *To Kill a Mockingbird* eight times. You told me your parents' names were Bruce and Wanda and that they died in a car accident when you were four years old."

"You know the truth now."

"You broke three fingers playing softball when you were nine years old."

"*That's* true."

"Your first crush was Enrique Iglesias."

"Can you blame me?"

"Not at all, he's fucking gorgeous." I ran my fingers along the inside of her thigh and she quavered. "Your favorite color is green. The first album you ever bought was *Fly* by the Dixie Chicks. You call being ten pounds overweight your 'Happy Zone,' and to hell with anybody who disagrees."

"Yeah, fuck 'em."

"You're not a vegetarian but you don't eat beef. You once marched on Washington with me for gender equality and—"

"Hey," Sally cut in, tilting my face toward her, placing a finger on my lips. "You don't have to remember everything at once. It's all there"—her finger moved to my forehead and tapped twice—"when you need it. So just relax. Breathe. Enjoy."

I nodded, closed my eyes, and sought composure—even the merest thread of it—amid the busy intersection my mind had become. I took slow and steady breaths, smiling as Sally ran her fingers over my recently smoothed skull.

"Your poor dreads," she said a moment later. "I'm sorry you had to cut them."

"It's just hair," I said. "I'll grow it out again. One day. When this is all over."

"I'd like that. Who cut it?"

"Dad."

Something about this tickled her. She giggled, cupped her mouth. "You're sweet, Harvey."

"He did an okay job."

"Yeah. It's okay."

My smile widened, remembering how Dad had delighted in snipping my dreads, forging me into a version of his younger self. This led me on a train of thought, taking me away from that busy intersection, if only for a moment. I went from Dad to his booby-trapped yard, to the clear water lapping at the edges of Spirit Lake, to the smaller lake within earshot of Mom's grave, to the *Sentinel* offices where she used to work—right beside the police department in Green Ridge, and from there to Chief Newirth . . .

I leapt out of bed as if someone had doused it with gasoline and dropped a match. My body grew rigid and loose at the same time—the oddest sensation—and I slumped stiffly against the wall.

"Oh, *shit*," I said. My voice was too loud.

"*Shhh*," Sally urged, and then, almost under her breath, "I was waiting for this."

"Jesus Christ."

"It's done, baby. In the past. No one will ever find out."

I pushed off the wall, paced for a moment, then sat on the edge of the bed. Sally shuffled closer, encircled me from behind. The shitty little motel room—which had taken a few woozy rolls—began to steady.

"Who was he?" I asked.

"A hunt dog," Sally said. "His name was Corvino."

My memory was particularly sharp at that moment; all the neurons were fully juiced and ready for action, and that name—Corvino—triggered another sequence: the cinderblock room, my body bruised and bleeding, feeling nauseous and violated after having Lang so deeply inside my mind. He'd beckoned Jackhammer close and told him to check out Asbury Park—to go gently.

Jackhammer: *You want me to go alone?*

Lang: *Is Corvino still MIA?*

Jackhammer: *Yes.*

Lang: *Then no . . . definitely don't go alone.*

Sally turned me toward her, kissed my face all over—Jesus, maybe a hundred times.

"You want me to take it away?" she asked between kisses.

"No," I said. "It's mine to carry."

I'd remembered what I'd done with the shovel.

The pieces were starting to fit, but there was still something missing. An *important* something. I looked at the clock. 4:42. Now was not the time to discuss it, but I couldn't wait.

"Corvino came looking for you," I said, holding Sally's face in my palm, always amazed at how perfectly it fit. "He knew where you were, which means you sent out a radar blip—you used your power."

"Yes," Sally said.

"You were forced into a corner," I said, speaking as the thoughts occurred to me. "You reacted. That's what started all this."

"Yes," she said again.

"Well . . . ?"

"We don't have time. I'll tell you on the bus."

"You can tell me now," I insisted, pointing at the clock. "We have sixteen minutes before the alarm goes off."

"That's not enough time."

"CliffsNotes, baby."

Sally sighed. She wasn't getting out of this—not without zapping my mind, at least—and she knew it.

"What did you do?" I asked.

She told me.

Just after five o'clock. Sally was in the shower so I took a moment to grab some fresh air. Hell, I needed it. It had been forty minutes—give or take—since she'd restored my memories and that intersection in my mind still purred. Not only that, but the information she'd just shared had set the room askew and I felt sick to the pit of my stomach. I leaned over the railing outside our door and took several deep breaths but it wasn't enough. I needed to walk out the jitters. A couple of minutes—to the other side of the parking lot and back—would help no end.

I started for the stairwell leading to ground level, dressed in my jeans, my Flaming Lips T-shirt, no shoes or socks. The lot was half-filled with bikes resting on their stands, chrome glimmering softly. I saw a TV flashing infomercials through the front office window. No one at the desk. A payphone was bolted to the wall outside.

I looked at it for a moment, then pulled my wallet from the back pocket of my jeans and flipped it open. There was the red feather, and behind it a scrap of paper on which I'd written Chief Newirth's number. It was after seven on the east coast. Chances were, he would've just sat down at his desk, coffee in hand, the back of his neck still smelling of soap.

I could give his morning one hell of a jumpstart.

If I paused, it was only for a second. I crossed the lot at a jog, grabbed the phone, and nestled it between my shoulder and ear. As I inserted my card (no worries about a digital footprint now, given Lang already knew where we were), I heard a car in the distance—its engine cutting through the stillness—but thought nothing of it; I was too fixed on making the call. There was no doubt in my mind I was doing the right thing. I wouldn't tell Newirth about the shovel, obviously, but this . . . *this* . . .

I tapped in the number. Waited. The car's engine got louder and now I looked toward the sound—coming from 66—with a frown; the dude was really motoring. The call connected. An automated voice informed me that I had reached the Green Ridge police department, told me to press "1" if it was an emergency, or, if I knew the three-digit extension of the person I was trying to reach, to enter it now.

I did.

Waited.

Come on, come on.

The car made a screeching right turn onto Guadalupe Avenue, headlights expanding as it approached the motel.

Chief Newirth's phone rang twice and went to voicemail.

"You have reached Chief Brian Newirth. I'm away from my desk at the moment, but please leave a message, stating your name and number clearly, and I will return your call as soon as possible. If this is an emergency, please dial zero for dispatch. Thank you."

BEEEEEEEP.

"Chief Newirth," I started, but only half of my attention was on the call. The rest was on those expanding headlights. "This is Harvey Anderson. Don't ask me how I know, just trust that I *do*. I have some information about the Green Ridge murders . . ."

And that was as far as I got. The car—another nondescript silver midsize—roared into the motel's parking lot, zoomed past me, hit the brakes. All four doors opened simultaneously and the muscle poured out. They flowed toward the stairway leading to our room, except for one—this thug a little slower, noticeably limping, one arm in a sling. I saw his face in the motel lights: dark with bruising, swollen and stitched together.

Jackhammer.

Nineteen

I dropped the phone. It bounced on its cord, clattered against the wall. Chief Newirth, the Green Ridge murders: gone from my mind. *Every-thing* was, except this new danger—the fact that I was outnumbered and unarmed. I didn't let that stop me.

There was maybe eighty feet between me and where the midsize had screeched to a halt, another ten to Jackhammer, who had started slowly up the stairway. I ran at him, bare feet slapping. I wondered briefly how they could have reached us so quickly. They hadn't arrived by helicopter or parachuted in like the marines, and there was zero fuck-ing chance they just *happened* to be in the neighborhood when Sally sent out her psychic signal. I didn't want to admit it—to even *think* it—but it strongly suggested they'd been following us all along, which meant that the tracking device wasn't on Dad's old truck. Maybe it had been stitched into the lining of my backpack, or maybe it was on me—*inside* me—implanted beneath my skin.

This flashed through my mind, there and gone in a split second, enveloped by panic and rage. I rounded the midsize with my arms pump-ing and ran at the stairway. Jackhammer was at the top now, his fellow thugs—I recognized one of them: Frankenstein's Boots—nearly at our door. My long legs took the stairs three at a time. Jackhammer turned toward me with a smiley kind of sneer.

"Harvey," he said, drawing out the second syllable: *veeeeeeey*. I balled two fists into one and swung it malletlike at his stitched, seeping face. He dodged, raising his good arm, and my knuckles deflected harmlessly off his solid triceps. As handicapped by injury as he was, it hadn't hindered his strength or quickness. He grabbed my wrist and yanked me toward him, raising his knee and driving it into the hollow of my stomach. It was like a small stick of dynamite had exploded in my gut. I crumpled to my knees with bulging eyes. Jackhammer planted his boot against my chest and shoved. Down the stairway I went, toppling twice, stopping halfway and sagging there like a discarded jacket.

Two thuds, followed by a splintering sound, a loud crack as they kicked our motel room door open—Frankenstein's Boots doing the honors, perhaps, with the sledgehammers he wore on his feet. I fought the pain and dragged myself up the stairs, staggering to my feet, then reeling crookedly down the corridor to our room. Jackhammer blocked the way, his back as broad as a road sign. I knew I couldn't go through him, but thought I might go around him—hoping that, if I could get to our room, and if, in all the confusion, I could free the .38 Special from my backpack, then the odds might swing in my favor. Whether or not I could pull the trigger hummed at the back of my mind, but Dad's words hummed a little louder: *What if your life—Sally's life—depends on it?* The revolver had a five-round cylinder, fully loaded, and at that moment I didn't think I'd have a problem evacuating every chamber.

Sounds from inside our room: the bathroom door crashing open; two screams, first Sally's, then a terrible male scream, full of horror, quickly followed by the *fzzzt* of a tranquilizer gun being fired. I'd reached Jackhammer by this point and tried ducking around him, but he clasped my upper arm, wheeled me one-eighty, and took me by the throat. I thought he was going to throw me over the balcony—game over, Harvey—but he slammed me against the wall so hard that the stucco cracked and flaked. Black spots swarmed my field of vision, busy as moths, and my teeth rattled. I didn't stop fighting, though; I rained blows on his pulled-together face until blood oozed from between the stitches. He roared and unleashed a blow of his own—one swift, ringing punch: that trademark jackhammer. It met my jaw and I folded.

I looked up at the strip of black sky between the balcony and ceiling, at scattered stars and the red winking light of an aircraft. These distant, dreamlike details were soon blotted out by the sole of Jackhammer's boot. He brought it down on my face as if stepping on a bug. I felt—heard—my nose crunch, the cartilage rupture, the skin break. He did it again and my lips smashed against my teeth and both split open. Then I heard Sally call my name, her voice pitched differently, horribly slurred: "*Uuurrvveeeee . . .*" I flipped onto my stomach, pushed myself to one knee. "*Saaahhh—*" I reached out, coughing blood from my throat, almost got to my feet, then Jackhammer booted me in the face and the world turned gray.

I saw this when I opened my eyes: two hunt dogs stepping over me, one supporting the other. He bled from his nose and ears, his eyes pinpricks, his jaw a slack band. *Sally,* I thought. *Sally did that to you, you motherfucker.* Any triumph was minor and short-lived; the next thing I saw was Frankenstein's Boots carrying Sally across his shoulders. She was naked, still wet from the shower, unconscious. The bright pink tailpiece of the tranquilizer dart lodged in her neck was unmistakable.

They headed to the stairway and I tried to follow, crawling first on my stomach then on my knees. I noticed a few of my neighbors' lights had flicked on, but not one of them—big and tough bikers, or not—came to help. *Also* motherfuckers. Maybe they'd call 911, but this would be over before the cops appeared. I was on my own, watching helplessly as the hunt dogs rounded the corridor and disappeared down the stairway. The panic and fear in my chest were too much to take and I tried to scream some of it loose, but then Jackhammer grabbed the back of my T-shirt, dragged me into my motel room, and threw me onto the bed. The clock on the nightstand flashed 5:14. Sally had stepped into the shower only eleven minutes ago. I couldn't comprehend how this had turned so bad, so quickly.

It got worse: Jackhammer pulled a pistol from his waistband and pointed it at me. His finger curled around the trigger and trembled.

"Harveeeeeeey," he garbled, his split face bleeding.

"Fuck you," I snapped, spitting blood of my own. My lips were ribbons. "I'm going to fucking *kill* you, motherfucker. I'm going to find you and fuck you."

He laughed. The swollen meat of his face strained the many stitches. *"Fuck you!"*

"Did you really believe a goddamn *haircut* could keep us from following you?" He rolled his eyes and sighed. "You're a resilient little cocksucker. I'll give you that. But you're also the stupidest cunt I've ever known."

I tried spitting at him but my lips were so torn that I could only spray blood over my T-shirt—my Flaming Lips T-shirt. Oh, the irony!

He lurched toward me, pressed the gun to my forehead. "I want to blow that dumb fucking head right off your fucking shoulders," he snarled. "You don't fucking *know* how bad I want to kill you."

"I think I do."

"But I promised you, Harvey, that if you crossed us, we would fuck you up—we'd crush everything you know and love. The reason I'm not going to kill you now is because I want you to know that I'm a man who keeps his promises."

My stomach turned to a pile of loose rocks as my mind shuddered with implications, echoed with screams.

"When my boss has finished with the girl, she's ours." A stitch actually popped as Jackhammer grinned. Blood trickled onto his upper lip and beaded there. "And let me tell you, Harvey, we're not interested in her mind."

The tip of his tongue exited his mouth and licked that bead of blood away. I wanted to dismantle him—drive my foot into his chest, roll off the bed, grab the .38, and punch all five rounds into his face. I couldn't move, though; the rocks in my gut weighed me down.

"I'm going to kill you," I said. There was a warble to my voice that undermined any threat. I stared him dead in the eye and said it again.

"No, Harvey, what you're going to do is feel a lot of pain. So much that you'll wish *I* had killed *you*. Knowing that will help me sleep at night." Jackhammer pulled the gun away, turned it on himself, dragged the muzzle across his wounds. "It'll make these scars easier to bear."

Outside, car doors opened and closed, then an engine ripped into life and revved impatiently. Jackhammer took that as his cue. He backed up to the door, limping, bleeding, but still so strong. Mother-fucker actually tipped me a wink before ducking out into the corridor.

"Fuck *YOU!*" I shouted after him, then managed to roll off the bed and crawl—aching, pissing blood all over the carpet—toward my backpack.

Still one trick up my sleeve.

The hunt dogs would exit the motel, turn south on Guadalupe, east on 66. If I was quick—if the rocks in my stomach loosened sufficiently—I could cut across the abandoned lot behind the motel and meet them, revolver in hand, in the middle of the road. *You want to fire it,* Dad had said. *You aim and pull the trigger. That simple.* One shot through the windshield, driver's side. The midsize would veer off 66 and slam into a doorway or maybe the silver pole marking the bus stop. A second shot through the passenger side window. Two more shots through the rear windows, then I'd drag Sally out of the wreckage and we'd fly.

Yeah, that simple.

I stumbled down the stairway into the parking lot, weaved between two Harleys toward the back of the motel. As I stretched my legs, worked my arms, picked up speed, I heard the midsize shrieking down Guadalupe—saw the red of its taillights between buildings.

It was going to be close.

I blurred across the abandoned lot, submerged in darkness, guided by the streetlights on 66. Short, tough breaths snapped from my lungs. Trash and dead brush whirled in my wake.

. . .

I both heard and saw the midsize approaching—the growl of its engine, its bright halogens pooling above the low buildings. I pushed harder, until my bare foot came down on something sharp. A jagged stone, perhaps, or a piece of glass. I stumbled and fell. Critical seconds lost.

The midsize was closing in. I staggered to my feet and lunged toward the entrance of the lot, then across the sidewalk and into the road. Headlights dead ahead. Coming on fast. I raised the .38—didn't have time to aim—and pulled the trigger. *Boom!* The gun kicked, sent a bolt through my wrist all the way to my shoulder. The car didn't stop. It didn't veer into a doorway or into the silver post marking the bus stop. I fired again. *Boom!* This time I saw a spark kick off the hood but that was all. I had time to think it was all over—that Lang had won and there was nothing I could do to stop him—then the car was upon me, all light and roar.

I don't recall moving but I must have because the car missed me by inches. Or maybe it had veered, chicken-style, at the last second— Jackhammer directing from the passenger seat, wanting me to live, to feel whatever pain he'd laid out for me. I felt the gust of it passing, re- minding me of standing too close to the edge of the platform when the express train rushes through. It rippled my clothes and sucked the air from my lungs. I reeled sideways, lost balance, dropped to one knee. From that position, I sighted down the revolver's stocky barrel, aimed at the car's rear windshield, but couldn't pull the trigger. I had a brief, graphic vision of the bullet striking the back of Sally's skull, exiting through her face, spraying the car's interior with blood and tiny pieces of psychic coil. Given that she'd be delivered to Lang, who'd reclaim every- thing she'd taken from him, I wondered if that would be the best thing.

The taillights disappeared. The sound of the engine faded. I kneeled in the middle of the road, too many emotions to process, so discarded them all. At least for now.

A coyote yowled in the darkness. Other than that: silence.

I dropped the revolver and lowered my head, shell-empty and hurting.

Cypress Police came to my motel room fifty minutes later, but not for the reasons I expected.

"Fights, gunshots," the younger of the two officers said, examining the door that had been kicked in. "Just another night in Cypress. Besides, you're someone else's problem."

I was sitting on the edge of the bed with one of Sally's sanitary napkins pressed to my nose. I'd done my best to clean myself up, but still looked and felt as if I'd been dragged across the desert by a wild colt. After the manager had colorfully informed me that I was responsible for all damages (he reverted to Spanish when he got excited—I picked out *dinero* and *mucho-mucho*, along with *chinga tu madre*, which I believe has something to do with fucking my mother), I took a moment to consider my next move—had barely got started when the cops showed up. As it turned out, they had my next move planned for me.

"Someone else?" I asked.

"We received a call from Chief Newirth of Green Ridge, New Jersey." The older cop had the ravaged look of a man who'd beaten cancer three or four times, wire-thin, his neck skin hanging in piscine folds.

"Right," I said. I'd left the chief on one hell of a cliffhanger. He'd tracked the number of the payphone—it likely showed up on his call display—then made a few calls of his own.

"Get your things together," the younger cop said. "You're coming with us."

The Cypress Police Department was small: one main room, two desks, three cages against the back wall reserved, no doubt, for the rowdiest of outlaws. The walls were mostly blank and yellowing. I sat at the desk and watched a lizard zip across the tile floor and disappear through a crack in the baseboard.

The young cop—Calhoun, according to his nametag—set about the very important task of brewing coffee, while the older cop—Randall— kicked the air conditioner to get it running. He then joined me at the desk, looked me over.

"Should we ask about this?" He drew a circle around his haggard face, indicating, of course, my broken nose and busted lips.

"I don't think so," I said. The sanitary napkin had been replaced by a handkerchief loaded with ice cubes. My head boomed and my eyes were beginning to blacken. "Put it down to girl trouble."

Randall appeared satisfied with this, as I knew he would be. To be fair, he couldn't help even if he wanted to (which, clearly, he didn't). *No* police could help. I had reflected on this since watching those taillights disappear into the distance. Yes, Lang was behind this, and there was a good chance Sally was being transported to his home in Tennessee, but it wasn't as if I could get a SWAT team to go kick down his door. One reason was that Sally didn't exist. She was the invisible girl. The police would look for her in the system and draw a spectacular blank. Another reason was that Dominic Lang was a for- mer senator who no doubt brandished residual influence. He would have friends in high places, so there was simply no way the authori- ties were going to storm his multimillion-dollar mansion—or even knock politely on the door—based on the accusations of some dirtball from New Jersey.

Randall grunted and began sifting through his general desktop clutter. "Cort, where'd you put that number?" His head swung left and right and his neck skin flapped.

"It's on the computer," the younger cop said.

"Well, shit." Randall swiveled his chair and peered at the half dozen or so Post-It Notes gummed to the monitor. He found the one with Newirth's number written on it and removed it with a flourish. "Four hundred dollars for a godsake computer," he said, picking up the phone, starting to dial. "Some schmancy Windows thing, and Junior uses it to stick our little notes on."

I nodded, as if I felt his pain, as if my own were not enough. What I really wanted was to scream and tear rocketlike into the sky, to explode in a ball of fire and shrapnel and rain down upon every motherfucker that had done me wrong. I thought I could do it, too. I really did.

Instead I pressed the makeshift icepack to my lips, watching as Randall reclined in his seat with the phone pressed to his ear. A moment later: "Chief Newirth, this is Officer Eli Randall, Cypress Police in New Mexico. We picked up your boy this morning. He's here with us now."

I reached across the desk for the phone. Caught within my emotion— and very much a part of it—were two pressing reasons for talking to Chief Newirth. The first was the Green Ridge murders. I would tell the chief everything I reasonably could and let him uncover the evidence he needed to make an arrest. The second reason—more crucial to me—was Dad. Jackhammer's promise had set its claws in my mind and wouldn't let go. I needed to make sure the old man was okay, and that he would *remain* okay.

The call didn't go the way I'd hoped.

"Chief Newirth—"

"You need to come home, Harvey. Right now. I don't care what you're doing or who you're with. You get on a plane and get your ass back to Jersey."

No more Mr. Nice Guy, apparently. The chief sounded harried. *Ugly*, almost. A far cry from the man who dressed up as Santa Claus every Christmas. I knew then that something had gone very wrong.

"Is this about my dad?"

"You know damn well it's about your dad."

The rocks in my gut returned. *More* of them, even heavier. I'm surprised they didn't drag me off the seat. Randall looked down the bridge of his nose with interest. Even Calhoun—sensing the atmospheric shift—momentarily stopped making the coffee.

"Is he okay?" I asked. My face was numb from the icepack. Everything inside was numb, too.

"Come home, Harvey."

"Is he okay?"

"You need—"

"Is my dad okay?"

Silence across the line, filled with terrible things. Randall's chair offered an inquisitive squeal as he leaned forward. Calhoun's coffee pot bubbled morosely. Several throaty choppers rumbled down 66. I heard these sounds all too clearly, but at the other end of the line there was nothing.

Until . . .

"We know, Harvey. We know everything."

"I don't understand," I responded timidly. But I did. I understood perfectly—knew *exactly* what the chief was going to tell me, because Jackhammer had made a promise to fuck me up, to crush everything I know and love, and simply killing Dad was not enough. Tears flashed from my eyes. I dropped the icepack and covered my face with my hand.

"He confessed, Harvey. To the murders." Chief Newirth's voice was rain-gray and each syllable felt like a bullet striking something vital. "We have it on tape. He confessed to them all."

Twenty

It's crazy how things work out; Sally and I were scheduled to arrive in Blythe, California, at 8:25 p.m. Instead, I—alone—touched down at Newark Liberty at exactly that time, to the minute. One of Chief Newirth's off-duty officers met me in arrivals. He was my age, prematurely balding. I remembered him from high school. We called him Jimmy Banana because he always ate a banana for lunch. Nothing else. Now he insisted I call him sir, or Officer Adams, even though he was out of uniform.

Walking toward the exit—pulling Sally's luggage along behind me, backpack hanging off one shoulder—I saw Dad's face on one of the airport TVs. It was his old post office photo. A nice shot of him; the lighting had softened his scars and he was smiling. The caption read: MURDER SUSPECT MISSING. The scrolling text: *Gordon Anderson wanted for questioning in Green Ridge murders.* And: *Police discover videotape confession in Anderson's home.* And: *Suspect's home a "den of violent contraptions."* I stopped and stared at the screen with tears of rage flooding my eyes. Officer Adams took me by the arm and tried to urge me along, but I didn't budge. I could have been bolted to the floor.

"Come on," he snapped.

My jaw was locked tight and my breath whistled as it exited my broken nose. Adams tugged me again and this time I moved, but stiffly. We stepped out of the terminal, into the fumy Jersey night. I didn't say a word until we were westbound on I-78, after Adams called Newirth to tell him that we were en route to the station.

"Call him back," I said. My voice could have produced sparks. "Tell him to meet me at the house."

"We're going to the station."

I gave him a look that depicted the earthquake inside me: a nightmarish landscape of destruction, where fires still burned and lost souls drifted. I imagine it was quite chilling.

"Why do you want to go to the house?" he asked.

I said, "Because I know where my father is."

A cackle of news vans had assembled at the bottom of Dad's driveway. I barely glanced at them. I focused, instead, on the house as it expanded in the headlights, thinking even then that it looked lonely. Chief Newirth's cruiser occupied Dad's parking spot—not that Dad would need it anymore, with his faithful old truck sitting at the bottom of a lake somewhere in Kansas—with a second vehicle, a beige sedan, off to one side. I saw Newirth talking to a couple of plainclothes cops with chiseled faces. The female's suit was crisper, and her hair shorter, than that of her male counterpart.

Adams pulled up behind Newirth's cruiser, shut off the engine. Before getting out, I took a second to look at Dad's house. It was odd to see it so lifeless; there were usually lights burning or windows open, drapes swaying in the breeze, or any number of cats arranged on the sills. And there were times I'd walked up the driveway to find Dad sitting on the porch, usually reading, but sometimes drinking lemonade and listening to the radio. I clung to the thin hope that these signs of life would one day return, but for this to be possible, and even assuming the old man was still alive, I had some work to do.

. . .

"Harvey, these are Detectives Sharpe and Lambert from the county prosecutor's office. They're leading the investigation. I need you to cooperate with them one hundred and ten percent. Do you understand?"

I looked at Chief Newirth and nodded, then turned to the investigators who were set to pin three sexual homicides on my innocent father. The earthquake boomed again and it was all I could do to keep from expelling smoke and rubble, knowing I needed to come across as a decent young man, raised by decent parents, to have any hope of clearing Dad's name. So I drove the anger deep, smiled at them both, and offered my hand. Only the female detective—Sharpe—reciprocated.

"What happened to your face?" Lambert asked. He had a front tooth missing, affecting his speech. *Face* became *faith*.

"I was beaten up," I said, thinking it a good idea to begin with the truth.

"Again?" Chief Newirth said. "The same guys as before?"

"Yeah," I said.

"Do you make a habit of surrounding yourself with bad people?" Lambert pressed.

"I try not to," I said. "But you can't help but run into them occasionally. That's exactly what my girlfriend did. And this"—I pointed to my damaged face—"is what happens when you get caught in the crossfire."

"You know where your father is?" Sharpe asked, bringing us back to the matter at hand. Her voice matched her name.

"I think so," I said, meeting her gaze while fighting to contain my emotion. "And rest assured you'll have my full cooperation. I *need* you to know the truth. But first, I'd like five minutes with Chief Newirth. Alone, if possible."

"Something you can't tell us?" Lambert's eyes drilled into me.

"It's not like that," I said. "I've known Chief Newirth all my life. He's known my father for over forty years. I need that kind of sensitivity right now. And Chief Newirth will tell you everything I tell him."

The two detectives exchanged a look. Something passed between them. An imperceptible communication developed through years of working together. Or maybe it was just a cop thing. Something wired into their DNA.

"Five minutes," Sharpe said, holding up five perfectly manicured fingers. "Clock's ticking, Harvey."

She and Lambert took several steps toward their unmarked car. Chief Newirth gripped my upper arm hard enough to bruise and dragged me in the opposite direction, toward Officer Adams, who was propped against the open door of his car, waiting to see if he was still needed. Newirth shooed him away with an impatient hand gesture. I'd never seen him like this before. He had an earthquake of his own.

"How long have you known?" he snapped, wheeling me toward him.

"*Known?*" I said. "Jesus Christ, Chief, he didn't do it."

"How long, Harvey?"

"He. *Didn't*. Do it." I looked the chief squarely in the eye. "You know my dad as well as anyone. He would never—"

"What I *know*, Harvey, is that your recent behavior has been suspicious, to say the least." He loomed closer, five inches shorter but filling my personal space as if he'd had to crouch to get in. "What I *know* is that you asked me to check on your father. I'm guessing you were struggling with your guilt—with how much you could tell me—because all you said was that he seemed crazier than usual."

"Yeah, but normal crazy," I said. "Not fucking serial-killer crazy."

"So I came over, like you asked me to. No sign of your dad, just a lot of spooked cats. The front door was open so I walked in, nosed around, and found the video cassette on the kitchen table. Imagine my surprise to see *my* name written on the label. I took the cassette back to the station, rolled the VCR out of retirement, and well . . . here we are."

"A confession proves nothing," I said. "Dad has mental health issues. He believes Obama is a reptilian overlord, for God's sake. That confession isn't worth the tape it's recorded on."

Newirth gestured toward the detectives. "That's not what they think."

I shook my head and stewed in the cruelty. I at least wanted to believe that Dad had put up a fight when Lang and the hunt dogs came, that he'd skulked through his overgrown, trap-infested garden—

KA-BAR knife locked between his teeth—like he was back in the Delta. Maybe he even took a couple of those motherfuckers out before they dragged him in front of his clunky old video camera. Even then he wouldn't have confessed. But Lang had crawled into his mind, placed all eight legs on the controls, and turned his scarred face toward the camera. *My name is Gordon Anderson.* Lang's words, Dad's voice. *This is my confession . . .*

Chief Newirth looked at Sharpe and Lambert, held up two fingers. The gap in Lambert's teeth was as distinct as a bullet hole. I kept my cool, knowing I could play my trump card at any time, but to do so at that moment would appear desperate. I needed to build my case, provide reason.

"This so-called confession," I said. "How detailed is it? I know police withhold certain information from the public in order to eliminate false confessors, and to ensure they catch the right guy. Did Dad offer any incriminating detail that only the killer would know?"

"Let me put it this way," Newirth said. "There's enough in that confession for our friends from county to want to question your father *very* badly."

"And the search for evidence . . ." I flicked a finger at Dad's house, where the only color came from the yellow police tape marking an *X* across the front door. "Did you find anything? Guns and knives, sure, but he's a former serviceman. I'm talking about evidence that links him to the murders. Blood samples, locks of the victims' hair, whatever crazy souvenirs serial killers collect."

"The search is ongoing." A muscle in Chief Newirth's jaw flexed as he clenched his teeth. "You have one minute, Harvey, then I'm handing you over to the detectives. My advice is that you quit playing Perry Mason and offer your full cooperation."

"They don't know me like you do," I said, lowering my voice to a whisper. "They want this case closed, and that confession has them running down a one-way street. I need you to help direct them."

"I think he did it, though." The chief's tone was detached, without any of the compassion and understanding I associated with him. "The confession may not be detailed, but it *is* genuine. I think he murdered those women, and if you knew about it—and your suspicious behavior suggests you did—that makes you an accessory after the fact."

"Is that why I called you from New Mexico this morning?" I asked, and there was enough emotion in my voice to make up for us both. "And why I jumped on the first plane back to Jersey . . . to confess to being an accessory?"

"I think this whole thing has left you confused and conflicted. Not remembering why you bought the shovel is evidence of that."

"You're wrong," I said, and imagined shell-shocked survivors clawing their way from my mouth and ears. "So fucking wrong."

"Really?" The chief's nostrils flared. "So tell me, Harvey, why are you so certain he *didn't* do it?"

I took a deep breath and wiped tears from my eyes. It was time to play my trump card.

"Because," I said, "I know who *did.*"

Twenty-One

Sitting at the edge of Spirit Lake, fishing for memories, I once asked Dad what he liked most about Sally. The first thing he said was that she danced spontaneously, that he admired her energy. He followed this by saying that she had a pretty singing voice. This triggered no memories at the time, but I remember now how Sally loved to sing. I would hear her around the apartment all the time, while she was fixing lunch, taking a shower, or just relaxing with one of her favorite albums. She had a breezy tone that was always cajoling, but threaded with a vulnerability that breathed realness into every note. I tried numerous times to get her to perform with me—there would have been a *lot* more money in my guitar case at the end of the day—but she never would. She didn't like the spotlight, she said, and now I know why.

She sang when she was distracted, or when she felt comfortable, which meant the customers at the Health Nut sometimes heard her while she stacked shelves or refilled the bulk bins. On one quiet afternoon in May 2015, Sally—singing quietly to herself—was approached by a customer who wanted to know where he could find the gluten-free bagels, but who was also keen to note that she had a wonderful voice.

"Thank you," Sally said, blushing. "I really shouldn't sing in the workplace." She offered the sweetest smile. "The bagels are in the freezer. There are some on the rack, but they're close to their sell-by date."

The customer thanked her, took two steps toward the freezer, then turned back.

"Have you ever thought about singing professionally?" he asked.

"Oh, no." Sally shook her head emphatically. "Absolutely not. My legs turn to jelly in front of a crowd."

"Well, that's a confidence issue, which can be remedied. But there's always background or session work." His intelligent eyes gleamed and he took a step toward her. "Do you know who I am?"

Sally nodded. "Swan Connor. You're a record producer. My boyfriend told me about you."

"My reputation precedes me," Swan said with a smile. "I launched the careers of Marlene Starr and Isaac Jefferson. I also took the Groove City Players from the Philadelphia club circuit to the biggest arenas in the world." He tipped an immodest wink. "I know a good voice when I hear one."

"You won a Grammy award, right?"

"Three Grammys," he said, and shrugged as if it were no big deal. "I retired a long time ago, but I still have contacts in New York, LA, and pretty much everywhere in between. If you're at all interested in developing your vocal talents . . ."

Swan left the invitation hanging but held out his hand. Sally—knowing the discussion was over; she could never do anything so brazen—took it out of politeness, and was about to thank him when she inadvertently tuned in to one of his thoughts. It was so clear and violent—*bitch I'll BLEED and FUCK you and BASH BASH BASH you*—that she leapt backward with a cry, as if Swan's hand had transmuted into a tentacle that coiled itself around her forearm. She bumped into the shelf behind her, spilling several cereal boxes to the floor.

"Is everything okay?" Swan asked.

She stared at him, cupping her elbows in her palms. Her mouth moved soundlessly for a second, then she managed to say, "A shock. Static, I think. You didn't feel that?"

—STAB and BLEED and STAB and—

"No."

"Maybe just me," Sally said.

"Or my electric personality," Swan said, and as he turned to leave she touched his mind and saw there just a few of the monstrous things he'd done—feral, soulless crimes that need not be detailed here, but that crippled her, and blackened her all over. She fell to her knees and stayed there until Joy Brady—the Health Nut's owner—found her. Sally said she'd suffered a moment's nausea, a small lie supported by her trembling and shortness of breath. Joy sat her down at the back of the store, administered a homoeopathic remedy, then sent her home for the day.

"Rest," Joy said. "Take tomorrow, if you need it."

Sally thanked her and walked the scenic route home, through Green River Park and up Chime Hill. Easily thirty minutes longer, but it gave her time to consider her predicament. She could take matters into her own hands: a red-bird lobotomy, turning Swan into a quivering vegetable. But doing this would place a blip on Dominic Lang's psychic radar, and the hunt dogs would come drooling. Goodbye, Green Ridge. Goodbye, Harvey. Her other option was to go to the police—an anonymous tip so she wouldn't draw attention to herself. But would the police take her seriously without proof? And even if they did—if they produced a warrant to search Swan's house and discovered all manner of incriminating evidence—would the wheels of justice spin truly? Swan wouldn't be the first celebrity to get away with murder. Or maybe, if the evidence was overwhelming, he'd plead insanity and spend the rest of his days in the kind of "psychiatric" hospital that offers mani-pedis, cable TV, and a choice of organic soups. She recalled what she'd seen in Swan Connor's mind—she heard those women beg and scream—and had to ask herself, what kind of justice was that?

"I knew what I had to do," Sally had said to me. Her eyes flicked to the clock on the nightstand, ticking steadily toward 5:30, when our bus—the bus we would never catch—was scheduled to leave Cypress. "I *always* knew, from the moment I saw those terrible things in his mind.

The only way to make sure Swan paid for what he'd done, and to ensure he never did it again, was to take care of him myself."

"You did the right thing," I said. I felt numb inside. Swan Connor, my dad's old pal, who'd always had a story and a smile, but who Mom—astutely, as it turned out—had never really taken to. Swan Connor, to whom I'd recently given a flower intended for Mom's grave. *Jub,* he'd said, and I'd actually felt good about that. Swan rapist-fucking-murderer Connor, who was now a driveling, sack-of-shit vegetable with nothing in his mind but old rags. The victim of a devastating stroke, or so everybody thought.

"You did the right thing," I said again.

"But it meant bringing the danger close," Sally said, clutching the bed sheets to her breast. "And, in all likelihood, saying goodbye to my life in Green Ridge."

"You had no choice."

"I didn't *want* to run away, Harvey. Not again. I didn't want to lose you." Another glance at the clock. She wiped her tired eyes. "So I decided to lure Swan away from Green Ridge, to where the hunt dogs would spend a long time chasing their tails."

"New York City?" I asked.

"Right," Sally said. "They would eventually spread out, of course: Yonkers, Westchester, Jersey, but they might never think to look in Green Ridge. Even so, giving Lang my approximate location was a risky move, but what choice did I have? Swan was a monster, and I had to stop him."

He lured all his victims the same way: with charm. He became a face they recognized and learned to trust, then he'd wait for the opportunity to strike. His first victim, Melissa Wynn, had been walking home from the grocery store and was crossing Reed Avenue—a quiet street with lots of tree cover and several properties set back from the road—when Swan pulled up in his spacious Cadillac. "You need a ride?" Melissa declined to begin with—she was only ten minutes from home, and it was a beautiful August day—then changed her mind. Perhaps she was running late for the babysitter. Or perhaps it was Swan's charming smile, or his propensity to share amusing stories about seventies R&B icons. Whatever the reason, she fatefully got into his car, and the next time anybody saw her, she'd been raped, beaten, stabbed twenty-three times, her body wrapped in garbage bags and dumped in the Shoe-Nuff parking lot.

Swan's second victim, Latisha Paffrey, was similarly abducted. Swan was a customer of the bank at which she worked, and would occasionally come in with a box of Munchkins from Dunkin' Donuts, and the tellers would uniformly trill and gather around and Swan would regale them with celebrity anecdotes and exhibit photographs of him with various luminaries from the music industry. One sleepy evening in July 2013, Latisha was standing on the sidewalk outside her apartment, waiting for a taxi that was running late, when a red Cadillac CTS pulled up to the curb. The passenger window buzzed down and Swan Connor smiled at her. "Hey, Latisha. You need a ride?" Eleven months had passed since Melissa Wynn's body was discovered, and Latisha—her guard lowered—accepted Swan's kind offer as readily as she accepted the Munchkins he occasionally brought into the bank.

Grace Potts—victim three—knew Swan from Dreams With Subtitles, a group for foreign film enthusiasts. It was a relationship Swan nurtured over many months, so it did not appear at all odd when he told her, in the utmost confidence, that doctors had discovered a tumor on his liver. He confided how frightened he was, and asked if she would accompany him to the aptly named Grace Medical Imaging in Newark, where he had to undergo a CT scan. "But please," he added, folding his soft hands over hers. "Given how sensitive this is, I have to insist you don't tell a soul." Grace had made a zipping motion across her lips, and then hugged him, and on the afternoon of April 12, 2014, met him at the agreed-upon location. "How are you feeling, Swan?" she'd asked, getting into his car. Swan told her it was going to be a wonderful day, and drove her not to the clinic in Newark, but to a condemned, isolated house on the outskirts of Green Ridge, where she screamed and screamed and screamed.

Swan was meticulous in his approach, attentive to the smallest detail. Colleagues in the music industry had often remarked on his patience—a quality he brought to every abduction. He was, then, taken aback when Sally leapfrogged several months of relationship-building and suggested they go out for dinner.

"I'd like to discuss my options," she said, and forced a smile. "I mean, being a session singer *has* to be better than stacking shelves, right?"

"Absolutely," Swan agreed, his own false smile firmly in place. He was thinking that being seen so publicly with a potential victim was not a smart move, and that a sixty-six-year-old man having dinner—not lunch, *dinner*—with a twenty-something-year-old woman was sure to draw attention. And attention, as Sally knew for herself, was not good.

"My treat, of course," Sally added.

"I would never *dream* of letting you buy me dinner," Swan said, and took a furtive glance around the store. Joy Brady was at the cash register, lost in her own world. There were a few other customers, equally preoccupied, not one of them within earshot of their conversation, and that was good. "This is a small town. Tongues wag. I'm afraid that if we're seen having dinner together, prior to you finding work in the music industry . . . well, that may send the wrong signal."

"We don't have to stay in Green Ridge," Sally said. "In fact, I'd prefer we *didn't*. And nobody needs to know about this. It can be our little secret."

She had put herself on a platter for him, and while he cautioned himself to be patient, another voice—*BLEED you and BASH you and FUCK you*—chugged through his mind like a smoky little train.

"I'll think about it," he said, selecting a packet of brown rice pasta from the shelf and dropping it into his basket. "In the meantime, we should keep this conversation between us."

"Shhhh," Sally said, and pressed a finger to her lips.

Swan returned to the Health Nut later that week and found Sally singing to herself at the back of the store.

"You really do have a special voice."

"Thank you."

"Little bird."

"You're not the first person to call me that."

He looked pale, tired. Sally saw in his mind that he hadn't slept much. He'd been thinking—obsessing—about her.

"So where do you want to go?" he asked.

"Manhattan," Sally said. "It's far enough from Green Ridge, and big enough that we won't easily be noticed. We'll find somewhere secluded, but classy . . ."

"Would you like me to drive you?"

"Let's play it safe and meet there."

"Yes. Good." Swan rubbed his chin thoughtfully. "I know a wonderful little Greek restaurant in the Flatiron District. It's tricky to find, but we can meet nearby and I'll walk you there."

He'll walk me to his car, Sally thought, and she didn't need to read his mind to know this. *He'll say he's remembered an even better restaurant, just a short drive away. And once the doors are locked . . .*

"Tomorrow night?" she asked.

"Perfect," Swan said. "We'll meet on the northwest corner of Madison Square Park. How does eight o'clock sound?"

Sally smiled. "I'll wear my prettiest dress."

And she did: a lace sheath dress the same color as the bird in her head. An expression of strength and femininity, Sally wanted it to flash in Swan's eyes as his wicked brain was crushed to all but a thread of light.

She arrived at the meeting point ten minutes early. Swan was right on time. He crossed Twenty-Sixth Street toward Madison Square Park, with his neat white hair combed across his scalp and his icy eyes glimmering. He wore a suit, with no tie and an open collar, revealing a sprig of silvery chest hair and a thin gold chain. A handsome man, no doubt, but about to become a deadened one.

He saw Sally—her red dress no doubt catching his eye—and the hunger in his expression was unmistakable. His lips sneaked up at the edges. The bridge of his nose wrinkled deeply. Sally waited for him to mount the sidewalk, then opened the cage door in her mind. She almost heard the flap of wings as the bird—furious—took flight.

Swan stopped, raised one finger to his temple, and gave his head a wee shake. His left eye twitched and blood trickled from both nostrils. "I need . . ." he said randomly, and these were the last normal words he ever spoke. His mouth collapsed and he teetered sideways, bumping into a punk-haired New Yorker jabbering into her cell phone, who brushed him aside without missing a beat. Swan slumped the other way, his legs sagging, but managed to stay on his feet. A single drop of blood dripped from his chin and splashed into the downy hair on his chest. "Flurp," he said, or something like that, then he shouted it, "*Flurp!*" and pressed his hands to either side of his head as if trying to keep it from splitting open. Several pedestrians were on alert by this point, most of them backing away. Swan rolled one eye toward Sally, and she saw amid the terrible confusion a world of agony and horror, nothing compared to what he'd inflicted, but deeply satisfying nonetheless. *Fuck you*, she mouthed, and Swan went down. He hit the sidewalk with a wretched, boneless thud. His legs scissored and shook. Someone shouted, "*Whoa, buddy,*" and laughed. Someone else screamed. Within moments a circle of onlookers had formed. Several people employed their cell phones to dial 911 or to immortalize the moment on social media. Sally lowered her head, gathering Swan's memories—his many cruelties— and locking them in the room at the back of her mind. Then she turned and slipped quietly from the scene.

Her heart trembling with emotion, and from knowing that somewhere, Dominic Lang was approximating her location, she hastened to Penn Station and caught a train across the river.

She looked over her shoulder the whole way.

The story I gave Newirth and the detectives was tweaked—to put it mildly—in places, but the bottom line was the same: Swan Connor was their man. When I'd finished, Lambert and Sharpe looked at each other for a long time. Their expressions told me nothing. I wished for Sally's ability to dip into their minds.

"Who is Swan Connor?" Sharpe asked Newirth.

"He's a killer," I replied on the chief's behalf.

"That's enough, Harvey," Newirth snapped. His brown eyes, always so calm, were now bulletlike. He inhaled through his nose and turned to Sharpe. "He's a local celebrity. Former record producer. A pretty big deal back in the day, but he had a stroke earlier this year and now all he does is sit on Main and wave at passing cars."

"Is he aware?" Sharpe asked. "Compos mentis?"

"No."

"Single man, living alone?"

"He was at the time of the murders," I said. "Now he has a live-in nurse."

Sharpe turned to Lambert. "Do we have anything on him?"

"I'll check," Lambert grunted, and sauntered over to their vehicle to run Swan's name through the law enforcement databases. I nodded at Sharpe to show my gratitude, but there was still a long way to go.

"Quite the ordeal for your girlfriend to go through," she said to me. Despite her willingness to hear me out, her voice could still cut through steel. "Abducted. Abused. Escaped by the skin of her teeth."

"Yeah," I said. I didn't feel bad about the fabrication; it was necessary to explain how Sally knew who—*what*—Swan was. I couldn't exactly tell them she was psychic.

"So why," Sharpe asked, "are we only hearing about it now?"

"I only found out this morning and called Chief Newirth right away. Then this happened"—I pointed at my face—"and everything went to shit."

"A remarkable coincidence that you should find out within hours of us coming across your father's confession."

"I know how it looks," I said. "But I'm telling the truth."

"Why didn't your girlfriend come forward at the time?"

"I asked her that. She was scared and confused, she said. Not the first victim of abuse to remain silent."

"We're talking about a serial killer. Not a heavy-handed husband."

"You can't categorize abuse," I said firmly. "It's all fucked up. It's all terrifying. From Sally's point of view, Swan Connor was a respected member of the community, and she was afraid no one would believe her—that she'd have to relive what happened and be vilified afterward."

"And the possibility of Swan killing again wasn't incentive enough for her to come forward?"

"It was all too raw, I think. Too close. Sally needed to pull herself together before she could consider anybody else." I hated making her appear so weak when only the opposite was true. "Anyway, Swan had his stroke a couple of days later. Sally figured it was God's way of stepping in. The son of a bitch got what he deserved."

"And where's Sally now?"

"I don't know," I said, and pointed at my face again. "This happened, remember? Sally was involved with some real douchebags."

"Let me get this straight," Sharpe said, taking a step toward me, her dark eyes narrowed. "You want us to switch our focus from a confessor with a clearly dangerous disposition"—she drew a circle in the air with her forefinger, indicating Dad's house, his garden, the whole shitshow—"to a stroke victim without the mental capacity to defend himself?"

"Yes," I said.

"Based on your troubled ex-girlfriend's accusations, who didn't come forward at the time, and who can't provide a statement because we don't know where she is?"

"All I'm asking is that you keep an open mind," I said. "And that you don't pull the trigger on my father until you've at least checked Swan's house for evidence."

"This is a very serious accusation," Newirth said.

"Do you want to catch the right guy?" I asked.

Lambert returned, perusing his notes, pressing his tongue against the gap in his teeth. "Douglas 'Swan' Connor," he began. "Born two-twelve, forty-nine, East Brunswick, New Jersey. Acquitted for rape in 1974. Was questioned in regard to the Green Ridge murders in August 'twelve, and again in July 'thirteen. Came out squeaky both times."

"Rape," I said. Acquitted or not, I thought it worth mentioning again.

"This is a waste of time," Lambert snapped. *Thith ith a wathte of time.* Asshole sounded like Sylvester the cat. "Where's your old man, kid?"

"But Swan—"

"We can't very well question him again," Sharpe said. "He doesn't even know his own name. And we can't search his property without a warrant, which means we need something more solid."

"Right," I said, and puffed out my cheeks. "Anybody got a cell phone I can borrow?"

Chief Newirth accessed the Internet on his cell and handed it to me. I brought up Google and entered "swan connor producer discography" into the search field.

"We're wasting our time with this," Lambert said.

"Swan Connor produced his first album in 1977," I started. "It was called *Breathe with Me* by Marlene Starr, a then-unknown African-American singer out of Detroit. It reached number twenty-three on the 'Top LPs and Tapes' chart—what is now called the Billboard 200." I flipped the screen, showing them the album cover and chart position. "Twenty-three. I want you to remember that number."

Lambert shuffled his feet. Sharpe inched a little closer.

"His second album as producer," I continued, "was *Get Down with the Groove* by the Groove City Players, an African-American band out of Philly. It was a big hit. A top ten album, peaking at number six."

I flipped the screen again.

"The stab wounds," Newirth said, the penny dropping with a sound like soul music. "Vic one was stabbed twenty-three times. Vic two, six times."

"Don't tell me," Sharpe said. "Connor's third album reached number eleven."

"*San Francisco Morning* by Sweetie Day, a Caucasian singer-songwriter from San Fran." I held out the cell phone so they could see for themselves. "So not only do the stab wounds match the chart positions, but the ethnicity of the victims matches that of the artists."

The three policepersons looked at each other, saying nothing, but I could almost hear their minds grinding through the gears.

"I don't like the word *motive*," I continued. "It suggests a degree of logic, when most homicides are acts of irrationality and anger. But if Swan Connor had a motive it was to express his disillusionment with the music industry. He was left behind in the nineties, and by the two thousands—the new media age—he was a dinosaur. But to hell with Swan; I don't want to credit him with any logic. These murders are an irrational, angry attempt for one shitty little man to reenact his greatest hits."

"Or it could be a strange coincidence," Lambert said. *Thtrange cointhidenth.* Even Sharpe rolled her eyes.

I Googled again. Brought up an image. Showed them.

"You know what this is?"

"A Grammy award," Sharpe said.

"Right," I said. "It has a wide, flat base so you can sit it on your mantel and show all your friends how great you are." I found a picture of Swan holding up the Grammy he won for producing Marlene Starr's *Ain't Nothin' Sweeter* in 1981. "It's a heavy little sucker, too—weighs four and a quarter pounds. That's about the same as four claw hammers strapped together."

"Are you saying that Swan Connor bludgeoned his victims with a *Grammy award*?" Sharpe frowned, her eyes flicking between me and the screen. "How would you know that?"

"He told Sally everything he was going to do to her," I replied smoothly. Another necessary variation of the truth. "I wasn't there, of course, so it's her word. But hey, you might want to revisit the forensic pathologist's report—see if the victims' wounds are consistent with the trophy's specs."

They looked at each other again, gears still grinding. I handed Newirth his phone with the picture of Swan brandishing his Grammy still on screen. He muttered something—thank you, I think—then gave his head a tired shake.

"We can look into this, Harvey," Sharpe said, still with that razor tone. I couldn't work out if she liked me or not—if she liked *anybody*. "But let me be clear: Your father is our priority. We need to find and interview him. We'll then proceed with Mr. Connor, as necessary."

"I understand," I said, although I was horribly certain Dad was in no position to be interviewed. I'd done what I could to defend him, though. I'd fought for him because I loved him. That's what you do.

"So let's get to it: the reason we're all here." Lambert found the edge of my personal space. His aftershave smelled like old watermelon. "Where is he?"

I took a deep breath, then stepped around Lambert and headed toward the back of the house.

"This way," I said.

Twenty-Two

led them to the backyard, stopping at a clearing between the shed and an old maple. I had Sharpe and Newirth train their flashlights on the ground and started kicking at the dirt and leaves.

"It's somewhere around here," I muttered.

"What are you looking for?" Lambert asked.

"Entrance to the bunker."

The three cops looked with me, dragging their shoes across the dirt until it hung in a low, brown mist around our thighs, and it was Newirth who found it—felt a hollow spot in the ground and thudded his heel against it. I helped him clear the area, kicking aside leaves until we'd revealed a five-foot seam in the dirt. I dug around with my fingers and found the trapdoor's handle: a flush-mounted ring pull. We lifted together. The earth separated with a creak, mud and stones rattling into the gaps. A moment later, the cops' flashlights shone on several narrow steps leading to a door.

"Well, Christ," Lambert said, brushing dirt from his pants. "You'd never know this was here."

"Dad wanted to make sure it was invisible to Russian drones," I said, emphasizing the fact that, yeah, Dad was crazy, but not the kind of crazy that raped and murdered women. "It's a storage container, re-inforced to withstand . . ."

I trailed off, recalling how I'd thought of Dad's bunker as a giant coffin. I licked my busted lips and shook my head.

"Any surprises waiting for us down there?" Lambert asked. "Booby traps? Ravenous dogs?"

"No," I replied, thinking the only surprise would be to find Dad alive and well. "It's safe."

Lambert didn't appear convinced, but he started down the steps with Sharpe behind him. Chief Newirth followed, but not right away. He hovered for a second, looking at me with a curious expression. I couldn't tell if he wanted to shake my hand or shoot me.

"Stay there," he said.

"I'm not going anywhere."

Lambert barked *"Police! Open up!"* and whapped on the door, then entered Dad's bunker with his flashlight and weapon drawn. Sharpe and Newirth followed him in. I waited with a sickness rising and a quickness of breath. I could reel off the clichés: time stood still; min-utes turned to hours. I watched dead leaves seesaw from the maple. One landed on my head, the stem snagged by my bristly hair. I plucked it free and remembered the leaf in Sally's hair on the day she met Dad, how it had accented her verve and color, whereas this leaf was curled and old. In many ways, it embodied Sally and Dad *now*. A red thing. A dead thing. I dropped it to the ground where it blended with the others, then lowered my head and wiped my swollen eyes.

I didn't look up until I felt a hand on my shoulder. Chief Newirth. I wanted to seesaw to the ground, too.

"I'm so sorry, Harvey."

Only Dad and I knew about the bunker, and while it wasn't as sacred to him as the lake, it was still special: his shelter from the storm. The reason he'd been killed—*violated*—here was because Lang and the hunt dogs wanted me to know that, in the end, Dad had no sanctuary, and no secrets. His mind had been torn apart.

We will *fuck you up, Harvey.*

Of course, it didn't hurt that leaving the body in the bunker meant it would take the police longer to find him, and a missing suspect—a *manhunt*—will always grab the headlines, stamping Dad's infamy, and his implied guilt, across the nation.

We'll crush everything you know and love.

I couldn't breathe. Couldn't move. My skeleton was granite, my muscles lead. Guilt and rage were two dogs fighting inside me. They growled and circled, equally vicious. I wanted to scream but there was no sound. I wanted to cry but everything was dry.

"Come on, Harvey," Newirth said. "You don't need to see this."

On some level I recognized Chief Newirth's voice—a distant interference, like the spikes Dad picked up on his radio telescope. I even felt his hand on my arm, but he was a thousand miles away.

"Harvey . . ."

Dad was slumped against the bunker's far wall, which had once been pristine white but was now marked with a russet stain, broad as a peacock's tail. The same reddish-brown color painted his upper body. The gun he'd used—that Lang had *made* him use—was still in his hand.

It was Lambert who broke the spell, stomping forward with a sheet he'd ripped from one of the cots. He draped it over Dad, clumsily nudging his shoulder so that he flopped to one side. I saw the exit wound toward the rear of his skull and a part of his brain, pulp-gray.

Lambert looked at Newirth but pointed at me. "Get him out of here."

"Let's go," Newirth snapped, taking my arm again.

I can't explain why I was there to begin with—why I'd blown past Newirth and down the bunker steps without pause for thought. I knew it was real; I'd known Dad was dead since being told that he'd confessed to the murders. Maybe I wanted to taste the pain, fuel myself for the fight ahead. Or maybe I wanted to witness what Lang was really capable of. *Know your enemy,* Sun Tzu had said. Seeing my father's corpse—the ragged hole in the back of his skull, and now his legs extending from beneath the sheet—I'd say I knew my enemy very well.

And on the back of this, my new violent mantra, having accompanied me from Oklahoma to New Mexico to New Jersey: *Kill him. Kill the fucker.*

Before it was a spark. Now it was a flame.

Detective Sharpe helped Newirth lead me from the bunker, but not before I'd claimed a photograph from the box Dad had packed for me—the box in which I'd found my Book of Moments. It was the shot of me and Dad at the shore, the one where I'm doing bunny ears behind his head. I pressed my lips together to keep my jaw from quivering, then showed Sharpe and Newirth in a wistful, absentminded kind of way.

In lieu of further condolence they nodded, then led me up the steps into the fresh night. I requested a moment alone and walked on jittery legs to the base of the maple, finding a comfortable spot among the roots. I looked at the photograph in the light pooling from the bunker, and the emotion finally broke through. Not a couple of thin tears and a whimper, but a body-clenching, mournful wail. Several of the more endearing Dad memories flickered in my mind, but the one shining brighter than all others was of the last time I saw him, standing at the top of his driveway with Michael Jackson clutched to his chest and one fist held defiantly aloft. It was a wonderful image—a real *Dad* image—and was accompanied by the last words he ever spoke to me: *I love you, Harvey.*

I wanted to believe he'd taken his own life, because the thought of Dominic Lang in his mind was simply too awful. But suicide was not in Dad's DNA. If it *was,* he'd have killed himself after losing his soul mate to cancer, or when the bandages were removed from his face, revealing the Halloween mask he'd have to wear for the rest of his life. No, this was Lang's doing, his revenge for going against him. *You're on my radar now,* he'd warned me. *If you try to run away, or even consider keeping information from me . . .* Staging Dad's suicide was a necessary part of the plan; a dead man couldn't retract his confession or reveal that his mind had been appropriated by the former Republican senator for Tennessee. All he could do was appear guilty, forevermore. Lang and the hunt dogs didn't count on me being able to incriminate Swan Connor, though, and hopefully clear Dad's name before it was dragged too deeply in the dirt. I'd like to say that lessened the pain, but it didn't.

I heard a sound in the grass to my left. A timorous mewl. Some small woodland creature, perhaps, separated from its parent or injured. I considered investigating when Chief Newirth emerged from the bunker, talking on his cell phone. I overheard the word *coroner* and imagined Dad's corpse being photographed, examined, then zipped into a body bag. I wanted to be gone before that happened.

I slipped the photograph into my back pocket and got to my feet. Stepping from beneath the maple, I heard the mewling sound again. I looked over my shoulder and saw a flash of pale fur. Despite my tiredness and grief, and every other emotion still rapping at the door, I knew exactly what—*who*—it was.

I approached carefully, parting the grass like a wildlife photographer closing in on a rare shot, and there, as expected, was Michael Jackson. He whimpered. His coat was grubby and his ears low. Even so, I smiled at the sight of him.

"Hey, Michael." I held out my hand so that he could smell me, *know* me, but I didn't need to. Maybe my voice was enough, because he sprang from the ground into my arms, nuzzling his face beneath my chin. "Okay, dude," I said. "It's okay now." And all at once I was bawling again, clutching him to my chest as if I'd never let go, suddenly the only good thing in my life. The only family I had.

Twenty-Three

There were dead flies on the windowsill and the leaves of my plastic banana plant needed dusting. Other than that, my apartment was how I'd left it—hauntingly so, as if I'd never been away. It didn't feel good to be back, either; I should have been in California, snuggled up with Sally in a comfortable hotel bed. Only my guitar—propped in the corner, where I'd left it—was a welcome sight.

Michael meowed and I set him down. He looped once around my ankles, then padded into the kitchen and nosed at a few crumbs on the floor. Newirth told me that the other cats had been taken to an animal shelter, which was understandable; it'd be next to impossible for the police to search Dad's property with them springing high and low. Michael Jackson had obviously been clear of the house during the roundup. Or maybe he'd been too afraid to return after Lang and the hunt dogs had visited. Judging from the way he'd been trembling in the weeds, I thought that quite likely. Whatever the reason, he'd avoided the cage and was temporarily in my care. I'd find him a new owner soon. Someone as crazy and affectionate as Dad, hopefully.

"Where do you want this?" Officer Mimes asked, indicating

Sally's luggage, which he'd carried up two flights of stairs because the elevator—as usual—was too slow.

"Next to the sofa is fine," I said, and Mimes wheeled it dutifully into place. I shook off my backpack, unzipped it, and took out the three tins of Friskies I'd persuaded Chief Newirth to remove from Dad's kitchen. I pulled open one tin, forked the contents into a cereal bowl, and set it on the floor beside Michael. He leapt at it and ate, his body tense and trembling, as if afraid someone would whip it away.

"That is one hungry pussycat," Mimes remarked.

"Yeah."

"I'm more of a dog person myself."

"Right."

Mimes had been assigned to me for the night. Newirth had said that I shouldn't be alone, but I think he was more afraid I'd run away again. I was still, from his point of view, a possible accessory after the fact. He wanted to keep a close eye on me. I didn't mind; it was better than spending the night at the station, and Mimes was another of the good guys. He'd been a Green Ridge police officer for over twenty years, never progressing beyond his current rank, and more than satisfied with that arrangement.

"I'll just park my old butt here," he said, choosing a seat by the window. "You should get some sleep."

I nodded. The clock on the stove showed 2:12, which meant I'd been awake for almost twenty-two hours—ever since Sally had woken me to restore my memories. I was halfway between exhausted and dead, given some semblance of life by all the emotion barreling through me.

Sleep wouldn't come easy, though. I found a box of Advil, downed three with a palmful of tap water, then hit the shower. I crouched beneath the spray until the back of my neck was raw, using the time to bemoan my fate. I must have bemoaned for a long time, because Officer Mimes rapped on the door and asked if I was okay, which was another way of asking if I'd used a razor blade to open my wrists. I assured him I was still alive, and a few minutes later crawled into bed with a towel wrapped around my waist. I thought I'd stare into the darkness for hours, but exhaustion won out. I slept until dawn, not deeply, but enough to smooth away the edges.

Officer Mimes had vacated the chair by the window and was sleeping—boots off—on the sofa with Michael Jackson curled up on his belly. They both purred contentedly, so I didn't disturb them. I left the apartment, bought coffee and bagels from the deli on Trenton Avenue, and took a stroll through Green River Park. It had been a long time since I'd been able to walk through my hometown without feeling the threat of the hunt dogs. I didn't plan on sticking around, so took a moment to savor it.

The smell of coffee roused my guests (Dad was a big coffee drinker, and I wondered if, for one heartbreaking second, Michael thought he was home again). Mimes sat up quickly, scratching behind one ear with a surprised expression on his face.

"Must've closed my eyes for five minutes," he said, looking around for his boots.

"Must've," I agreed, handing him his coffee and bagel. He nodded sheepishly. I went into the kitchen and fixed breakfast for Michael: water and Friskies, which he consumed more patiently than the night before. Then I grabbed my guitar and played a few tunes while they ate.

I spent most of that day at the station. I was questioned by Sharpe and Lambert before giving my statement to Officer Adams. There followed an agonizing wait, during which my thoughts went everywhere and nowhere was good. I sat on a hard chair in a small interview room. There was no clock on the wall but I felt every second.

Finally, the door opened and Chief Newirth walked in, as drawn and somber as I'd ever seen him. He carried no file, no handcuffs, only a steaming mug of coffee, which I took as a positive sign. He sat opposite me, slurped from the mug—spilling some on the table, further evidence of his tiredness—and said:

"I'll begin with an apology."

"Okay," I said. My jaw trembled and my voice cracked; I knew where this was going.

"I didn't believe you," the chief said, "and I'm sorry."

"Okay."

"Swan Connor's vehicle—the red Cadillac CTS—was sold shortly after he suffered his stroke. We tracked it down, and although it had been fully detailed, forensics lifted blood residues from the trunk, as well as a human hair that is confirmed to have belonged to Grace Potts."

"Jesus Christ," I said. Hearing it from an officer of the law gave it a haunting weight, a *realness*. It conflicted with the relief flooding from me. I lowered my head and imagined Dad smiling down at me.

"You mentioned last night how police withhold certain information from the public," Newirth continued, and I turned my bleary eyes back to him. "In this case, we withheld that the killer cut a square section of material from his victims' clothing. Searching Swan's house today, we found those swatches hidden behind the gold discs Swan was awarded for"—he took his notepad from his pocket and read from it—"*San Francisco Morning, Breathe with Me,* and *Get Down with the Groove.* We think the square symbolizes a record sleeve or album cover."

"Makes sense," I said, and then shuddered. "No, it doesn't. It makes no sense at all. It's crazy shit. Did you check the Grammys?"

"Blood is incredibly difficult to remove," Newirth said. He took another slurp of coffee, spilled it again, down his shirt this time. "So is coffee. Shit." He wiped it with his fingers, then shrugged. "Luminol revealed blood traces on all three Grammy awards. We're still running tests, but there appear to be multiple blood types—as in *more* than three. We think Swan has been murdering women for a very long time."

"That sick son of a bitch," I said.

"We'll take this as far as we can."

"Maybe you should look into that rape from '74, too," I said. "Some bullshit got him acquitted."

"I think all of Swan's evils will be revealed." Newirth shook his head, blinked his red-rimmed eyes. "I probably shouldn't say this, but Sally was right: That stroke was such perfect justice."

I didn't know what to say to that, so I said nothing at all.

"Although it *does* mean he'll avoid prison and spend the remainder of his days in a high-security hospital," Newirth said. "He'll have his food cut up and his ass wiped for him. There's nothing we can do about that. Even so, we'd like Sally to provide a statement. I know she's . . . wayward, but if she gets in touch when this goes public, you can assure her she doesn't have to be afraid anymore."

I thought that, wherever Sally was, she was more afraid than she'd ever been.

"I won't hold my breath. Sally is clearly on the run, and in deep with some bad people." The chief leaned across the table and whispered, "Man to man, I think you should take a step back from that relationship. You've been beaten up twice. *Badly*. Next time, you might not be so lucky."

"I know that," I said.

Newirth nodded before continuing, "A press statement is being prepared, in which your father is cleared from any and all involvement. He made a false confession in the midst of a suicidal depression, and the press will be made aware of that. I'll personally make sure he gets the respect he deserves."

"Thank you," I said. "And thank you for listening to me. I know you didn't believe me, but you listened, and I appreciate it."

"We follow all leads, Harvey. That's the job."

"And you're good at it," I said honestly. "Always have been. Although you might want to put some eye drops in before you go on TV. And change your shirt. You look like hell."

He smiled, which brought a smile to my face, too. I reached across the table and he slapped his palm into mine. We shook. His grip was strong and assuring, despite his tiredness.

"Am I free to go?" I asked.

"Absolutely," he said, grabbing his mug again and taking another slurp. "Go home. Rest. You've got a lot of healing to do."

I nodded. Rest sounded good, but the healing would have to wait. I got to my feet and started toward the door.

"Harvey?"

I stopped, turned slowly. I knew what he was going to ask me.

"The shovel, right?"

"Right," he said.

I scratched my head. My lips twitched. I knew exactly what I'd done with the shovel but couldn't tell him. Not ever. I didn't want to lie to him, either, but opted for the theory that false closure was better than *no* closure.

Newirth sensed my hesitation, cocked an eyebrow. "Well?"

"It doesn't matter anymore." I shrugged.

"What doesn't matter?"

"My reasons." The sadness in my smile was genuine—the only thing about me in that moment that was. "I never forgot, man. That was a lie. I bought that shovel to help Dad lay the last layer of sod on top of the bunker. I swore I'd never tell anyone about its existence. I knew it was just his usual crazy, but I've always tried to keep my promises."

It was a slick lie. A plausible lie. It had dropped into my head so effortlessly that I could almost believe it had been sent by Dad. Horseshit from beyond the grave. A little thank-you, perhaps, for clearing his name.

Newirth nodded. "Right, and if I were to go looking for that shovel I'd find it . . . where? Your dad's garage? His shed?"

"I guess. Yeah. Probably." I shrugged again, knowing the chief had better things to do than go hunting Dad's property for a shovel that really didn't matter anyway. "Good luck finding it, though. If you think Dad's house is a shitshow, just wait until you see his shed."

Newirth ran one hand down the side of his face, where a day's worth of grime and stubble had bloomed. He shrugged, then nodded. It was as weary and resigned a gesture as I'd ever seen.

"Okay, Harvey," he said. "Okay."

"So you're not going to arrest me for keeping a promise?" I tried another smile, but it was a timid effort. "I hear it carries the death sentence in some states."

"Go home."

"And the question mark?" I pointed to a spot above my head.

After a moment's consideration, Newirth replied, "Given what you've told me, and with everything that has happened, I think that question mark will always be there."

The crazy thing: I agreed with him.

. . .

Something Sally had said—that she'd taken from Lang's notes—suggested it could take weeks, even months for the antipsychotic drugs to suppress her coil, thereby weakening her enough for Lang to get into her mind. I wasn't going to wait that long. Besides, I had another reason—a *burning* reason—to catch the next flight to Tennessee.

Kill the fucker.

It was all I could do to keep from going directly from the station to the airport, but there were a few things I needed to take care of. Top of the list: sleep; I had reached near-hallucinatory levels of exhaustion and would be good for nothing if I didn't launch my head into a pillow. I stumbled the half mile home, my hands driven deep into my pockets and my face stiffening in the chill evening breeze. My landlord was on the entranceway steps with his guido blowout shimmering. He tried engaging me in conversation—something about getting the Cadillac logo tattooed across his chest. I nodded politely a few times, then went up to my apartment to find that Michael Jackson had shit all over the kitchen floor. I cleaned it up, fixed him dinner while he curled around my ankles, then collapsed on the sofa. I woke up at midnight with cricks in my neck and back, as if I'd been lifted by gigantic hands and twisted. I dry-swallowed Advil and staggered into the bedroom. The last thing I remember is thinking that my pillowcase smelled like it could use a wash, and that I'd get on that if I made it back from—

And then sleep. Deep. Dreamless.

Swan Connor was coast-to-coast news the following morning. There was no mention of Dad; he'd been muscled from the story entirely, and that was fine by me. I semi-celebrated with some lazy-ass yoga and a bowlful of quinoa flakes two weeks past their sell-by date. Almost like old times.

Next on the list: Find Michael a new home. I could have dropped him at the animal shelter with his celebrity brothers and sisters, but I had somewhere else in mind.

"Isn't he adorable?" Marzipan said, tickling beneath his chin. Then she screwed one eye shut and tilted her head—an allergy, I wondered, but no: her tic. She made the zipping motion across her lips, fighting it, losing it: "Shit and fuck. Scumbag. Fuckity."

"He belonged to Dad," I said.

"Oh," she said, and touched my forearm gently. A perfect gesture of kindness and sympathy. Then she tickled the cat again. "Does he have a name?"

"Michael Jackson."

"Like the singer?"

"He *is* the singer," I said. "Dad believed that when Michael Jackson died, his troubled spirit soared the breadth of the country and landed in the body of this cat."

"Amazing."

"I know, huh?"

"Can he moonwalk?" Marzipan asked seriously, and I could have hugged her.

"Only when you're not looking," I replied, and it was my turn to touch her arm. "Will you look after him for a few days? Maybe longer? I have to . . . do something, and I guess there's a possibility I won't be back. Michael was real important to Dad, and I can't think of anybody I'd rather have take care of him."

Marzipan held out her arms and I handed Michael to her. He rolled his head against her chest, getting snug, the way cats do. His purr was engine-loud.

Marzipan beamed. "I think he likes me."

"I think so, too."

She hugged him, kissed his face. "This could be the beginning of my crazy-cat-lady phase."

And I said, "I hope so."

Next on the list: Starbright Medical Imaging.

Sally sent out a signal whenever she let the red bird fly, but that wasn't how the hunt dogs found us in Cypress. They were there too quickly,

which meant they were tracking us—tracking *me*. I'd been unconscious in that cinderblock room for I don't know how long, and that
was when they'd done it: a tiny implant near my shoulder or thigh,
somewhere I wouldn't feel it. Then they let me go and I'd led them to
Sally, dumb idiot that I was.

I told the tech what I expected her to find, but that I didn't know
where she'd find it.

"Go whole body," I said. "Run me through the big machine. I don't
care how much it costs."

"How about we start right here?" the tech said, indicating the scar
on my left cheek. "It's a fairly recent wound by the looks of it. Heck, if
I were a tracking device, that's where *I'd* be hiding."

I started to refute that. It was too conspicuous. *Too in-your-face*, was
what I was going to say, but was stopped by the unintended aptness of
it, then by the tech's eyes, which were blue and deep and far smarter
than mine. So I shrugged and told her to have at it. Minutes later, she
held an X-ray image of my skull up to a light box, and sure enough, an
inch below my left eye socket, was a piece of hardware no bigger than
my pinky nail.

"Those sons of bitches," I said, running my fingertips across the scar
and feeling the solid little lump beneath—what I'd always thought was
a knot of damaged tissue. "They really did it."

"It's thin, too," the tech said. "Thin as a dime. Could be some kind
of micro GPS tracker. I wouldn't even say it's hi-tech; it's likely being
tracked by a cell phone."

"Sons of *bitches*," I said again, and recalled Jackhammer's warning:
We can get to you anytime, anywhere. Of course they could; they'd slot-
ted the device into my open wound while I was out cold. It was too
easy, and—for all my precautionary measures—I was too stupid to even
consider it.

"At least you know where it is now," the tech said.

"Right," I said. "And I need to get it out of there."

"Yes, well . . ." The tech shrugged, her expression caught between
regret and amusement. "There's only one way for it to come out, and
that's the same way it went in."

. . .

The smart thing was to have the implant surgically removed, but I didn't have time for that and didn't want to answer a bunch of awkward questions from medical staff. The alternative was to take care of it myself. A fairly simple procedure, I thought; it was just beneath the skin, after all.

I arranged my makeshift surgical apparatus on the edge of the bathroom sink, everything placed on a clean cotton napkin. Two ice cubes (a spare, in case I dropped one). A sterilized razor blade. A sterilized pair of tweezers. Antiseptic swabs. A tube of superglue. I took several steadying breaths, wheezing through my busted nose, then looked at myself in the mirror.

Ready.

Using my left hand, I pressed one of the ice cubes against my cheekbone until it had half melted and I could no longer feel the cold. It slipped from my fingers and clattered into the sink. With my right hand—still dry and warm—I picked up the razor blade and ran one edge along the scar, following its curve. I did it quickly and didn't feel a thing, but blood flowed from the incision, obscuring visibility. I used a swab to wipe it away, then separated the wound. More blood pooled, dripping down my face, onto my chest. I swabbed deeply and felt the implant move. Then I saw it—one slick edge. I tried plucking it free with my fingers but it was too slippery and I only lodged it deeper. I winced; my skin was still numb but the subcutaneous tissue was not and a thumbtack of pain caused my eye to water. I blinked, wiped more blood away, grabbed the tweezers with a trembling hand. Gritting my teeth, I peeled the incision wider and poked the tweezers inside. I worked by feel more than sight (there was too much blood and now both eyes were watering), digging around with the prongs until they tapped against something solid. The pain expanded to my lower legs, making them quiver and sweat. It was impossible to ignore but I didn't buckle, I didn't quit; I tweezed the tracking device and pulled. There was some resistance where my tissue had fused to it—a wet sound as it dislodged—but I yanked it free with a triumphant cry.

My head howled and pounded. Blood streaked my face and chest. I dropped the tweezers and the tracking device, grabbed the antiseptic swabs and pressed them to the wound. More pain, but I wasn't done yet. I pinched the incision and ran a bead of superglue across it. The fumes stung my left eye but that was the least of my concerns. I counted to sixty, then trickled another line of glue across the wound.

I didn't move again until the pain had faded.

The implant was on the bathroom floor, smeared with blood. I picked it up and placed it on the toilet seat. A tiny chip—yes, it really was as thin as a dime—responsible for so much hurt and damage. I was tempted to destroy it, but didn't want the hunt dogs to know I'd discovered it. Let them think I was huddled in my apartment, playing guitar and jerking off.

I lifted my gaze to the mirror. With my busted-up face, and with this new battle scar, I barely recognized myself. I recalled Dad saying—after he'd sheared my dreads—that I looked like I could win a fight, but right then I looked more like I'd fought a war.

I touched my new wound and sneered. It was ugly and tender, but I didn't care in the least; the tracking device had been removed. I was sure Dominic Lang—having found what he desired—was no longer interested in me, but now I was truly off his radar.

The son of a bitch wouldn't see me coming.

After cleaning up, I called Skylands Funeral Home and told them I was out of town for a few days, but that I'd begin arrangements for my father's service as soon as I returned. I added that Dad had reserved a plot at Rose Hill next to Mom, wanting them to know this just in case I didn't return.

With this taken care of, there was only one thing left on the list. But first I had to wait until nightfall.

Then I needed a shovel.

I took a cab to Newark Liberty the following morning. I'd packed only a few clothes, figuring this would be over—one way or another—within forty-eight hours. I didn't pack the .38 Special, either; I planned on securing more powerful weaponry in Tennessee, not necessarily of the aim-and-shoot variety.

My success incriminating Swan hadn't healed me; the same emotions continued to push and pry. I sat in departures switching between the photograph of my father and the red feather, focusing on what each meant to me: love and family, justness and determination. I was faced with a do-or-die task, but I wasn't backing down.

It didn't have to be a suicide mission, though. I had the element of surprise in my favor, and while Lang had too much influence—and I none—for the authorities to be any use to me, that didn't mean I had to fight alone. Jesus, I wasn't *capable* of fighting alone. I may have looked like a warrior with my new haircut, scars, and bruises, but the only weapon I brandished with any confidence had six strings.

I needed help. No doubt about it. My own little army.

And I thought I knew where to get it.

Twenty-Four

Tinsel, Tennessee, was a dismal patch of not much on the western edge of the state. Population 650, it was bordered to the north by redolent swampland and to the south by a landfill as large as the town again. Its main through road—the erroneously named Colorful Boulevard—was dotted with empty stores with FOR LEASE and EVERY-THING MUST GO signs posted in the windows. It was difficult to imagine a time it had ever flourished.

Employment came by way of a waste management facility and a sheet metal company. I had a feeling the town would give up the ghost if either of these businesses folded, like a diseased body with some vital organ removed. There were several nicer homes, but most were minimal style with faded siding and junked lots. I estimated that half the population lived in Outer Town (the sign adjusted to read Out*house* Town), a cluttered trailer park that boasted its own fundamentalist church and shooting range, and was bordered to the west by the Mississippi River.

No public transport. No hotels or other accommodations, which was fine because I didn't plan on staying the night. I took a bus from Memphis to Dyersburg, and a cab from there into Tinsel. I was dropped on Colorful Boulevard and walked three blocks before finding what I was looking for: a dusty bar with neon in the windows and live music Fridays and Saturdays.

I went inside and asked if they knew Elvis.

Five words: *Mom took care of them.* Five words that had drummed through my mind loudly and often since the hunt dogs took Sally, and that formed the basis for my plan of attack. *Mom took care of them.* Five words, five syllables, one simple sentence upon which everything hinged, and while it wasn't up there with *Kill the fucker* in terms of mantra, it ran a respectable second.

We packed our bags and laid low at a hotel just outside Memphis, Sally had told me. *But Lang found us within a few days and sent his muscle. Mom took care of them—made them turn their guns on each other—but it was a close call.*

I walked from the dusty bar to the trailer park on the west side of town. It was a pleasant day—clear skies, mid-seventies—but not a pleasant walk. I wore sunglasses to disguise my bruised eyes but still earned uncomfortable stares from the locals. One of them called me a "tall-drink-of-motherfuck" and spat between his boots. I was glad I no longer had dreadlocks; I may have been burned at the stake.

It wasn't long before I smelled char and sourness, and saw a riot of aluminum flashing in the afternoon sunlight. I took a cracked path between stunted tupelos and came fifty yards later to the park. There was a dead armadillo at the foot of the OUTHOUSE TOWN sign, rocking on its carapace in the breeze. I skirted two grimy toddlers hitting each other with sticks and headed toward the park's office, only to find it closed. No sign of when it would open, so I carried on walking, following dirt roads fringed with trash. I heard country music, a child crying, dogs howling. A pickup with mismatched doors and a plastic Hulk toy strapped to the grill passed me at a crawl, its driver eyeing me from beneath the peak of his baseball cap. A few minutes later, I stopped outside a trailer where a middle-aged woman with one arm curled a twenty-five-pound kettlebell. An older man sat in a lawn chair beside her, feeding live mealworms to an albino rat perched on his shoulder.

"Whachoo want?" he drawled.

"I'm looking for someone," I said.

I was there because of something else Sally had said, and which also drummed through my mind. When I'd asked if her parents were still alive, she'd replied, *Last I heard, Mom had shacked up with an Elvis impersonator in Tinsel, Tennessee. I don't know where Dad is.* A gin-soaked regular in the dusty downtown bar told me—in exchange for a drink—that the only Elvis impersonator he knew of lived in Outer Town. He wasn't sure where, exactly, so I'd have to ask around.

"Elvis?" the woman snapped, grunting as she curled the weight. The vein in her bicep bulged. "You mean Lou Shipp? That ol' cock basket?"

"Maybe," I said. "Does he live with a woman named Tatum?"

"Miss Patches, we call her. And she ain't no woman."

"Where can I find them?" I asked. I removed a twenty from my wallet and let it ripple in the breeze. "It's important."

Moments later, I stood outside a trailer as stained and dull as an unwashed kitchen sink. Its torn awning flapped in the breeze and a faded US flag covered one window. I wrinkled my nose as I approached the front door; the smell of trash and old cigarettes was nauseating.

I knocked twice, loudly, to be heard over the TV, and looked down at a sign almost buried in the weeds.

I had to smile. It read WELCOME TO GRACELAND.

Lou answered the door, almost knocking me off the orange crate that doubled as a step. He was a big unit. Bigger than the real Elvis, even at the end. The top half of a heart-surgery scar poked from the neck of his grubby white vest.

"Lou Shipp?" I asked, and thought, *You ol' cock basket.*

"Who wants to know?"

"My name is Harvey Anderson." I held out my hand. He didn't take it. "I need to speak with Tatum. I have some news for her."

Silence from inside the trailer as the TV's volume was cut. The rest of the park seemed amplified. I heard three kinds of music, gun shots from the nearby range, the *tap-tap* of a crow knocking a snail against a broken garden ornament. Then Lou was gone, pulled out of the door-way by the woman behind him. She was in shadow to begin with— I caught the flash of her teeth and a gold necklace—then she emerged into the light and I saw the damage. If I hadn't been so used to Dad's disfigurement, I may have blanched. As it was, I didn't even blink.

"I need your help," I said.

I detected a frown amid her many scars, and—deeper still—saw Sally in her eyes.

"This can only be bad news," she said.

It wasn't as trashy inside as I'd anticipated, although it had its share of clichés: empty Busch cans lined up on the kitchenette countertop; *Judge Judy* playing on TV; a leopard-print rug on the living room floor. These were offset by several surprises: a Thomas Pynchon novel on the coffee table, for starters, and two abstract paintings I recognized, but couldn't put a name to, on the walls.

Tatum told Lou to take a hike, which he did, slipping into his shit-kickers and exiting without a word. The door slammed behind him. Tatum turned off the TV and sat opposite me, feet on the coffee table.

"Elvis has left the building," she said. "That big rack of shit ain't much to look at, but he can sing like a bird."

I had removed my sunglasses so that I could see inside the gloomy space, and noticed now, as she grabbed her smokes and struck a light to one, that the pinky and ring fingers of her right hand were missing.

"I'm something pretty myself, huh?" she said, exhaling a band of smoke into the air between us.

"I know you're angry." I tapped my chest, where my own anger rumbled and shook. "That might be a good thing. A *usable* thing."

"I'm too tired to be angry, hon."

"Too tired to fight?"

I told her everything, beginning with how I'd met Sally (occasion-ally remembering to call her Miranda), and ending with my decision to come to Tennessee. This was the first time I'd divulged the full story without having to adjust truths, and every word—floating in the open like Tatum's cigarette smoke—felt less crazy than it had in my head.

It took a while. At least an hour. Tatum listened intently, occasionally wiping saliva from her chin with a washcloth she'd secreted up her sleeve. I tried reading her expressions, but there was too much smoke, too many scars. I heard her, though: a whimper, a sigh, always in the right place. At one point she sobbed and lifted the washcloth to her eyes. Sally had suggested that her parents only cared about themselves. I wondered if time had altered her heart.

"That poor girl couldn't run forever," she said when I'd finished, touching a light to yet another cigarette. "We were crazy to think she could."

"There was only ever one solution." I leaned forward in my seat, inhaling a chestful of secondhand smoke. "Putting an end to Lang."

"Easier to run." Tatum tapped ash into a chipped coffee mug.

"Easy isn't always best."

"You've got a lot of spunk, sweetie, but your head's in the clouds." She fanned at the smoke and loomed toward me. "This is what happens when you mess with Dominic Lang."

She'd been pretty once, I could tell. Her hair was lined with gray, but it still had bounce, and her hazel eyes were kindly shaped. Her face, though, was a diagram of torture, cut into irregular sections, as if removed from her skull one piece at a time, then stitched back into place. There were circular scars on her throat. Cigarette burns, I assumed. Her lower lip was gone—sawed away like a strip of fat.

Miss Patches, we call her. And she ain't no woman.

"I'm a goddamn monster," she said.

"All the more reason to stop him."

She said nothing for a moment, sucking her cigarette down to the butt, smearing spit from her chin. I looked around the trailer. Four small rooms divided by plywood walls. I could see into the bedroom, festooned with dirty laundry. One of Lou's jumpsuits hung from the back of the door, its myriad sequins shimmering. A draft made the flag in the window ripple.

"We were shitty parents, but we loved that girl," Tatum said, breaking the silence. She leaked smoke like a broken machine. "I swear, putting her on that bus—knowing we'd never see her again—was the worst heartbreak. A kind of dying."

"Really?" I couldn't keep the edge of disbelief from my voice.

"You doubting me?"

"You deserted her."

"We did what we had to—what we thought would keep Miranda safe. Shit, we *wanted* to go with her, protect her, but the truth is we'd only have slowed her down. Realizing this was perhaps our one shining moment as parents."

"Yeah, well, Miranda didn't see it that way," I said. "She felt scared. Betrayed."

"She got tough in a hurry and learned to survive. At least until you decided to play superhero."

"I wanted to help her," I said.

"Give that man a cigar." Tatum could sneer just fine with one lip. "It comes down to this, Captain Clusterfuck: Miranda removed herself from your mind to keep you from following her—to keep you both safe. We removed ourselves from her heart to keep *her* safe. If she believed for one second that we cared about her, she would've come home, and Lang would've been waiting. I say again: We did what we had to. It was a heartbreaker, but we did it."

"You introduced her to Lang in the first place," I countered. "Trying to make a quick buck, right? You let him abscond with her for days at a time, and the things he made her do . . . I don't know how it didn't break her."

"We were living in a car," Tatum growled, pointing one of the existing fingers of her right hand at me. "I was whoring myself out. We were desperate. Some parents send their kiddies off to Hollywood, or dress them up as little dolls and have them parade around a stage. We didn't see this as being much different, and as soon as we found out what was going on, we put a stop to it."

I inhaled deeply. In the fresh air it would have pacified me, but the smoke and trash smell only made me feel worse. Still, I nodded and held up both hands in surrender. Nothing she could say, no excuses, could explain her actions, but I needed her help, her power. Pissing her off wasn't a good idea.

"I took these scars for her," she said a moment later. Her voice was softer, but still laced with emotion. "We tried running. Steve went north. I went south. They found me quickly—tranq-darted me from behind. I woke up in a small room, strapped into a chair, a plastic sheet on the floor."

I flashed back to my own room of pain—Disneyland, compared to what Tatum had been through.

"Lang ransacked my mind, then turned me over to his goons." She sobbed again. Her pain was as thick as the smoke. "I knew they wouldn't kill me. As long as I'm alive, I'm a link to her. Same reason they didn't kill you. But I took these scars, and I got some more you'll never see, so don't you suggest—not for one goddamn second—that I don't love my little girl."

I lowered my eyes.

"Doing nothing is hard, honey, but sometimes it's the best thing."

"We don't have that option anymore."

She got up, opened the door to let some of the smoke escape, then poured us both a shot of cheap bourbon. I wasn't sure it would help with my nausea, but I took it just the same.

"To mutual pain," she offered.

We touched glasses. I sipped. Tatum knocked hers back in one, then slid her empty across the coffee table. It clinked against the mug she'd been using as an ashtray. She ran the washcloth across her wet chin. Had to wipe her eyes again, too.

"Sorry about your daddy," she said. "That's tough, sweetie."

"Yeah, it's . . ." I drummed a fist against my chest, as if this would convey everything—the complicated tangle of emotions. "He was on a different level of crazy, but his heart was gold and I'm going to miss him like hell."

"Were you close?"

"Not especially. We could have been, if I'd tried harder. I always felt we had nothing in common, that I was more like my mom. Make love not war, you know? It's taken all this for me to realize that I'm very much my father's son."

"And your mom . . . she still alive?"

"She died when I was sixteen," I replied. "The worst pain I've ever felt. They say time heals but that's not true. Time dulls, it softens, but it doesn't heal. I feel as much grief today as I did ten years ago."

"Cancer?"

I nodded.

"These?" Tatum tapped her packet of cigarettes.

"No. Mom may have tried pot in college, but that was about it. She was a health-food advocate and clean-living vegetarian. So put it down to shit luck. Or fate, if you prefer. And hey, there's nothing you can do about that."

"Nothing at all," Tatum agreed.

"I guess that's why I'm in this situation." I lifted my arms, indicating the shit-storm my life had become. "I couldn't do anything for Mom. Her pain—and mine—was out of my hands. But I *could* do something for Sally. I didn't have to sit there feeling helpless."

A diesel engine clattered to life outside. A dog howled nearby, followed by a man's high-pitched remonstration: *"Getchoo, you ol' sumbuck!"* The engine grew louder for a second, then faded into the distance. I heard those popping sounds from the range once again.

Tatum sniveled. She wiped her chin. Her eyes.

"They're going to kill her," I said with no inflection in my voice: a matter-of-fact statement. "Lang is going to weaken her coil, then crawl into her mind. He'll be like a thief in a museum with the security system shut down. He can help himself to whatever he wants, and destroy whatever he doesn't. Then he'll hand her over to the hunt dogs, and they'll do to her body what Lang did to her mind."

"I know that," Tatum said.

"I wouldn't be here if I could do this on my own, or if there was any other way."

"I know that, too."

"Will you help me?"

She sighed, then shook another smoke from the packet. When she popped the Zippo, I saw how badly her hand was shaking.

"Look at me: living in this goddamn stinkhole with a man who doesn't much love me, who rarely fucks me, and when he does he calls me Priscilla." She barked a chesty, mirthless laugh. "Miranda is just about the only good thing I've done in life, and that was by accident. So yeah, I'll help. You know goddamn well I will. But it's suicide, hon. Plain and simple. We may as well head over to the range and offer ourselves up for target practice."

"It's a mountain to climb," I said, finishing the bourbon, burning inside in more ways than one. "But without you it's impossible. You're my only hope. And Steve-O, too, if you know where he is."

She laughed again. Louder, but equally humorless. Her upper lip flashed another sneer.

"You got twenty bucks on you?"

"Yeah," I replied. "What for?"

"Gas money," she said, wiping spit from her chin. "Come on, sweetie. We're going for a drive."

The sun had dropped into the west, burning through cobwebby cloud, and there was an edge to the breeze. I followed Sally's mother through a maze of trailers, stepping around junk, ducking beneath washing lines and the cables from satellite dishes affixed to trees. "*Miss Patches!*" some dirt-faced kid yelled, and threw an empty Pepsi can at her. He howled like one of the many raggedy dogs we saw tethered to posts, then ran away, managing maybe a dozen steps before veering inexplicably left and bouncing headfirst off the window of a burnt-out cargo van. I looked at Tatum. She looked back at me and smiled.

Mom took care of them, I thought.

We came soon after to a fenced-in parking lot with some of the spaces taken up by broken appliances. Tatum's—or rather Lou's—vehicle was easy to spot: an old Chevy Malibu, hand-sprayed pink. A bumper sticker read: WHO DIED AND MADE YOU ELVIS?

"It's an hour's drive," Tatum said. "If you're hungry, there's a Mickey D's across the road from the gas station."

"I'll be fine," I said.

"Good for you, but I'm hungry enough to eat the balls off a low-flying duck. I'll take a Big 'n' Tasty with cheese. Go large with the fries."

"No problem," I said, thinking that an hour in a car with the smell of cigarettes and McDonald's might be the longest hour of my life. "The window rolls down, right?"

"Sometimes," she said. "Get in."

"Where are we going?"

"Where do you think?" Tatum popped a smoke and climbed behind the wheel. "We're going to meet the bonesnapper."

Twenty-Five

We drove northeast toward Union City, then cut straight east through Martin and on to the town of Glowing, which was anything but. Tatum chomped her burger and fries and played one of Lou's tribute CDs. It was awful. If there'd been a way to travel outside the car—strapped to the roof, perhaps, like a kayak—I'd have taken it.

There was little conversation because of the music and the rush of air through the open window. During the few quieter moments, Tatum told me more about herself. She was orphaned at three; her entire family—both parents, her grandmother, five brothers and sisters—were killed in a house fire, and she went to live on a farm where her "new daddy" made her feed the chickens and collect the eggs, which was fine, but also parade naked for him on occasion, which was definitely *not* fine. Tatum realized she had a special gift when, at eight years old, she made this sorry excuse for a human being place both his arms in the wood chipper. "It's like this," she said, taking her hands off the wheel to light a cigarette. There was a bend in the road and I instinctively reached across and steered us through it. "You got it, sweetie," she said, blowing smoke over the scar tissue where her lower lip used to be. "You're not driving, exactly, you just *steer* for a second or two. And

I steered that ol' cocksucker's arms directly into the chipper." She nodded, took the wheel again. "We had pigs used to scream when they were taken off to slaughter. They knew what was coming and rightly opposed. Sometimes the farmhands had to break their legs and drag them on the truck. And that's what he sounded like in the last minutes of his life: a broke-leg pig."

Tatum explained that she felt different, *not* powerful. "Alone," was another adjective she used. She moved from the farm to a new family, kinder in all ways, although they never treated her as their own. At school she was an outcast, behind in her studies, relentlessly bullied. By thirteen she was dependent on antidepressants, and then it was cocaine.

"It's a constant battle," she said, "between wanting to express your power, and wanting to hide it. The coke numbed both sides. It allowed me to walk down the middle, but for all those years I was walking dead. I got pregnant at nineteen—gave birth to a boy as still as stone. That was when I decided to turn my life around, but first I needed to make some peace with this thing inside me."

After writing the parapsychology departments of several universities, Tatum was put in touch with Dominic Lang. He ran his tests and told her about the psychic coil. "He made me feel kind of special," she said. "Something I'd never really felt before." A few years later, Lang invited her to the Coil In Harmony support group, where she met a certain bio-PK by the name of Steven Farrow.

"I know the rest," I told her.

This conversation used up seventeen of the sixty-three minutes we were on the road. The rest of the time I had my head out the window, entranced by the rush of air over my skull. We finally stopped a mile outside Glowing, beneath a neon sign that flashed POOL BEER MUSIC, with an arrow pointing at a single-story building with mesh across the windows and a sign at the door requesting that firearms remain holstered at all times. The several exclamation marks suggested this was a zero-tolerance policy.

Inside, it was grim and beer-smelling, a chain of old TVs showing blood sports, Waylon Jennings drifting from speakers I couldn't see.

There was a darkened wooden stage with a Tennessee flag backdrop and a bed of red-felted pool tables at the far end of the room. Tatum walked toward the bar with her boot heels clicking—a little extra sway to her hips, I thought. If she was at all self-conscious about her appearance, she didn't show it.

"Tate!" the bartender exclaimed. He was a strip-thin man with flamboyant red sideburns. It looked like someone had set fire to his cheeks. "Christ alive, how you doin'?"

"Fair," Tatum said. "Is he here?"

"He's always here." The bartender gestured toward the pool tables.

Tatum nodded, kept walking. She said to me, just above a whisper, "That's Rusty—Steve's half brother. He sued an insurance company after he got stuck in their elevator. Claimed psychological damages, even though there wasn't a whole lot to damage in the first place. Anyway, he got a chunk of change and bought this shithole outright. Steve lives here rent-free. I think he does a little work around the place, but not much."

"Lucky Steve," I said.

"You're about to see how lucky he is."

Three of the six tables were in use. We weaved toward one where a middle-aged man in a wheelchair hoisted himself onto the rail and shot a striped ball into a corner pocket. "*Hoolah!*" he shouted. He had bull-thick, tattooed arms and no legs. His jeans had been cut off at the knees, tied into knots. He scooted to where the cue ball settled and lined up his next shot.

"You're supposed to have at least one foot on the floor when shooting," Tatum said, and the guys around the table jeered, except for Steve-O, who looked up from the tip of his pool cue with narrowed eyes and teeth showing.

"Potato," he said. "Your jokes are about as funny as your face."

"We need to talk," she said. "But finish your game first."

He sneered, went to take his shot, but at the last second adjusted his cue by a few crucial degrees and straight pocketed the eight-ball. The guys jeered again, but Steve-O only looked at Tatum with one eyebrow lofted.

"Thanks for that," he said.

"Game over, hotshot," Tatum said. "Let's go."

She found a quiet table and I joined her. Steve-O dropped from the rail into his chair and wheeled along behind. He pulled up beside Tatum but swiveled to face me. His gaze felt as blunt as an elbow.

"Who do we have here?"

"This is Harvey," Tatum said. "Miranda's boyfriend."

"Oh," Steve-O said, and then, when it sunk in, "That ain't good."

"Lang found her." Tatum's voice was dry enough to kindle in the sun.

The muscles in Steve-O's forearms tightened and the cords in his neck showed. With her humorless laugh, Tatum had intimated that Steve-O wouldn't be able to help, perhaps because of his disability, but from what I saw in that moment, there was nothing wrong with his heart.

"We're going to get her back," I said. "And we're going to put an end to Dominic Lang while we're at it."

"Well, hallelujah," Steve-O said, and the light in his eyes was borderline crazy. "Where do I sign up?"

The music changed from Waylon to a string of Johnny Cash favorites and the bar steadily became rowdier. Steve-O shouted salutations on a semi-regular basis, proving that having no legs hadn't hindered his popularity. Mostly, he gripped the armrests of his wheelchair and seethed.

"So what's the plan?" he asked me.

"First off," I said, pointing to the bottle of Budweiser sitting on the table in front of him. "Go easy on the booze." I flicked my finger toward Tatum. "You, too. You need to be focused, ready for anything, which means not drowning your coils in alcohol."

"When are we doing this?" Tatum asked.

"As soon as we can," I said. "Hopefully tomorrow."

"Suits me," Steve-O said, his lip curled. "Rusty's got some hardware behind the bar. We'll load up and go get her."

"Take guns, take weapons, whatever," I said. "But don't use them unless you have to. Be smart about it. Gunshots bring cops. Bullets can be traced. You have more effective weapons in your minds."

"I wouldn't go that far," Tatum said. She took a swig from her bottle, wiped the drizzles from her chin. "I don't know what you expect of me, honey, but I'm no superhero. A few blasts from the coil"—she brought the bottle to her forehead and tapped twice—"and I'm likely to piss my britches and pop a nosebleed. Maybe pass out, too."

"Same here," Steve-O said.

"Which is exactly why you need to stay sharp," I said. "Listen, we have two objectives: rescue Sally—"

"Who the hell's Sally?"

"Miranda. Jesus. Rescue *Miranda*, and get Lang. We do whatever it takes. I'd just prefer we don't get arrested or killed."

"That don't faze me," Steve-O said, and that crazy light was in his eyes again. "I've spent too long thinking of ways I can destroy that son of a whore—everything from slow torture to taking him out with a scoped rifle. I might've done it, too, if his goddamn gorillas weren't watching my every move."

"They're not watching anymore," I said.

"He took my legs away." Steve-O flapped the knotted bottoms of his jeans. "Worse still, he's ruined my little girl's life. I'll go to my grave a happy man—shit, I'll *boogie* into my coffin—if it means I can park a bullet in his wicked ol' skull."

"I understand," I said. "Just be smart about it."

"You boys need a reality check," Tatum said. "Psychic powers. Guns. It don't matter. Unless you can pluck Sylvester Stallone and the rest of the Expendables out of your asses, I say we've got a snowball's chance."

"Maybe," I said. "*Probably*. But let's take a deep breath and strip it back. We're not breaking into Fort Knox. This is an old man in a house with a few fat bodyguards for security, some of whom are either injured or out of commission."

Seriously stripped back, but technically true; Jackhammer was walking wounded; Brickhead had been next to him when their vehicle flipped during our demo-derby through the farmlands of Mid-Kansas; Sally had zapped another hunt dog at the motel—turned his brain to

Jell-O, judging from the blood leaking from his nose and ears; and then there was Jackie Corvino, who'd been removed from the equation some time ago.

"We can *do* this," I insisted. "Middle of the night. Element of surprise. We go to wherever he's keeping her. I'll be the decoy—lure the hunt dogs away, which should leave Lang mostly unprotected. Find him. Take him out. Then grab Sally and run."

"You make it sound easy," Tatum said. "But those 'hunt dogs' will be armed. Heavy caliber machinery, I bet. There'll also likely be real dogs, security cams, and light sensors. You say 'element of surprise' but chances are Lang will have one eye open. He'll see us coming and pick us off like wooden ducks."

I'd thought of all this, of course, and more: snipers on the roof, thermal imaging scopes and cameras, sensors that trigger the house into lockdown mode. With more time, we could have reconnoitered the property and devised a stronger plan, but every second lost was a second that Lang could burrow deeper into Sally's brain. We had to act.

"We'll recon to the best of our ability," I said. "And without drawing attention. I'll go in first, create a diversion, then it's down to you."

"So you're basically going to run away and leave us to do the dirty work," Tatum said.

"I'm going to *lure* the security away from the target," I said. "It's called a strategy."

"It's called bullshit."

"Then it's a bullshit strategy, but it's the only one we've got, and we don't have time for—"

"Hit the rewind button, bub," Steve-O cut in, looking at me from beneath a furrowed brow. "*Wherever?*"

"Huh?"

"You said, 'We go to *wherever* he's keeping her.' You mean you don't know?"

"No," I replied. "Not yet, but—"

"Well, Christ *shit*," Steve-O said. He threw his arms up so forcefully that his wheelchair rolled back six inches. "This bullshit plan just turned into no plan at all."

"Listen, I have—"

"You know how many houses Lang owns across Tennessee—how much property?" Spittle flew from Steve-O's lips and a warm little glob caught me just below the eye. "She could be in any one of those places. Or in *none* of them. What are we going to do? Start knocking on doors?"

I used my shoulder to wipe the spit away, then grabbed my bag from where I'd parked it beside my feet.

"Forget decoys and diversions," Steve-O continued, managing to keep his voice to where it wouldn't be heard over the music. "The first thing we've got to do is find out where he's keeping Miranda, and he's not exactly going to post that on his goddamn Facebook page. Only way of getting that info is to grab one of those—what did you call them?—'tracker dogs,' and shake it out of him."

"Hunt dogs," I said, unzipping my bag, reaching into it. "It's Lang's terminology, not mine."

"Whatever the fuck. Those sons of bitches can hide as well as they can seek. You ain't going to find them unless they want to be found."

"Boy," Tatum said to me, wiping her chin. "You're just one step behind stupid."

"And one step ahead of you."

I took the wallet from my bag and threw it on the table. It still stank of the corpse it had been buried with.

Twenty-Six

Sally hadn't been herself for a couple of months. She'd been distracted, out of sorts. When I asked her about it, she only shrugged in her secretive way and said it would pass. I asked if she was going to leave me—if the walls in Green Ridge were finally closing in.

"Let's hope not," she replied.

On my part, I did everything I could to make it—whatever *it* was—right; I busted my ass in the kitchen and produced several above-average meals; I administered scalp and foot massages until my fingers ached; I was considerate and giving in the bedroom; I even wrote half a song for her (I struggled with the lyrics, but the melody was pretty).

On the day it happened, we had decided to pay Dad an impromptu visit. He could always be relied upon to shake up the mood, and put your own concerns into perspective. It was a shimmering August afternoon and the inside of the bus felt like a box of sweat. Sally suggested we get off and walk through the woods, join the trail south of Spirit Lake and follow it to the edge of Dad's property. It was a route we took every now and then, when time and weather allowed.

So Sally pulled the cord and we hopped off the bus. I remember thinking that she looked beautiful. She had a red bandanna in her hair, which brought her eyes to life, and she'd smiled more than once that day—a sign, I hoped, that she was on the flipside of whatever had been getting her down. She even kissed me as the bus pulled away, and whispered that I made her happy.

"I don't tell you that enough," she said.

"You don't need to."

We crossed Buckhorn Road, letting go of each other's hands to negotiate a snarl of bushes and weeds. The woods were water-cool and alive with earthy color. The sun pushed through in thick arms of light and insects purred. We linked hands again and started toward Silver Rock Trail.

Neither of us noticed the man stepping into the woods behind us, pistol drawn.

The man was Jackie Corvino, a former bodyguard and US Marine, and Lang's number-one hunt dog. He had hastened to New York City after Sally had fried Swan Connor's brain, responding to a psychic tremor that Lang had felt nearly eight hundred miles away.

In a city so vast and vibrant, Corvino should have been chasing his tail for a very long time. He got lucky, though; after ten weeks of fruitless searching, a YouTube video emerged showing Swan Connor collapsing at the northwest corner of Madison Square Park. The date and timestamp on the video matched the exact moment Lang received the psychic signal.

Coincidence? Maybe, but it was too great for Corvino to ignore. He proceeded under the assumption that Sally was behind the incident, and that she and Connor were acquaintances (she didn't just attack him, randomly, in the street). Having determined where Swan Connor lived, Corvino armed himself with a tranquilizer pistol and Glock .45, and crossed the Hudson to the Garden State.

Sally never told me how long Corvino was in Green Ridge before making his move—I assume she had that information; she had access to all his memories, after all. She also never told me why he didn't call for reinforcements. Perhaps he had to act quickly and simply didn't have time. Or perhaps, after nine years of searching, he wanted all the glory.

Whatever the reason, going it alone was a big mistake.

. . .

We heard him behind us. The forest floor was mostly soft, carpeted with needles, but he was a hefty guy and something—a pine cone or strip of bark—cracked beneath his foot. We turned and saw a dark figure duck behind a tree twenty or so yards away.

"Hey, I think someone's—"

That was as far as I got. Sally snatched her hand from mine. "*Run, Harvey!*" she shouted, and was gone. She zigzagged between the trees, pulling the bandanna from her hair to reduce visibility. Within seconds, she'd disappeared.

"What the fuck?" I said, turning again to where the shady figure had ducked from view. He had reemerged into a strip of sunlight and I saw him clearly: fifty-something, with the bland, grapefruit expression I would come to associate with all hunt dogs. I noted the pistol in his right hand and the muscles packed into his shirt. He broke through a tangle of branches and bolted toward me, his thick legs working like pumps. As confused as I was, I made a series of split-second connections, all of them loose, but they felt *right*: this was Sally's mysterious past (which I'd always avoided in conversations) catching up to her. The reason she'd been so distracted was because she sensed this was coming.

They had found her. Whoever *they* were. Whoever *she* was.

"What the fuck?" I said again.

The guy didn't even *look* at me. He would've barreled past if I hadn't made my move, and I'm guessing the reason he didn't tranquilize me was because it would take critical seconds to load another dart. To put it another way, he underestimated me.

He shouldn't have.

I lowered my center of gravity like the football player I'd never been and lunged at him, socking my shoulder into his midriff and knocking him off balance. He made exactly the sound I hoped he'd make— "*Hoomph!*"—and we both spilled to the ground. The tranquilizer pistol popped out of his hand and clattered through the understory.

"Bastard," he growled, staggering to his feet. He hesitated—caught three ways, I think, between coming for me, finding the tranquilizer pistol, or chasing Sally down. I made the decision for him; I grabbed a fistful of dirt and needles as I rose to one knee and threw it at him. He turned away, shielding his eyes. I sprang to my feet and lunged again.

This second attack was more successful than the first in that we hit the ground again, but this time I came down on top of him. He grabbed my dreads and pulled. I drove my thumbs into his eyes. He called me a dirty whore and shook my head from side to side. I pressed harder with my thumbs, meaning—so help me God—to scoop out his eyes. I'd never experienced such violent intention before. It bubbled quickly from some darkened place inside me, the first proof that I wasn't the quinoa-eating hippie loverboy I thought I was.

He writhed beneath me, then let go of my hair and rained fists on my arms, my shoulders, my skull. I pulled back and his knuckles grazed my nose, causing blood to spout. It dripped onto his white shirt and into the creases of his throat. He punched me again, caught my chin and I wobbled. The next strike—a looping haymaker that chimed off my left ear—took all of the tension out of my arms. He pushed me backward and I rolled off him. When I tried getting to my feet, he planted the heel of his shoe in my stomach. I collapsed onto my side and gasped.

Corvino pushed himself to one knee, reached behind him, and produced the Glock .45. It was uglier and meaner than the tranq pistol, and guaranteed a more effective level of sleep.

He pointed it at me. Curled his finger around the trigger.

"You're dead, motherfucker," he said.

And then Sally attacked.

The light went out of his eyes. I saw it happen. The simile is cliché, but accurate: like a candle being blown out—a flutter, and then nothing. The gun drooped in his hand and he stumbled three steps sideways. "*Krup,*" he said. A line of spit hung from his lower lip. "*Furpy . . . sploo.*" He laughed at something. My blood on his throat looked too red, too vital.

What the fuck is going on? I thought.

"*Sklump!*"

I scrambled backward and managed to find my feet, then the branches parted and Sally appeared beside me. She was crying, trembling. I took a step away from her.

"I forgot to tell you," she said. "I have one of the most powerful psychic minds on the planet. Oh, and these guys are looking for me."

I don't know if she was trying for humor, but she failed. There was only bleakness and pain. I wiped the blood from my nose, shook my head. My mouth moved but no sound came out.

"I have to go now," she said, and the tears spilling down her face were painfully bright. "My life is too dangerous, and there's only one way to make sure you don't follow me."

"*Snurgle . . . burrup.*"

"I'm so sorry, baby."

She was about to zap herself from my mind when Corvino parked the gun in his mouth and blew the roof of his skull away.

The report shook the trees and birds clattered through the branches, squawking. I barked with alarm and Sally screamed. Corvino teetered for one horrible moment. Blood rushed from his nose and mouth. He folded at the knees and hit the ground with his arms spread. Wet stuff trickled from the window in his skull.

"No," Sally said. "Oh, no."

I backed away from her, bumped into a tree, stumbled over the roots and fell. Sally stepped toward me with her hands raised. Her eyes were dark with tears.

"Listen to me, Harvey."

"No," I said.

"I want to protect you, but you have to do what I say."

"No."

"That corpse has got *your* blood all over it." She pointed, as if I wasn't quite sure which corpse she was referring to. "This doesn't look good for you. We need to bury him. And quickly."

"Fuck that," I said.

"Harvey—"

"I'll go to the police." I picked myself up but kept some distance from Sally. "I'm innocent. Newirth will believe me."

"What are you going to tell him?" Sally asked. She was trying to be calm but the anxiety in her voice was tight and telling. "That this guy attacked you and then shot himself?"

I shook my head, clutched my dreads and wrung them. It's impossible to explain everything I was feeling in that moment. I wanted *something* to make sense, but nothing did. Even the late afternoon sunlight, angling through the canopy, seemed wrong.

"He's a bad man who works for a worse man. No one is going to report him missing." Sally's wet eyes flicked from me to the corpse. "Bury him, Harvey, and I'll help you forget it ever happened."

"I'll never forget this."

"You will."

I swiped more blood from my nose. It's realness—its *redness*—made me realize Sally was right; this bad man's corpse was covered with my DNA. Not just my blood. My sweat and hair, too. I could wipe some of it away but I'd never get all of it. The quickest and easiest solution was to make the body disappear.

"I'll drag him to the lake," I said. "It's deep and still. I'll put rocks in his pockets—"

"It's two miles away," Sally cut in. "Up steep inclines, over boulders, through thick woods. He weighs two hundred and sixteen pounds. You'd never make it."

"So you want me to dig a grave with my bare fucking hands?" I picked up a stick with a pointed end. "Or with this? You think that would be quicker?"

Sally approached Corvino's body. She dropped to her knees, dug into his pants pocket, and threw a set of keys at me.

"His car is parked close to where we got off the bus," she said. "Take it. Get a shovel. Be quick."

"How do you know where he parked his car?"

"I know everything about him. Where he went to school. The first person he killed. How he found me." She lowered her eyes, as if disappointed in herself. "All of his memories are in my mind. I can tap into them as if they were my own."

I started to say something, then recalled the way the light—the *essence*—had been blown from his eyes.

This was real. Terrifyingly real.

Corvino's cell phone started to rumble. Sally and I both leapt backward, but it was Sally who reached into his pocket and pulled it free. She tapped the screen twice, read what was displayed there, then flipped the phone so I could read it, too.

It was a text from someone called Mr. L: I just got another signal. Bitch is in North Jersey. TELL ME YOU'RE ON TOP OF THIS!!!

"Who's Mr. L?" I asked.

"Dominic Lang," she said. "He's the *worse* man I was telling you about. And he knows where I am."

"He'll send more guys after you?"

"Yeah, but I might be able to throw him off the scent."

I read over Sally's shoulder as she replied to the text: One step ahead of you. Target tracked to Morristown NJ. Hang tight, Mr. Lang.

She hit send and closed her eyes. I felt the energy pounding off her. It made me feel very small.

"Shovel," she said. "*Now*, Harvey."

"I don't know you," I said distantly.

"You know my heart, Harvey. You just don't know my history." She swept toward me and planted a firm kiss on my cheek. I felt her body trembling, and despite everything, all the fear and confusion, I wanted to wrap my arms around her—fly upward, through the canopy, and away.

"I want to help you," I said. "Whoever you are."

"I'll tell you everything," she said. "Whatever you want to know. But first you need to dig a hole. A deep one."

So that's how I ended up buying a shovel on the day Sally disappeared. I went home first, washed the blood from my face, and changed my T-shirt, then stepped across the road and made the purchase at Cramp

Hardware. It was the quickest way to get one, better than stealing from someone's garage or driving out to Newton, and I didn't think it would come back to haunt me. I was buying a *shovel,* for God's sake, not a Tec-9.

I made it back to Sally within an hour. She had covered Corvino's body with branches and leaves and was hiding in a tree. She leapt down beside me, landing silently, like a cat.

I started to dig.

I had buried a rabbit once, when I was thirteen. I found it in our garden one morning, stiff and crow-pecked, and decided to make it a grave. I thought that burying a human would be *sort of* the same. A bigger hole, that's all. I was wrong. Each swoop of the blade was darker and more damning than the last. I kept glancing at the mound of branches covering the corpse. He was a bad man, no doubt about that, but I imagined his life in kinder colors—a life of love, laughter, and achievement. It added weight to every shovelful of earth I tossed over my shoulder. The depth of the hole mirrored the darkness in my soul.

I knotted my T-shirt around the handle to keep from getting blisters. My back, shoulders, and neck throbbed with pain. "Deep enough," I said when the grave was up to my waist, then Sally took the shovel and made it a foot deeper. She emerged smeared with dirt and tears. I absorbed some of her strength, jumped into the grave, and dug for another thirty minutes. Water pooled around my sneakers. I struck flint, fossils, and roots as thick as my forearms. I kept digging.

The woods dimmed, full of shadows and fiery light.

"Okay," Sally said.

I scrabbled from the grave—it was as deep as my chest—and lay panting on the ground. Sally had located the tranquilizer pistol when I went for the shovel and she threw this into the hole first (I didn't see her remove the dart and slip it into her pocket). The .45 was next. I got wearily to my feet and helped her strip the branches from Corvino's body, then we dragged him by the legs and rolled him into the grave. He hit the bottom face-first and settled with his legs splayed and one shoe hanging off. It was as far from repose as I could imagine.

I used the shovel to scoop up the pinkish-gray matter that had spilled from his skull—tossed this into the hole, too. Sally threw Corvino's cell phone in, but not before I saw that he had six missed calls and nine unread messages. I guessed all of them were from Mr. L. The alarm bells were ringing.

"I'm sorry I got you into this, Harvey," she said.

"I don't understand any of it."

She replied by wiping her eyes. She'd been crying for so long. I held her until she said, "Let's fill it in," then I grabbed the shovel and pushed the dirt into the hole. Sally took her turn, working quickly, and with angry little grunts. I finished the job. It took us an hour. I dispersed the excess earth around the area and covered it all with pine needles, leaves, sticks. It was full dark by the time I'd finished.

We used the traffic sounds to navigate back to Buckhorn Road. Corvino's car was parked where I'd left it. My blood was on the steering wheel and driver's seat and we used a bottle of water we found in the cup holder to clean it off. I drove us back to Green Ridge, stopping briefly on Firefly Bridge to ditch the shovel in the deepest part of Green River.

Sally sat in the back the whole way, ducked low, out of sight. She had me check the apartment and give the all-clear by flashing the living room lights twice. Once the door was double-locked and the security chain in place, she peeled off her muddy clothes and stepped into the shower. I joined her. I washed her and she washed me. The water ran brown to begin with, then clear.

I sat on the edge of the bed afterward with a towel around my waist, another around my dreads. It was my turn to cry. Sally sat beside me, her head on my shoulder.

"Help me," I sobbed.

She did.

I didn't see the tranquilizer dart in her hand. There was just a flash of something bright—I actually thought it was her fingernails—then I felt it puncture my throat.

"I'm sorry, baby," she said.

I once read that it can take *minutes* for a tranquilizer dart to take effect, depending on the drug used and the physical makeup of the person being immobilized. That wasn't the case here; I instantly felt my muscles grow numb. Sally swam in and out of focus. I tried to touch her—to cup her exquisitely shaped face—but my hand only trembled.

"Oh . . ." I said, and blinked tears from my eyes.

Sally removed the empty dart from my throat, kissed me sweetly. My lips were too heavy to respond.

"I love you, Harvey."

"Oh . . ."

She let go. I tried holding on. I fell.

While I "slept," Sally removed herself from my mind (deliberately leaving a partial memory of her dancing on the boardwalk at Asbury Park), from my computer, and from my apartment. She then drove Corvino's car to Frederick, Maryland, where she hopped on the Greyhound and made her way to Abilene.

I woke up late the following morning with my reality skewed. I ached all over and there was blood crusted around the inside of one nostril. I rolled out of bed feeling like I'd been drugged or hit by a train. My reflection in the bathroom mirror was gray and bloodshot. I recognized only half of myself.

I tried calling Dad, if only to hear a familiar voice, but of course he didn't answer the phone. I then spent an hour rearranging the furniture in my apartment, trying to alleviate the feeling that something was missing.

The daylight hurt my eyes. I went back to bed.

Jackhammer and the remaining hunt dogs were in Green Ridge by the end of the day. They could have knocked down my door at any time but favored a more cunning approach. They watched from the periphery, waiting to see if I would contact Sally.

When after a few days I didn't, they made their move.

Twenty-Seven

Steve-O emptied the wallet and arranged the contents on the table. Credit cards. Driver's license. Social security card. There were a few other cards along with a wad of sales receipts and $190 in cash—which he and Tatum made disappear in a hurry.

"Can't buy shit-all at the bottom of a hole," he declared, stuffing the rolled-up bills into the front pocket of his jeans. He looked at me and grinned. "Boy, you're full of surprises."

Tatum pocketed her share of the money, then picked up Corvino's driver's license and spat at the photo. "This nasty bastard took my face." Tears welled in her eyes. She used the sodden washcloth to dab them, then flipped the license onto the table. Steve-O folded one of his tattooed hands over hers.

"Oh, Potato," he cooed. "Sumbitch is Jersey worm-food now."

"Get *owf* me," she hissed, pulling her hand back. She popped a light to a cigarette and speared smoke across the table. "Dead don't bring the prettiness back."

They had listened to my story with expanded eyes and slack mouths. Neither uttered a word. I'm sure the bar—in all its blue-collar splendor—faded around them, and they traveled with me to the heart of the

North Jersey woods. There was even a moment's silence after I'd finished, which lasted until Steve-O cracked the wallet open and shook
the moldering tens and twenties across the table.

"I guess those presidents were too dead for you," he said to me, angling his head from Tatum's stream of smoke.

"I didn't dig him up for his money," I replied. "I wanted information, and that's what I got."

It had been easier the second time around. The earth was looser, for
one thing, and I didn't have to dig *as* big a hole. I just needed to uncover
the ass pocket of Corvino's pants, where I recalled seeing the shape of his
wallet when Sally and I had thrown him facedown in the grave. Also, I
grabbed the tools from Dad's shed—a shovel, a pickaxe, the battery-
powered lamp we'd used the night we went UFO spotting, and some
work gloves to prevent blistering. My saving grace was a deep-seeking
metal detector which Dad employed to search for alien relics, and which
I used to make sure I dug in exactly the right spot. It located Corvino's
.45, cell phone, and tranquilizer pistol five-and-a-half feet underground.

After a solid hour, the shovel's blade thudded into Corvino's spine.
I dropped to my knees and dug the rest of the way by hand, retrieving
the wallet quickly and clambering from the hole. It took twenty minutes to fill it again and blend the area. I returned the tools to Dad's
shed, then changed into clean clothes and took a cab to my apartment.
I touched down in Memphis fourteen hours later.

"So what've we got?" Steve-O asked, indicating the contents of the
wallet. "MasterCard. Amex. Driver's license. Could be worth checking out the address."

"I already did," I said. "It's a rented house. I called the owner to see
if it would be available anytime soon. She told me that a young family
had recently moved in."

"No hunt dogs there," Tatum said.

"No, but this . . ." I pointed at a white card with a magnetic stripe
on one side and a plain company logo on the other. "It's a keycard,
the same as you get in a hotel. But what's it for? There's no company
name or telephone number, right?"

Steve-O flipped the card both ways and shrugged.

"I figured there's a reason it's in Corvino's wallet," I said. "So I pho-tographed the logo using the camera on my laptop, then ran a reverse image search on Google."

"Lookit you," Steve-O said. "Bill fucking Gates."

"It's actually very simple," I assured him. "And it works; the search results revealed that the logo is for Lyon Security. That's Lyon with a *Y*. They're a private security firm out of Nashville."

"*Lang's* private security firm," Tatum ventured. "That was his boy-friend's name, right? Gene Lyon. With a *Y*."

I held my hand up over the table and she slapped me five (or *three*, to be precise). Even Steve-O nodded, acknowledging the speed at which she made the connection.

"The office is by the airport," I said. "This card gives us access to the building, but we don't know what we're looking for or how many hunt dogs will be there. My preference is to stake it out, wait until someone leaves, and follow him. Tatum can use her power to steer him to an isolated location, then we'll grab and interrogate him."

"Sounds like a plan," Steve-O said.

"*If* I can get a latch," Tatum said.

"You will," I assured her. "You *have* to."

"So we wait, we follow, we interrogate." Steve-O grinned and spread his hands. "What can possibly go wrong?"

I didn't want to answer that question, but Tatum had no such reser-vation.

"Every goddamn thing," she said.

I'd learned a few things from Sally about being invisible, and knew that driving to Nashville in a pink Chevy Malibu and parking it across the street from the Lyon Security office was not the smartest move. This meant renting a car—something suitably nondescript, I thought with a wry smile—which in turn meant waiting until morning.

"I'll see you both tomorrow," Steve-O said as Tatum and I stood to leave. "Meantime, I'll hit up Rusty for some firepower. Whatever he can spare."

"And get some sleep," I said, then pointed to the fresh Bud in Steve-O's hand. "No hangover, either. You'll need your A game."

"Roger that," Steve-O said, saluting me with the neck of the bottle.

We left the bar. Tatum struck a light to another cigarette the moment she was behind the wheel of Lou's Malibu, then drove us through the deep Tennessee night. She didn't turn the stereo on, and we spoke very little. After thirty minutes or so, she left the Interstate and navigated an overgrown trail that wound first through sparse forest, then into a clearing beside some nameless, noisy river. She killed the engine and shut off the headlights.

"We're parking?" I asked.

"Don't get your hopes up, bucko." Tatum popped the door open, then sat on the hood, cigarette in one hand, damp washcloth in the other.

I joined her.

"No light pollution here," she said. "Look up."

I did. The stars were spilled across the night sky, outrageous in number, cooling on the eye. I sat beside Tatum on the hood, then reclined against the windshield and lost myself for a moment. It was edifying, to feel both vital *and* insignificant. I was just another ball of gas—a shimmering fusion of fear, anger, guilt, and love.

"I know why you brought me here," I said to Tatum. "You think this is the last time we'll see the stars, don't you?"

"I take back what I said about you being stupid," she said, and opened her arms. "Drink it in."

"You don't think we can do this?"

"Honey," she said. "I *know* what Lang can do."

"So do I." His evils—those I knew about, or had experienced—flashed through my mind. One image lingered: my old man, slumped against the wall of his bunker with that jagged exit wound in the rear of his skull. The flame burned inside me, as brightly as any star above. "It's the reason we're doing this."

She didn't respond. Her eyes glimmered. We looked at the stars and listened to the river roll. It was so serene—or maybe I was just so tired—that I drifted along the edges of sleep, then Tatum elbowed me to full alertness. We got in the car and rumbled back down the trail to the Interstate. There was no more conversation, and that was fine by me. Twenty-five minutes later, she dropped me outside a Days Inn in Dyersburg. I exited the vehicle, breathed air that wasn't ruined by secondhand smoke, then leaned toward the open window.

"I'll pick you up tomorrow morning," I said. "Before ten. Then we'll get Steve-O."

Tatum nodded. She pumped the accelerator and the Malibu's engine made a shrill sound. No doubt she wanted to get back to her trailer, to Lou, to her normal, if lowly, redneck life.

"We can do this," I said to her. "I'm not going to pretend it'll be easy, but we *can* do it."

"You going to tell me we just need a little self-belief?"

"Wouldn't hurt," I said. "Self-belief, and a lot of luck."

She nodded, pumped the accelerator again.

"We *have* to try."

"Yeah, we do." Tatum ran the washcloth across her chin and I saw how she trembled. "But I'll keep my grip on reality, if it's all the same to you."

"Whatever gets you through."

"We saw the stars tonight," she said. "Tomorrow, I'm going to wake up early to watch the sunrise. I suggest you do the same."

I nodded and she pulled away. Her taillights blended with the city lights, and I wondered how tempted she was to keep driving—to stop in some faraway place where the night sky wasn't filled with the last stars she'd ever see. I imagined rolling up outside her trailer the following morning, Elvis answering the door dressed in nothing but gold-rimmed sunglasses and dirty underpants. *She didn't come home last night,* he'd say, then break into a hip-shaking rendition of "Heartbreak Hotel." While the image was somewhat amusing, it didn't make me smile.

I checked into the Days Inn and slept until a nightmare shook me out of bed at close to 5 a.m. I showered for an hour, trying not to consider the possibility that this would be the day that I die. Just in case, though, I slipped into my jeans and went outside to watch the sun come up.

I would have chosen a more appealing vista for my final sunrise: Uluru, perhaps, in all its spiritual wonder, or the ancient ruins of Machu Picchu, teasingly revealed as the sun rose over the Andes. You take what you can get, though, and I stood with my heart locked in my throat as the sky above the Walmart Supercenter turned from mauve to deep crimson. It was exactly the same color as the bloodstain on Dad's bunker wall.

Once this was in my head, I couldn't shake it. I could have said it was the same color as the feather in my pocket, or the bird in Sally's mind. But no . . . it was blood.

Blood in the east—the direction we were heading.

Blood, as far as the eye could see.

I rented a white Honda Accord—not as nondescript as a silver Camry, but virtually invisible compared to a pink Chevy Malibu—and drove to Tinsel. The dead armadillo was still rocking on its carapace beneath the Outer Town sign, but now there was a large raptor pulling red strings from its exposed stomach. I tried not to view this as an omen. As I approached Graceland, I again imagined Lou answering the door in his underpants, informing me that Tatum never came home. The thought of me and Steve-O having to go this alone made my stomach clench, but there was nothing to worry about; Tatum was ready and waiting, sitting in a haze of cigarette smoke beneath the torn awning. She winked when she saw me. I thought, *Mom took care of them,* and almost wept with relief.

"What's in the bag?" I asked. It was a grubby Nike sports bag that she'd tossed onto the backseat.

"Kleenex. Change of clothes. I figure today could get messy."

We drove to Rusty's bar with the radio tuned to raucous country. Tatum burned through cigarettes and still trembled. She told me it was adrenaline, not fear, and I held out my hand to show her that I was shaking, too.

"It's good to feel something," I said.

Steve-O sat at the bar dressed in the same clothes as the day before: those leg-knotted jeans and a Kix 106 T-shirt. I was relieved to see a soda in his hand, not a beer, although the bloodshot in his eyes told me he hadn't gone easy on the booze. The reek of his breath was another giveaway.

"I'm fine," he snapped when I asked if he was hungover. He hopped from the barstool to his chair and wheeled himself outside. Before transferring to the rental, he showed us what he'd brought in lieu of a change of clothes.

"Rusty's got a sawed-off behind the bar he won't part with. He calls it Ma Barker. He let me have Bonnie and Clyde, though."

He pulled a revolver from the left pocket of his wheelchair that made the .38 Special that Dad had given me look like a toy. From the right pocket he pulled a .45 eerily similar to the one I'd buried with Jackie Corvino.

"By the end of the day, either Lang will be dead or I will." Steve-O blew across each barrel. He wasn't trembling at all. "But one thing is for damn sure: Bullets are gonna fly."

We drove to Nashville.

I'd done my research and found an extended-stay motel in the Elliston Place neighborhood of Nashville. I didn't plan on extending my stay, of course, but the rooms had kitchenettes and I needed a stove. I checked in under a bogus name. Paid cash.

"One bed?" Steve-O asked, checking around the room. "You expecting we're all gonna get cozy?"

"If everything goes to plan we won't be sleeping here," I replied. "We—that's all of us, including Sally—will be hightailing it out of state. If everything goes tits-up . . . well, we won't have to worry about sleeping at all."

"Then why the room?"

"It's our meeting point, should we get separated—which is likely, given the plan." I walked over to the stove, cranked all four knobs to check that at least one of the burners worked. "Also, I need to make something."

Steve-O and Tatum stayed at the motel room and rested while I went shopping. I bought a pound of Garden Chief stump remover—100 percent potassium nitrate—from a downtown hardware store and nearly everything else, including a jumbo pack of bang-snaps and a magnesium fire starter, from the Dollar King.

When I got back to the room, Steve-O and Tatum were curled up on the bed, fast asleep. They had their arms around one another, getting cozy, after all.

I didn't wake them.

I made ninja smoke bombs.

Five o'clock. We packed everything up and drove to the Lyon Security office in Donelson, ten miles east of downtown, where the air was scored with the sound of aircraft taking off and landing. This part of the neighborhood was an even mix of commercial and industrial, with stores and restaurants sharing lot space with modern office buildings. Lyon Security was one of these: single story, glass-fronted (mirrored, so we couldn't see inside), set back from the road. There were a dozen cars in the parking lot but their owners might be in any of the adjoining buildings. One of them—a silver Nissan Altima with tinted windows—looked like a hunt dog vehicle to me.

We parked on a side road maybe fifty yards from the office but with an unobstructed view of the door. This too was mirrored glass, decaled with the Lyon Security logo. Like the hunt dogs themselves, it blended with its surroundings, not designed to attract attention. This particular security firm wasn't interested in acquiring new business; it was a front for Lang's army of henchmen, killers, and torturers.

"Now we wait," Steve-O said.

I sat behind the wheel with Steve-O next to me, Tatum in the back. We watched through the windshield as vehicles came and left, but the door to Lyon Security never opened. Time passed slowly. We opened the windows to let Tatum's cigarette smoke escape but also to keep them from steaming over. We drank water but not too much—didn't want to fill our bladders. The clock on the dashboard ticked from 6 p.m. to 7 p.m. and beyond.

"They took my feet first," Steve-O said. "First the right, then the left."

I watched the mirrored door as Steve-O told me how the hunt dogs had tracked him down. It had been seven years ago. He was living with his then-girlfriend in Madisonville, Kentucky, hoping that being one state to the north would keep him safe.

"I spent the first few months after we skipped town looking over my shoulder," he said, "I swear my head was on a swivel. Then I met a girl—a meth head, but something fierce between the sheets—and got too comfortable. I lowered my guard and they came for me."

Eight of them, in the dead of night. They kicked down the door and beat Steve-O's girlfriend into a coma she would never recover from. Steve-O fought back but was outnumbered.

"I snapped a few bones," he said, "but was too fucked up to do much more. They threw me in the trunk and drove me to Lang's mansion in Belle Meade. This was the first time I'd seen him since Miranda had near emptied his mind, and it wasn't a reunion I took any pleasure in."

An exterior light flicked on above the Lyon Security door, probably on a timer but maybe someone inside was about to exit the building. We held our breaths and waited. The dashboard clock showed 9:03. The Print 'n Save next to Lyon Security closed its doors for the night. The proprietor left in a blue Dodge Durango. Only three vehicles in the lot now. The silver Altima was one of them. We waited another ten minutes.

Nothing.

Steve-O continued his story.

"Lang was weaker, but more determined. *Crazier*, if that's possible. He pumped me with antipsychotic drugs then wreaked havoc in my mind. Three weeks he was in there, off and on, looking for Miranda. He finally gave up and threw me to the dogs. They used a chainsaw—took my feet first, like I said. They cauterized the stumps with a blow-torch, left me for a day or so, then cut me off at the knees. The only advantage with a chainsaw is that you can't hear it cutting through the bone."

I cranked my window wider, took a gulp of the cool night air.

"I don't know if it's possible," Steve-O said, "to die of pain, but I came close. When it started to fade—Jesus, maybe three, four days later—they came back and took the rest of my legs. Do you know how long it takes to cauterize wounds that big? It's no fuckin' party, believe me."

Tatum reached from the backseat and squeezed his shoulder. He covered her hand with his own. *Now* he was trembling.

"They didn't have to take my legs." A muscle in his jaw throbbed as he clenched his teeth. "It wasn't about information; Lang had already turned my mind inside out. They did it because they're coldhearted sons of bitches."

"Evil," Tatum added. She wiped her chin with her free hand.

"I've waited a long time to make them pay."

Ten o'clock ticked around. Tatum fell asleep across the backseat. Steve-O drummed his fingers on the dash. At 10:30, the deli next to the Print 'n Save shut out its lights and another vehicle exited the lot. Now there was just a tan Buick Century and the Altima.

"Every other unit on the lot has gone dark," Steve-O noted. "That Buick is too old to be driven by a hunt dog, and it's parked too far from the door. That leaves the Altima. I think whoever drives it is inside the building."

"I think the same thing," I said.

"One guy. Maybe two."

I nodded.

"We should use the card," Steve-O said. "Go in."

"Too much could go wrong," I said. "We don't know the layout of the building. There could be an alarm system, cameras. We need to stay in control."

"Or *take* control," Steve-O said. "Just as much could go wrong following them. We could lose them in traffic or get stopped by the cops. Worse still, they might spot us and notify Lang. I say we—"

I held up one hand. Steve-O buttoned his lip. I used the same hand to point toward the mirrored door. In the five hours we'd been wait-ing, I'd barely taken my eyes off it. I was so used to it being closed that I was momentarily thrown by seeing it open. Two hunt dogs appeared. I recognized one of them from the cinderblock room—the smudge-faced man who'd cut my binds and warned me about talking to the police. He got behind the wheel of the Altima. His partner got in beside him.

"Two of them," Steve-O said. "What do we do?"

"We stick to the plan," I said. I gunned the ignition, leaned over my right shoulder. "Wake up, Tatum. It's time to get messy."

Twenty-Eight

Taillights bright as drops of paint. Mostly empty roads. It made them easier to follow. That was good. But there was also a greater risk they would notice us, and that was definitely *not* good. I imagined the driver checking his mirrors, frowning, making a few random turns to see if we'd follow, then reaching for his cell. *Mr. Lang, we have a problem.* Lang would take no chances. He'd increase security, go into lockdown mode. Any slim hope we had would be gone.

This had to be done quickly.

"Can you get a latch on both of them?" I asked Tatum.

"Yeah, but it'll be weaker," she said. "Like splitting a signal."

"Do it."

"You need to get closer."

"How close?"

"Whites of the eyes."

I put more weight behind my right foot and the speedometer crept from thirty to forty. The distance between us and the Altima's taillights narrowed.

"Closer."

Tatum leaned between the front seats. Her eyes were wide and focused. I edged to within three car lengths and kept it there, afraid that the streetlights, or the high beams of an oncoming vehicle, would illuminate us like actors on a stage. I glanced at Steve-O. He'd sunk lower in his seat and played nervously with the knots in his jeans. The muscle in his jaw pulsed quickly.

Red light up ahead. The Altima slowed down . . . stopped. This was a bright, busy intersection with a Mapco station on one corner and a Starbucks on the other. Rock music thumped from a nearby bar and the sidewalks were dotted with pedestrians. I pulled up behind the hunt dogs and disguised my face with one hand.

"Tatum," I hissed. "Get that latch."

"I'm trying."

"I can't get any closer than this."

My heart roared. I imagined it booming from the rental like a high-end subwoofer, drawing all kinds of unwanted attention. The light turned green and we rolled west across the intersection. I dropped back two car lengths and scooped sweat from my eyes.

"Hope you've got a plan B," Steve-O said.

"This'll work," I said, but I was losing faith.

The Altima made a right onto a quieter street and we followed. It ran a mile to another intersection. Another red light. I rolled up to their bumper again, hoping they were too preoccupied to realize the same car had been following them for the last four miles.

"Come *on*, Tatum."

"It's no good," she said. "I need a line—a bridge. I can't even see them."

Green light. The hunt dogs pulled away, straight through the intersection. We were right behind them.

"Better do something, hotshot," Steve-O said. "Run them off the road if you have to."

"No," Tatum said, smearing sweat from her brow and saliva from her chin. "I have an idea. Pull alongside them."

"They'll see us," I said.

"Yeah, and I'll see them."

The two-lane street was lined with shuttered stores, punctuated by service roads and alleyways. I saw no pedestrians and only one other vehicle, this some distance ahead of us.

"One swing of the bat," I said. "That's all you get."

"That's all I need."

I gripped the wheel and took a deep breath. I would later reflect on that morning's sunrise—a deep, gruesome red; blood, as far as the eye could see—and how prescient it turned out to be.

"Don't fuck this up, Potato," Steve-O said.

"Shut your damn fool mouth," she said.

I put my foot down, screeched into the oncoming lane, pulled alongside the hunt dogs. I was amped, evidently; my heart pumped up through my eyeballs, turning the streetlights to cold ribbons and Tatum's eyes, glimpsed in the rearview, to pits as deep as bullet holes.

Tatum latched on to the driver the moment he looked at us. I almost *heard* the connection, I swear, like something clicking into place. The hunt dog in the passenger seat barked something, looking from the possessed driver to us. Tatum dealt with him, not by getting a second latch—perhaps she didn't want to split the signal—but by having the driver reach for the semi-automatic tucked into his shoulder holster. He leveled it at the passenger. Pulled the trigger. There was a flash, a muffled crack. Blood painted the inside of the Altima and the passenger flopped against the door.

"*Jesus!*" I shrieked. I jerked the wheel and the rental bumped against the Altima. Both cars wobbled and I switched my attention to the road. There were headlights in the distance, coming our way. Beyond this, another intersection. I wondered how close we were to the downtown core—to SoBro, Music Row, the Gulch. A city full of life and noise.

"Tatum," I said, trying to keep the panic out of my voice. "Hit the brakes. Steer him down one of these alleyways."

But her focus had been disrupted when we'd traded paint with the Altima. Her eyes twitched in their sockets. Blood poured from her nose, over her mouth and chin.

"He's . . . fighting me," she groaned.

I looked at the driver. He thrashed in his seat, head snapping from left to right. Saliva bubbled from the corners of his mouth. He was streaked with his partner's blood.

". . . *fighting* . . ."

We tore down the street at fifty miles per hour, six inches between us. Everything trembled. The pit of my stomach was a block of ice.

"Slow him down, Tatum. *Now!*"

She gurgled something—coughed and sprayed blood. The Altima slowed but not enough. I watched the driver thump his head against the steering wheel, trying to get Tatum out.

"*Harvey!*" Steve-O screamed. His right stump jerked as his phantom leg stomped on an imaginary brake pedal. I snapped back to the road. The headlights of the oncoming vehicle bore down on us. A horn sounded, angry and long. I slammed the brakes and the car wobbled again. We came close to spinning out, but I touched the accelerator, regained control, swerved in behind the Altima.

"Jesus fuckin' Christ," Steve-O barked.

"*Tatum!*"

"Gone," she said. "I . . . I lost him."

I glanced in the rearview. Tatum's eyes had rolled to whites and more blood spurted from her nose. She had lost control of the hunt dog, but worse still, was on the verge of passing out.

"Stay with me, Tatum," I said. "I can't do this without you."

But it was no good. She gurgled something nonsensical and slumped across the backseat. Seconds later, I smelled the bitter tang of urine.

The hunt dog floored it. The Altima tore away from us.

"What now?" Steve-O asked.

My mind whirred. The hunt dog wasn't going home, and he wasn't going to the police—not with *his* bullet in his partner's skull. What he wanted was to shake us. Then he'd call the rest of the hunt dogs. They would assemble. They would *hunt*. It would be over for us. And for Sally.

"We can't let him get away," I said. "We have to stop him. Whatever it takes."

. . .

I floored it, too. The rental responded, but gradually; it was a Honda Accord, not a Ferrari. The engine whined and the needle edged from fifty to seventy. We saw the Altima make a right at the intersection and followed seconds later, cutting in front of a truck that had the right of way. It braked hard and laid on the horn.

"Shit on *me!*" Steve-O exclaimed.

The Altima's taillights zigzagged as it weaved between traffic, then cut across the other side of the street. It missed a motorcycle by inches as it made a hard left into a parking lot. We weren't far behind. I rubbed sweat from my eyes and hammered the accelerator. A car suddenly reversed out of a parking space and I swerved around it with tires squealing. The seconds I lost were regained when the hunt dog exited the lot's north side; he came out fast, mounted the curb, struck a newspaper rack and sent it spinning into the air. Pages of *The Tennessean* exploded around us. The Altima crunched back onto the road, sparks bursting from its back end. I was close enough to see the blood on the rear windshield.

"You know what you're doing, right?" Steve-O gasped.

I didn't. This was seat-of-the-pants improvisation. The one thing I *did* know: With the inside of the Altima splashed with blood and brains, and with a corpse lolling around in the front seat, the hunt dog would avoid the busier neighborhoods. This worked in my favor. My half-assed plan was to run him off the road, then drag him from the wreckage. I'd throw him in the trunk with Steve-O's wheelchair, then drive to an abandoned lot to bleed—or *break*—the information out of him; I had a feeling the bonesnapper would want to get involved.

A tight left turn, leaving rubber on the blacktop. We blazed down a near-empty street, bumpers touching, across an all-way, then over a series of uneven railroad tracks that almost bounced me off the road. These were the backstreets of South Nashville, mostly industrial and residential, with police and pedestrian presence at a minimum. The reckless way we were driving, though, it was just a matter of time before I saw red-and-blue lights flashing in the rearview. I had to end this.

I tore into the oncoming lane, foot to the deck, edged alongside the

Altima. We traded more paint and I lost the passenger side mirror. The steering wheel jolted in my hands and the car's interior shook.

"Whoa, *fuck*." Steve-O had both hands pressed to the roof. I'm sure his phantom legs were similarly extended to the floor.

I eased off the gas, jerked the wheel right, trying to catch the Altima's back end and spin it out. There was a metallic crunch as I buckled the rear door. The Altima swayed but kept control. I was about to hit it again when the driver's window scrolled down and the semi-automatic appeared.

"Harvey . . ."

"I see it."

I jumped on the brakes—saw two flashes. The first bullet struck the hood. The second went wild. I rolled back behind the Altima, punched the gas, and thudded into its rear bumper. One of my headlights exploded and a deep crease appeared in the hood. The Altima veered into the left lane, then back into the right. I thought it was about to lose control, but the hunt dog braked hard, threaded the needle between two parked cars, then ripped through a chain-link fence and across a patch of scrub.

The maneuver was sudden. It took me by surprise and I couldn't follow. I lost sight of him momentarily—made a right at the next intersection and howled down a narrow street lined with low-income houses. Another right turn—cutting across someone's yard, hitting a garbage can—and I saw the Altima burst across the road ahead of me, trailing a strip of chain link.

I got the rental under control and followed, the needle rising from thirty to sixty miles per hour. We tore down streets not much wider than our cars, tires rumbling off the cracked asphalt. We made mazy right and left turns, hitting fences and mailboxes, occasionally causing pedestrians to spring out of our paths. Tatum groaned on the backseat, sliding this way and that. The last time I was involved in a high-speed chase, her daughter—also unconscious—had been flopping around in the foot well. It had ended favorably for me on that occasion. I prayed for lightning to strike twice.

Also on the backseat, secured somewhat by Tatum's prone body:

the ninja smoke bombs I'd made at the motel. I'd packaged them sensibly—in an egg carton, on little cotton wool pillows, just like Dad had shown me—but was acutely aware how volatile they were. One too many bumps and the car would be filled with blinding smoke.

The Altima steered off-road, popped over the curb, smashed through a wooden fence. I was right on its ass. We careened across what looked like a graveyard for trucks, with old Macks and Peterbilts sitting on their rims. I avoided a trailer with a collapsed landing gear, then put my foot down and took another swipe at the Altima's back end. We bounced off each other, shimmied, veered in opposite directions around the remains of a semi. As I sped toward him again, I saw the handgun reappear. There was a sequence of muzzle flashes. Two bullets pocked the rental's front fender and a third struck the A-frame on the passenger side.

"*Motherfucker,*" Steve-O screamed. If his guns—Bonnie and Clyde—had been within reach, he would have fired back. One good tire shot and he might have ended this where I could not.

"Can *you* get a latch?" I asked desperately, swinging behind the Altima again. "Break his arms, or something?"

"Are you fuckin' kidding me?" Steve-O replied. His balding head glistened with sweat. "I need to be close. Eye to eye. And ideally *not* getting shot at."

The handgun slid through the window as the hunt dog switched his attention back to driving. We exited the lot the way we'd entered it: by crashing through a flimsy wooden fence. On the backstreets again, we made wild left and right turns, our dented panels clattering, tires smoking. We motored through another residential area and came out on Lafayette Street. This was a busier road, four lanes, plenty of traffic. I saw a university campus, a McDonald's, a news station—a *fucking news station*. Cop presence was inevitable. Live coverage was possible. The hunt dog wouldn't want to be on this road for long.

"Abort fuckin' mission," Steve-O said. "This is bullshit, Harvey. We'll think of another plan."

"There is no other plan."

The hunt dog turned off Lafayette, narrowly missing a city bus. I roared up behind him and slammed his bumper again. He lurched, almost lost control.

"We'll get him," I said unconvincingly.

"This is bullshit," Steve-O said again.

We flew across an all-way, then the road swept right into an industrial zone. It was partially blocked by a truck reversing into a loading bay. Off-road again, through one empty parking lot, then another. There was a factory to the right and a warehouse to the left. Directly ahead, the lot was enclosed by chain-link fence with thin trees and bushes beyond this. The hunt dog would have to brake unless he wanted to drive through them. I saw the chance to make my move.

I swerved right, came up on the Altima's passenger side so that the hunt dog wouldn't get a clean shot at us. He slowed like I knew he would and I crunched into him. The impact was impressive. Our airbags ballooned, driving us back into our seats, coating us with powder. One of the rental's tires blew and we spun out of control. The Altima spun, too. We crashed together through the fence and our momentum carried us through the trees and bushes. There was a ten-foot drop on the other side into—ironically—a junkyard, where I assumed our vehicles would remain. We hit the ground hard. The Altima rolled onto its side and skated twenty feet trailing a comet tail of sparks. The rental landed on all fours and bounced, and even then I may have gotten it under control if not for the smoke bombs.

They spilled from their comfortable pillows and detonated simultaneously. A single earsplitting crack. White smoke flooded the interior. I dimly heard Steve-O—"*Whafucksat?*"—but couldn't see him. I couldn't see *anything*. My heart exploded from my mouth. My fears and failures leapt onto my chest and stomped. I turned the wheel hopelessly, struck something too hard, and the rental flipped, first onto its roof, then back onto its wheels.

Blood as warm as bath water filled my left eye and the ringing in my ears was more like screaming.

. . .

I unbuckled my seatbelt, threw my shoulder against the door. It jammed, then opened with a creak. I spilled onto the ground, coughing, crawling through broken glass and fluids. All I could think about was dragging the hunt dog from *his* wrecked vehicle and getting Sally's whereabouts out of him. It wasn't too late, I could still—

A gunshot halted me. The bullet met the ground an inch from my right hand, spraying me with glass and chips of concrete. I fell backward with a cry, then fanned at the smoke still swirling from the rental and saw the hunt dog standing ten feet away. He was injured, poised crookedly. Some of the blood on his smudged face was his partner's but not all of it. The hand holding the gun was remarkably steady, though.

"You are one stupid bastard," he said through gritted teeth.

"Where is she?" I asked.

Steve-O dragged himself from the rental. Needles of glass glittered in his face and a flap of loose skin hung across his brow. I wondered if his psychic coil was amped and ready to deal some damage—snap every bone in this motherfucker's body. Even then I believed we could pull this off. One stupid bastard, indeed.

"Where is she?" I asked again, pushing myself to one knee.

The hunt dog switched the sights from me to Steve-O.

"Move and I'll kill him," he said.

"WHERE IS SHE?"

Another gunshot, and this wasn't designed to miss. The bullet caught Steve-O high in the chest and drove him backward. He cracked his skull on the rental's buckled wheel arch and flopped loosely to one side.

"The bitch in the backseat will be next," the hunt dog promised, then leered through the bloody mask of his face. "Although the guys will want to have some good ol' hokeypokey with her."

I raised my hands. My stomach clenched and my groin turned to ice.

The hunt dog staggered a little, wiped blood from his eyes, then with his free hand pulled his cell phone from his pants pocket. He dialed someone, never taking his eyes—or the gun—off me.

I lowered my head and conceded that it was over. I was beaten. Sally was beaten. The bad guys would win, and not for the first time.

"Where are you?" the hunt dog spoke into his phone. "Okay, listen: MNPD may be en route to Big Jim's Auto Salvage in South Nashville. Have them redirected. Then get your ass out here. Call the rest of the guys. Fuck yeah, all of them. You're not going to believe this shit."

He ended the call, slipped the phone back into his pocket, staggered toward me. I indulged in the fantasy of Tatum springing from the backseat, taking control of the hunt dog's mind, then having him point the barrel at his own head. This didn't happen, of course. No Hollywood moments for this kid. Instead, the hunt dog raised the gun to shoulder height and hammered the grip off the top of my skull.

I saw stars. Again. They were brilliant and many.

Twenty-Nine

This all began in a cinderblock room. Made perfect sense that it should end in one.

My cheek was flat to the cement floor. I tasted blood and oil. My eyelids fluttered and I saw a pair of polished shoes with blood on the soles. Beyond these, a pair of boots large enough to belong to Frankenstein's monster, also with blood on the soles.

Ah, fuck, I thought.

"Get him up. I want him to see this."

I recognized that voice. Characterless, emotionless, as nondescript as the car he drove and the clothes he wore. My eyes followed the polished shoes up. Jackhammer, with his stitched-together face and low fists swinging.

Ah, fuck.

Two sets of arms dragged me to my feet. The room pirouetted. I moaned, screwed my eyes shut.

Bright pain, suddenly. An open-handed slap rocked my head to the left and I would've dropped if I wasn't being held up. My face filled with heat. Someone laughed and said, "Oh mama, that was a tasty slap-cake." More laughter and murmuring. I wondered how many hunt dogs were in the room.

Another slap, backhanded, not as hard, but again I would have dropped if those meaty arms hadn't been keeping me upright. This was followed by a rapid *slap-slap-slap* on my glowing right cheek. I groaned, shook my head. One eye cracked open.

"That's it, loverboy. Wakey-wakey."

I didn't recognize the hunt dog slapping me, but he had the same tough hands and blank face as his counterparts. I pulled away from him. My head rolled back. I blinked and looked at the roof. It was high and wide, crisscrossed with steel girders. It was the roof of a building that didn't have neighbors. I could scream for as long and loud as I wanted, but no one would hear me.

My head rolled back down. Mr. Slap had gone and now Jackhammer stood in front of me. I blinked again, cleared my vision. His face was still healing—stitches across his forehead and cheeks. The sling had gone, though. He had use of both arms.

"Mr. Lang apologizes for not being here in person," he said with a smile. "He's somewhat preoccupied at the moment, but he asked me to extend his warmest regards."

"Where . . . is she?"

Jackhammer made a grunting sound that was almost a laugh. "That's what I like about you, Harvey. You're a tough, ballsy little prick, and you stand up for the things you believe in. There's simply not enough of that . . . that *tenacity* in the world today."

I licked blood from my lips, still split from the last beating he'd given me.

"Sadly, it won't do you any good." Jackhammer gripped my shoulder and squeezed, like an uncle offering advice. "In fact, it's only going to hurt you."

I doubled over, the air exploding from my chest, as he drove one of those signature fists into my solar plexus. Both pairs of arms strained to keep me from dropping, then heaved me upright again. Jackhammer clasped my jaw, setting my head on a tee for his next punch. It came. A wide, dull fist booming off my cheek. It reopened the incision I'd made to extract the tracking device. Blood spouted. I spilled to my right and this time the arms, muscular as they were, couldn't hold me up. I hit the floor in a shower of pain. I spat out a tooth.

"Get him up."

I was hoisted to my feet. Everything was limp and hurting. Jackhammer gave my face a couple of crisp slaps.

"Eyes open, Harvey. You need to see this." He clasped my jaw again, cranked my head to the left. "This is all on you."

Steve-O was slumped in his wheelchair, coated in blood. That flap of loose skin drooped over his left eye and the hole in his chest oozed slowly. He didn't appear to be breathing; I'd have believed him dead if not for his right forefinger twitching. He *should* have been dead, of course—he'd taken a bullet to the chest. I wondered if he was using his bio-PK power to slow his heartbeat, slow the blood flow.

Tatum was next to him. Clearly more of a threat, she had a burlap sack over her head and her wrists had been duct-taped to the arms of a wooden chair. I couldn't tell if she was conscious or not. Judging by how still she was, I didn't think so.

More disturbing than their condition: the bright red jerrycan on the floor between them. It stank of gasoline.

My eyes widened. So did my focus. That's when I saw the hunt dogs. They circled us, penned in by the cinderblock walls. I looked from one unremarkable face to the next.

I counted eighteen—most, but not all of them—and passed out again.

Slap-slap-slap.

"The fun is about to begin, Harvey. You're not sleeping through this."

My eyes shot open. I screamed and struggled, kicking my legs, pulling at the gorilla arms still holding me from behind. Jackhammer pacified me with a swift, brutal blow to the stomach. I curled and cried.

"No . . . please, no."

Jackhammer used a blood-spotted handkerchief to dab his stitched face, then gestured at one of the many hunt dogs. He—smooth-skulled, blank-eyed—stepped forward, grabbed the jerrycan, and splashed Steve-O with gasoline. It poured over his wounded face, over that raw flap of skin, onto his shoulders and chest. Steve-O writhed in his chair. The wheels rolled back and forth.

"Don't do this," I begged. "Please."

"Fuck you, Harvey," Jackhammer said.

"I dragged them into this. They didn't want to do it." I freed my arms and clawed at Jackhammer. He slapped my hands away. "I blackmailed them."

"What part of 'fuck you' don't you understand?"

"Please."

He rocked me with a stinging backhand slap that started my nose bleeding. I looked at the cement floor, then at Steve-O—still writhing—then back at Jackhammer. He was holding Corvino's wallet.

"We found this in your bag. Where'd you get it?"

I shook my head.

"Did you kill him?" Jackhammer raised his eyebrows. "Nah, I can't believe a little pissant like you killed Jackie. Your girlfriend, maybe. But you had something to do with it. Why else would you have his wallet?"

"*They* had nothing to do with it." I pointed at Steve-O and Tatum.

"Jackie was my best friend," Jackhammer said. "We were in the marines together. We were like brothers."

I looked at Tatum. She was awake now—roused, no doubt, by the gasoline fumes and Steve-O's whimpers. Her arms strained at the duct tape binding them. Her head moved inside the burlap sack, scrolling steadily from left to right. I thought of Dad pointing his radio telescope at the sky, trying to get a signal.

"How long have you known these redneck assholes?" Jackhammer asked, jerking his thumb at Steve-O and Tatum. "A day? Two days? Not exactly friends for life. Killing them doesn't begin to make up for Jackie."

Tatum's head moved this way and that. I knew what she was doing: registering the sounds—not just Jackhammer's voice, but every breath, sniff, and cough in the room. She was gauging her targets. Not that it would do any good; there was a reason that sack was over her head.

I need a line—a bridge, she'd said as we'd followed the Altima through the Nashville streets. *I can't even see them.*

I looked at the twenty-plus hunt dogs gathered around us. Even if Tatum *could* see them, how many could she take out? Three? Six?

All of them?

"You've caused a lot of problems, Harvey," Jackhammer continued. I smelled his pungent breath, even over the reek of gasoline. "We're down numbers—lost another man tonight. A damn good soldier. This is where we get even."

I gestured toward Steve-O and Tatum. "They've suffered enough."

"But you haven't."

"Don't do this."

"Once again: fuck you."

I lowered my arms, discreetly ran my fingers over the cherry-sized pellet secured in the lining of my front pocket. Jackhammer bumped his chest against mine, growled like a real dog, then pointed at Steve-O.

"Light him up," he said.

The hunt dog who'd been holding my right arm stepped around me, walked toward Steve-O. He took a Zippo from his pocket, flipped it open, spun the wheel.

Snick.

I made my move. My only move.

When Dad had handed me the egg carton filled with smoke bombs, he'd advised me to keep one in my pocket. A *loose* pocket, he'd said. Away from keys and coins. I hadn't heeded that advice, and when Jackhammer and Brickhead had jumped us in Kansas, it was only luck—the fact that I happened to be within arm's reach of the carton—that saved us.

Having made a fresh batch at the motel in Nashville, the first thing I did was slip one into the pocket of my jeans. Then I forgot about it. At least until I saw Tatum gauging the position of the hunt dogs from behind the burlap sack.

I thought it would buy us three seconds. Maybe five. Surely not long enough for Tatum to achieve multiple latches and clear the room, but it was the best I could do.

Snick.

All eyes were drawn to the flame. Nobody noticed me slip my right hand into my pocket and pull out the smoke bomb. I waited for Mr. Zippo to get closer to Steve-O, then threw it on the floor between my dirty sneakers and Jackhammer's polished shoes. I *spiked* it like a football, making damn sure it went *BOOM*. And it did. A skull-shaking sound, amplified within the cinderblock walls. Jackhammer staggered backward, quickly veiled by smoke. I spun clear of the hunt dog to my left, lowered my shoulder, and body-checked Mr. Zippo. He was a big dude—they were *all* big dudes—but I lifted him off his feet just the same. He went sprawling into his hunt-dog friends, knocking two of them to the ground.

Unbalanced, I stumbled into Steve-O's wheelchair, rolling him backward, then lunged at Tatum and ripped the sack from her head.

"*Now!*" I screamed.

Her eyes were wide. They crackled with power.

Mom took care of them, I thought.

She came close.

Tatum's crackling gaze snapped from one side of the room to the other. She knew exactly where her targets were.

She latched. Controlled. Released.

Again.

And again.

This happened: A total of seven hunt dogs lifted handguns from their holsters, shot the compadre opposite, then turned the barrels on themselves. In the time it took to draw a breath, fourteen hunt dogs lay dead on the floor around me, holes in their skulls, in their chests.

Fourteen.

That quick.

This moment has run through my mind a thousand times since,

always chaotic, defying belief. I think now that Tatum drew upon her many pains and disappointments, the unsteady tract of her life. She went deeper than she'd ever been—a maelstrom of psychic energy, not without consequence. Her face palsied. Blood bubbled from her mouth and nose. It even trickled from her eyes. Even so, I like to believe she could have taken out a few more—Jesus, maybe even cleared the room—were it not for the smoke. It had provided a critical diversion, but it also obscured several targets, Jackhammer among them.

I didn't see him until the smoke had mostly cleared, with Tatum a breath away from collapse and me struggling to make sense of what had just happened. He appeared gun first, then his face floated into view. He screamed. It came from the pit of him. A terrible sound. He had three hunt dogs to his left. Four to his right. Frankenstein's Boots was one of these. So was Mr. Slap. All had weapons drawn.

"I'm sorry, honey," Tatum managed. "I tried."

I flashed back to her trailer, with its leopard-print rug and abstract paintings on the wall, and to what she'd said when I asked if she'd help me: *But it's suicide, hon. Plain and simple. We may as well head over to the range and offer ourselves up for target practice.*

There were eight guns aimed at her.

Jackhammer fired first.

His bullet met her mid-chest and rocked her back in the chair so forcefully its front legs momentarily left the ground. He fired again. They all fired, multiple times. Tatum—already dead—jerked and bounced, deep red holes appearing in her chest and stomach, in the scarred web of her face. Her chair skated backward, through blood and gasoline, until it struck a dead hunt dog and toppled onto its side. Tatum sagged like something torn. The duct tape kept her from spilling to the floor.

The thunder of gunfire faded, replaced by Jackhammer, still screaming. Some of his stitches had popped. His face seeped and throbbed. He holstered his gun, splashed across the floor, took me by the throat.

"*Motherfucker.*" He rained blows upon me. Clumsy, numbing blows that rang off my shoulders, neck, the back of my skull. I huddled, trying to protect myself. He threw me to the floor, kicked me in the ribs, then picked me up with one powerful arm and tossed me to the other dogs.

"Hurt him," he said.

I tried fighting, afraid they'd hollow my eye sockets or chainsaw my arms. But I also tried for Dad, who taught me never to underestimate myself, and who'd always believed in me. I tried for Tatum, who'd surrendered so much to amend her mistakes. And for Steve-O, still slumped in his wheelchair, barely breathing. Mostly I tried for Sally, not because I believed I had any hope of rescuing her, but because she deserved nothing less than everything I had.

Any one of these guys could break me in half with one arm tied behind their back, and I faced *eight* of them. I smeared blood from my face and raised my fists.

"Fuck you all," I said.

I'm not a coward.

I threw laughable haymakers and not one landed. I kicked and clawed as I was pinballed from one hunt dog to another. It wasn't a beating. Not *yet*. It was torture. They were toying with me.

"I said *hurt* him," Jackhammer said. "Like this."

He punched me. I hit the ground hard. Spat another tooth from my mouth.

I got to my feet.

He knocked me down again.

"Little *fucker.*"

I looked through the hunt dogs' legs and saw, twelve feet away, a handgun that had been dropped by one of the dead men. I found it cruel, more than anything, that I should obtain a thread of hope: to retrieve the weapon and fire eight rapid, accurate shots before Jackhammer and his accomplices could fire but one. It was the kind of bullshit move that only worked in action movies. The reality would be catastrophic;

if I didn't drop the gun—assuming I managed to clamber through the hunt dogs' legs and retrieve it—I would likely miss eight times, or catch a bullet in the head before my finger even touched the trigger.

Alternatively, I could do nothing. Let Jackhammer kill me. Slowly.

I was enclosed by the wall on one side and a semicircle of hunt dogs on the other. I had to go through them if I had any hope of reaching the gun, which meant looking for a weak point. I found it: Smudge Face, aka Mr. Altima, still dazed and crooked from the accident. I crawled in his direction, hand over elbow through the blood. My breathing was labored, wheezy, and that was good; I wanted them to think I had nothing in the tank. I made a show of collapsing facedown, took a moment to gather myself, then sprung to my knees. As I did, I planted my fist fully in Mr. Altima's balls. It was as perfect a punch as I could have dreamed. I felt them first squish, then separate around my fist. "*Smooooh,*" he said, and hit the ground.

Nothing between me and the gun.

I lunged for it, knowing I could take a bullet at any time. My heart drummed. My focus narrowed. I splashed through the blood and gasoline, reached out . . .

My fingers brushed the grip. I had time to think that I just might do it, that I'd catch them by surprise and kill them all, then Jackhammer grabbed me by the waistband of my jeans and yanked me back. I clawed hopelessly at the floor but was thrown against the wall. The semicircle reformed around me.

"Get up," Jackhammer snarled.

"Fuck you."

He covered my face with one hand and pulled me to my feet. I threw wild punches that buzzed but fell short. He threw one—a classic jackhammer—that briefly shut out the lights.

I'm sorry, honey, I thought, stealing Tatum's final words but thinking of Sally. *I tried.*

I opened my eyes. The cinderblock room rolled and yawed. When it settled, I saw Jackhammer pointing a gun at me. His grin was insane.

"I'm going to enjoy this," he said.

I turned away, and that was when I noticed Steve-O. In all the death and excitement, I'd kind of forgotten about him.

At their peril, so had the hunt dogs.

I'm sure they'd frisked Steve-O for weapons, but when they pulled his wheelchair from the trunk of the rental, they'd neglected to check the side pockets.

He was seriously wounded but managed to roll up behind the hunt dogs, his wheels silent on the cement floor. His hands moved to the pockets. He reached for the revolver—Bonnie—first. Then Clyde joined the party. For some reason, they looked roughly the size of cannons in his hands.

Bullets are gonna fly, he'd predicted that morning, and he was right.

He started in the middle of the semicircle and worked his way out. The sound was bone-rattling. Hunt dogs dropped one after the other, some dead before they realized what was happening, others reaching desperately for their weapons. I saw Mr. Slap take a bullet to the neck and die on his knees. Mr. Altima caught one to the shoulder that spun him one-eighty, then another to the chest that wheeled him back around. Jackhammer—his gun already drawn—turned and fired frantically. He accidentally shot Mr. Zippo between the eyes (another damn fine soldier lost) and popped one of the tires on Steve-O's chair. That was as close as he got.

He was the last man standing. The other hunt dogs—twenty-one of them—were either dead or dying.

Steve-O aimed both guns at him and opened up.

One shot from the revolver, blowing a hole through Jackhammer's right flank and dropping him to his knees. Three shots from the .45. The first tore through Jackhammer's gun hand, sending the weapon and two of his fingers spinning through the air. The second hit him high in the shoulder and knocked him onto his back. The third was a gut shot.

"You took my legs," Steve-O slurred. He wheeled himself closer, steering around Mr. Zippo so that he could look down at Jackhammer. "Took your turn with the chainsaw, huh? *Two* turns, if memory serves. Did you honestly think I'd kill you quickly?"

Jackhammer didn't scream. He twisted in pain and growled. Blood oozed through his clenched teeth.

"You and your goddamn boss have made the last nine years of my life a living hell." Steve-O's voice was fragile but his eyes were intensely bright. I imagined his coil running, keeping his heartbeat slow, his blood from flowing. "You tortured—killed—the only woman I ever loved. Made *her* life hell. But worst of all, you've *hunted* my little girl, taken everything away from her."

Jackhammer gurgled something. His eyes darted wildly, as if trying to look anywhere but at the juggernaut of death rumbling toward him.

"You say something, handsome?" Steve-O asked, leaning forward in his chair.

"Arrgah . . . doolay."

"You're right, payback *is* a bitch."

"Too late," he managed. He drew his knees to his stomach, curled in pain. "He . . . already got to her. You're . . . you're too late."

I had slumped against the wall, mostly feeling nothing, riding the numb wave of disbelief. Now I stood upright, staggered toward Jackhammer.

"Where is she?"

"Fuck you."

"Where is she?"

The sound that rose from his chest was nightmarish: part scream, part laughter. He slammed the back of his head against the cement floor, manic with pain, but in the midst of it all managed to flip me the bird. I knew he wasn't going to tell us anything.

"Do what you've got to do," I said to Steve-O.

"Yeah," he drooled. He lifted the .45, squeezed the trigger twice, popped one bullet into Jackhammer's groin and another into his left thigh. His scream was louder than the gunshots.

"You think that hurts as much as a chainsaw?" Steve-O asked.

"*Faaahk ooooob.*"

"I don't think so, either."

Steve-O pulled the trigger again but the .45 clicked empty. He switched to the revolver and that was empty, too. He sneered, opened his hands. Both guns clattered to the floor.

"Out of bullets," he said.

He started snapping bones.

The peace-loving hippie was long dead. Exorcised by necessity. Mom once told me that violence is how stupid people negotiate, and I had followed that like a not-so-wise man following a star—something shimmering, but unattainable.

Changed, battle-hardened, desensitized to violence, I nonetheless turned away when Steve-O began breaking Jackhammer's bones. I'm not sure it helped; hearing the crisp, snapping sounds was just as bad. It went on for a long time, too. Maybe ninety seconds. I know that doesn't sound very long, but you can break a lot of bones in that amount of time. I couldn't believe Steve-O had that much psychic—or *physical*—energy left inside him. I'm sure, like Tatum, he went deeper than he'd ever gone before, drawing on all his emotions. Or perhaps his coil had strengthened after the hunt dogs took his legs, like the muscles in his arms.

Eventually, the breaking sounds ended. So did the screams. I turned, looked at Steve-O, collapsed in his chair, then at Jackhammer. I expected him to look like he'd been thrown off an overpass, but most of the breaks were subtle, hidden by his clothes. There was a dip in his ribcage, though, the size of a footprint, and there were multiple fractures to his skull. His face had fallen inward. It collected the blood still pouring from his nose, like rainwater in a tarp.

I stepped over him and scanned the fallen hunt dogs, looking for movement. Someone groaned. I thought it was Steve-O, but then heard it again and placed it nearer the back wall. Shuffling closer, I noticed a pair of broad shoulders rise and fall. I approached the hunt dog, grabbed his upper arm, rolled him onto his back.

It was Frankenstein's Boots. He looked up at me, his eyes wide and shocked. He'd taken a bullet to the abdomen. He clutched the wound. Blood seeped between his fingers.

I took his wallet and cell phone from his jacket pocket. The name on the driver's license read Richard Black. There was a photograph of a woman in the wallet, too. I saw no family resemblance. A wife, then, or girlfriend.

"Are you going to help me, Richard?" I asked.

His eyes flicked away from me. He gritted his teeth.

I fished the photograph from his wallet, flipped it toward him. That was all it took.

"The red house," he blurted. "That's what you want to know, right?" He grimaced, eyes closed. "Lang . . . is there. With the girl."

"Red house?"

"It's Lang's . . . private retreat." He arched his back, gasped. Tears squeezed from his closed eyes. "It's in Casper Creek. East . . . Tennessee."

I powered on his cell.

"Password," I snapped.

He gave it to me. It worked. A good sign. I accessed the Internet.

"Give me an address."

"I don't know it."

"Then give me directions."

He did. I brought up a satellite image of Casper Creek and zoomed in on a sizeable lakeside property a mile west of the village. It was accessible by a narrow road wending through deep forest. There were no neighbors for at least three hundred yards in either direction.

"Security," I said.

"You just annihilated it."

I looked around the room, taking in the bloodstained walls, the floor littered with corpses. *I* hadn't annihilated anything. It was all Steve-O and Tatum, their rage and suffering. It was as if they had saved everything for this.

"Anything else?" I asked. "Alarms, attack dogs . . . ?"

"An alarm, yeah." Spittle popped from his lips. His eyes flashed open and closed. "Light sensors . . . in front. Nothing lakeside."

"Any other surprises?"

"Only Lang himself."

"What do you mean?"

"He's . . . different."

"How?"

"Powerful," Frankenstein's Boots gasped. "*More* powerful. You don't . . . stand a chance."

I thought of Jackhammer garbling that we were too late, that Lang had already gotten to Sally. My blood couldn't run any colder, but I felt something like a brick in my chest, pulling everything down.

I lowered my eyes, but not for long; I didn't want him to see that he'd rattled me.

"I'd better find her there," I said, showing him the photograph again.

"Why would I lie?" He almost grinned. "He's going to kill you."

I pocketed the wallet and cell phone, then stepped over more bodies and crouched in front of Steve-O's chair. His eyes flashed in the red mask of his face. The smell of blood and gasoline was sickening.

"I'm going to drive you to a hospital," I said. "I'll have to leave you at the door, though. Someone will take—"

"No," he said. "No doctor in the world can help me now, kiddo. Just wheel me over to Potato and I'll die satisfied."

"But—"

"No buts." He shook his head. More blood pumped from the hole in his chest. "I'm almost out of juice. I'll keep my heart rate down—or try—until the police show up. All this . . ." He flapped a hand at the corpses strewn around him. "This shit is on me. Ballistics can't link anything to you. I'll tell the cops that me 'n' Potato stole your rental, too."

"Steve-O . . ."

"What are they going to do? Throw me in jail?"

I shook my head. I didn't know whether to cry or scream.

"You're in the clear, kid," Steve-O said. "Now get out of here."

I placed my hand on his shoulder and squeezed gently, then wheeled him through the maze of bodies, righted the chair Tatum had been duct-taped to, and positioned them side by side.

"Together again," Steve-O said, placing his hand over Tatum's. "Elvis can kiss my ass."

I recovered two semi-autos from the bloodbath. I checked they were both loaded (I'd read enough thriller novels to know how to release a magazine and count the rounds), slipped one into my waistband and gave the other to Steve-O. "Just in case he tries anything stupid," I said, pointing at Frankenstein's Boots. I then opened the door and took a dose of the cool night air, so clear it made me lightheaded. From what I could see, we were in an industrial lot, probably not far from the junkyard where I'd wrecked the rental. There were fewer vehicles outside than there were corpses on the floor, so I began digging through their pockets for keys, hitting the unlock button on the fobs until headlights flashed outside, indicating a match.

"Not too late for the hospital," I said to Steve-O, showing him the keys.

"Yeah, it is," he groaned. His head lolled to one side. I saw what looked like tear tracks in the blood on his face. "Don't sweat it, kid. I'm next to my soulmate and surrounded by my fallen enemies. That ain't a bad way to hop on the last rattler."

"I didn't want it to end this way."

"Nothing's ended," Steve-O said. "Go get our girl."

Outside, I washed the blood from my face with water scooped from a dented barrel. It was warm, full of bugs. I then took the cell phone from my pocket. The map of Casper Creek was still on screen.

The red house, I thought, and imagined Lang inside. Isolated. No security. But powerful, Frankenstein's Boots had warned me. *More* powerful.

You don't . . . stand a chance.

Maybe, but I'd gotten this far. Something—some crazy mojo—was working for me. Also, it was the dead of night. Lang might be tucked up in bed, dreaming his wicked dreams. I could give him one hell of a wake-up call.

I adjusted the gun in my waistband, then pulled the keys from my pocket and pressed the unlock button on the fob again. Lights flashed. I walked to the car and saw without any surprise that it was a nondescript midsize.

I got behind the wheel. Cranked the ignition.

My turn to play hunt dog.

Thirty

I t took two hours to reach Casper Creek. I drove the speed limit the entire way, stopped at every amber light—couldn't risk clipping a red and perhaps getting stopped by the cops. The engine hummed: a calming sound that didn't calm me. I ached and bled. My heart thumped so hard I imagined it glowing, like an element about to overheat.

Casper Creek was nothing, really. A convenience store (closed). A gas station (closed). A stoplight (red). I consulted the cell phone, made a left onto the rurally named Coyote Pup Pass, which looped through the dense woods and led me to Lang's property. I had expected a wrought-iron gate, locked, perhaps an intercom. What I found was a wooden gate haphazardly splashed with red paint. It was wide open.

The driveway was broad and paved, bordered with towering pines. My headlights picked out more splashes of red paint on some of the lower boughs. I followed the driveway—this also splashed with red—until the house came into view. My plan was to ditch the car, snake through the trees, approach from the rear so that I wouldn't activate the light sensors. This didn't happen.

I walked directly to the front door, bathed in light.

· · ·

The house was ranch style with a modern edge. All dark wood and glass. Any hope of sneaking up on Lang while he slept was gone; every light blazed, outside and in. I heard music playing—something eerie, distorted by distance. The front door, like the gate, was wide open.

I had a feeling he was expecting me.

I stepped toward the front door with the gun clenched in one trembling fist, my heart doing its now regular mad gallop. The steps were stained near-black. The red paint daubed across them was fresh. The door—a mahogany slab—had been wildly painted. It was tacky to the touch.

I stepped into the entranceway and saw why it was called the red house. The décor was largely red: the walls, the ceiling, the trim. There was a standing vase festooned with synthetic red feathers. I saw two paintings on the walls. One was of a naked man with red wings, elevated godlike above a devout people. The other was a Pollock-style piece, red drips on a black background. There was a tall lamp with a red shade, a soapstone carving of a woman cradling a red infant. Stepping deeper into the house, I saw that some of the non-red décor—the doors, the light fittings, the hardwood floor—had been recently marked: a red *X* here, a red brushstroke there. The words *BLISS* and *ME* and *BIRD* were scrawled all over.

No sign of Lang, but I sensed he was close. I stepped cautiously down the hallway with the gun raised, following the music. Something from the roaring twenties, I thought, but not at all Gatsby-esque. The warbling gramophone sound gave it a nightmarish quality, as did the lyrics: "*T'ain't no sin to take off your skin and dance around in your bones . . .*"

I'd been in the house seconds and felt like screaming.

The hallway was L-shaped and led to an open-concept kitchen, dining, and living room. Floor-to-ceiling windows faced the lake, although nothing could be seen now but light glare and reflections. I followed the reek of fresh paint from the kitchen to the living room. This was where the music came from—that jaunty, scratchy melody that made me want to claw out my eardrums. I had expected a gramophone with a dripping red horn, but it was a sleek stereo system, one of the few things untouched by Lang's bright red brush. The paint was splashed across the floor, the leather sofa, the coffee table. It plinked from the light fittings and bookshelves.

This was the work of a very sick man, one whose mania had recently deepened. Lang wasn't only tyrant-dangerous, though God knows that would be bad enough; he was consumed with power—Sally's power, specifically.

He didn't just *want* the red bird . . . he wanted to *be* it.

"Harvey," he said. "I'm so glad you're here."

He stood on the other side of the living room, naked but for a pair of boxer shorts and an ornate bird's mask—red, of course—with a long, hooked beak, the kind commonly worn at a masquerade. He had red feathers in his hair, stark against the silver. I watched as he dipped his brush into a pot of red paint and slapped the word *BIRD* across his chest.

I took two staggering steps toward him. More red feathers swirled around my bloodstained sneakers.

"Where is she?" I asked.

"Broken," he said. "Unquestionably."

He looked at me. His fierce eyes flashed through the holes in his mask.

I had a gun in my hand but couldn't use it. The lines of communication between my brain and trigger finger had been disrupted. I could no more shoot Lang than I could crawl lizardlike along the wall.

Lang appeared barely to notice the gun, but of course *he* was the disruption. He was stopping me from pulling the trigger and it was effortless. This was not the same man who'd spidered through my mind back in Jersey—a psychic effort that had left him withered and in need of oxygen. He was now replete with power and energy. He almost glowed.

I watched as he dipped his brush again, drew it across his mouth. A broad red smile. He spread his arms wide.

"Do you like the new me?"

"No," I replied. "But then, I didn't much like the old you."

"Oh, Harvey. I'm just another American with a dream."

I wondered how I could get to him—if I could short-circuit his psychic coil just long enough to point the gun and shoot. I didn't care for his *glow*, though. Or his smile. The real one. The one beneath the paint.

"They're all dead," I said in an effort to unnerve him. "Your army. Your dogs. I buried Jackie Corvino in New Jersey. The rest are stinking up a warehouse somewhere in Nashville."

"Yes, I know." Lang nodded. The red beak went up and down. "I can see it in your mind. I don't even have to *spider* inside." He wiggled his fingers. "You *project* it. Everything you're thinking . . . I'm one step ahead of you."

The music switched. Another roaring twenties number. Equally maddening. Lang didn't think so; he broke into an impromptu Charleston. It was as unsettling as it was ridiculous.

His attention diverted, I focused on my trigger finger, trying to take back control. I couldn't do it, though. The gun could have been in someone else's hand.

"It's barely a loss," Lang suggested a moment later, shrugging indifferently. "The dogs had served their purpose. They had nothing left to hunt. You saved me the awkward task of firing them. Not *all* of them, of course; I have security for my presidential campaign to consider."

I placed one hand on the back of the sofa to steady myself.

"I should be ready for 2020," he said. "I'll reestablish Nova Oculus, earn favor on the Hill, maybe another short spell in the Senate, and then . . ." He put down the paint pot and drew a banner in the air: "LANG 2020: I HAVE THE VISION. How's that for a kick-ass slogan?"

I brought to mind a different vision, one I'd had before: of a tyrannized people rising up, of broken streets and shattered lives, of desperation and anarchy. I saw a post-apocalyptic cityscape: collapsed buildings, smoke, fire . . . a single red feather in the foreground.

"A little dramatic, don't you think?" Lang asked.

"No," I said.

"We are a nation bathed in blood, Harvey. Always have been." Lang took a step toward me. "We don't need fifty stars on our flag. Only seven: one for every sin we represent."

"I don't believe that."

"You look at me and think—"

"Tyrant," I finished for him. "Madman. Beast."

"We are all beasts," he said. His teeth appeared in the strip of paint across his mouth. A horrible grin. "We don't need a good man to run this country. We need a strong man to control it."

"You're not strong," I said. "You're insane. You'll destroy us all."

"Not destroy, Harvey. *Change.*"

The Orwell quote occurred to me: *Power is in tearing human minds to pieces and putting them together again in new shapes of your own choosing.*

"Exactly," Lang said.

"It's demonic," I said.

"It's entirely necessary." He snapped his fingers, as if suggesting how easy it would be. "And long overdue."

I considered my trigger finger. Useless to me. So I turned from hate to my other reason for being there: love. The reason I fought.

"Where's Sally?"

"It doesn't seem that long ago I was asking you the same question." Lang dropped into another hot-stepping Charleston—the swift, elegant moves of a man in fine physical condition. "I won't be quite so difficult, though." He stopped dancing and held out one hand. "Come with me."

I took his hand. Not because I wanted to, but because he *made* me. He clutched it like a lover, and as he turned I saw the bright red markings on his back. They started at his shoulder blades and stretched along the backs of his arms.

He'd painted himself wings.

We walked hand in hand down a short red hall, through a red door, down a flight of red stairs. The basement was comfortably cool. It smelled of sawdust and something sour. I heard the birds before I saw them: perhaps a hundred of them, agitated and crying. They were packed into a dozen cages that formed a narrow corridor at the foot of the stairs. Their feathers had been dyed red.

Lang let go of my hand and strode between the shrieking birds toward the far end of the basement where a red curtain hung from a *U*-shaped rail. He snatched it aside, revealing a steel bed fitted with arm and leg straps. They were no longer employed—no longer *needed*. Same with the IV. A half-empty bag with the word CHLORPROMAZINE hung from the hook, but the drip wasn't connected.

"Sally," I whispered.

I didn't know what to expect. I'd envisioned many macabre scenarios, from her being blindfolded, tortured beyond recognition, to finding her facedown on a slab with a hole drilled through her cranium. I also recalled Sally telling me that Lang used to fantasize about eating her, and braced myself to find her carved into deli-thin slices, served on silver platters.

My darkest fears were not realized. Nor was it a best-case scenario, of Sally being alert and aware. She lay naked on the bed, on a red satin sheet, still as glass and paper-pale. Her breast moved too delicately to know if she was breathing. Only the thinnest vein, ticking in her left eyelid, told me she was still alive.

Red feathers were scattered around her.

"Fallen," Lang said.

I limped toward her, pushing the IV stand aside so that I could get close, take her hand. She was as cool as she was still. Lang went around the other side, took her other hand.

"Don't touch her," I said.

"A little late for that."

The birds screeched and whirled. They enveloped the music from upstairs, though. No small relief.

"Sally . . ."

Only that thin vein moved.

"I've taken everything I can," Lang said. "She isn't completely void; her coil has some flicker yet, and I left her with the memories of rapists and killers. There may be a few of her own memories ghosting around, but she'll never be the woman she was. She'll be more like a dog, I think. Stupidly faithful. Shit anywhere. Haven't you always wanted a dog, Harvey?"

Tears welled in my eyes, spilled onto my cheeks. "Sally . . ." I lifted her hand to my broken lips and kissed her fingers. "Sally, baby . . ."

"I reclaimed my powers, of course," Lang continued. "And learned a few new tricks in the bargain. Wonderful news: I'm stronger than ever. Most importantly, I recovered the sequences for *my* memories. Had to dig deep to get them, but it was worth it. I remember *everything*, Harvey. Oh, bliss!"

He let go of Sally's hand and pirouetted. The birds sang furiously.

I used Sally's fingers to wipe my tears away. She didn't react. *Broken*, Lang had said. *Unquestionably*. And I feared he was right. I wondered if she'd simply given up—if she was too tired of running, of fighting, and had let Lang in.

"Not at all," Lang said. "I compromised her coil with a steady drip of antipsychotics." He gestured at the half-empty bag hanging from the IV stand. "Not without risk: The required dosage could result in tachycardia or neuroleptic malignant syndrome, which would almost certainly prove fatal. Fortunately, I discovered a new weakness and was able to exploit it."

He looked at me. A bead of light winked off his glimmering beak.

"*You*, Harvey. You're her weakness." He spread his arms—his wings. "The antipsychotics started the process, but threatening to kill you accelerated it. She broke so easily in the end."

I tried raising the gun again. Still nothing.

"Quite romantic," Lang said, "what you've sacrificed for each other." He swept a strand of hair from her brow. "Maybe I left some love behind. A morsel. A *crumb*. If so, Harvey, I hope you find it."

"My dad was right about you," I said. "You're a fucking reptile."

"I'm a *bird*," he said, sneering. "And don't think me unfeeling. I may change my mind about letting you take her."

I dropped Sally's hand. It landed on the bed with a soft thump. Feathers lifted and swirled.

"What?"

"You heard me," he said. "I don't need her anymore. So take her. Just go."

I shook my head, looking from Sally to Lang, then beyond the noisy birdcages to the short flight of stairs. I imagined carrying Sally up them, through the red house, then out to the car and away . . . *away.*

"What?"

"You're a fighter, Harvey. You've earned this. God knows so has she."

I stared at him, considering the other fighters: Steve-O and Tatum, and Dad, of course. They'd all gone to battle. They'd all fallen.

The mantra rumbled. I wasn't going anywhere yet.

"Ah, yes," Lang said, smiling. "How foolish of me. You didn't come here just for Sally, did you?"

"No," I said.

"Kill the fucker . . . is that how it goes?"

I nodded.

Lang squawked laughter—actually *squawked,* then all the mirth, affected or otherwise, dropped from his demeanor. His eyes burned inside the mask. He stepped around the bed with long strides, pounding his chest with his fists.

"So come on," he screeched. "Kill me, Harvey. I'm right here. Let's *do* this."

I imagined it: aiming the gun at his chest, curling my finger around the trigger, squeezing off a single deadly shot, blowing him across the room as easily as blowing a feather from my palm.

"That's it," he said. "One shot. *Come on.*"

He stood in front of me. I looked at the word *BIRD* on his chest, thinking I would aim for the *R.* The gun trembled in my hand. I couldn't lift it.

"Kill me."

"You're blocking me."

"Kill me."

And suddenly the block was gone. I felt the life return to my hand— to my trigger finger. I lifted the gun, stared down the sights, about to shoot when my vision blurred. I shook my head and blinked, wiping my eyes with my free hand, and when everything swam back into focus I saw my mother standing in front of me.

"*Baby boy,*" she said.

Except it wasn't Mom; she had red feathers in her hair.

"No," I said. The tip of the gun wavered.

"*Baby,*" she said. "*You should have let Sally die . . . just like you let me die.*"

"*No!*" My finger trembled on the trigger. I closed my eyes and took a faltering step backward. Mom laughed, a maniacal sound that turned into a scream and then cut to silence. I opened my eyes. Dad was there.

"*Kill yourself, Harvey,*" he advised, and grinned. His scarred face was daubed with red paint. "*It's the only way out of this. Trust me.*"

I felt a *tugging* sensation in my brain. My right arm tingled. I flipped the gun on myself, opened my mouth, and lodged the barrel so deep I gagged.

"*There you go,*" Dad said. He walked a slow circle around me. I followed him as far as I could with my eyes and when he came back into view it was Lang again. The mask was gone. His dark eyes sizzled.

"Just like Daddy," he said. "Boom."

Tears squeezed from my eyes. My finger twitched against the trigger.

"Orwell was right." Lang took a whistling breath and spread his hands. "Power is in fucking people over and reshaping their minds." He winked, plucked a feather from his hair, ran it from my cheek to my forearm. "But sometimes it's better to destroy them completely."

My finger exerted pressure on the trigger. I closed my eyes and waited for everything to end. Instead I felt that tugging in my brain again and drew the pistol from my mouth. Lang dropped the feather and held out his hand.

"Give me the gun."

He didn't need to ask. I slapped it into his palm.

"Psychokinesis," he said, caressing the grip, the barrel. "The ability to interact with, affect, or alter exterior matter through the power of thought."

I coughed up threads of pinkish bile, tasting steel on my tongue and someone else's blood. Lang smiled and focused on the gun's barrel. His eyes narrowed and the brows above them hooked upward. I recalled watching Uri Geller on television when I was a kid, bending spoons and house keys out of shape. This was nothing like that. This was subtle, but *real*. I watched the barrel of the gun first crimp, then buckle.

"You're a fool. A weak fool." Lang handed the gun back to me. I looked at its warped barrel, then dropped it on the floor. Its shooting days were done.

"Monster," I said.

"So what now?" he growled. "How are you going to stop me, Harvey? How is *anyone* going to stop me?"

I lowered my head and he slapped me. It was a cold, *human* gesture that shocked more than hurt me. I held my face and looked at him through the tears in my eyes, then directed my gaze over his shoulder. Sally lay in her cradle of red. I hoped this would be the part where I'd see her eyelids fluttering or her pinky twitching, something to assure me that she was close—she was *coming*. But there was nothing. She was glass.

Lang was in my mind a second later. He didn't fly in. He wasn't a bird, despite what he thought.

He was a spider. Still.

He crawled.

I felt the *scratch* of him. The *skitter* of him. Before he had been slick and plump, dragging his abdomen across my memories as his eight legs worked to connect damaged connection points. This time he was harder, larger, so that when he burrowed it felt like my brain was unspooling.

Am I cold, Harvey?

"Yes," I blurted.

And deep?

I shrieked, shaking my head as if that would knock him loose. He laughed and went deeper, his stiff legs spidering through the rope of my brain. My body trembled. My eyes scrolled inside my skull and locked there. He skittered through emotions and instincts and emerged above the brainstem. The pressure was excruciating. I imagined blood vessels ballooning, weakening, all set to rupture and flood the deep tissue of my brain.

That would be too easy, Lang said. *Too quick.*

He wriggled down my spine, looped around my ribcage to my heart. He clambered onto it, legs braced, his swollen abdomen bouncing as everything thumped. I clamped both hands to my chest and staggered.

Now this could be fun, he said. *Acute myocardial infarction. Or a heart attack, in layman's terms. Whatever you call it, I can make it looooooong. Every beat will feel like a hammer falling, and you'll wish each one was your last.*

The strength went out of my legs. I sagged to my knees.

"Get out," I wheezed. My heart mirrored the birdcages: choked red and full of cacophonous sound. I saw them in my peripheral vision, swinging and rattling. Small feathers bled to the floor.

I don't think so, Harvey, Lang said. *You don't come into MY house, looking to kill ME, and expect to get away with it.*

He squirmed back to my brain and started assembling memories, but bastardizing them as they formed. Here was Mom on her deathbed, not beautiful, even in her frailty, but monstrous. She had crow's talons for hands. Black smoke plumed from her mouth and eyes. *You were always such a weak little cunt,* she said to me, and coughed glowing coals onto her breast. Another twisted memory: Dad standing at the top of his driveway, clutching a dead cat to his chest and holding his fist aloft. *I believed in everything except you,* he said. *I should have thrown you into the lake when you were a baby.* He disappeared and another memory formed: Sally dancing on the boardwalk while the band played "Abilene." *You were never strong enough for me,* she said, and blew away in a swirl of feathers.

SALLY—

I recalled lying beneath the stars with Tatum, her mouth wrapped around my cock while blood dripped from the bullet holes in her chest. Then I was thirteen years old again, eating breakfast with Mom at Cadillac Jack's. I had the Brando omelet while Mom feasted on a bowlful of dark, gristly flesh. *Yummy cancer,* she said, then pushed a bleeding tumor into her mouth and came in for a kiss.

I screamed for Sally. I *needed* her.

She's broken, Harvey. She won't find you.

My skin scrawled. My teeth rattled. Lang turned my sweetest memories into nightmares but I refused to break. I clamped my skull between my palms and roared, and the more I defied him, the harder he pushed—the more monstrous he became.

I'm going to kill her while you watch, Harvey.

I slumped onto my side, knees drawn to my chest.

No . . . I'm going to make you kill her.

Lang scurried deeper, squeezing his engorged body between the folds of my brain. I saw my parents hand in hand at Spirit Lake, and everything was exactly how I remembered except they had curled horns and swishing devil's tails. And there was something else, only glimpsed: a ribbon of red light over the mountains beyond. I remembered my first day at school, where every kid wore a bloodied pig mask and we pledged allegiance but Lang's face was on the flag. I looked out the window and briefly saw that red light again. More "memories"— snapshots of my life, every one buckled or cracked. I glimpsed that shimmering red ribbon in all of them. I thought it was Lang. His anger. His wickedness. But there was a familiar delicacy to it. Something in the way it *danced.*

I'd seen it before, I realized; I'd followed it through my mindscape when my memories were restored.

Sally.

Her coil had some flicker—Lang said so himself—and she was using it. Not to look for me, but to track Lang's psychic signal. *We're connected,* she'd said at the motel in Cypress. *It's a thin thread, but it's there—it's* real. She rarely used her power because it gave away her location. I had a feeling that line of communication worked both ways.

I pushed against Lang, trying to get him to amplify his signal, but I couldn't keep this revelation—or the *hope*—from my mind. He tuned in to it. I felt him recoil, then retreat.

Too late.

My head filled with red light. The ribbon flowed. It turned into a bird.

Sally found him.

She swooped.

He was snatched from my mind in a blur of red feathers. My eyes shot open and I staggered to my feet. Lang pirouetted across the room, but not deliberately this time—certainly not *gracefully*. He held his head and shrieked.

The birds cried. Tiny red storms.

Sally stood at the foot of the bed, head low and shoulders hunched. She glowered at Lang, using what precious power she had left to smash his wicked brain. But it *was* just a flicker, as Lang had said, and she faded too soon. She took a faltering step and raised one hand to her temple. Blood bubbled from her nose. This was all Lang needed. He pulled back his shoulders and hissed. Sally quailed beneath the force of it. He swept toward her, struck her twice across the face. She fell to one knee.

He went for her mind.

He was, however, completely out of *my* mind. If the gun hadn't been twisted out of shape, I could have retrieved it, aimed, and blown him out of his dirty old skin. It remained the only weapon close to hand, though, and I knew I had to do *something*. I picked it up and ran at him, intending to drum it off his skull. It might damage him enough for Sally to regain control. Finish the job.

I didn't get close, though; Lang turned toward me, eyebrows flared, and I bounced backward as if off an invisible wall. I went sprawling to the floor. The gun popped from my hand, spun out of sight.

Sally shuddered and moaned. Her lips were skinned back and her eyes twitched.

"*SALLY!*" My throat ruptured; I put everything into that cry. She didn't hear, or didn't appear to. Lang loomed over her and increased the pressure. I staggered to my feet, approached him again, bounced off the same invisible wall.

"Watch me kill her, Harvey," he said. "Watch me *crush* her fucking skull."

Sally held her hands out. Blood trickled from the corners of her eyes.

"Help me," she said.

I did then the only thing I could think of to do: I ran at the cages, every one of them. I opened the doors, and let the birds fly.

They didn't attack—they were canaries and finches, dyed red, not buzzards—but they *did* distract. They swarmed Lang in a bristling cloud, breaking his concentration. He turned away from Sally and flapped at them, scowling. Some were batted from the air and stomped on.

In the commotion I watched Sally get to her feet. The birds whipped around her, too. They thumped off her shoulders and arms, brushed against her hair, but she didn't flinch. Her attention was on Lang. She wiped her eyes and staggered toward him. I'd like to say that what happened next was spectacular—that Lang's head exploded in a shower of blood and bone, or that his heart was ripped still beating from his chest. His violent life deserved a violent conclusion, but this wasn't the case.

He didn't even bleed.

Sally managed two shaky steps before collapsing to her knees. Urine squirted from between her legs and more blood bubbled from her nose. She didn't lose focus, though, and Lang stiffened as she took hold of his mind. I don't know how strong the latch was, but he made a deep gurgling sound and his upper body trembled. The birds darted and sang. Red feathers swirled around him. Sally clenched her fist and Lang dropped to one knee.

"No," he said. "It can't . . ."

She *pushed*. I saw it in her eyes and in the way her muscles tightened. The red bird in her mind may have had its wings broken—torn off, even—but it wasn't dead. It hopped from its cage. Its beak was still sharp.

"The clouds don't know," Lang said bizarrely. "It's all *fuckles*."

I knew then that she had him. She might empty her soul in the process, but nothing was going to stop her from finishing Lang once and for all. He toppled onto his back and Sally put the pressure on. She crawled toward him, pushed *harder*. More blood dribbled from her nose and eyes.

"Over," she snarled. "No more hate."

Her hate, or his . . . I didn't know. Both, I supposed. He reached for her, maybe to strangle her—shit, maybe even to *caress* her—but his arm flopped loosely to the floor. His eyes rolled. They wept.

"No more," Sally said.

"Hate," Lang said, as if to finish Sally's sentence. He then uttered his final words: "Fucking bird."

It wasn't quick. It was the mental equivalent of smothering someone with a pillow. In movies this is done in seconds. In real life it takes much longer—in this case eight-and-a-half minutes. Lang twitched and moaned. At one point he tried to sit up. Then, finally, and without fanfare, his eyes closed and he never moved again.

A bird landed on his chest, unexciting but felicitous.

This is how I'll remember you, I thought.

Sally rolled onto her side and wept.

I don't know how long it was before the birds found their way out of the basement and dispersed throughout the house. The first I knew was that I heard the music from upstairs again. Something from the *Great American Songbook*. That's what got me moving.

I stepped around Lang—broken, unquestionably—and crouched beside Sally. I touched her shoulder, then her hair.

"Sally . . . it's me: Harvey. I'm here."

She wept behind her hands. Didn't look at me.

"You're safe now."

I asked if she could walk. She didn't reply, made no effort to get up, so I scooped her into my arms and staggered to the steps. If I hadn't been so weak, I would have made it out of the house and to the car without stopping. As it was, I rested four times. In the kitchen, I found a non-red tablecloth to cover Sally's nakedness. We drank water. Two tall glasses each. I cupped her face. It complemented my palm perfectly.

"Do you remember me?" I said.

"I don't want to remember anything," she said.

I carried her down the driveway with a fierce sunrise lining the horizon. By the time I reached the car, it had robed the lake and Lang's house. It soaked through the trees.

Everything red.

I drove in the opposite direction.

Moment: How It Begins

Four years have passed since you last wrote in your Book of Moments. Most of that time was spent going through the motions. From average Monday to slightly-better-than-average Friday, you'd get up, eat breakfast (quinoa flakes with blueberries and almond milk), then roll into your day. The evenings were spent with Miranda (Sally, as you knew her then), reading, listening to music, making love. Life was . . . you know . . . life. It was simple, but you dug it.

The last few months have kicked the ass out of almost everything. The moments have gone from average to unimaginable. That's putting it mildly. You haven't been reshaped—*you're still* you—*but you have been adjusted. You're like the feather in your pocket: a symbol of justness and determination. Damaged but storied.*

This Book of Moments is similarly damaged, in part from having journeyed with you across the nation in search of a girl you couldn't remember, but mainly from having been read so many times. You gave it to Miranda, hoping it would trigger some memories, but it didn't. "I'm in this, but it's like reading about somebody else," she said, which is exactly how you felt when you discovered it in Dad's bunker. She's read the second half—the Sally years—eight times, but nothing has stirred. On her last read-through, she pointed out the several blank pages at the end of the book.

"You should fill these in," she said. "One final moment."

So here you are, with your unusual second-person narrative, to better detach yourself from emotion and focus on memory.

It is, after all, what we're made of. When we think of the soul, we imagine an ethereal essence separate from the physical. That's exactly what it is, but this is also true: "Soul" is the collective noun for memories.

Late afternoon, the sky smoky with cloud, except for a patch to the west where the sun hangs in a spill of color. You sit on the porch, guitar on knee, the fretboard as familiar to your left hand as the shape of Miranda's face. She sits in the chair next to yours. Michael Jackson is curled on her lap in a near-perfect circle. You have him on weekends, then he goes back to Marzipan, who adores him. She has replaced the pictures of spooky nineteenth-century dudes in her restaurant with pictures of Michael Jackson—the cat and the superstar. People come from miles around to have their photograph taken with him.

A breeze whirls along the porch boards and a loose shutter taps softly. It has already become a familiar sound. You moved into Dad's house a few weeks ago. You made it comfortable—a place for you and Miranda to feel at home, but it isn't home. It is now and will always be Dad's house. You don't have a problem with that; the memories are mostly magical. You just can't live here.

It needs to be a place of rest, you realize, like Dad's grave. He is buried at Rose Hill, next to Mom. You visit most days, usually with your guitar, and you sit with the whisper of the lake and the wind piping through the sculpture, and sing their favorite songs. Something else: Totally stealing Dad's idea, you leave little notes—memories, glimpses of the life they lived, and what they meant to you. The last one, placed beneath Dad's headstone, reads:

The distance between boulders is greater than your little legs can manage. You hesitate, then feel yourself being lifted into his arms. You look at his face as he strides effortlessly across the gap and know he is your father. You hold him tighter. He never stopped carrying you.

"*Play my favorite song,*" *Miranda says.*

You do. "*Ruby Tuesday*"—*the Melanie Safka version, with its spirited chorus. Miranda only knows it's her favorite song because you told her. She closes her eyes and listens, but doesn't sing along.*

"*It's quite dark,*" *she says when you finish.* "*And sad. I should get a different favorite song.*"

"*I can help you with that.*"

You laid Sally Starling to rest and Miranda Farrow was born. Or re-born. She doesn't have to hide anymore. You obtained a copy of her birth certificate from Tennessee Vital Records, then got her a social security card and driver's license. She has an identity for the first time in nine years.

What she doesn't have is a past.

Dominic Lang said that she might have a few of her own memories ghosting around, but that she'll never be the woman she was. It's still unclear how much of her mind he damaged with his power, not to mention the excessive dosage of antipsychotics. She is present enough to know her name, and there are snapshots of her parents, her childhood—a tenuous sense of self. She recalls elements of your relationship ("*You used to have long hair,*" *she said to me last week), and knows you would never hurt her.*

She knows you love her, but doesn't remember what that means.

Yet.

You have told her as much of her past as you know, not all at once, but in reasonable increments. You assured her that her parents loved her immeasurably. "*They weren't always the best parents,*" *you said.* "*But you were the most precious thing in their life, and they did everything they could to protect you.*" *You showed her the news stories about the* "*Ragin' Redneck*" *couple that waged war against the mobsters that disfigured them. Steve-O and Tatum have achieved cult status. Their faces adorn Internet memes and wallpapers and T-shirts, and their unofficial social media pages have* "*fans*" *and* "*followers*" *by the millions. Your favorite image is the* Scarface *movie poster with Tatum's face Photoshopped in place of Al Pacino's.*

In the aftermath, and for the two hours that Steve-O was still alive to regale his story of bloodthirsty revenge, your name was never mentioned. Nor Miranda's. No one is going to play you in the movie of their life.

You're okay with that.

You took Miranda to Asbury Park, had the band play "Abilene" while you danced with her on the boardwalk. It was sweet and silly, but no memories were triggered. You read To Kill a Mockingbird*—her favorite novel—to her, but she had no recollection of having read it before. You bought strawberries and bubbly wine, took her to Buttermilk Falls and played Van Morrison's "Someone Like You" while wearing a long chestnut-colored wig you borrowed from one of Marzipan's mannequins. She laughed and held you, even kissed you, but no connection points were repaired.*

The gaps in Miranda's memory are broad. You have tried to fill them, but for now all you can do is lift her in your arms and carry her across.

Keep carrying her.

Part of it, you think, is that she's afraid to remember. Lang left her with the memories of others, Jackie Corvino and Swan Connor among them. There are cruelties in her mind that surface all too easily. She cries every day. Sometimes for hours. She wakes screaming from nightmares, slippery with sweat, and you hold her until she is sleeping again. There's so much darkness inside her and none of it is her own.

"Your power," you said yesterday. "How much do you have left?"

"A flicker," she said, and smiled. "I sometimes know what you're thinking."

You were at Spirit Lake, skimming shale across the water. It was cold, that first hint of winter in the air. You took Miranda's hands and warmed them in your own, pulling her toward you, opening your mind.

"No," she said.

"Yes," you said.

"I can't."

A flicker, she said. And yes, maybe that's all it is. But it was still enough to defeat Lang. Miranda is still a powerful young woman.

You wanted her to transfer the darkness. Every scream, every drop of blood, every wicked memory she has appropriated. She could upload them into your brain, just as she had your memories. You would carry the load.

"No."

"You can do this," you insisted.

"I'm not going to," she said. Her breath plumed the air. Her hands were still cold. "You've done so much for me, Harvey. I could never do that to you."

She kissed you, drawing on those feelings not associated with memory. Her mouth was soft and warm and she pressed her body close. You, as ever, cupped her face.

"Never," she said again.

Maybe she *does* remember what love means.

Strumming your guitar, watching the sun leak across the west and listening to the loose shutter tap, you consider the darkness she carries. It occurs to you that the life you have been trying so hard to rekindle was really no life at all, and that maybe—just maybe—Lang did her a favor by hitting the reset button.

You will hold her when she cries. You will wipe her tears away. And together, you will create new memories—collaborate on a new Book of Moments—bright and abundant enough to eclipse the darkness.

Michael Jackson purrs tunefully. You expect nothing less. Miranda strokes behind his ears and you play another song. Something raw but soulful.

This time, Miranda sings along.

You strum the final chord, let it fade, then look at Miranda and say with absolute seriousness, "You want to run away with me?"

"Yes," she replies without hesitation, and then, "Let's get bicycles. We'll take the back roads—it'll be wild."

You set your guitar down, hold out your hand. She comes to you, sits on your lap, and rests her head on your chest. Michael Jackson watches you with pleased, sparkling eyes. His tail flaps rhythmically.

"Where shall we go?" she whispers.

"As far as we can pedal," you say.

You kiss, and the darkness—hers and yours—fades, if only for a moment. You look toward the trees and Spirit Lake beyond, and recall the words of a very wise man: I'm more afraid of *not* believing than I am of not finding what I'm looking for. He'd been talking about UFOs, of course, but it counts for everything.

You hold Miranda closer and realize something else: that whatever it is you're looking for, and however long the journey, finding it is just the beginning.

Acknowledgments

Mickey Choate agented this novel, and in so doing agented (by which I mean: brought to life) a dream I'd harvested for over twenty years. I'll never forget the joy in his voice when he called to tell me that the deal was final. It seemed, for all the world, as important to him as it was to me. This enthusiasm continued as I went to work; Mickey requested I send him chapters as I wrote them, which I did. His valued and thoughtful responses fueled the early stages of the novel.

Make no mistake: This is Mickey's book, too.

I was midway through the first draft when I received news of Mickey's death. It came out of nowhere: a most terrible bolt out of the blue. Mickey had been battling a particularly aggressive cancer. I had no idea. I finished the book heavyhearted, but with Mickey at the forefront of my mind. He accompanied every word, every decision, every edit. I'm so proud to be associated with him, and to be one of his authors.

You changed my life, Mickey. Thank you.

Endless thanks to Laurel Choate, Mickey's widow, for her kindness and understanding. And a huge thank-you to my new agent, Howard Morhaim, whose good grace, generosity, and professionalism have been nothing short of inspiring. I wear my tuxedo with pride, Howard. Now and always.

Jaime Levine acquired this novel for Thomas Dunne Books. Like Mickey, she read the early chapters and steered the book in a stronger, better direction. Thank you, Jaime. I owe you so much. Will Anderson saw *The Forgotten Girl* through its editorial stages. He was strong and ruthless where he needed to be (but always considerate and kind), and I am so damn grateful to him. Quressa Robinson took the reins and championed the book through publication, with no shortage of patience. Quressa also came up with *The Forgotten Girl* as a title, after I'd spent nearly two years slamming my head against the wall trying to think of one. Thank you to Michael Homler, Lauren Jablonski, and Cam Jones, who arrived late to the party but brought all of their care and attention with them. My thanks, also, to Pete Wolverton and Thomas Dunne, for taking a chance on me when chances are in short supply. I'll forever be grateful.

Many thanks to Christopher Golden, Sarah Pinborough, F. Paul Wilson, and Joe Hill—terrific authors, all—who read advance copies of this book and had nice things to say. Chris, in particular, has been a staunch supporter of my work for many years, and I love him for it. Extra special thanks to Paul and Joe, who offered suggestions in a couple of vital places, and helped add an extra layer of shine.

Love and thanks to Pete and Nicky Crowther, who published several of my earlier works and opened so many doors for me. As did the great Peter Straub, who gave me my first blurb (told you I'd never forget it). Thanks, also, to Sean Daily at Hotchkiss and Associates, who has shown *The Forgotten Girl* the kind of enthusiasm any author would dream of.

With my first major publication, I would be remiss not to thank the friends who have demonstrated such huge levels of support and encouragement over the years, including but not limited to: Richard and Lisa Buck, Joel Sutherland, Owen King, Mark Morris, Tim Lebbon, Stephen Volk, Brian Keene, Michael Rowe, Ron Eckel, Brett Savory, Sandra Kasturi, Ian Rogers, and Chris Ryall.

The list goes on, believe me.

A huge thank-you to my mother, Lorraine May, who bought me a typewriter (a Brother AX-10—I loved that rackety thing) for my eighteenth birthday (it was all for this, Mum). Also to Sandra and Andrew Marsh, who have been there for nearly every page I've written.

And of course, eternal love and thanks to my wife, Emily, and my children, Lily and Charlie, who fill my world with wild, beautiful, essential light. This is the light I write by. More importantly, it's the light I live by.